TORCHED

Putrid, acrid, choking. It smelled like something out of a war zone.

Brannon put on the filtered mask and seeing the driver's-side window tinted with blackened smoke residue, he steeled himself and opened the door to the wrecked interior. The driver's seat was incinerated. . . . It was as if the ferocity of the flames had centered on a contained area, the area around the driver alone.

"Told you it was weird," said Ames from behind him.

"From the smell of it, someone's flesh burned off here, but we've got no body."

"That's the most puzzling aspect of this whole damn thing," replied Ames. "There is no body, only a few fingers."

"Fingers?"

"Have a look at the ignition."

Brannon stared at what was left of human fingers fused to an ignition and keys that had become one mass of metal in the superheated explosion. "God . . . what could have caused this?"

fire & flesh

evan kingsbury

JOVE BOOKS, NEW YORK

FIRE AND FLESH

A Jove Book / published by arrangement with
the author

PRINTING HISTORY
Jove edition / January 2003

Copyright © 2003 by Robert W. Walker
Cover art by Craig White
Cover design by Rita Frangie
Book design by Kristin del Rosario

Visit our website at
www.penguinputnam.com

ISBN:0-515-13440-6

A JOVE BOOK®
Jove Books are published by The Berkley Publishing Group,
a division of Penguin Putnam Inc.,
375 Hudson Street, New York, New York 10014.
JOVE and the "J" design
are trademarks belonging to Penguin Putnam Inc.

PRINTED IN THE UNITED STATES OF AMERICA

10 9 8 7 6 5 4 3 2 1

1

Drought-driven peasants, successive waves of peasants, arrived daily now in scorched Calcutta, many to die
here. Some Buddhist monk remarked that the newly arriving
peasants shimmered in the heat like human torches, their images floating in the heated river of air rising off the pavement. One old scryer named Kalie proclaimed amid the
bustle of humanity, "If the Kundalini serpent god had its
original power today, it would feed on these peasants like
flambéed delicacies."

No one knew what the old man meant; his religion had
separated itself eons before from the infamous serpent god
rooted in antiquity, and the young, even the middle-aged,
knew nothing of the Ancient One. The scryer ambled the last
few steps to his kiosk, opened it up for the final few hours
of business—fortune-telling, a prosperous profession here
that people felt more comfortable purchasing by night. Scryer
Kalie settled in behind his booth, and from there he watched
all the poverty and squalor and broken limbs and broken
souls and the walking dead about him. This had become his
ritual, his each day. He wondered if the Kundalini god would
not have been kinder than the pantheon of gods the religion
had been left with; he wondered how a man could follow
gods who allowed so much suffering. Then he reminded him-

self that he must be content within to find peace and understanding, applying serenity of acceptance and what that
serenity betokened: acceptance as a balm over the wound
called humanity.

The destitute formed a human carpet all around the scryer,
a carpet weaved with disease and pestilence, poverty and
suffering; knit one, purl two. . . . Calcutta, a city consumed
by Decay with a capital *D*, yet millions inhabited the decay,
swarming to it like flies over the decapitated head of a boar.
The flies swarmed over Calcutta's small squares and market-
places, her avenues and narrow, pinched alleyways. The
swarm moved like one animal with one mind, moved it
seemed in a constant flux, an unthinking, unmindful human
river of dreams washing away, dreams of nirvana, of perfection, visions just out of grasp of the zombie horde.

It moved with a kind of half-life, this single-minded thing
in the heat wave. Although the smallest fragment of pavement was occupied at all times, the old man, respected by
all, did not have to fight for his space; somehow the living,
breathing thing opened up and allowed him to pass whenever
he came near it. Still, all around him lay kiosk after kiosk,
and even the smallest snail's space in this universe was occupied, settled upon, covered with squatters, hawkers, beg-
gars, lepers, and homeless families.

Every few feet another cardboard box or other makeshift
"space" marked someone's territory or shelter. So much human refuse, the scryer thought, and yet all life remained sacred, down to the lowliest vermin crawling on six or eight
furry legs. So these humans, each and every one, must as-
suredly be sacred as well, but then why do they disgust me
so? Am I too old to any longer feel any humanity toward
my own?

Alongside the disturbing thoughts that filled the scryer's
tired mind stood the streets, littered with stalls, altars, small
temples, chairs, tables, signs, smokers, gamblers, tricksters
and hucksters; it all resulted in a lunatic chaos, and without
adequate trash collection services, seventeen-hundred tons of
garbage accumulated daily all along the roads, in turn attract-

ing flies, rats, cockroaches, mosquitoes, mice, creating a feast for the eyes of any and all vermin. But here, even the vermin was taboo as food, for even vermin life was sacred. Still, a man hungry enough will eat, even if it led to his soul's end—condemnation.

This summer the proliferating filth brought with it a parade of epidemics: cholera, hepatitis, typhoid, rabies, and encephalitis. At the center of India's most arid land, now combating a drought worse than any the scryer had ever known in his seventy-odd years, the City of Joy looked and played the part of a gargantuan refuse heap, the city choking under a poisonous cloud of fumes. The old man's thoughts ran to the fires that had rocked the city. Some of the overcrowded buildings in the oldest sections of the city were powder kegs—explosions waiting to happen. The nauseating gases sometimes turned into actual discharges that left a neighborhood looking like the aftermath of a SCUD missile attack, a devastated landscape of twisted and torn building materials, leaking sewers, bursting water pipes, dangling telephone wires, all adding to the growing number of disemboweled tenements in Calcutta.

The extreme of the extremely poor in the city lived among such ruins, and out of such a dangerous place stepped Dhashid Ramar, and even from this far, the old scryer could make out Dhashid's sad features.

Poor Dhashid. If ever a man was beset by troubles, at the end of the proverbial rope of his resources, Dhashid was, and so again this evening he meant to sell his blood to one of the hundreds of the city's blood merchants.

It must be a city of joy for vampires, mused the old man.

The need for blood in the hospitals and clinics amounted to thirty- to forty-thousand vials a year, and since the seven official State of Bengal blood banks proved incapable of meeting such demand, private enterprise flourished, even this late in the day.

It seemed lately that anyone could become owner/operator of a new blood bank in Calcutta. All a fellow had to do was to gain the help of a physician, and physicians of the sort needed had also proliferated. Everyone's hands greased, the one calling himself a doctor merely had to do the paperwork—place a request at the Health Department for his protégé in the blood business. Step two: rent premises, purchase a refrigerator, a few syringes, and vials—all reusable—and voilá, a man was in the blood-bank business overnight.

Result: a wild trade in human blood on the streets, and an annual turnover in excess of twelve-million rupees per anum. The scryer had told Dhashid, "You are a fool to be selling your blood, when you rather should become a blood buyer! Never go to dig gold, but rather sell the tools needed!"

"How? How do I do this?" Dhashid had pleaded, thinking the near-blind old man knew something he did not.

"You must find a physician who will sponsor you."

Dhashid laughed hollowly in response. "Old fool, I know no one even approximating a physician, and given my circumstances, I am not likely to come across one soon."

"Calcutta is a hard place. Cultivate serenity, peace within. It will lead you to a solution, to wondrous riches beyond your dreams."

"Now you treat me like one of your customers? I tell you, old man, if I had your wisdom, I would be penniless just the same," Dhashid had said that evening before walking away disgusted, while the old man riddled out the insult.

Now here was Dhashid Ramar going to feed his family by selling his blood once again. What next? His spleen? Pancreas? Liver? Heart? His skeleton? The blood and body merchants had a stranglehold on the likes of Ramar, and it sickened the scryer, who kept asking himself, "Why should I care? Why should I give a single goat-fuck?"

Dhashid Ramar entered the marketplace coughing; in fact, he coughed up blood with his sputum. He'd been ill with cholera on and off for most of the season, and the disease still held him in its grasp. The acrid air of the marketplace filled his lungs, threatening to burst them. Half a dozen funeral pyres slowly lit the now darkening sky, struggling to end the world's darkness, an impossibility.

Dhashid walked in an ambling fashion, like a man not anxious to arrive at his destination. Only the day before, he had buried his youngest child. Only the day before this, Dhashid had met a man belonging to the Dom caste, a man who specialized in cremating the dead, and since there were always pyres burning with several corpses alongside every pyre, each corpse waiting for its return to nirvana, this man had offered Dhashid what he had called a trifling compromise for his financial situation. The Dom would slip his daughter's inconsequential body in among others for a lower price, but he could not guarantee her soul's well-being. Instead, Dhashid had made a deal with another type of devil, a hospital physician to whom he had signed over half his body parts on the event of his death. Not unlike Visa or MasterCard, some joked of the arrangement between the hospitals and the poor here in Calcutta, the adopted home of Mother Teresa until her death. But even now, even after having found the money for a proper funeral, Dhashid felt the constant press of the terrible loss of his nine-year-old daughter, Ilyana, the angel of his and her mother's heart. Poor Ilyana's disease could only be ended in the arms of peaceful death.

Since they had come to Calcutta when the child was a mere infant, the little girl had had no inkling of their true homeland, the open countryside of East India; instead, she had lived all her life in the grim glow of the funeral pyres. As young as she was, even she knew that for the wood alone, her funeral would cost a hundred and twenty rupees. She knew that cremation wood was far more expensive than ordinary wood, that it had been consecrated, treated and blessed by the Brahmin attendant, who would also pour ghee over her forehead as he recited the holy mantras. This holy butter-oil had been purified five times; such purification did not come cheaply. The butter had created a wax mask of her features so that she would be recognized in the next life.

Being highly combustible, it also hurried Ilyana's cremation along to its final end.

The cost of the white linen shroud, the stick-mesh basket she lay in, all of it was absolutely necessary, yet Dhashid must think of his other, living children. Money, always a problem.

He had still not been paid the full amount by the hospital doctor. So he had come into the open marketplace to seek out a blood merchant to help out his immediate needs. No matter how hardened Calcutta had made him, he still felt for his children.

Now, as he searched the faces in the throng for a blood merchant, his mind drifted back to the pitiful stash of belongings left behind by Ilyana: a few utensils, a change of *longhi* and trousers, and a battered little umbrella with an empty Mickey Mouse key chain attached to it. This was all that he had of her to feed the fire and to go with her into eternity. His wife and Ilyana's little brothers and sisters had sung hymns, verses from *The Bhagavad Gita,* sacred book of their religion. Every Hindu learned the verses when still a child, as had all of Dhashid's children, all to proclaim the glory of eternity.

Today eternity had had a steep price tag, and now the costs he was bearing for Ilyana preyed on him like a viper that had wrapped itself around his brain, a viper with an unquenchable appetite, ever biting at his soul. Yes, he said to himself now, like the fabled Kundalini, this constant financial beast eats away at one's peace of mind and his very entrails. In fact, it was taking his entrails by signed contract, so that on the day of his death, the hospital physician would be first in line for his body, the Dom second, if at all.

Legend had it that the fabled Kundalini, the serpent god, wandered about the burning pyres and robbed many of the souls of a place in nirvana, feeding on their burning gases, sucking them into itself. They said it fed on the poor deceased children in particular, since they seldom had the luxury of parents who prayed for them. If not the poverty stricken children, it fed on those who had died without an attending Brahmin, his holy appointees, and their anointments.

It was said that the evil serpent god fed on those improperly cremated, that it sucked in all the burning fumes, feeding on the noxious gases, short-circuiting any plans for eternity. All men who gave any credence whatsoever to the old ways feared such things might happen to their dead or even to themselves. Prayer, fasting, and rupees proved the only safeguard against such demons, but the fates were so capricious, Dhashid knew that even after taking all the correct steps, one could lose to the whim of the gods. . . .

And so those unable to afford the Brahmin and the funeral pyres must simply place their dead in the Ganges River, where, it was rumored, the dirty waters of the filthy river worked to stave off evil spirits almost as well as the Brahmin's mantras and butter.

Since Dhashid was Ilyana's father, the Brahmin had instructed Dhashid to stab the lighted torch into the carefully prepared and treated pile of wood on which her basket lay. Five times Dhashid had stepped around the pyre, following ritual, and then he plunged the roaring torch into the wood below the basket holding his daughter's remains. The force of heat sent him back, stumbling, almost falling, the pyre erupting in flame like no one had ever witnessed before. The burning pyre sent up a cascade of cinder and ash like a river of rising butterflies. "Ily's soul is rising," he told his wife and the girl's siblings.

"Ily." He muttered her name several more times, creating his own mantra. "Ily, I am sorry for this world; perhaps in the next you will find far better karma, and far more beauty. Perhaps you will be reborn as a Brahmin, a doctor, a government official—anything, even a blood or body merchant— anything other than a starving peasant child."

The cremation ran just under three hours, and when only a handful of ashes remained, one of the overseers sprinkled these ashes with water taken from the Ganges but blessed by the Brahmin.

The ashes were scooped up and placed in a drab, baked

clay pot. It was turned over to the grieving parents, and it was then, for the last time, that Dhashid had carried his little girl—no longer in her earthly form—as the family proceeded to the river, where Dhashid scattered the ashes on the pre-dawn current.

"It is beautiful," his wife had said in his ear, "to see the cinders of her spirit borne away to the sky, and the ashes of her body borne away by the current. From here she goes to eternity."

He'd responded, "It is good to see her in no pain."

"She is in a better place, my husband."

The final ritual had them all wading hip deep in the river for a purifying bath and to give thanks to the Hindu gods.

Dhashid walked into a woman without arms, but she had none of the usual marks of a leper. He instinctively rushed on. Women had a horrible time in this place, he thought, many having to sell their babies to be assured the child would be fed, and if not selling the baby outright, then selling the child's future off, one organ at a time, since Mother had run out of organs to sell. Records were carefully kept. The various sold organs and bones and whole skeletons sold for thousands and thousands of rupees to medical schools in the United States and elsewhere around the world.

The running joke had it that more Indians "saw" America via the organ and the bone trade than all the Indian tourists put together. Livers and hearts for transplants, bone marrow, bodily fluids, infant T cells. "It is a strange world we live in, Father," Ilyana had often reminded him.

"And my karma in it, just as strange, and never good," he'd often reply. He missed just talking to her. She had been the most understanding creature on the planet.

From afar, the old scryer Kalie watched Dhashid with more than curious interest when a tall, imposing dark-skinned man with strange features approached Dhashid from the throng. The stranger appeared as if from nowhere and as if from all around, capturing Dhashid's full attention.

"I have watched you with much interest," said the man in their native tongue, in fact, in the same dialect Dhashid had grown up with. It made him recall the happiness of his childhood, the happiness Ily had never known. The shoulder-to-shoulder crowd in the marketplace disappeared, as if Dhashid and the stranger from his homeland were the only two in the milling humanity here. He found himself staring into the single most hypnotic pair of eyes he had ever seen, and yet the other man, dressed in rags no better than he, appeared no more important than a rickshaw puller.

"Do I . . . do I know you, sir?" Dhashid's own dialect had become rusty, as he had blended even his speech to go about Calcutta as a native; there was more work for natives.

"Of course," the man replied. "Everybody knows me, even those encased in ghee." The other man's smile turned into a curling grin that was both playful and sinister at once.

"You speak like someone from my village."

"Do you wish to better yourself? To do better for your family, your remaining children, your wife and yourself?" he repeated, his dark eyes penetrating. "Better that is than you have your Ilyana?"

His daughter's name coming off this stranger's lips came like a blow. He felt stunned. "What . . . what do you know of my daughter?" Does everyone in the area know of my painful loss? he wondered.

"I offer you a way from this hell." His arms went up and out to include all of Calcutta and every black hole within it. As he spoke his eyes grew in size, his dark pupils enlarging. A hungry gleefulness took hold of the man and it attempted to take hold of Dhashid, attempted to infect his mind with itself, but something deep inside told Dhashid to resist this giddiness that threatened to overtake him.

"What're you? A body merchant? Forget about it. I have already sold my organs. You're too late. Find another pitiful soul."

"I want you, Dhashid, all of you, not just one piece at a time, but all and now."

"I have a contract on the event of my death."

The stranger appeared suddenly to have gone deaf, ignoring what Dhashid had told him. His arms expanding, he said, "I want it all; the whole package—the full meal deal." Smiling, the strange, dark man pointed to a sign high overhead in the air, a billboard of the giant yellow arches of McDonald's.

Dhashid laughed. "You want to treat me to an American hamburger on Kama Sutra Boulevard?" Dhashid thought of the tourist section with its recently renamed streets, where KFC and McDonald's resided along with the high-rise hotels, where people who had service jobs lived a halfway decent life.

Today the heat that filled the Calcutta street overpowered even the hardiest of natives at 122 degrees Fahrenheit. The tourists trade suffered this summer due to the drought and heat. Yet the stranger who had promised Dhashid a free meal appeared without the least discomfort, not so much as a drop of sweat. This fact, combined with the growing eyes and the man's tongue darting in and out, added to the bizarre behavior and odd mix.

"How do you do that?" Dhashid suddenly asked, fascinated with the snakelike tongue, the growing eyes now with a fire inside their black, shining seeds. "How do you keep from sweating?"

"Cold-blooded," the stranger replied and laughed.

Dhashid did not laugh, but he managed a smile, a nod, and he wondered why he had not simply rushed away from this eccentric fellow.

"I am like the snake," the man added. Something like truth flitted across the pupils, something frighteningly wrong, supernatural even.

"I am looking for rickshaw work." Dhashid wiped his brow of glistening sweat.

"You have tuberculosis," countered the stranger. He seemed to know everything about Dhashid. "It will be extremely difficult for you to drag a carriage around in this heat for a few rupees; you are already coughing your lungs out.

Look, my name is Hari." The stranger extended his hand for Dhashid to shake.

Dhashid looked at the hand as if it were diseased; some instinct he did not recognize told him not to take the hand offered, or accept a meal from this man, or any other hospitality. *Under certain conditions, what is normal common courtesy can get you killed,* his intuition screamed. Rather than take the man's hand, Dhashid asked, "What province are you from?"

"My name is Hari . . . Hari Shakir."

"The name means nothing to me. Shakir is a common name, Hari."

"What province would you guess me from then, Dhashid?"

"How do you know my name and so much about my business?"

"I keep close to the ground." Again his smile held a silent hiss, and his tongue darted about as if doing the job of keeping him from perspiring. "Come now, Dhashid. What if I were to offer you more money than you can earn in two months sweating your ass off between the two shafts of a rickshaw that does not even belong to you, without . . . without your having to do anything—anything?"

The magic word now: *money.*

"How much . . . how much are you talking about?" stammered Dhashid, as he mentally calculated two months work on a rickshaw after everyone took his cut and all hands were greased, how much in rice and beans for his poor family, but to do nothing for it? This was some sort of hoax, a street scam; he just didn't know yet how Hari Shakir operated.

The noise of the Basra Bazaar had stilled, magically, inside Dhashid's head. A peacefulness resided there, a peace he had not known in over a decade. Something about Hari, the strange one, remained fascinating to the degree that Dhashid saw and heard no one else, not even the old scryer who suddenly recognized Hari and screamed at the top of his lungs for Dhashid to move away quickly from the other man.

"It's my blood you're after, isn't it?" asked Dhashid, not

cognizant of anything but the now-bulging black eyes with the fire deep within each onyx orb.

"Your blood is rotten, useless in and of itself. It's not your blood I'm interested in. I don't feed on blood. I'm not a fucking vampire."

"What . . . what exactly are you then?"

The man toyed with Dhashid, enjoying his confusion and fear, like a vulture standing over wounded prey.

"My bones; you want my skeleton?" Dhashid had finally figured it out. The weird, gaunt man who stood a head taller than he was a procurer in the bone trade; a trade that made India the world's largest exporter. Each year, twenty thousand intact skeletons and tens of thousands of carefully packed skulls and other bone parts were shipped UPS and via the mails from gigantic warehouses filled with skeletal remains here in Calcutta. It afforded passage on a plane or a ship abroad for the teeming poor, so the joke went. The bones were destined for medical schools in the U.S., Europe, Japan, Australia, Germany, anywhere doctors plied their trade. The principal exporters were well known, and it was entirely legal, so long as proper authorization and paperwork verified the certificate of origin. It merely needed the signature of a police official of the superintendent rank.

"No, I am not interested in your puny skeleton. It is only one part of you, Dhashid. I am interested in the whole man." Again came the curled smile.

"My soul? Are you telling me that you are a Dom?"

"No, I am not a Dom in the sense you take it to mean, no."

"What then? Who the hell are you?"

Dhashid did not see the old scryer, his stick raised as he fought his way through the crowd to get at him and the stranger, and he did not hear the old man's shouting.

"Kundalini, Dhashid . . . I am the ultimate body and soul merchant."

"What?"

"And yes, I want your body parts and your soul parts; I will take all parts of you into my being; and you? You will become a part of my power, a part of the solution to this wretched existence you lead. You will become a part of something larger, greater than yourself, if you but take my hand and ask . . . ask . . . ask . . ."

Dhashid did not remember taking the man's hand, but his palm was clasped between each of the stranger's now, and the grin had curled full again, creating a supernormal mouth that consumed the face. Dhashid's mind screamed for the man to let go and get away from him, but his words came out in his native dialect. "I offer you my being . . . soul and body, heart and head as yours. . . ."

It was a long-forgotten plea that had resided over the years in Dhashid's subconscious, a prayer he had heard in childhood, repeated by the old ones in his village, forgotten by all others. Somehow the man-creature holding Dhashid's hand and turning it white hot had sucked the thought from his brain, and somehow this Hari Shakir made Dhashid's tongue work, made his vocal cords create the words that the Kundalini wanted to hear.

"I like that," said Shakir.

"Get away! Get away from it!" shouted the old scryer, but someone knocked into him before he could strike the stranger with his cane.

Dhashid, feeling his hand burning away inside the grasp of the monster, fought to pull away now, but the throng all about kept him in place, the odor of scorched and seared flesh having no effect on the crowd familiar with such odors from the pyres. The perspiration that had bathed Dhashid's body turned to a white vapor cloud hanging over him, awaiting more gases to join it.

Fear gripped him, causing his stomach to spasm, his entire epidermal layer of skin now smoking and frying, the odor filling Dhashid's nostrils as the fire worked through him like an electrical current, taking the next layer and then the next, like peeling an onion, he thought of the effect. He shivered not from cold but from the sudden heat, every muscle twitching. He felt the flesh of his face shrink over the cheekbones, his skeleton forcing its way to the surface, as if it meant to escape him. It was now impossible for him to work his mouth or jaw even to close it. Nor did his eyes obey his brain, as he so wished to close them now but could not. His entire body froze in a flash point of heat, spasms rocketing through him.

Dhashid's skin had turned a curious ice-blue pallor. With the speed of a motion picture, the skin on his hands and forearms turned toasty and then brittle, completely dehydrated, giving off gases, the wrinkled, hardened veins popping under the pressure of heat.

It all happened in the blink of an eye. All around him the few who actually noticed what had happened fought to distance themselves. Others seemed not to want to notice, save the old, near blind seventy-year-old scryer, and now even he fought to distance himself from the odorous explosion of gases resulting from Dhashid's instantaneous human combustion.

The scryer saw only a soot-filled smoke cloud, greasy with human fatty tissues, all that remained of Dhashid, and he saw the strange-eyed one *inhale* like a mighty being to take all the acrid smoke, soot and much of the grease into his flaring nostrils. The ghost plume that had been Dhashid Ramar was all that remained, and it disappeared into the throat and nostrils of the creature that had claimed his life.

The stranger held firm to Dhashid's right wrist, however, and he lifted it now to his eyes, a dehydrated piece of jerky on a bone that a dog would find hard to chew, and he smiled and said, "Wonder what the body merchants would pay for this?" He tossed the bone and desiccated skin fragment to the old scryer and winked at him where he sat amid the throng of passing humanity. It had all happened so fast that the few standing closest did not know what had occurred or what they had seen or not seen. Many, the scryer included, did not believe their eyes, and those who did turned their gaze from the man calling himself the Kundalini.

*   *   *

The old man had safely averted his eyes from the scaly thing at the center of the white fire he had seen, and when he looked again, the monster was gone. The stranger had evaporated into the crowd as if the creature existed in the throng of humanity *at all times*, always ready to strike. Beside the scryer lay the bone fragment. He feared taking hold of it. Instead he scrambled away, returning to his kiosk and tent, back to a reality that he'd momentarily lost.

In a world inhabited by the severely depraved and ill, those suffering from encephalitis, tetanus, typhoid, typhus, cholera, infected abscesses, severe burns, amputations and leprosy, the sight of a spontaneous human combustion in Basra marketplace stirred a great deal less interest than it did a healthy fear.

Dhashid Ramar's cremation hadn't cost him a single rupee, but there had been no Brahmin to bless his departure or to pray over his journey, and no family to wish him better karma in his next life. A serious problem. *You get what you pay for*, the old scryer thought, his attempt to make light of it falling flat even after a chuckle. "I told Dhashid to get off the street, get into the blood business," he reminded himself. "This is the price he pays. Sad . . . very sad."

An ancient beggar in rags, who had also witnessed the death, found the scorched wrist and hand fragment left behind in a pool of waste at his feet. He knew of Dhashid and he wondered how much his wife would pay for the fragment of her husband. He would ask for a hundred paisas. If not, he would settle for fifty—five cents U.S. When he picked up the bone, it was hot to the touch; he couched it in his garment to keep from burning himself. A kind of acrid gas coming off the thing burned a hole through the beggar man's garment. He located a discarded tin can and placed the fragment inside for safe transport.

2

Florida Memorial Hospital of Miami was woefully understaffed and underequipped, and for this reason Dr. Renea Stanton gave of her time and energy in the Miami ghetto, where Memorial stood like an ancient fortress under siege. But the more time she spent at Memorial, the more defeat she saw at every turn. The hospital's only cobalt bomb had remained out of use for sixteen months, and all because no one could find funds to repair it. Elsewhere a cardiac resuscitation unit was shut down due to the heat wave, which had effectively killed the air-conditioning system in that wing, where peeling wall paint littered the worn tile floor. Two defibrillators and ten of twelve electrocardiogram machines—the older sort without computer interfacing—were shut down, as had been the bedside monitors.

Brownouts and the occasional blackout had become the norm over the past two weeks of intense heat, the drain on Florida Power and Light like the proverbial black hole citywide. No matter how much people conserved, the plague of heat Miami faced proved simply too long and too great a depletion on the systems in place.

It'd been impossible to open the new surgical wing because the Health Services human resources department, the personnel people, had not gotten off their red-tape asses to approve the hiring of so much as a goddamned elevator attendant. Meanwhile a general lack of technicians and materials had the labs and the X-ray division backed up for weeks, delaying any analysis. To further complicate matters, several of the ambulances had this very morning been found with their windows shattered, batteries stolen, and wheels stripped, along with valuable equipment that'd been in the rear of each van. *Community involvement* or so the joke went.

In its third week now, the heat wave was breaking all records, and for Miamians to complain of heat, Dr. Stanton, a Bostonian by birth, knew it must be beyond scorching. The weather reports filled the airways and TV stations with the figures on heat-related deaths and strokes, the number astronomical—war-zonelike.

Tonight Dr. Stanton felt a wave of exhaustion hit her when she had finished her list of needs going unmet, the last being finding time for herself. She'd gone about each surgical unit for her report, and she had found empty containers everywhere. What was needed? Everything. Forceps, scalpels, clips, and sutures. Reserve blood supplies proved nearly nonexistent, which made Renea wonder if the blood plasma packs, like all else in the hospital, were being pilfered—for what reason she dared not wonder. Even the food intended for patients. Meals now had to be transported in padlocked carts. Even some of the electric lightbulbs had turned up missing. She had complained about all this to hospital administrators, to doctors, nurses, even relatives and friends, hoping for donations from personal acquaintances, all to little avail.

Meanwhile outside the hospital the late summer had become vengeful, inflicting unimaginable suffering and heat-related fatalities, and as always, it struck hardest at the most destitute, those in the most miserable slums. These past few days had become an atrocious torture, worse than any cold or hunger or homelessness.

The combination of record-breaking heat-wave statistics and humidity levels off the charts had conspired to bring many a mind to a boil, so that large portions of the populace sat in the brutal heat awaiting what local and nationwide preachers of doom termed the final Armageddon. For others—true believers—the holy Rapture had at last arrived, and so too (she thought it ironic in the extreme) had come a breakdown in morality and concern for others.

Dr. Stanton could hardly blame people for their extreme views, given the extremeness of the weather and given the rhetoric of local TV evangelists, mediums and self-appointed prophets of the airways. Still, through it all, there remained a core of good souls at Memorial who bonded together to fight the awful horrors of the long day and night of this heat wave that continued to boggle the imagination even as it continued to break all previous records.

As Dr. Stanton made her silent round of checks on the surgical supplies, she thought of poor Mrs. Evey Tyler; poor woman had had a spinal fusion of the rachis, which involved a lot of pain and a grafting of the vertebral column. She thought of how incredibly hard the nurses and doctors here had worked to help her to gradually regain the use of her legs. Every time Renea Stanton stepped foot in Memorial, she visited Mrs. Tyler, the dear, sweet octogenarian, nearing eighty-two now. Evey had spent the better part of her last decade in and out of hospitals, unable to walk until now, thanks to Drs. Anatoli and Painter, two pathologists who normally worked with the dead downstairs in the basement morgue. Evey, as the staff had come to call the elderly miracle, had become a symbol of many things at Memorial, not the least being: When all hope is lost, don't give up hope. However, more than hope played a part in Evey's care. Chance had come into play, as it was by a fluke that Drs. Anatoli and Painter had seen Evey's X-rays. It had been her X-rays, sent mistakenly to the morgue, that had turned the trick for Evey. The two pathologists had recognized her problem, diagnosed it, and asked why hadn't the woman gotten help before dying?

Anatoli and Painter conferred on the case with Dr. Wilson Lambert, Evey's attending physician, after they discovered the error made by the X-ray department. The two pathologists had been surprised and pleased to learn that they'd diagnosed the problem of a living person still in a bed upstairs. Meanwhile Dr. Lambert had thoroughly misdiagnosed Mrs. Tyler, and he had blindly worked on with the missent X-ray of a dead woman, making no distinctions between the two.

Dr. Wilson Lambert silently slipped into the ER surgical supply room behind Dr. Stanton and he said, "Why don't you call it a night, Renea?" He startled her. He normally came on as she was going off, and they had bantered about any number of subjects, and Wilson had repeatedly asked her out and she kept turning him down in what had become a cat-and-mouse game with him. He didn't take rejection well, and his physical advances in dark little corners like the supply room had continued.

"I've got two tickets to see *Annabelle* at the Arts Center Friday night. Would you care to join me?" he asked.

"Sorry, Wilson, but I promised Jake and Sara I'd take them to the RollerRama Friday."

"Who's Jake and who's Sara?"

"My two kids."

"I didn't know you had children."

"You never asked. Look, I'm out of here," she replied, glistening with perspiration as she exited, stepping into the half-light of the empty surgical room. The air-conditioning had been set at half-life at the hospital to avoid another blackout. Withering and tired now, she thought of home, a cold bath, her air-conditioned apartment, some provolone and Chianti. As she gave thought to the coolness of a bath with wine and cheese, she felt his arm slither around her waist. She immediately freed herself from his touch.

"Children or not, we ought to do something about this thing between us, Dr. Stanton," he said, his palms open, supplicating.

She had never had any serious interest in Lambert, but since the story of Evey's misdiagnosis she had also lost respect for him. Besides, her clothes were sticking to her, and she felt uncomfortable already. She didn't need him sticking to her, too.

"You look especially beautiful tonight," he said to her. "Smell good, too."

"You've got to be kidding. I must smell like a longshoreman."

"I wouldn't say that. A little pungent is ... nice."

She wondered if he was into toilet sex or something nastier. "I'll take that as a warning." And in her mind a bell tolled.

"What about Saturday, dinner and a movie, or a walk in the moonlight?" he asked.

"My crazy schedule at St. Sebastian's and here doesn't really leave me much room, Wilson. You know how killing it is, being a doctor running between two hospitals."

"You're spreading yourself too thin, Renea. If you were a patient of mine, I'd advise rest, relaxation, some time away with a handsome colleague, maybe at Club Med, take a cruise together, you and me."

Arrogant bastard, she thought. "Can the kids come along?"

He attempted a smile at this.

"Truthfully, Wilson ... *hmmm.*" She hummed, buying a moment before telling him a white lie. "I'm involved right now with a man, Wilson, an exclusive relationship, if you know what I mean." She guessed he did not know *what* she meant.

"I see ... I hope it works out," he lied.

"But thanks for the invite, Wilson, and ... and good night."

"Night ..."

At her locker she dressed down, exchanging the suit she'd had on all day beneath the white lab coat for a pair of khaki shorts and a pullover top, a pair of new Nikes—running shoes—replacing the old Nikes she preferred over anything else to spend all day in, the pair she'd sweltered in all evening. Her final "casual-down" touch was to put her hair into a ponytail. At thirty-four she could look in the mirror and worry at the first signs of wrinkles with a hope she would favor her mother in old age. Jake and Sara spent more time these days with her mother than she did, what with all the causes she had gotten behind both here and at the other hospital.

She soon pushed past the ER doors as someone with a gunshot wound was wheeled past her. The usual peaceful boredom of the place turned to pandemonium before her weary eyes. She heard someone shout, "Gunshot to the chest!" and she knew the black kid on the gurney would most likely not survive the night, and that the already short supply of plasma packs would be lost on him. A part of her scolded herself for the negative thought, while another part thought of the DEA's latest war on gang drugs, the city's crackdown on gang violence, and the state's new "Say No To Gangs" program, none of which had proven particularly effective. Death by gunshot for young black males in Miami had only risen to more startling numbers than ever; more young men died of such than of all the diseases combined.

Indeed a mad world, she thought, going now for her car in the hospital lot. As she fished for and fumbled at her keys somewhere at the bottom of her purse, she felt the press of the blighted area around her. The area seemed to have eyes, a breath and a life of its own, like a living creature. Not two blocks distant, in wealthy Coral Gables, people partied at the Granada Country Club and at the historic Vanderbilt Hotel, and she gave a moment's thought to the new Dali museum opening, which she'd been unable to make due to her commitment here tonight.

"Dr. Stanton . . . Renea Stanton?" came a voice from behind her. She gripped her car door in one hand, her mace key chain in the other.

"Wilson?" She steeled herself to rebuff the man again, but on turning, she found a dark-skinned man standing too close, invading her space, making her uncomfortable. "Harry?" she asked.

The Indian maintenance man had been working at the hospital for nearly two weeks now, doing his janitorial work in a stiffly silent manner. Renea had to drag words from him when she first noticed the newcomer, and he struggled painfully with English. "What is it, Harry?"

"Hari, madam doctor. It is Harr-ree, Hari Shakir," he said, pronouncing his name distinctly for her while his dark eyes bored into her. His white uniform made his skin even blacker than it actually was. He spoke with a distinctly East Indian accent, but he scarcely spoke at all, seemingly very shy. She had never seen him initiate a conversation, yet his eyes were always curious, always watching, the black centers always questioning.

Yet here he was tonight seemingly *changed* somehow.

He tossed aside a pungent Indian cigarette that had burned at its tip like a flare.

"What . . . what can I do for you, Hari?" He had never corrected her on her pronunciation of his name before now, so she took pains to get it right.

"I see you . . . as you left hos-spit-tal. I was there," he pointed at the lighted ER bay where everyone stepped out for air and a smoke, some foolishly thinking they could get both at once. Hari smelled; he smelled of India—Indian food, Indian cigarettes, Indian blood and perspiration, yet he didn't appear to be perspiring, despite the horrid wall of heat that made up this night. The air was so still and thick with heat that she had felt her body pushing it ahead of her as she'd walked out to the car.

"Yes? So you saw me leaving; so you see me now leaving. How can I help you, Hari?" She mentally chastised herself for talking to him as if he were a child, a knee-jerk reaction to anyone who spoke with a thick accent and worked in a service position.

"It is *I* who wish to help *you*, Dr. Stanton. This man Lambert. He is not right for you, and this place," he said and paused to look around, a hand gesturing to the surrounding slums, "it is not safe for you. I thought best someone walk you to your motorcar."

A product of the British school system, she thought. *Motorcar* sounded so Continental. But what did he know of her and of Lambert? Had he overheard their banter from some corner or shadow? And what right had he to presume? *God, I'm too tired for this shit,* she thought.

"It is a danger to be here," he continued, "alone."

Man but his English has improved fast, she thought. "But I'm not alone, Hari. I'm with you, and thank you for your concern, but really, I'm all right."

"Allow me, madam," Hari said, taking the keys from her grasp, plopping into her seat and starting the car and the AC, saying, "It is far too stuffy and warm inside, sitting out in the sun since three."

He knows precisely when I come on.

"I am pleased that it is your day to be here," he added from the cab of the car.

She only came twice a week from St. Sebastian's, a real hospital, where the staff did not steal supplies and plasma packs did not mysteriously disappear along with X-rays, and there were no mad instances of the occasional misplaced food tray, instrument tray, scalpel, patient, or corpse.

"I am told you only come here sometimes," he said.

"Yes, only part time when I can."

"It is so kind of you to take time away from St. Sebastian's to be here."

He knows a lot about me. He's asked a lot of questions. "Thank you, Hari, but won't you be missed?" She indicated the hospital with her index finger.

He climbed from the car and closed the door behind himself. He stood leaning against the door now, his large, imposing and dark form between her and the car, and *something* in his manner made her feel for a moment like a frightened child. She tried to shrug it off as foolish, but then what did she know about this man? She tried to concentrate on the idling car, his chivalry in helping her; she imagined how wonderful it would be to slip into the air-conditioned interior he'd prepared for her, if only she could get past Hari, who *still* stood too close.

Renea wished that the silent custodian's assistant had remained silent, that she had never heard a word from him.

"It's all relative, don't you suppose?" he asked.

The question confused her. "I'm not at all sure I follow you, Hari. What do you mean?" *Damn it,* she silently cursed herself for asking him anything at this point. *Just get in and take off,* she thought.

He thoughtfully replied, "All the suffering in the heat, the hardships, the strokes, the dying."

"How do you mean . . . *relative?*"

"For one, all the victims have relatives!" He smiled, showing gleaming white teeth. "Is a joke."

It was a lame joke, but one to be expected from a nonverbal, freshly off the boat, wanna-be American from New Delhi or . . . or . . .

"*Calcutta* is the place I journey from; I am on a quest, you see. Something I must have."

Is he reading my mind? she wondered. "Calcutta? Really? I would love to hear more about it but—"

Something about his eyes stopped her; she thought she saw some slight movement of light or was it shadow, deep in the pupils, and the pupils—dark as rosary beads—enlarged with each passing moment. Something fascinating, mesmerizing about Hari, but what was it? A part of her wanted to chat with him. *Be nice,* said her right-side brain. *Screw being nice,* said her left side.

She found herself saying something about the heat and the conditions under which the doctors and nurses, and Hari himself, had had to work this past week. He only laughed in return and said, "You American doctors whine so much, yet you have not one idea what is true suffering, what is faced every day by doctors in India."

"Really now?"

"To approximate the suffering in Calcutta, you would have to multiply your ghetto here ten, twenty fold."

"I didn't mean to sound complaining or—"

"*Ahhh,* it is nothing. Like this so-called heat wave is *nothing.*"

"Nothing? This is record-breaking heat we're dealing with, Hari. The dead wheeled through those doors over there, they wouldn't call it nothing. It's the worst in all of—"

"This heat you call heat . . . it is like the spring breeze in Calcutta."

She managed a light laugh at this. "Tell *that* to my body. And at the moment, my feet are killing me. Been on 'em for ten hours running."

"My homeland is a place of many secrets and mysteries and antiquities and architectural wonders."

She realized he was coming on to her. Two in one night. Neither proposal feasible. Still, she felt flattered, but at the same time, she wanted nothing to do with the janitorial help. *What a story it'll make for the nurses. Day after tomorrow when I return, it'll be all over the hospital, a garden for gossip.* Out the corner of her eye, she saw some self-absorbed interns smoking at the ER bay turn and reenter the hospital. No doubt the rumor mill would begin on this grist the moment they got to Nurse Murray.

"I would love to hear more about Calcutta, but right now, I am—"

"Dead," he replied, "merely a *walking* dead."

The remark sent a new wave of eerie feeling jolting through her being. She was not unfamiliar with the prison term for death-row inmates. Not for the first time a small voice in her brain gave alarm, like a screeching, vibrating panic button, screaming for her to get away—while another voice, strangely unfamiliar to her kept chanting "be nice to the immigrant fellow."

Ignoring this last pitch to be nice to Hari, she reached for the car door handle, but she found that his hand was quicker, as hers now overlaid his.

She instantly pulled her hand away as if burned, and Hari then opened the door for her and bowed. Such manners she hadn't seen since going on a teen date.

She awkwardly nodded at his gesture and rushed to get into the Olds Cutlass as she kept one eye on him. Her attention still on him, she slowly slid into the car, finding the interior as hot as a baking kiln. "Damn it . . . Hari, you turned on the heat, not the AC!" *Damned fool,* she thought, but when he was suddenly in the passenger seat beside her, she realized that he'd also unlatched the passenger-side door earlier while in the cab. All to what end? Why this curious behavior, this curious rendezvous?

"Get out! You are not wanted here, no!" she shouted.

"I thought you could give me a lift. I'm off now, too, and who wants to be alone? We could have drinks, cool down."

She grabbed the ignition key, burned herself on the hot metal, and let go. Part of her mind ciphered out why the metal was so hot, while she carefully switched off the car and removed the keys. She fumbled with the mace canister attached to the keys, pointing it at him.

He merely smiled, his white teeth opening for a darting tongue.

She realized only now that he hadn't a drop of perspiration on his entire being, and that he basked in the heat of the oven he'd created of her interior. "No, no lifts," she firmly said.

"Yes, of course, and I am most sorry if I have in any way offended you, madam, most apologetic."

"Apology accepted, now please . . . please, just get out of my car," she replied, her keys lightly ringing one another as she continued to point the bad end of the canister at him. *He must see I mean business,* she thought.

Hands up in the universal gesture of retreat, Hari opened the passenger door, readying to leave. She stabbed the key back into the ignition, anxious to crank up both the engine and the AC and get the hell away from him. This place got weirder by the hour. She breathed in the hot air with some relief when she heard the car door slam, Hari telegraphing his own frustrations. Then her driver's-side door opened and Hari was on his knees just outside the car, their eyes at the same level.

She saw a snakelike intensity in his eyes, and the venomous eyes enlarged from their small black orbs to large red ones before her. His tongue flicked in and out, a darting viper's tongue. Then his enormous tongue found her cheek and licked at it, all the way from his crouching position outside the car. She wanted to crawl across the seat, tear open the passenger-side door and race back into the hospital, but somehow the act of his touch, his tongue touching her, held her in a kind of suspended animation.

She fought him for her mind and an end to the paralysis, fought by thinking of her Jake and Sara. But there was something *preternatural* about his tongue, the size of it, the strange odor of bile as if it had crawled up from his stomach, the feel of the snakelike creature it had become, slithering along her skin. The flicking touch of it caused a quaking shudder in her, and only now did she feel the stinging, acidic burning sensation in the epidermal layers of her face.

Hari no longer looked human, merely a conduit for this monster rising from him.

A fire ignited below the lowest layer of her skin, and it intensified as if from within, one layer upon another, each fueling and eroding the other in a silent, invisible flame that crawled now like lice all over her body. She felt a tight hardness overtake her torso and face, the extremities following.

Her skin became shoe leather, dehydrated, brittle. In the rearview mirror she caught a glimpse of the smoke coming off her body, turning her clothing to soot, and in a moment all clothing was gone the way of each layer of skin and hair, and then she felt the soft tissues of her eyes become hard, blind, blistered orbs milliseconds before they exploded into flame.

At the same instant, Renea Stanton's bodily fluids and fatty tissues exploded into a gaseous form inside the car. The chemical reaction threw off large pellets of black soot and human creosote in its wake, bathing the steering wheel and column with it. This along with the cushion of her seat.

The Kundalini man smiled to see her—from jogging shoe to ponytail—become the coalesced gaseous cloud trapped within the confines of the motorcar. The creature living within Hari had replaced him with itself, and now Hari appeared as an enormous snakelike dragon, and the dragon opened its enormous jaws and flaring nostrils to inhale the cloud of blackness made of Dr. Stanton's molecules, sucking powerfully, swallowing her essence deep into its enormous chest.

When it was over, the monster sat in the lotus position just outside the driver's-side door, straight and tall, with a feeling of power, and a sense of unleashed giddiness coming over him as he reshaped into Hari Shakir. "And the Kundalini shall laugh the laugh of the mortals," he said, recalling an ancient story about himself.

"I am all that the great dark god of my people has promised, am I not, Dr. Stanton?" he said with a sneer. "The Kundalini does not lie to any of us. He has put your troubled mind to rest; no more turmoil with respect to life's problems. And he has made you part of us, and he has made me all powerful, and when I find my brother, then the last of my kind, the last *Shakir* will be one and whole again with the last *Shakar*. Then the power of the two ancient families united will create the *true* Kundalini. Then . . . then his will be done . . . then will be released on this world all of the god's power, and then everyone will know the ultimate truth."

She did not answer him. In time, she would, for so long as he lived, a part of her soul resided in the snake god.

Hari casually made his way back to the hospital doors, smoking a Camel as he went. *American cigarettes,* he thought, *could not be beaten the world over.* He wondered how long it would be before seeing his long-lost spirit brother, Shakar. How long before his snake god could take full possession of him and use his body for its true purpose?

3

Detective Lieutenant Eric Brannon recalled that it was his mother's birthday, that he hadn't gotten her a card much less a gift, and when would he find time to get it in the mail? She lived in San Bernadino, California, with her new husband. He pushed the personal problems aside even as he pushed through the crowd in the Delta terminal, keeping an eye on the suspect at all times. The suspect wore the blue uniform and breastplate of a Delta skycap, but Brannon knew better.

The Delta skycap, wheeling a late arrival in a chair through the crowd, anxiously looked over his shoulder every few minutes, as if feeling eyes on him. The last-minute arrival in the chair had to be wheeled down a special ramp, down a flight, and out onto the teeming black asphalt. The man sat beneath a blanket.

The airstrip and surrounding asphalt at Miami International pushed a hundred and forty degrees Fahrenheit. The people in the control tower were stressed; the heat wave created wind sheer that swooped about the airfield like unleashed ghosts. Men working about the airfield blessed any breeze, including a wind sheer, as they worked in the sweltering heat rising off the blacktop. The men working the Delta terminal ground crew had been reduced to slow-motion puppets in this weather.

Heat stroke had already claimed a number of baggage handlers. No one was taking any chances.

Brannon kept his eyes on the mischief afoot. Both skycap and wheelchair victim were suspect at this point.

Brannon's partner, Jackie Hale, also in plain clothes, hung back, prepared to back any play Brannon might make. They had teamed with Stan Castle's vice squad to get close to their prey.

Assignments had been gone over a hundred-and-one times, along with the complete layout of the Delta terminal, the area where Brannon had expected Castle's men to take their suspect down. Still, with men stationed all over this wing of the airport, there was no way Enrico Garza could possibly slip out of Miami with the drug money destined for Bogotá and a Colombian cartel. No, this time Enrico had made murder, and he had made murder on an undercover cop.

No way was Enrico going to waltz out of the country with a cop killing on his head.

The cop had been the seventh in a line of people killed by Garza and his men, who had left a trail of bodies in their wake in search of some white powder that had gone astray. Thanks to a sister of one of the victims, angry as hell at losing her brother to torture and murder, Brannon and Detective Sergeant Jackie Hale had reliable information on Garza's movements. The brother had left his sister with a little black book filled with information on Garza's operation, to be used in the event of the man's death.

The team remained on radio silence, knowing that Garza's people routinely listened in on police frequencies. They closed in behind Garza, believed to be in the skycap's chair. A free and easy ride at the moment.

Earlier flights had been delayed due to tires bursting as they taxied about the sweltering runways, and so the Delta crew sprayed the plane's tires with a coolant to keep them from overheating.

"Where're Garza's bodyguards?" asked Jackie, catching

up to Brannon, who remained close on the skycap and chair. Delta had been contacted earlier to board everyone on the Columbian flight off the tarmac. They now followed the chair down the ramp to the oven of Miami morning.

"I think the guy pushing the chair is one of his guards, and the decrepit one in the chair is Garza in skin-mold makeup and white wig."

"Garza? Suppose you're wrong, Eric?"

"It's got to be him. Everyone else has boarded the plane."

He held back, peering out through the glass partitions at the wheelchair and the man pushing it. Something new struck Eric as odd about the man in the chair: the way his legs were crossed, or the size of an ankle that showed. He could not be sure what bothered him, but something just didn't appear right. Maybe it wasn't Garza after all.

Then one of those sudden gusts blew away the seated man's hat, and a cascade of jet-black hair showed through the back of the wig. "It's Garza's woman," said Brannon, realizing now that his eyes had registered the fact long before his brain. "Garza's pushing the chair."

It was time to act or lose them. The pair need only make their way up the steps to the waiting plane. Once on the plane, they could take hostages. From all sides of a baggage train that divided them police acting as baggage handlers appeared, and Garza's bodyguards materialized from the plane wearing airport security uniforms, all brandishing firearms smuggled past the detectors.

Brannon saw the entire scheme in his head. Garza's men had overpowered and likely killed a pair of armed guards and had made their way to this position earlier. Garza and the woman followed. Brannon now burst out onto the tarmac shouting, "Miami PD! Hold it, Garza!"

Seeing the Uzi come out of the wheelchair, Brannon hit the hot pavement and opened fire on her moments before she fired, striking her left forearm, but the impact set off a chain reaction in her, and she squeezed off repeated rounds from the AK-47. And as soon as Garza's woman had opened fire, so had the bodyguards.

Bullets rained on all sides of Brannon. The baggage handlers who were cops, like Brannon, hit the sunbaked deck, ignoring the scorching pain to exposed skin, and opening fire. From somewhere behind him Brannon heard his partner, pinned down in the open like him, cursing.

Gunfire blazed all about the idling plane in all directions, from Garza's men at the top of the ramp, and from the woman who acted as a human shield for Garza, and the return police fire.

The woman with the Uzi continued to fire as she backed up the ramp, shielding her man. She gave credence to the song "Stand by Your Man," Brannon thought, knowing he'd never command that much devotion from any woman, not in this life.

Baggage handlers continued firing back at Garza's people atop the ramp. One by one, Garza's guards at the top fell, hit by return fire. Some of Castle's people fell back also, bleeding, hit. Garza's two guards lay dead on the ramp.

Meanwhile Garza had evaded the gunfire, protected by the beautiful, dark-haired woman with the Uzi to make it to the top of the ramp only to find that the flight attendant had locked him out.

Brannon, an imposing, tall man at six foot two, took careful aim, and with his next shot he sent the deadly woman cascading over the ramp to the jumbo jet, her skull silently cracking below the noise of the idling engines.

Suddenly the sound of gunfire became a waning echo, all of Garza's people dead and bleeding, leaving him exposed and alone. Garza's woman lay on the searing pavement, her blood already baked against the blacktop. Garza cursed and banged on the hatchway, cursing at the attendant who had bravely unlatched the metal steps from the open doorway and shut him out. Garza screamed for those inside to open it up, finally firing a handgun into the hatchway. The plane then pulled away from the ramp, and the metal staircase that had represented Garza's freedom now toppled over, making Garza a flying target as some of the cops continued to fire at him. He hit the scorched pavement with his face and head first, blood everywhere.

Eric Brannon got to him first and held his gun steady on Garza, knowing him as he did, knowing he had at least one other concealed weapon. "Give me one reason why I shouldn't blow your fucking head off, Garza."

But Jackie, Castle, and the others had all gathered round the immobile Garza, thinking him dead. Jackie said, "Forget about it, Eric. He's outta here."

Castle kicked away at the man, trying to get any reaction. "She's right."

Garza was bleeding enough that he should be dead, but Brannon checked his pulse at his neck. "The son of a bitch is still alive." He then searched him and found another concealed gun. Garza had sustained a vicious facial laceration, which, combined with the skull fracture, along with two gunshot wounds, would land him in a prison hospital ward for some time before he stood trial.

He had sixteen guns still trained on him, some shaking. "Filthy cop killer. I say let him die where he fell," said one of Castle's men.

Nobody disputed him, but Castle got on his radio and ordered in the waiting medic wagons. Castle said to them all, "I want to be there to see this guy go to the chair."

In the distance a pair of city slab wagons wailed, and they soon bullied their pachyderm selves onto the airstrip and to the waiting wounded and dead. Several of Castle's baggage handlers had sustained minor injuries and gunshot wounds.

"How did you know the bitch in the wheelchair was packing an Uzi?" asked Stan Castle as he came up to Brannon.

"Something in her eyes spoke volumes."

"So, my report will say you fired first to warn, detain or to subdue?"

"Subdue, of course. She fired first."

"All right; guess that's the way your partner sees it?"

Jackie Hale nodded on hearing this, backing Brannon up.

The cops congratulated one another, slapping one another on the back, laughing, coming down from the adrenaline high. Jackie Hale took Brannon aside, even as he studied the amazed crowd looking down on them from the terminal windows, some passengers no doubt fearful that their bags had been among those destroyed in the fray. Jackie forced his head around and stared into Brannon's snow-blue eyes, saying, "How'd you know the woman was carrying the Uzi in her sitting position?"

"We all did the same research on her; she grew up a soldier in Bogotá, started as a mule and rose through the ranks until she hooked up with Garza, who made her his queen. Knowing what I knew about her, it was no big stretch, not really."

"Yeah, but you fired first, Eric."

"Me? No . . . no way."

"I saw the whole thing from my vantage point, and you fired first."

"She opened fire, and I returned fire. If I'd fired first, she wouldn't've gotten a round off, much less—what?—seventy-nine?"

"She hadn't got off her first round when your first bullet grazed her, spinning her. She continued firing, almost hitting Garza with that pirouette, and then your second bullet sent her over the side."

"Just pray no one up there at the terminal was filming. Hate to see this SOB get off on a technicality."

"I ordered them to halt, identified us."

"Yeah, and then you opened fire. Lucky thing in the long run. Firing like that bitch did with only one good arm, we would've all been mowed down."

"His lawyer would be screaming police vendetta, if you're right."

"You read her body language perfectly, Eric. She was about to fire. You got *blue* is what you got, the blue sense."

He smiled at the familiar cop's term for knowing *before* knowing, a kind of instinct that came with experience that some saw as a near psychic ability to foretell an event. It was often a cop's lifeline on the street.

Already internal affairs division cops had shown up and were pouring over the scene, attempting to understand to the second what had led up to the use of deadly force, whether or not it'd been warranted, and if anyone on the force had acted unwisely in the situation. Eric Aaron Brannon had had brushes with IAD men and women in the past, and they never forgot an incident, a face, or a badge number.

Jackie, noting the IAD officers as well, punched Brannon in the arm and said, "Play nicey-nice with them. Don't piss anyone off, OK?"

"No problem here."

"You just assume I'm going to back you a hundred percent."

"The bitch had an Uzi; she was opening up on us. I saw it in her crazy eyes. Who knows, maybe she and Garza had a fight this morning. Maybe she wanted it to end this way."

"All right. You know I'll back you."

"We were successful. We got payback. That's the important thing."

"We didn't let him slip out of the country this time. We got the slimy lizard."

Brannon again smiled at his partner. "Yeah. Feels good, doesn't it?"

After listening to and answering a series of questions, Brannon and Jackie felt drained from the drilling process, and each had begun to smart off at the internal affairs officers. Each detective was interrogated by a different IAD detective, as was Castle and his men—*divide and conquer*. When their questions could shake no unhappy conclusions or confusing testimony from anyone at the scene, the partners were at last allowed to leave. The plane that had been riddled with bullets had been grounded. Passengers would be placed on another flight.

Brannon and Hale walked off amid police squad cars that had huddled about the area now. Brannon looked back at the mob that'd been brought in to mop up after. Castle had gotten hold of the all-important valise that Garza had been carrying when the gunfire had erupted. Everyone knew it was filled with drug money for the waiting lord back home in Colombia. For the moment it would go to a police lockup. The amount, while staggering, wouldn't surprise a choirboy in today's drug-infested Miami streets.

Brannon and Jackie arrived at the car that had brought them to the airport, huddled in the corner of a Flying Tigers cargo hangar. "Why don't you join some of us for drinks tonight, Eric? Castle says we deserve a celebration for today's work. O'Banyan's about eight."

"If I can make it, it'll be late, around eleven," he told her.

"Bring her along, whoever she is."

"It's not like that. Seeing Dr. Stanton tonight. We finally found a hole in our schedules that will allow it."

"Bring her along," repeated Jackie.

"She's doing me a favor; it's not a date."

"Helping you with that lower back pain, is she?"

"Sure . . . sure . . . having that lumbar thing taken care of." He knew it was easier to go along than to do otherwise. Together they laughed.

Finally he said, "All kidding aside, I gotta see Renea tonight, and if she's interested, I'll ask her to join me at O'Banyan's, OK?"

"You thinking of funneling some of Garza's drug money into I-CARE or to some other community service helping crack-head mothers again?"

"The concern is for the crack-head mothers' *babies*, Jackie."

"All right . . . all right."

"You know, every kid deserves a crib maybe, maybe a toy or two?"

"Yeah, well, Mr. Goody Three-shoes, either way, you wear your heart on your sleeve, someday it's going to get you into—"

He cut her off, saying, "Trying to work out a proposal for a regular program that funnels money like Garza's into helping people, and Dr. Stanton's interested in the idea. Helping me couch it in the right terms for the politicians."

"*Couch* being the operative word?"

He glared, then broke into a laugh. "Nothing of the sort."

"I should think you'd need a lawyer for that."

"Dr. Stanton knows a lot about the law. She was gonna be a lawyer before she locked down on doctoring."

"So . . . she knows a few people in the system."

"A goodly few, yes."

Jackie leaned in across the hood of the car and smiled across at her partner. "Real tough bastard, aren't you, Brannon?"

"Yeah, bad to the bone." He slid into the driver's seat, and she into the passenger seat. "Let's get back to the one-five."

"Got a lot of reports to fill out," she replied.

The car radio came instantly alive with static broken by a voice trying to get through. Eric lifted the receiver, the static magically disappeared, and the voice trailed off. "This is Brannon. Say again."

"Urgent call for you, Brannon. They want you at Miami Memorial. Something about a suspicious car explosion and a possible abduction."

"Memorial on Elm and Flagler?"

"That's the one."

"OK, we're on it," he repeated and stared across at Jackie. "That's ironic, huh? That's where Renea . . . Dr. Stanton puts in a lot of her time."

He slipped on his rainbow Oakley shades against the glaring sun. The heat was sucking away at the detectives' oxygen, but at least the car had been sitting under shade. Jackie caught her breath as the air-conditioning finally began to kick in, saying, "We gotta get this thing looked at."

She located a pen and began chewing on it. She took a deep breath and said of the pen, "Poor substitute for a good cigarette." She then muttered curses at her addiction, and then at her resolution to quit smoking.

But Brannon wasn't hearing her. He mulled over his own thoughts; felt his initial fear—that something had happened to Dr. Stanton—a foolish thought, he reassured himself, a foolish one indeed. Still, they had spoken many times about how dangerous it was for her to be in such an area at night, and he had talked to her about carrying a gun, but she only argued that she'd wind up shooting herself, saying that her mace would be protection enough. It was daylight now, but hadn't dispatch said the car explosion occurred the night before? Why were they just getting to it now? he wondered.

He got back on the radio. "Dispatch, can you give me any particulars on that explosion at Memorial?"

"A doctor has gone missing under unusual circumstances."

"Unusual circumstances?"

"Her car is in the parking lot with fire damage."

"A female doctor?"

"Looks like maybe a bomb went off. Fear is someone's abducted her and torched her car. Suspect for now is an old boyfriend. Captain Ames wants you there. Says you've had some history with the missing woman."

"Christ, it is Renea." He hit the siren and placed the strobe light atop the unmarked police car all in one swift motion while accelerating. Jackie stared across at the burning concern creasing his features. He was an active, strong man with a muscular build, and he stood six foot two, but as Jackie looked across at him, he had suddenly taken on the appearance of a frightened little boy. He knew the worst had happened; he knew that his friend's vanishing act was far from a simple disappearance. Somehow Jackie knew that he knew: his friend's life had come to an abrupt end under *unusual circumstances*.

Every cop in America knew that when dispatch characterized something as unusual circumstances that the translation read murder.

4

Find him . . . find Shakar . . . find Shakar . . . The
words of the beast within him were always the same demand.
It hammered out its message incessantly now that time was
running out. It had driven him all over India, to Europe,
London, Paris, and finally here, crossing the sea to America,
and now here, the city of Miami. Adib Shakar had been
clever in so long eluding his fate; and shrewd to hide for so
long in Calcutta, and now to have escaped to America, but
what would save him now? Soon the *Shakir* and the *Shakar*
would be joined as their destinies dictated. They would join
and then Hari Shakir's life would forever change.

So many years upon years of this kind of half-life alle-
giance to the Kundalini within, since childhood, having been
the chosen one.

He had returned to his flophouse after finishing up at the
hospital, going off his shift an hour after ingesting Dr. Stanton. He might need the job a bit longer as a cover. Now he
lay in a coiled position on the floor, preferring it to the mattress, and he stared up at the whirling ceiling fan.

He wanted closure as much as the snake god wanted it,
and he had no misgivings about the final resolution in which
he would have a franchise portion of the ultimate power in
the universe. He would become part of the one ultimate force

of energy, the all-powerful being from whom an entire pantheon of gods from India's most honored and ancient past
would be spawned anew.

Hari and the creature within had walked until dawn about
the Miami streets, contemplating the long journey to get here,
so close to Adib Shakar, his end goal. Still, it was a large
city with many places to hide, not entirely unlike Calcutta,
despite the riches here. From what Hari had gathered before
even leaving India, Adib Shakar had something to do with
medical work, or that he worked in a medical place like a
hospital. That was all he knew.

It kept no secrets from him, and he could not keep a secret
from it. In this, Hari knew the genesis of the growth within
him. When only an infant, his family had prepared him to
enter the tomb of his ancestors. There he was infected by the
unseeable viral cell that had become the scaly tumor which
doctors had told him he should have removed, but the virus
had cocooned itself, the tumor its safe wall, its fire wall in a
sense. Within the confines of the tumor, over the years, it
metamorphosed into a larvaelike state. Finally, at age thirteen, Hari had voluntarily returned to the tomb, as per the
ritual, which required his willing sacrifice. It was then the
creature, in its infancy, formed into a worm-sized serpent,
weak and coiled deep within his scrotum, where it exercised
a circular path about the area, causing great sexual excite-
ment and pleasure, beyond anything Hari had ever known or
imagined possible. The sentient white worm within then began a physical teasing, comingling a mental teasing, and the
sensual distraction had its own allure and addictive quality.
It became his obsession, his allure, his distraction from the
world. He became its slave early on, enjoying the plentiful
pleasures it provided unbidden.

Somehow it fed on his sexual arousal, so that the give and
take between it and the human mechanisms for pleasure became more than any need fulfillment, but a basis for communication and a full-blown symbiotic relationship in which
Hari was made to feel important as an integral half. Yes, it
fed on his sexual arousal, but it also provided for his sexual

arousal, and nothing else would do. The thing within next began communicating its intent *cerebrally*, and its voice grew in strength and intensity with the level of sexual arousal—at least that had been the case at first, in its early stage. It told him how to withhold his sexual peak, to sustain the climax in a circle of eddies of joy and ecstasy. Eventually, it trained him to—at the last instant of ejaculation—direct his semen not to spurt and spill outward but to flow inward instead, in *reverse* and into its waiting mouth. Coiled and contented then, the thing drank often of his semen in a phase of nourishing necessary to its continued growth—and his own. And when it grew stronger, it grew a second head, one at each end now, so that it could go in two different directions at once. By now it had stretched itself all along the course of his spine, from scrotum to brain stem. It could now coil about his every nerve, muscle and organ. After this stage, it rested comfortably wrapped about his spinal column, and its communication with him through his cerebral pathways had come into full-blown conversations. It spoke to him in his native tongue, and since Hari knew English, it spoke to him in English at times as well.

Now with its two-headed aspect, it took in the semen at one end and carried it up to the brain, where it spewed it out in a wash of mental juices that Hari had only heard about. Most people believed such a thing, restricting the semen to go through the various chakras of the body and to ultimately spray forth over the cerebral cortex, was pure nonsense put forth in books written by priests and purveyors of abstinence, but here was the miracle, and it was the most satisfying, luscious five-senses-pulling experience of Hari's life.

He thought of the millions on the planet who had no conception of a sexual experience that was indeed cosmic perfection, reaching to the kind of pleasures usually ascribed to the gods alone. And he once again was honored by and taught by the Kundalini fire serpent within him that perfect lust was as close to godhood as the human creature could ever hope to become, that nirvana was reached not by prayer and fasting and beating one's self with a whip, but by perfect sexual harmony through the sexual power inherent in mankind—as the gift of the gods. But mankind as a whole remained blind to this fact, that they held such power within. So the ignorant creature called man seldom understood its own sensual orgasmic supremacy.

The serpent of fire within Hari Shakir held out promises far greater yet, should he locate and join with the body and serpent god within his brother family, Shakar.

There was no going back from the course Hari had set himself on. Not now. For now *it* stood as tall as him, perhaps taller, as it coiled in places and stretched in others the full length of its human host. It not only reached the length of him along his spine, it now *was* him. Its desires, its goal was his own. In the meantime, it required carbon, lots of carbon, and hydrogen, nitrogen, potassium, quicklime—all the minerals making up mankind.

It took its nourishment from the combustible human form, somehow using its enormous mental power and converting it into an incredible electrochemical flare that in an instant consumed whatever Hari's eyes focused on. It was like living with a controlling, powerful poltergeist with a unique ability to control a chemical combustion without igniting itself.

The first time he had combusted something, Hari had been a child. He'd been terrified by the sudden rush of supernatural heat energy. While his every sensation was eerily put on hold, his eyes registered how the alley rat he'd focused on was turned into a little gaseous ball, and how instantaneously it had been consumed down his mouth for the waiting serpent.

And so it began with small animals, dogs, cats, goats, until Hari was *made* to inhale and ingest the gaseous cloud of a derelict woman. He had seen the fear in her eyes, and had enjoyed the power as never before. With the animals, the *fear* in them had hardly registered with Hari, but the human horror-filled eyes. . . . He found these to be an added charge to his own system, that he—Hari Shakir—might hold on to something of himself, for he did so bask in the newfound power shared with the creature within. And so when Hari had begun to call himself the Kundalini, the fire serpent was not displeased but rather encouraged the boy's pleasure.

Again he thought of the horror he had himself felt the first time it had happened. Yes, he had heard all the tales of the magnificent and mighty serpent god, but until the Kundalini displayed its power, it hadn't actually been real to Hari. To artfully and at will turn matter from solid to gas in the blink of an eye? It was a terrifying force for a boy to be carrying about within him, with no idea how it could possibly be. To hold within him at age thirteen the power over life and death for other humans. Now, at age forty-eight, he had nurtured and developed the power for long enough. It needed to go to its next stage.

He had since his thirteenth birthday fed on many lives in Calcutta, including that of the old scryer in Barsa marketplace, who knew the Shakar family, the same old fool who had shown too much interest in Dhashid Ramar's fate. From the scryer's lost memories, he learned that Adib Shakar was hiding somewhere in America.

He had joined a cargo ship as a crewman on the *Pegasus*, and on board the ship coming over to Miami he had fed on more mortals as they cruised through the Bermuda Triangle, and now he would feed on a multitude here until his *brother* could be located. According to the thoughts of the old scryer, who knew an uncle of Shakar's, Adib had met a woman while in London, had fallen in love and had followed her to America. The uncle did not know the woman's name or what name Adib traveled under. He had a vague notion that Adib worked in medicine or around medical people. That was all.

Somewhere in this teeming cesspool called Miami, hiding in this strange cultural desert, was Shakar, his spirit brother, who both feared and hated him. Shakir could feel Shakar near; no doubt Shakar could feel him nearby as well. If only Adib Shakar could know of the jeweled promise held out to Hari as Hari knew and understood it. The promise of life as an omnipotent being, power without limit or end, power to rival that of the sun.

If only Adib Shakar would cooperate; allow the fusion.

Only then would life for Hari become the celestial wonder that the creature had promised. As it was, the Kundalini spent most of its hours now in an angry, foul mood, hungry at every turn of the clock, as if feeding sated its hunger for its ultimate and final stage. If it joined with Shakar, then perhaps it would return to its old self, have a sense of having been sated and spiritually fulfilled as well.

Somewhere in this organized chaos called Miami, Adib Shakar resided. Together, fused as one, they could inherit the four spirits of the elements—earth, wind, fire, and water, and so rule earth, and rule over all mankind and the lower forms.

"You, Hari, will be part of it all," the thing within him kept reassuring him. After all, he had not only been the chosen one, to carry the seed of fertility for a god within him, he had not shirked his responsibility—to allow the creature to incubate within him—as had Shakar.

Patience, he constantly told himself, was both his greatest virtue and his weakness—for he had allowed too many years to pass without any result. But those same years had allowed the fire serpent within to gather strength and knowledge of the world as it fed. Hari must continue to be patient, to endure the torture and the honor of the god's occupancy and growth within him, like a child in the womb.

The often difficult, often painful insults to his unimportant human body and psyche must never dissuade him from the true and righteous path he had set himself on, or to ever interfere with the evolution of a god.

Hari cursed the time it had taken to hone in on Adib Shakar, and he rolled onto his back, displaying a large tattoo encircling his abdomen, his belly button at the center of the coil, a tattoo that had grown in size with him, given to him at birth.

He fell asleep in the flophouse apartment he had taken over when he had consumed its occupant, an elderly man living alone. Streaks of sunlight filtered through the curtains dark with a greasy residue, the light weaving a crazy mosaic about the floor and foot of the bed, a mosaic reflecting the thick black and sooty material on the curtains where, at the window, he had consumed Mr. Jeffrey Long.

The air-conditioning unit in the unmarked police car hammered out a rhythm that Louis Armstrong could sing to; the thing sounded as if it would soon choke to death on its own coils in a losing battle with the heat wave that had laid siege to all life—including mechanical life—in Miami. A few weeks earlier a monster hurricane had passed close to shore, sending the thermometer plunging to twenty-nine degrees, and since then, the mercury had steadily risen to its current record-breaking 124 degrees Fahrenheit, making Miami the nation's oven: too hot, too steamy, too stifling even for the Canadian tourists, who had begun to disappear in droves.

The city of sun and fun baked under the usually welcomed eye of God—suffering beneath an intensity like none that Eric Brannon, a native of Florida, had ever felt. Drought conditions even threatened the tough saw-grass lands of the Everglades just west-southwest of the city. One careless match, one lightning strike in the state known as the lightning capitol of the world, and hundreds of thousands of acres could go up in smoke. In fact, the saw-grass lands of the 'glades were set afire almost daily, so that firefighters were kept on a constant vigil and roadways were clogged with ground smoke—a tinderbox ready to ignite. So Sun City wasn't fun anymore, not this summer; the beloved season of tourist and merchant alike had become a season of despair, Miami hopeless in the relentless grip of the worst heat wave in its history.

Brannon fought to keep his mind off the horrible and diverse possibilities of what awaited his arrival at Miami Memorial Hospital, where Renea Alice Stanton worked twice a week, volunteering her time to the near defunct place. Dr. Stanton was a longtime friend, who had helped Brannon when he was a mere rookie cop. Renea was a sparkling, energetic spirit from whom others took energy and enthusiasm; she had more to spare than she could ever give away. She was a woman of the sort seen nowadays only in old black-and-white films on the all-night movie classics channel. She exuded class, yet she was neither superior nor overbearing in her thinking, in her directing of others, or in her manner; in fact, she had a genuine humility about herself and her accomplishments found in few doctors.

"How long have you known this missing doctor?" asked Jackie, beside him, the car careening toward Memorial.

"Met her in ninety-four."

"That long, huh?"

"Yeah, that long."

"How'd you . . . you know, meet?"

"Why's it every woman wants to know how a guy met another woman?"

"Why're you being evasive?"

"We met in a hospital!"

"Oh, that tells me a lot."

He sighed heavily, his chest swelling. "We met just after the first time I had to use deadly force on the street."

Jackie bit her lower lip, contemplating this. "Oh, so she's a shrink. That explains a—"

"No . . . no, she's no shrink. Just a caring, sensitive person's all. Met her at the hospital where she worked. Kid I shot was under her care's all."

"Kid . . . you shot a kid?"

"Kid with a zip gun that fired twenty-two caliber bullets, yeah. Kid forced me to shoot him, Jackie. Damn it, I don't need to justify it. IAD already did that in ninety-four."

"So, let me picture this. She—your doctor friend, Stanton—was patching the kid up—did he live or die?—and she gives you a shoulder to lean on? That's pretty decent," Jackie replied.

"No, no . . . this was no little kid. The kid lived to stand trial for forcible rape, three counts. As for Renea, we got into an argument, right there in the ER. I wanted to choke her to death, the way she talked to me. The way she coddled that rapist."

"So you fought? Give me the damned details."

"We somehow got into a fight about police procedure, street tactics, politics, sociology, and she knew a hell of a lot about what I . . . what *we* do, Jackie. Anyway, she sensed how shaken I was, and she more or less insisted she take me for a drink. We debated all night, till dawn. Didn't know where the time went, and she was good, damned good . . . well-read, a walking encyclopedia, and a most persuasive lady."

"And since then you've remained friends all these years?"

"Not a sexual thing, Jackie. We just connect as friends. Since ninety-four she's moved up through the ranks, and she has a lot of pull with community groups and politicos alike. She kinda works as a linchpin now, getting things that're choking on red tape untangled. She gets results."

"Gotta respect that."

"God, I can't believe something's happened to her, but I can all the same. She places herself in danger every time she goes down to Memorial."

"Real armpit community, I know."

"God, if she's been abducted, raped . . . murdered . . ."

"We don't know that, Eric. Don't get ahead of yourself." She placed a calming, supportive hand on his.

"If some brainless street punk *has* harmed her, I swear, Jackie, he'll live to regret the day."

"All we know is she's disappeared. That's all we know at this point."

But they also both knew that Miami had already broken over a dozen records in criminal statistics this year. While gunshot wounds, muggings, rape and murder had fallen off in Chicago, Detroit, LA and New York, Miami's stats spiraled upward, partially due the boiling point of brain fluid, Brannon believed. Guns and drugs, the never-ending story of violence, the twin snakes of poverty and addiction, it all appeared rooted in a twisted love affair Americans had with it all. It had all to do with a basic and pervading disregard for the value of human life, Brannon believed, and it made him, among others in law enforcement, wonder in what sick direction the world was now pointed and heading.

When he was a kid, growing up on 125th in north Miami, the boys played football in the street, and when he'd run into someone's car, or dive over the hood, an *excuse me* settled the matter, and the ballgame went on. *Nowadays, you touch someone's car, you're killed*, he thought.

As they entered the destination area, Brannon thought of how the slum fields around Memorial always looked, felt, and smelled hotter than the rest of the baking city, and he realized, as always, the most destitute and miserable were the most cruelly treated by nature and adverse weather. In the absence of electricity, no AC, not so much as a fan. Not even opening a window helped in this still, dead heat. Besides, all manner of vermin—including the human kind—were attracted to open windows.

Opening a window proved useless at best anyway, since the air somehow felt like the heated torrent that poured forth from a furnace door; it caused one's breath to come up short. The humidity had risen to a hundred percent, making the least movement an exercise in lathered perspiration. The least effort—going up a flight of stairs, sweeping a stoop, walking a dog, stepping out for groceries or a drink at the corner tavern, often resulted in heat stroke, heart attack, or death. The warnings to the elderly and infirm had gone forth, blaring across the radio waves and TV screens alike.

Brannon felt that both man and dog found themselves petrified in an incandescent stew of boiled air. Renea Stanton had warned Brannon to be on the lookout for an increase in crime with the heat wave, that heat brought on passions and anger and temper and frayed nerves, along with boils, carbuncles, psychosis, socioeconomic-cosis, mycosis—*skin diseases and disorders*—as both physical and mental pressures rose sharpest in the slum areas, understandably so.

"Three days to go," he said to his partner.

"Three days?"

"Three days and the temp's supposed to drop."

Jackie laughed and replied, "Yeah, but for now it's a hundred twenty-four in the shade, and you factor in the humidity like that annoying little blond thing on Channel Two News, and it's the equivalent of a hundred thirty f-fing degrees. A hundred forty on a black surface like tarmac."

They pulled into the hospital parking lot with tires screaming, and Brannon leapt from the car, going for the crowd of fire officials and blue-suited cops milling about Stanton's car. Jackie hurried in his wake, taking in the scene as well. Two squad cars with strobing lights twirling looked like grazing animals, and to one side stood a big Jimmy van with the logo of the Miami coroner glaring back at them.

Knowing instinctively that something terrible had happened to Dr. Stanton, Brannon had too quickly rushed from the AC of the car and through the thick, choking heat before remembering to slow down and recall his last mountain-climbing expedition. Concentrating on that mountain in Colorado with its snow-covered peaks kept his internal temperature to a manageable level.

He was welcomed by Ken Scarsdale, a uniformed cop with whom he had lifted drinks on occasion. Ken stood red-faced, his tie choking a thick neck; he looked as though he might keel over at any moment, yet he blocked Brannon's body and said, "You want to go easy, Eric. This is bad, really bad."

Brannon pushed past Scarsdale and moved on to Louis Ames, his tall, imposing black captain, who had been talking to Carl Osterman—one of the oldest guys on the fire department's payroll, an experienced arson investigator. Ames and Osterman saw Brannon coming on fast now, and Ames, wearing a filtered breathing mask across his dark features, stepped from Osterman and grabbed Brannon by the shoulders. "It's bad, Eric."

"Doesn't look that bad. Car's intact."

"Strange detonation, real weird. No one heard an explosion, but it looks like a bomb went off under the driver's seat, but it didn't set off the gas tank, not even an alarm."

"And you say the owner's been abducted? Do we know if she's alive or dead?"

"No, we don't."

"No calls or notes left?"

"Nothing like that, no. It's strange, Eric."

"I need a closer look." He pushed past Ames, going for the vehicle, which stood against a parking lot wall. It didn't look so bad from the exterior. The paint hadn't been burned off, and approaching from the rear, he saw no scattered glass, that while all the windows were smoke-blackened and spider-webbed, but holding.

"Heat was concentrated over the driver's seat," Ames said, catching up to him. "Never seen anything like it."

Behind him, Jackie followed. Ames turned to her and said, "It was maybe a mistake to call Brannon in on this."

Brannon's each step toward the vehicle increased the ugly odors infiltrating his nostrils. Captain Ames called out, "It's the odor of burnt flesh, Brannon."

5

Putrid, acrid, choking. It smelled like something out of a war zone, bringing back memories of Brannon's stint in Desert Storm. And there lingered a thick metallic odor as well. The captain pushed a face mask into his hand. "Take it!" ordered Ames.

Brannon put on the filtered mask and seeing the driver's-side window tinted with blackened smoke residue, he steeled himself and opened the door on the wrecked interior. The driver's seat was incinerated, while the rear seats and the passenger seat had been left darkened by smoke but intact. On the passenger seat lie a purse atop a file with papers, again dusted by smoke residue but intact. The amazing sight defied anyone to understand how the purse and papers could have survived such an inferno untouched and unmoved. It was as if the ferocity of the flames had centered on a contained area, the area around the driver alone.

The next thing to strike him as odd was the steering wheel. It had half melted, forming an awkward, twisted, crying circle like a drunkenly misshapen object escaped from a junkyard. He again stared at the blackened driver's seat, mere tatters of cloth left hanging, as if blown off in a Nagasaki explosion.

"Told you it was weird," said Ames from behind him. "Had to close the doors on the odor."

"From the smell of it, someone's flesh burned off here, but we've got no body. If Dr. Stanton were killed here, where's the body? Dr. Katra's people whisk it away before I could get here?"

"That's the most puzzling aspect of this whole damn thing," replied Ames. "There is no body, only a few fingers."

"Fingers?"

"Have a look at the ignition."

Brannon did so, pulling back from the sight; three finger bones with blackened flesh cut at the knuckle had been caught up in what looked like a small lava flow where the metal around the keyhole had melted. Perhaps a bomb poorly constructed that didn't go off properly. Or the work of someone who wanted to make it look so? Again Brannon stared at what was left of human fingers fused to an ignition and keys that had become one mass of metal in the superheated explosion. "God . . . what could have caused this?"

Ames said, "They're having to remove the column; take the whole thing, fingers and all. Fact is, they're fighting over who gets it, Katra's crime lab, or Osterman's fire lab. I think Osterman won the argument to do a chemical analysis. Katra is leaning toward a freaky theory about its having to do with spontaneous human combustion anyway, so—"

"Spontaneous human combustion?" Brannon looked across at Jackie, who had opened the passenger-side door and now leaned in from across the other seat, trying to get a look. She saw the column and fingers in the molded metal. "Never seen anything fucking like it in my life."

"Freak explosion that no one in the hospital or neighborhood heard. . . . It makes no sense. And the best ME in the city is talking shit about human combustion. It'll make the news by noon," said Brannon.

"Neither Katra nor I want any leaks to the press," said Ames.

"I can understand that, Captain!" said Jackie, choking on the odors.

Ames rubbed his bearded chin. "First time I've ever seen Adib Katra completely stumped."

"But spontaneous combustion? A theory like that is going to leak tons," said Brannon.

Unlike most MEs, Adib Katra shunned publicity as if it carried some sort of disease, and everyone in law enforcement respected him for it. Most MEs enjoyed the limelight of unusual cases played out in the press, and most were liked by the members of the press. Adib was the exception.

"Where is Dr. Katra now?"

"Back inside his van. Hiding, I think. He didn't look so good. Never seen him go white before but this . . . this really got to him."

Brannon saw Dr. Adib Katra emerge from the crime-scene van arguing with his pretty, busty, auburn-haired second-in-command, Dr. Angelica Hunter. They argued a lot, Brannon had noticed over the few years he'd worked with Katra and Hunter.

"Look at the gas pedal, Eric," instructed Ames. "Something else Adib found."

Brannon looked down at a tiny patch or swath of cloth peeking from beneath the gas pedal, jammed there, it seemed. "What the hell is it?"

"Adib surmises it's a piece of a shoe, toe area of a sneaker. Says there's a partial Nike logo showing. Says for us to touch nothing. Look but don't touch."

"Dr. Stanton usually wore sneakers when on duty," Brannon muttered, using a pen to poke at the object below the pedal.

"Don't disturb it, Brannon," said Ames. "Dr. Katra's on his way back."

"Not sure what we're looking at."

Brannon's initial reaction was shared with the others. "Appears maybe he used some sort of torch . . . one of those totally-crazy-outta-control-maniac lover's spats, in which one partner feeds off destroying the property of the other, but it got out of hand, and he burned her here where she sat, dragged the body off. It's the only explanation for the odor of raw, burned flesh."

"Check out the windshield and windows," said Captain Ames, a red-haired, brown eyed, burly, thick man—thick in the limbs, the chest, the stomach and face. Cops under his command jokingly called him Malcolm X, and he not so jokingly spread it around that Malcolm was an uncle of his.

Brannon and Jackie stared at the strange configurations in the windshield. Against the spiderweb of the cracked windshield something had spattered like blood, but this was black hardened ooze, a kind of mudlike substance that when touched, as Brannon unconsciously did, cracked, revealing air pockets inside. When it crumbled at his touch, it fell away like ash. Apparently Brannon was only the latest in a string of people who had touched the stuff, as the dashboard was littered with the ashen results. It gave the appearance of someone's pouring out cigarette ashes.

Jackie asked, "What the hell is that stuff?" as Brannon, sniffing his fingers, picked up a highly concentrated odor of ozone. The same odor that came with lightning.

"ME figures it to be a kind of . . . oil . . . fat," replied Captain Ames.

"Fat? It looks . . . hell, it feels like blackened Styrofoam, and it smells like—"

"ME says it's superfried, superheated human *creosote*."

"Which means what?" asked Jackie.

"That's what Dr. Katra called it. The fire was so intense it splattered the interior with the stuff—greasy black smeary stuff, you know, like when you smear a cigarette ash with your finger and it becomes like ink."

"Stuff? What kinda stuff are we talking about, Captain? I've never heard of this . . . human cree-o-sote stuff," said Brannon. "What does Osterman say?"

"Osterman's scratching his head. Says he's going to need time to figure this one out, and he feels Dr. Katra has no clue either."

"What else does Katra say?"

"Human fatty tissues, Brannon. Of human origin. Like I

said, Katra believes it's a case of spontaneous human combustion."

"It can't be animal?" asked Jackie.

"Katra clearly said spontaneous human combustion. Claims he has seen it in India—that is the results of it."

They all frowned and stared at one another, disbelieving. Brannon asked, "And what'd Carl Osterman say to that?"

"Says it's a staged scene," replied Ames. "He doesn't believe in spontaneous human combustion. This grease and the odor, he says, could be animal fat; says Katra has no way of knowing without testing it, while the little ME from India says he has the odor *imprinted on his mind* from birth, having grown up in India where they cremate the dead in open-air pyres."

"Is he suggesting that someone . . . that Dr. Stanton was somehow . . . cremated inside this Cutlass Olds?"

"That's what Katra says, but I'm leaning toward Osterman's theory of the crime."

Brannon knew Dr. Katra as well as anyone on the force. The man was an acknowledged genius in forensics, a guru. "Interpol came to him for help on a case last week," said Brannon.

"Ok, so we're fucking lucky to have him in Miami, and I know his reputation is sound, but this . . . it sounds too weird to believe," countered Ames.

Jackie added, "I think for the time being, I'll put my money on Carl Osterman, that it's some sort of weird setup. Maybe we'll get a ransom demand soon."

Ames replied, "Osterman says it may have been an incendiary device of some sort. Set to go off when she turned over the ignition, but it was a controlled explosion of some sort. He admits he doesn't know."

"A bomb? That sounds nuts, too. The whole car would've gone up, not just the driver's seat." Brannon shook his head over the scene before him. He brushed against the driver's-side door panel, dislodging more of the blackened Styrofoam material that Adib Katra had, in essence, summed up as Dr.

Renea Stanton's mortal remains. His back created a dust cloud of ash caught on the wind.

"Damn, be careful, Eric!" said Ames. "You're losing evidence. Whatever that stuff turns out to be, a chemical foam explosive maybe, we need enough for analysis."

Like the windshield, the panel had caught the spatter of black fried grease—animal or human fat—that had solidified into air and ash.

When Jackie had backed out of the car, unable to take the odors any longer, fire investigator Carl Osterman poked his head inside. Osterman's white eyebrows bobbed as he spoke. "I tell you, Ames, it's some lunatic playing out some scene in a fucking movie he's seen, staging what he thinks will make us cry spontaneous human combustion, a hoaxster."

"Then where is Dr. Stanton?" asked Brannon.

"Who knows? On a cruise, maybe? And those bone fragments are likely going to turn out to be from some lab chimpanzee or gorilla."

"Dr. Stanton was on duty here last night, Carl," said Brannon. "And this is her car. And now no one can locate her."

"He's holding her hostage then, like I said before." Osterman stepped off and walked around the back of the car. He spoke now directly to Ames. "All right, let's say he abducted Dr. Stanton and torched the car and threw in the fingers to make it look like some sort of *X-File* thingy, to, you know, throw us off," continued Osterman, chewing on an unlit cigar. "Fact is, we've had a couple of similar type incidents, one in a warehouse not far from here, one in an alleyway back of the Bennigan's eatery on Bell and Kensington. Both have been under investigation as arson."

"Whoa, what're you saying, Chief Osterman?" asked Brannon. "That we have some sort of serial lunatic setting fires to body fragments and staging spontaneous human combustion scenes?"

"Yeah, that's what I'm saying."

"And it's all a hoax, using animal bones?"

"Not all the tests have come back yet, but I'm sure bones will prove to be old. Could be from any number of sources."

"So we're just dealing with some nutcase who's staged all of it," said Ames.

"What the ME's proposing, spontaneous human combustion, well it only just happens in science fiction, right?" replied Osterman.

"Yeah, science fiction," muttered Brannon, one hand squeezing the other. "Tell me, Carl, just how hot did it have to be inside the car to melt the ignition column and burn out the passenger seat and yet not touch the other seats or disturb items on the seat next to the passenger?"

"It'd have to be like the fire in a g'damn kiln, that intense, maybe higher, certainly at flash point."

"Flash point, the temperature at which the seat flashed over?"

"Right. Higher than flash point."

"Maybe it was more like a crematorium than a kiln then?" replied Brannon.

Osterman considered this. "That'd bring the temperature over fourteen thousand degrees."

"That's strange . . . that's what Adib Katra put it at," said Ames.

"Yeah, but his theory is absurd," countered Osterman.

"Yeah, and no guy with a wand torch could turn an Olds into a crematorium," Ames agreed.

They all stepped away from the overwhelming odors emanating from the car. "Yeah, science fiction," Brannon repeated. "Meanwhile, how long has Renea gone missing?"

"Can't say for sure," replied Ames, Osterman stepping back. "But the car's been here all night. No one made anything of the car or its condition, not in this neighborhood, until this morning."

"Even though it was torched and running all night?"

"Gotta consider the area; it's like Beirut down here."

Brannon told Ames, "Worst-case scenario, Osterman is right and this guy is a collector."

Ames looked intently into Brannon's eyes. They both knew how horrible it could be if this were an abductor who held on to his victim until he had no more use for her. "But to stage a scene to make it look as if she just imploded in the heat to have us chasing phantoms? If so, this guy's gone to a hell of a lot of trouble."

"That'd take a lot of time out here in the open. Somebody had to have seen something. The perpetrator torched her here where she sat in the car, then wrapped her in something, tossed her into a van or trunk, then he spread all this chemical gunk all over? Yet no one saw a thing. . . ."

Ames raised his shoulders. "Heat wave like this, it does strange things to people's brains."

Brannon asked, "Intense fire, charred remains? The guy makes off with her body? What the fuck for?"

Lou Ames dropped his eyelids, shook his head and answered, "Hey, detective, with the kind of muck-fucks, necrophiliacs and nutcases we see, who knows? Why should it surprise you two that a guy torches someone and wants to sleep with the charred skeletal remains?"

"Sick SOB . . ." Brannon stared again at the lopsided steering wheel. Half melted, again it made him think of those strange Dali paintings with the melting clocks.

"I think I've seen enough," said Ames, but Eric once again studied the charred bit of remains on the floorboard; what was left of the shoe showed blue beneath the sooty matter, the tip of the navy blue sneaker seemingly jammed below the pedal, as if forced there by human hands. Part of the staging.

Only one fact seemed a constant in all the disparate theories that had been put forth—a distinct odor of ozone permeated the air along with the distinct odor of charred human flesh.

Brannon said to Ames, who tugged at him to come away, "What about that odor like an electrical storm? You can't bottle that shit and carry it around with you."

"Can't say, Eric. Nothing here makes any sense."

The odor and the sight of the windows smeared with grease—grease presumably from a human source, if the ME could be believed—conspired to make Brannon ill. He felt his stomach lurch, hold, and threaten him again. He willed himself to handle this.

Captain Ames patted him on the back and said, "Despite Carl's theory and his bravado, none of the fire guys have any idea what's going on here, no more'n we do. No one's stepped up to take charge. I've sent for Shelby Harne. He's the best fire investigator I know. Retired but nobody's as good. He's an expert in this sort of thing, a guy who kinda troubleshoots for bizarro-shit fires. . . . I mean Carl's a good man, but I think he's out of his depth here."

Brannon stepped away from the car with Ames. He saw that Jackie was leaning against a fence, a Coca-Cola in her hand, still trying to get the stench of the vehicle out of her nostrils. Brannon asked her, "Are you OK?"

"Hell no, I'm not OK. This . . . this is too damn motherfucking weird, Eric, weird."

"Tell me about it."

Eric stared again in the direction of the crime-scene van, where the ME, Adib Katra, still stood in debate with his assistant. Obviously, Dr. Hunter did not agree with his rash assessment of the crime scene any more than anyone else here. The dark, little man looked pained and anxious as he continued to engage in heated discussion with Dr. Hunter. His body language translated to irritation and anxiety. He looked in Brannon's direction as if he didn't want to come near the car again, but he slowly did so, stepping away from Hunter, who held on to a small cooler marked by the familiar medical insignia of two snakes coiled about a lance, a cooler normally used for transporting human body parts.

The short, dark Dr. Katra returned to Stanton's car, the cooler in one hand, his cane in the other. Brannon quickly joined him, Jackie reluctantly following. "We'll lift some of this creosote from the windshield and door panel," he said as he worked with Acrylophane tape, putting the substance into a plastic bag. "We'll analyze it at the lab."

"Looks like a freakin' car bomb went off here," said Brannon to Katra, feeling him out, trying to get him to open up about what he thought had happened here. "But wouldn't a car bomb have created your normal inferno of the car? It defies logic."

"Look for nothing logical here," said Katra, "and no hope of understanding."

"What is that supposed to mean?"

Katra replied with nothing, not a single word, and his entire body had stiffened. Dr. Hunter had joined them. She looked on with a mix of emotions coloring her features, her cheeks still red from the spat with her boss.

Katra lifted the cooler and placed it on the metal frame of the burnt-out driver's seat. He tried to pry loose one of the finger bones with a long steel awl, and when this failed, he worked a scalpel between two of them. All to no avail. "Damn," he cursed, "I wanted one of these for analysis before they take it all to Osterman. Whose jurisdiction is this, anyway? It's murder, not arson!"

Failing with the embedded fingers at the ignition, he took a pair of thongs and reached in under the dash for the shoe part. "As for the ignition, we are awaiting an automotive mechanical genius to find the best way to remove it intact for the fire department. Your captain's idea, not mine."

"I still think we must insist, Dr. Katra, that it *all* go to our labs," said Angelica Hunter.

From her tone, Brannon extrapolated the crux of their earlier argument. Still, Brannon felt baffled at Adib Katra's lack of enthusiasm for the fight. It was not like him at all to give in to the fire department demands. He would normally be scrapping tooth and nail for all of the contents of the car in this uncanny mystery.

Brannon continued to closely observe Katra. The ME was indeed subdued, perhaps distracted, absorbed with something going on in his head. He'd have normally been like the proverbial Jack Bull terrier, captivated and intrigued and determined all at once by such bizarre case findings. He now simply stepped in as a man going through the motions, Brannon thought. Personal problems, deep and troubling, the detective guessed.

Dr. Katra had knelt on the hot pavement in order to reach

far into the car for the shoe fragment. However, he suddenly
dropped to his rump, scraping his hands on the scorching
pavement as he did so. His dark face had blanched, and he
announced in his accented voice, "I cannot do this. Dr. Hunter, please . . . please take over here. I . . . I must find my
pills." He held his stomach as if in pain.

"Dr. Katra . . . are you all right?" asked Dr. Hunter.

"I am fine. Do the work; do not attend to me. I am fine;
just . . . must . . . need find my medication." He grabbed hold
of Eric Brannon's outstretched hand, climbed back to his
feet, and then pulled free of Brannon's help. Their eyes met,
and Brannon saw something lurking deep within the black
pupils. What was the man hiding? And what had it to do
with the crime scene? The ME's eyes broke from Eric's, and
now he stared for a moment at the others *as if* calculating
who might be conspiring against him. Yes, it was the look
of the paranoid, Brannon told himself.

Brannon thought the ME appeared overwhelmed by the
crime scene, shaken, unnerved, rattled. Shaking his head,
Adib grabbed his snake's head, silver-tipped cane, which
he'd left against the car. He then made his shaky way back
to his crime-scene van.

Brannon and the others watched Katra with some concern
for the small, dark Indian doctor. Brannon had known Dr.
Adib Katra now for some seven years. A moody, brooding
man at times who only occasionally took a drink. Katra only
showed fire when he was deeply involved in an interesting
case. The ME had a habit of speaking in cosmic terms about
the slightest things. Cops joked that he could make a salt-
cellar a celestial palace if given a few drinks. Still, Brannon
had never known him to be anything but cool, collected, and
professional while on the job. Dr. Katra, knowing that his
alcohol limit was two, stayed away from the juice, as a rule,
but Brannon had picked up the whiff of bourbon on him
today.

"Prolonged gastroenteritis bothering him, I think," said
Angelica Hunter, noticing Brannon's interest. "Been after
him to take care of it. He keeps putting it off."

Brannon had noticed the man grab for his abdomen more than once. "Yeah . . . saw you two discussing it. Must be serious." Brannon wondered if there could be more to the problem plaguing the ME as he continued watching the other man stagger off.

Was it a badly ulcerated stomach, or something else entirely? Had he gotten bad news about a loved one? Had he been diagnosed with an incurable disease? Whether he'd received such news or not, the message his countenance telegraphed to Eric Brannon could not be clearer. The medical man was in great, sustained depression and woe, and Brannon believed it had something to do with what he saw inside Dr. Renea Stanton's car, as he had twice now walked off while in the midst of examining the crime scene.

"Please, out of the way, Detective," said Angelica Hunter to Brannon.

Brannon watched Hunter uncomfortably kneeling where Katra had been, smartly cushioning her knees with a mat made for such occasions. The cooler that Dr. Katra had left on the burnt-out seat tumbled when she leaned in with the forceps and brushed it. The cooler landed in her lap, spilling out ice. She cursed and worked to replace the ice into the cooler.

Her emotions, Brannon thought, were in disarray. Again from her kneeling position just outside the vehicle she reached deep in under the dash for the sneaker fragment. Her white lab coat smeared with soot, the assistant to the chief medical examiner for the city of Miami-Dade took on the ice-veined objectivity of her profession. She lifted the fragment with the care of moving a Tiffany egg. It felt heavier than she'd expected once it came free, and as a result she'd gasped. Then it slipped off the prongs, as if alive, tumbling back onto the floorboard, scurrying in mouse fashion to remain free of her grasp. She swore, whipped out a handkerchief, and, damning the thongs, grabbed up the shoe fragment in her gloved hand. "No tool ever invented can replace the flexibility of the human hand," she said.

Once more she noticed the weight of the small toe end of

the shoe in her hand. It's weight was unexpected.

With Brannon looking in over her shoulder, Hunter turned the forensic prize in her hand. The handkerchief created a collar around the open end of the shoe fragment. Something was embedded, deep in the toe of the cloth and rubber scrap of the tip end of a woman's sneaker that'd somehow survived the inferno.

Dr. Hunter erupted with a gasp and a shudder. She then said, "Oh my God!"

Brannon kneeled beside her, asking, "What is it?"

"I was expecting a sneaker tip, not this." She held the evidence she'd gathered so he could make it out. Five intact toes rested like packed sardines inside the shoe fragment. Only slightly discolored by the fire, the toes looked like fat brown tomato worms inside a cocoon.

6

"Ever see anything like it in all your years on the force, Detective?" asked Dr. Hunter of Brannon.

"No . . . can't say that I have," he replied, helping her to her feet. She still held on to the shoe fragment and its contents.

"What the hell've you got there?" asked Ames, rejoining them.

"Toes," replied Hunter.

Ames stared down at what she gently lay atop the ice in the cooler. "Toes?"

"Human toes—not monkey, not chimp, not gorilla, human."

Ames took a deep breath. "My God. Any other surprises? *Ripley's Believe It or Not* time." He pulled out a radio that had come to life on his hip. "I've got to take this. Got men in all the surrounding buildings and in the hospital searching for anyone who saw anything." Ames grabbed Jackie Hale, asking her to assist him with some chore.

"What's next, Dr. Hunter?" asked Brannon.

"I'll analyze the bones against what we know of Dr. Stanton's makeup."

"How long will that take?"

"What with the backlog . . . a month to six weeks, but

since this is so unusual, I think I can talk Adib into putting it at the top of the pile. Give me a day or two. We'll speed up the process, make it as soon as possible, OK?"

"Suppose . . . you know . . . you don't think maybe this is maybe . . . some sort of—"

"Hoax? Like Osterman says?"

"Intentional disappearing act, you know . . . a magic trick."

"Magic trick?"

He gritted his teeth. "It's what people who are financially and emotionally in over their heads do; they disappear. I worked Missing Persons for six years."

"You think Dr. Stanton faked all this? To get out of her life?"

"Well, I admit that part doesn't figure. She loved her work, was devoted to it. She's got two kids. I don't know; drawing at straws, trying to make sense of . . . of this craziness."

She nodded, biting her lower lip. "Was she depressed? Upset?"

He stared long at her emerald eyes and at her auburn hair, tied in a neat bun. She wore glasses, but it didn't detract from her heart-shaped face and smooth skin.

"Not that I was aware of, no."

"Do you know her well enough that she'd confide that someone might've been stalking her?" asked Hunter.

"No . . . I mean, yes, but she never said a word that anyone was making trouble for her."

"But that's the way to truly disappear, isn't it? To tell no one you're about to."

"Right. . . ."

"I hope the bones don't turn out to be hers, Detective."

"Same here."

"Give us time. We'll let you know as soon as we know. Sorry for . . . the lack of answers."

He realized she'd almost said *sorry for your loss*—the policeman's standard phrase for dealing with grieving relatives. "Apparently, we weren't as close as I'd thought. If *something* was troubling her, or if *someone* was troubling her, you'd think she would've come—"

"Careful of assumptions at this point, Detective. We really are shooting in the dark here. We need more information, all of us."

"Yeah, maybe . . . guess I ought to know better."

"Well, this isn't an ordinary case for you; you're emotionally involved."

"Let me know when and if you learn more, Dr. Hunter, and I appreciate your concern."

Angelica Hunter waved Brannon off with a slightly upraised hand and a nod, turned to the cooler and tightened down the latches. In a moment she disappeared into the waiting crime-scene-unit van.

Eric Brannon felt now that the phrase *unusual circumstance* barely fit the situation, given what he had seen here. The phrase had become an understatement in the case of the missing Dr. Stanton.

Carl Osterman had pulled his team off, deciding to let the ME and Ames's people take care of this one. All he wanted was the steering column delivered to the lab. He was satisfied that the crime here fit with the serial nutcase fire starter that he and his team had been pursuing for a week and a half now. And from what he saw of the car's interior, he didn't think the evidence at all compelling except as his theory allowed. Besides, Ames said he was calling in Harne. Harne would tell Ames and the others the same damn thing, but who listened? And sometimes, the closer you were to someone, the less they really listened to what you had to say; he and Ames went a long way back, but if he wanted Old Shelby Harne's woefully lacking two bits, then so fucking be it. As for Osterman, he had a Miami Dolphins away game and a beer waiting at home.

Osterman said his good-byes to Ames. Carl was a head shorter than Ames's five-foot-nine height, placing him right around five four. Round of build and solid like a barrel bulging at its seams, Carl Osterman's hair was white at the temples, gray and black elsewhere. The man's shoulders seemed permanently bent forward, as though trained to it from so many years working on hands and knees in fire rubble. To his friends, he knew that he seemed both unshakable and set in his ways, and once he made up his mind to a thing, there was no budging him. He was opinionated on every subject and people liked to buy him a drink and listen to him rant and philosophize on issues ranging from the city sewage treatment plant to who was paying former president Clinton's rent.

Captain Lou Ames waved at Osterman as he watched the man calmly walk away with that signature limp and slight bowlegged gait that amounted to a duck waddle. His straightforwardness and appearance reminded Ames of the actor James Whitmore, who now did ads for Miracle Grow.

Without a word Osterman signaled his crew, and they began to disappear from the scene, only too happy to turn it over to Miami PD. Osterman promised to send over reports on the last two similar such cases he and his men had been chasing.

So much for fire and police cooperation, thought Ames.

Dr. Hunter had finished with the car, and the city pound tow truck was now backing in up against it. The steering column would be taken care of at the impound. The crime scene was shut down, the only body parts carried off in Hunter's icebox.

"I want to know about these other fires Osterman's talking about. Could they be the work of the same guy?" asked Brannon.

Ames nodded. "There were bone fragments in the rubble of each fire, yes. Extremities like what we have here."

"Do we have anyone working the case?"

"Osterman's only just now disclosed all the details."

"Is that right?"

"First fire was in a warehouse. Nothing like this, 'cause the whole place went up. Bones were thought to be animal until they were analyzed. Second fire in an alleyway left a little more, hand and foot bones that're still being analyzed. Now this."

"Were there any earlier identified victims?"

"Nothing whatever in the rubble of either fire to ID the victims. As to the bones found, strange thing."

"What's that?"

"Well, while they haven't finished running tests, they did determine that the bones were shorn off with *heat,* not a bone cutter or cleaver or anything of that nature."

"Heat . . . like a laser, you mean?"

"Something like that, yes."

Brannon scratched his head, confused, wondering. "Laser-intensity heat. You think we may have a guy with some kind of new high-tech laser torch, going around burning people up?"

"I don't know what to think, Eric," Ames replied to the noise of the wrecker pulling off Dr. Stanton's car for the impound. "We need to ask around about blowtorches, what's on the market, how available they are, who would be using one on a daily basis."

"So that's how it's shaping up, and the SOB's getting bolder with each murder."

"Sounds a sight more logical—*even though it's crazy*—than Dr. Katra's thing about spontaneous combustion. Adib writes this up that way, he'll become a departmental joke."

Carl Osterman drove off certain of his ground, all save the ozone odor; there was that one mystery remaining. He thought how strong it was at all three scenes, in the alleyway, the warehouse, and now the vehicle, that mellow, timeless odor, as sure as that scent coming on the wind before a powerful electrical storm, the smell of supercharged air, ozone.

"I gotta puzzle that mother out before Shelby beats me to it," he told the empty cab of his Ford Ranger. Still, whoever touched off the fires in all three locations had done minimal damage and had killed no one with fire, at least not on scene. . . .

The perpetrator was, however, using human body parts, scattering bone fragments, stuff like that, and now at least one person appeared to have come up missing.

Some deranged fool who lived with Mommy Dearest until the old lady kicked off, and it sent him into an emotional tailspin, no doubt. Maybe it was pieces of Mommy he was scattering about the city. But as to the odor of ozone, he couldn't say, not yet. That meant an electrochemical charge on the order of lightning.

Then too, there was the odor of human flesh in a flashover. He had a nose for odors after so many years of fire investigation, and he knew the smell and the lingering taste in the mouth of charred flesh from a fire victim. A charred body, even if dragged off by an arson-killer, left a distinct odor, and this was there in the car along with the ozone scent. And all this nonsense floating around about people going up in spontaneous combustion—SC—was instantaneous *bull-swallop*. The only proven spontaneous combustion happened in nature to organic materials, in forests littered with decaying matter, just waiting for the catalyst of a match or a lightning strike. No concrete evidence existed in all of fire history and fire investigation of a human being spontaneously combusting, despite all the anecdotal tales. Even when hit by lightning, the human body remained intact!

The flash point for such a thing happening, theoretically, would have to be in the range of Fahrenheit fourteen thousand. That kind of heat could only be generated by a manmade kiln, a crematorium, and he didn't know anyone who could lug one of those around on his back.

He had told Ames all of this, and he felt confident that he would pass it along to his detectives and the task force Ames meant to put together as a result of this latest fire disappearance.

Osterman saw the downtown off-ramp and thought of catching what was left of the game of the week at Paddy O'Shea's pub and oyster bar. He had friends there who didn't second guess him. Friends who respected his professional opinion on matters. The wife could wait. He swerved and tore down the ramp, making for the pub.

It had been at Paddy's, a hangout for firemen, police, and city employees, that he laid out his take on the so-called SC deaths that they'd all begun to speculate on.

After a few drinks, he expounded on the true nature of the horrendous crimes—crimes worse than anything in nature— hatched as they were, molded and put into action by what Osterman referred to as a "warp-oid" individual.

He recalled how he'd summed it up in a single phrase which lifted eyebrows all around: "All the horror and anger of nature, at any given time, is no match for the perversities of the human brain."

Someone asked for clarification, and, inebriated, the old fire chief felt duty bound to spread the word. "There's no need for panic or speculation over some wild-hair notion about an epidemic of spontaneous combustions. It ain't upon us. We've got enough to worry about with AIDS and VD. It's just like I told the chief, some sick son of a whore's going around planting human body parts, most likely dug up from vandalized graves, and he's making it look as if they've imploded in a ball of flame, when he's just blowtorching a handful of bones is all. It stands to reason. Worse case scenario, the man's scattering body parts from a body he's keeping in his freezer, sprinkling body parts around the city in a desperate plea to be caught and stopped."

The small crowd he'd gathered about him at Paddy's seemed well placated to learn the truth; they got the message. They heard what they needed to hear, and he hoped the solace of his message would be spread by each and every one of them. A lot of silly departmental rumors had begun to spread about the two previous fire deaths; he could imagine what would come of the missing doctor and the torched car.

One or two of his listeners in particular felt great relief in his theory, and they bought him additional drinks to hear more. He had hit on a reasonable explanation, and somehow they could all sleep better at night knowing there was no exponential rise in mysterious cases of spontaneous human combustion. Osterman believed he saw relief in their faces when he had left to go home to the wife.

Back in his car and on 1-95 North, he chuckled at the gullibility of the cops he'd met at the scene of the charred vehicle in the lot across the street from Memorial Hospital. Still, the ozone odor and the intense smell of charred flesh lingered in his brain, and he again puzzled over it. It was a greater odor than merely torching a few body fragments, and what the hell was all the grease about? His own lab had no grease, human or otherwise, to analyze until now with the car. The warehouse fire had obliterated everything, and the alleyway fire investigation turned up nothing of the sort. But then everything in that alley was awash in oils of one kind or another. No one was looking for grease.

The confined space of the car had been altogether different. No handheld torch with wand could explain it away. What that funny little Indian ME Katra took for human bodily fluids and fat, the same as Osterman took for animal fat, could simply have been part of the contents of the incendiary device, although Carl had never seen a "fat bomb" before. As for the bones, they weren't that hard to come by. But again, he couldn't figure the ozone in such concentration. No aerosol can could dump that much raw ozone in the air, the smell of highly charged, bombarding electrons—electrified air.

He found himself across the centerline, weaving into the other lane. A tractor-trailer came within inches of clipping the side of his Ranger. He swerved, overcompensating and going off onto the shoulder, his truck flipping.

The thing was restless, and it twisted inside Shakir, anxious for closure or simply for more humankind to feed on. Sometimes it seemed one and the same, the feeding, the hunt for his kindred soul, Shakar, the hope for touching immortality.

Hari Shakir and the serpent had located the addresses listed in the Miami phone book for a Ronald Shakar, but the place was empty, and from the six or seven newspapers on the stoop, no one appeared home. Shakir broke in through a back window anyway, only to confirm that the place was empty. There were no Indian furnishings or trinkets. It didn't feel to either of them—serpent or man—as if it were Adib Shakar's dwelling place.

Frustrated by yet another failure, the serpent within wanted feeding again, now. Feeding gave it some quick gratification that calmed it, but the more Hari arranged to feed it, the more it required. It was gathering more than sustenance, however; it gathered information, past lives, as it took the human meal. It took memories and knowledge, childhoods and facts, Kodak moments, names, numbers, whole dialogues, stories of lives, gossip and lies, the chorus of a person, that which refrained in the being—the core self: be it kindness and compassion, as in Stanton's case; shrewdness, as in Kalie the scryer; or bitterness, as Dhashid Ramar.

Dr. Stanton had no inkling of knowledge of anyone named Shakar working as a doctor in the city. The creature mined her memories but found nothing of a Shakar in them. Her mind was filled with her children, her mother, deceased father, home, work, community projects.

The old scryer had given Hari the notion to look in plain sight for his kinsman. The scryer had been Adib's confidant while Adib yet lived in Calcutta. The dead scryer inside the serpent had whispered something about a woman Adib had fallen in love with while in London, who lived now in New Jersey and taught at Princeton. But Adib's old friend was strong of mind and will, and Hari feared he held some magic that allowed him to miraculously lie to the serpent. Certainly, Hari had never before consumed a person with so much resistance.

All evidence still pointed to Miami, and so Hari and the serpent decided that Shakar must be in Miami in some capacity as a medical professional or working in a medical environment.

Not long now . . . not bloody long now, he kept mentally reassuring the serpent. "We both sense with every fiber how close we are to finding Adib Shakar; we can hear the other man's frightened breathing, and we sense that Shakar also knows how close we are to a final resolution, a final blending of our powers."

The telepathic connection with Adib was not between Hari and Adib but between Hari's serpent and Adib's serpent within. They could sense one another's energy. It knew ... it sensed even his—Hari's—nervous energy at the reunion of the two snake gods. When they would finally entwine, they would breed a single, all-powerful being from their heads. The hundred-thousand-year histories of their two houses had all come down to this time, this place, amid a heat wave—one remaining Shakir, one remaining Shakar— two supernatural beings inextricably drawn to one another, to interlock in a battle that would bring about the true, all powerful Kundalini.

As a boy, Hari Shakir had gone to the tomb of his ancestors, in search of himself—his history, his roots, his purpose. His family told him that inside the tomb resided the bodies of previous men like him, all who had failed the serpent god. Opening the tomb, he felt imbued with the spirit of those who had gone before him. On successive visits to the tomb, he began to feel the seed of the serpent take greater and greater form. He began to feel the movement of the snake god within, and finally, for the first time, he heard it speak to him through his brain in a tender voice, pleading for his help.

Imagine it, he told himself now, *a time when it needed me, when it pleaded for my help*. It had told him how lonely it was, and that for too many years it had lived in limbo, within the desiccated flesh of Hari's forefathers, none of whom had succeeded in uniting with their counterpart Shakars in the allotted time, fifty years.

Now today it was nearing Hari's own fifty years, and he had begun to fear failing the god within. He feared dying with its wrath directed at him; feared being tormented, eaten slowly from the inside out back in that filthy tomb of his ancestors, where the serpent would feed for an eternity on the last Shakir's carcass. Hari would not be so lucky as those he had smoked.

With little choice in the matter as a child, and then with the spirit of a crusader at age thirteen, Shakir had taken on the quest at first with great gusto, and he still enjoyed wielding the power of incinerating people of his choosing, as there was something addictive and seductive about being at the center of such enormous cyclonic heat and being given resistance to it at the same time.

But of late, with time running out, he worried a great deal, sometimes to the point of making himself sick of mind and spirit.

The serpent within knew this . . . knew it all, every thought he paraded by himself, as it was also paraded through the creature's mind. They were neither of them ever completely alone, and that meant twenty-four hours a day, seven days a week. There was no private place, not even in Hari's head; he had forfeited that luxury when he allowed the beast its power over him, when he invited it in to take control of him. Since then, Hari had learned to control any doubts or misgivings about his early choices. The thing within didn't want to hear any doubts. To cover them, Hari often kept up a mantra, and in it, his thoughts projected over and over that he alone, after generations of Shakirs, had taken on its cause as a religious crusade to which he was fully, completely devoted, and that he did not expect anything in return save to see the glory and power of the fire serpent returned to its original prominence.

The modern world had made the crusade more difficult. Adib Shakar had more places to hide; more means of transportation; radio, television, newspapers, computers, and more to tell him of Shakir's approach; for wherever Hari went people were smoked, and in many places, the event made headlines in his wake. No doubt this would be the case right here in Miami, and Shakar might again bolt.

So Adib Shakar could trace his spirit brother's movements via news of spontaneous human combustions around the globe, Calcutta to Paris to London.

The Shakars had for a hundred generations now thwarted the final union of the two beasts. They did so through a terrible ritual suicide. If Adib Shakar were not caught and stopped, he might again end the serpent's quest today for completion.

It was the only thing the fire serpent feared, the resolve of the Shakars, who had taken an oath never to allow the union of the two houses. Hari knew full well of its fears. Hari knew it because each time it relived moments of near completion and closure with its brother snake god, the serpent within him gnarled up as if flinching, as if curling into a ball-like position, its melancholy unrelenting, sending both it and Hari into month-long depressions.

Another downside to being Hari Shakir, he mentally told his parasitic other self. Hari reassured the serpent that this time would be different; that he was not like the serpent's other lovers. That together they had become strong enough to overcome any adversity, including Adib Shakar.

Still, they both worried that Shakar knew of their being near him now. Each side felt the closeness. Adib's own abdomen must be crawling in circles with the knowledge that Shakir had found his new hiding grounds. Adib must be strong to detect them as he had. How frustrating that he always knew when they were within striking distance.

To compensate for its frustration, it wanted more gaseous food.

Get me someone who can help us locate Adib. Bait him in, the serpent of the dark ordered.

"I'll do what I can . . ."

Hari stared out the apartment window, which belonged to the absent tenant named Ronald Shakar. From the window, he saw a man in a light brown service uniform beside a truck with the logo SEMINOLE AIR CONDITIONING and a large-faced American Indian firing an icicle from his bow painted on the van.

The man in uniform had stepped from the van and had gone to its rear for some tools. He looked weary. It was after six. The van was parked in front of a tall apartment house across the street, and Hari made his way quickly to the van.

The man had not seen him until he turned around, startled.

"Jesus!" said the Seminole serviceman.

"Got a cigarette?" asked Hari.

"Sure . . . here." He handed Hari a cigarette and went back to lifting and rearranging tools, searching for something. Behind him, Hari blew a breath on the end of the cigarette and lit it.

When he turned the serviceman found Hari blowing smoke rings around him.

"You are having a problem at this address?" Hari pointed to the apartment house some fourteen or fifteen stories tall. "Do you need a worker? I am a good worker."

"I don't do the hiring. Get the number off the van, make a call."

"My name is Hari."

The uniformed man sized up the dark man who'd so startled him, replying, "Yeah, OK! I gotta get to work now, mister."

"Whole city is having problems, I know."

"Power outages—hospitals, police precincts, grocery stores with freezers. Some old lady here's got an air conditioner on the fritz, so . . ."

"Fritz?"

"You know, *busted.* Anyway, the company's got me spread damn thin, so if you know anything about cooling systems, give 'em a call, unless you own the building or something."

"No . . . I live on the street. Homeless." Hari indicated a causeway with a refrigerator box. "My home for now. I see paramedics carry off a lot of old *geezers*—is how you say it?—from this building." Hari said it with a little too much grin.

"OK, so what do you want from me?" the man asked.

"Look, sir, I'm on the street, no food, no shelter and well . . . we're looking to be the same size."

"So?"

"I am thinking maybe you could find clothes in your van for me?"

The serviceman smiled. "Hey, this uniform doesn't make me Goodwill."

"Maybe I look good in what you wear, uniform, yes," suggested Hari.

The heavyset man looked exasperated now. "You want a company uniform?"

"Yes, that would be good thing."

"Regulations say I can't do that. Sorry."

Hari looked down, his head bowed.

"Tell you what I can do. I can give you a twenty. Help you out."

"You are too kind."

"Never you mind. Been down and out myself. I know just how it feels."

Hari read the stitched on letters of the man's name on his uniform patch: Randy. He saw that another institutional beige brown uniform lay in a metal locker in the van. As Randy searched his wallet for his generous offer, Hari took him by the arm and said, "Now is time for good-byes, but not to worry. You will always be with me. . . ."

The man smiled at the quaint sentiment a millisecond before Hari felt the power of the fire snake run through him like a lightning charge and spew forth from his fingertips, his mouth, his eyes to electrify the victim and alight him into combustible timber. Flash point was reached in the blink of the victim's eye, and as Hari sucked in the smoke and gases, a passing pair of kids on bikes screamed and fled.

The errant greases created by the combustion smeared everything in the van as the rush of superheated air blackened the interior. Hari felt the warmth of the thing within him feeding. He leaned into the van and lifted Randy's other uniform from the smoking metal box. The uniform felt warm as if straight from the dryer, only a few smudge marks over the name.

He returned to Ronald Shakar's apartment, kicking newspapers from his path as he did so. Inside, he quickly changed into the beige uniform and emerged as the air-man Randy. On the front seat of the van, he found a clipboard with the work order Randy was filling. It read *126 Magnolia Street, apt. 14-C.*

"You have won the lottery," Hari said to the name on the clipboard, Samantha.

7

Samantha Krueshicki preferred to be called Sam, and had she any friends, she would insist they call her Sam. She had always considered her life an obscene joke played on her by a disagreeable god, and that she ought to have been born a man. She had the build of a man—thick from head to toe, muscular back, wide shoulders, a wrestler's reach on her. A thick-necked, capable, tough, elderly woman, she had grown accustomed to her strength, and she believed herself capable of taking down any man anywhere, any time, until now. Until the heat wave. It had drained her of all energy.

She had fought her entire life to live on her own terms, and now, nearing seventy, feeling decrepit for the first time in her life, she was in battle against her own children, Hilda and Gerta—who had always condemned her for one thing or another, including the names she'd given them. They wanted her in a home for the elderly, to give up living on her own. She just wanted to be left in fucking peace.

Some cursed person was now knocking at her apartment door. With the heat wave, of course, her air-conditioning had gone out, and with it her last breath of patience. "Go away! Leave me!" she shouted from the bathtub where she lay in tepid water, desperately trying to gain some relief from the heat.

But the pounding continued, insistent and demanding. So much so it angered her. She tried to ignore it, but the *thud-thud-thud* had become a pounding in her head now. She lifted from the tub and threw on a flowered light robe.

"Who the hell is it, and what do you want?" she shouted across the room as she made for the door, her fists balled up.

She looked through her peephole and saw a scary-looking dark-skinned man outside her door. He held up a work order on a clipboard and wore a brown uniform. She went to the window and stared down at the street where she saw the Seminole Indian logo on his van.

Feeling confidant now, she returned to the door and opened it, staring out at the dark man, a foreigner, she thought, by the look of him. "Damn, it took you long enough! I gave up on you, mister! Andy, is it?" She poked at his name sewed onto his shirt, smudged with grease.

He touched the name with a finger and said, "A loan. I am Hari, Hari Shakir. I have come for you."

"For me?"

"To repair you."

"Repair me?"

"Fix you."

"Oh, oh . . . yeah, the air, right? The air conditioner. Better not cost me a dime. It finally took its last breath yesterday." With a motion of her hand, she invited him in while still complaining. "But I've bitched to the landlord about it for weeks. Giodello's so damn cheap," she finally muttered.

The dark man smiled, showing large white teeth, nodding repeatedly as if he understood her. In fact, she thought him sympathetic. He held up his clipboard again. "I have work order here."

Samantha Krueshicki waddled to where she had left a drink, the ice having melted. "How soon you think you can put me back in business?"

"Business?" he asked, confused.

"Ahhh . . . how soon it fixed?" she replied in broken English, thinking he might more readily understand.

He nodded several times up and down but failed to answer,

instead pointing to her cat, a long-haired Persian, and said, "I always like cat."

"She's my only joy, that little thing. Only living creature on this earth that gives me no grief."

He began petting the cat even as it hissed at him.

"Now be nice to the man, Lemondrop. That's her name, Lemondrop."

The cat stood on the kitchen counter, and Hari crouched to come eye to eye with it. Lemondrop's back arched, its hair electrified. Hari and the cat stared into one another's eyes, and in a moment she relaxed under his gaze, calmed. Hari then easily lifted the cat to his bosom, petting it, smiling.

"Funny . . . I didn't think she'd take to you, not after hissing like that. She's normally shy anyway."

"Cats like me, and I like cat."

"You maybe ought to take one of them English classes for people who speak another language," she suggested.

"I am in the class of nature; I learn from the world every day," he countered, "and have many secrets to convey. I will show you a trick, if you will allow me to use your cat."

Samantha Krueshicki shrugged. "I guess, but maybe first you *fixie* the air-conditioning unit?"

"First trick with cat. It is fast . . ."

"All right, all right . . . do it and get to work on the air."

"Already trick is working, and you won't need any air soon."

"Damn it but you talk funny."

With the small animal extended in both hands, Hari and the old woman watched Lemondrop make one final hissing sound moments before a growl of sheer pain, and suddenly she burst into a gaseous ball of flame. The gaseous ball of chemicals floated between the man's dark hands. He had transformed Lemondrop into a smoke cloud, bits of black, inky gruesome stuff splattering her owner's face. In shock, Samantha watched as Hari proceeded, before her eyes, to ingest the gases, sucking the noxious little cloud of chemicals into himself. It had all happened in the blink of an eye, but the old woman caught a blinking glimpse of the snake god.

Samantha's terrified features pleased Hari. It was the result he had sought.

"Where . . . where's my cat?" She foolishly scanned the places in the apartment Lemondrop favored. "Where is she!"

Rubbing his belly, Hari replied, "She is with us . . . inside here."

"You bastard."

"Come . . . come . . . you join with Lemondrop now." He reached out to her.

She had waltzed her way around the strange man, trying to get closer to the door, her only exit aside from the window, the fire escape and a fourteen-story fall. But he stopped her progress, coming closer, his eyes riveting in their unnatural light, a dim but green light in the black pupils, like something she'd never seen before, certainly not human. They suggested the eyes of a snake, and now, like Lemondrop, he began a playful hissing noise as he backed her into the Pullman kitchen, until she came to a stop, her back against the refrigerator.

Once cornered here, she determined to take a stand. She waited for his final step toward her, and she lashed out with a blow to his head, but he absorbed the blow as if it meant nothing, and he grabbed hold of her forearm, holding it now in a viselike grip.

"What I did for your Lemondrop, I now do for you."

"Bastard!" she cursed and screamed even as her cells began overheating, and even as the cells pulled away from one another at the molecular level, until she became a gaseous ball of burning fat. The heat in the apartment soared to incredible temperatures, but concentrated at the center of the old woman's body, the heat rose to fourteen-thousand degrees.

Hari Shakir opened wide and he inhaled deeply. He literally smoked the old fighter. What spirit she had. He admired that in one so old. Now she was part of him like those who had gone before her to the snake god. He saw and felt her wasted life spread out before him. He felt her bitterness and saw her raw, angry memories. While she filled the serpent's pit for the time being, she knew nothing of Shakar or why she had died.

Hari stared at what was left of her human shape, an outline in grease that had splattered black against the white refrigerator uneven only at the crack between refrigerator and freezer doors. It made an impressive silhouette, but an even more impressive calling card. "Well, my lady, who says secondhand smoke is not good for you?" he joked.

He stepped on some teeth that had not combusted, and he backed up only to kick a shredded ankle and whole foot, blackened but intact. "Damn, when am I going to make it to that perfect burn? Does it require the fusion of myself with my brother?"

Angry, he kicked the body fragment farther across the room, the ankle and foot lifting in flight. The fragment knocked over a picture of two younger versions of the old woman, presumably her daughters. Hari lifted the photo and brushed away the shattered glass and stared for a moment at the two women, wondering if either had half the grit and spirit of the old one. "Not bloody likely," he muttered, "but then one never knows." He ripped the picture from its frame and folded it into his beige Mr. Fixit uniform shirt.

He returned to stand before the refrigerator and, reaching up to the ceiling, he dipped his index finger into the greasy soot of a circle of blackness left there. Using his finger as a pen, he wrote a message on the refrigerator to Adib.

Dr. Adib Shakar, aka Katra, stared at toe fragments and the melted ignition and fingers sitting on the table in the lab. They had gotten the prize only because Carl Osterman was no longer in a position to fight them for it; the fire investigator lay in a coma at General. Adib knew of only one force on earth capable of spontaneously combusting Dr. Stanton, but who would believe such a conclusion here in the sleek, modern world of Miami, Florida? Adib intensely stared into the molten metal, and within it, he saw the movement of a shadow, Hari Shakir. He saw him cremating yet another victim outside an apartment beneath a street sign that read: MAGNOLIA 120W BLK. The sighting of images in the molten metal, emanating from his brain, deposited there via a strange telepathy between him and Hari Shakir meant that Hari could sense his closeness to him as well. It could all be over in a moment, should Shakir find him.

Others worked around Adib here in the lab, but no one knew what he was going through. The serpent within Adib restlessly sent signals to his mind, and Adib, sickened by his own taste for the odors that had infiltrated his system while working over the Stanton crime scene, felt a pull, an urgent need to investigate this one-hundred-and-twentieth block of west Magnolia.

The tug at him was dangerous, and he knew going there would be foolish, yet he was drawn to it.

"Are you all right, Dr. Katra?" asked Angelica, looking up from her microscope.

Adib thought her a lovely young person and a first-rate medical examiner. "I must leave . . . get some air," he replied, rushing out. "Please cover for me until Dr. Slater gets in . . . thank you."

"Yes, of course, and I hope you're feeling better."

Adib rushed from the lab across town to the location in his head. When he pulled onto the block, he could smell the odor of ozone. Hari had been here, but Adib's heightened senses told him that Shakir had long before left. While he feared getting to near Shakir, he continued to feel the psychic plea from his own inner serpent to investigate.

Dressed in a white suit, he followed his nose and rang all the bells at once in the apartment building at 126 Magnolia Street, and, as expected, at least one person responded, asking who it was as he buzzed the lock. Adib didn't answer, simply pushing through. He stepped to the elevator, his cane tapping against the broken tiles. He knew nothing of the occupants here, knew nothing of the victim. He was certain only that there was one—a body metamorphosed into a ball of flame and gas, leaving only a small fraction of herself behind, perhaps a gnarled foot, a knuckle bone, some fingers like Stanton's, as this new victim was consumed in a spontaneous combustion brought on by the beast chasing Adib Shakar.

He had felt the beast close, and he had seen this place in a confused vision, and while he had come to view the results, to satisfy some need in him to do so, he feared where his feet led him; he feared going near the result of Hari Shakir's unrelenting hunger. Still, something within had driven him here.

A lifetime of struggling to keep the snake within him in its pit, to keep control of it so that it did not control him, had aged Adib Shakar. People thought him twenty years older than he was. He'd had to begin use of a cane now, a searing arthritis in his hips. His hair was gray, turning white. His skin dry and brittle.

Even before getting off the elevator on the 14th floor, he smelled the raw, acrid results of Shakir's having been here. His snake within had been right. The elevator doors opened and the odor was stronger still. Adib inched closer, cautious of everything around him, sensitive to every sound, which all seemed heightened inside his ears along this corridor. He followed his senses to 14-C, where his hand trembled over the doorknob. He turned it, finding it unlocked, and with his snake's-head cane, he pushed the door open. It creaked as it went inward.

Adib silently prayed that Vishnu, the god of all things, would be merciful to the serpent's latest victim. He hesitated at the open door as the pungent odors wafted out to him like the index finger of a fiendish ghost, enticing him on. The odors of burnt flesh and ozone. He found himself enticed enough to breathe it in with a deep effort, and it pleased the snake within him that he'd done so. Something about the acrid odors of a combusted victim made Adib *want* to taste of it himself, and he knew the hunger Hari Shakir felt to be as real as it was hideous.

He finally forced himself to step through the open door when he heard someone whistling on the landing below.

Then a voice from there asked, "What is that stink? Who's burning sauerkraut?"

Adib now took the final footfall in what had been a kind of psychic abduction of his will, and yet he knew deep, deep within that part of the reason for being here instead of on a plane for anywhere else was his own morbid fascination with the power, a power that he, too, could wield if he chose, and a power that would be multiplied tenfold should he ever succumb to Shakir's advances. All it would take from Adib or Shakir was a touch.

Looking around at the empty apartment, seeing the scorched roof and the black silhouetted figure in smoke-smudge outlined against the refrigerator, told the ugly story of what had unfolded inside the shabby little apartment. He continued to stare at the blackened outline of the victim against the white refrigerator door, and written in the grease were the letters he feared: *H-A-R-I*.

"So, my ancient and evil other half, you are truly afoot here in Miami." Adib had known it when viewing the scant remains of Dr. Stanton. There remained a weak unbidden psychic tug between them—a psychic link between the two serpents—always and forever uniting them, and if not them their offspring. It was why Shakar chose never to have a child, to never put another soul through the torment of his life, and to end the bloodline once and for all.

Shakar knew that he must not be seen here by anyone, at least not yet. How might he explain how he had honed in on this place, that the victim was discovered here by him?

Looking on at the unmistakable evidence of the serpent's having come and gone here, Adib felt no shock of surprise, not after what he'd seen in Stanton's car, but rather a feeling of recognition and acceptance. Still the sight shook him to his core; no one knew the far-reaching consequences of having the knowledge he possessed, and no one could imagine the burden of the centuries that lay now squarely on his shoulders. No one could begin to guess at the horrors that he and Shakir—if united as one—could bring into this world.

It had only happened once before, before the dawn of re-corded history, when the Kundalini god had consumed the world's population in its lust for absolute supremacy. The only thing that had ended its power on earth had been its having nothing left to feed upon but itself. At least this was what the ancient ones wrote about, a kind of flood of fire that engulfed every living thing on earth until the only thing left to consume was itself. Vishnu had then looked down upon the ruins and had planted the seed for mankind to re-generate, but the serpent seed remained hiding and dormant as well.

Adib knew in his veins, in his bones, in his body and soul that a return to power for the Kundalini meant that all the world's population would become its cattle to feed upon at its leisure until yet another end of days came. The germi-nating seed of the thing could not ever be completely killed, but Adib knew that he could keep it from growing beyond its present stage if he could keep it from fusing with him. And Adib was running out of places to hide as the beast pursuing him grew stronger with each feeding. He and Hari both knew that it must join with Adib within the next two years or it would take Hari back to the tomb with it, to lie dormant until the next rising. Two years didn't seem like much, but now with its nearness to him, its growing strength, Adib feared the worst. He must act.

"My own death is the only cure," he muttered to the empty room, his eyes still on the refrigerator.

Adib Shakar began to contemplate the best death for him-self, for his half of the monster. It was not the first time he had contemplated it, but it must be carried out properly. Who in this place might he trust? With whom could he entrust his remains, for if the Shakir got hold of his uncleansed and unexorcised body, he could still *join* with it to become the Kundalini with all the power that entailed.

He thought of the alternative, to flee once again, but it was so close that he feared it would know his plans. And where could he go? The damnable thing would find him again. It was desperate now. It only had two years. It had cornered him here in Miami, positing psychic messages for him in its wake, perhaps in hopes of getting him to make a rash act, a foolish mistake, or to rush to the airport to once again run away.

Hari's actions would soon be front-page news. The Stanton death scene and the one he now saw in his mind would make sensational photos in the press. Was it all in order to flush Adib out? Did Hari know already that Adib would be called on to clean up his mess in a professional capacity? Did he know Adib was a medical examiner?

Adib had read about the suspicious warehouse fire and the alleyway fire in half-inch stories on the back pages of the local newspapers. The stories made references that authorities were hiding something, that they had found bone fragments and body parts from unidentified individuals in the rubble of each fire. The stories had gotten no attention, no play on TV, but they ended with questions about spontaneous human combustion. The public's awareness of the danger would soon change if Adib did not act. SHC cases would be dominating the airways, and more lives would be lost.

Although Adib was not surprised at what he found in the apartment, he couldn't stop quaking, as he felt completely isolated in his realization of how damnably close to the final edge all humanity stood at this moment. A powerful sense of duty mingled with an equally powerful melancholy, as his own serpent worked to suck in the aftereffects of the murder, taking over his autonomous reflexes so that he breathed deeper and deeper of the odors pleasant to the beast within. It threatened to please Adib's mind as well. He struggled for control. For should he himself fall prey to the near irresistible snare of the beast—should they blend and become a united one—the result would be catastrophic, all life on the planet fodder for its insatiable appetite, until once again it consumed itself. What choice had he but that prescribed by the ages, prescribed by the scrolls?

Adib backed from the apartment. The odors had brought people out into the hallway, curious. He found himself surrounded by complaining tenants who wanted to know what the fire odors were and if they should vacate the building. Adib held up his credentials and shouted for everyone to remain calm. "There is no danger," he assured them, realizing the irony of his statement. "I am a doctor, and I am calling authorities now." He got on his cell phone and dialed Lou Ames's private number. Ames was immediately out of bed and on the phone with Eric Brannon, giving him the street address.

Adib next called Dr. Hunter at the office, telling her there had been another suspicious fire death, and that he needed her at the location.

"But you're already there?" she asked, wondering how he had gone from the lab to a crime scene that had not been reported to the ME's office.

"You have to do it. The odors . . . they are overwhelming for me. Try to understand. I cannot remain long here." In fact, he stood out on the fire escape, sucking in all the fresh air he could get, while deep within him the serpent coiled around his spine in a kind of ecstasy over the odors it had taken in on the inside.

"I've got to end this before it takes complete hold of me," he told the night sky.

Brannon hadn't felt like celebrating, and so after his shift, he had gone home for a shower and rest, and he had fallen asleep in his La-Z-Boy. He was awakened there by a call from Captain Ames, who told him of Adib Katra's call. "One twenty-six West Magnolia, apartment fourteen-C. You will find another victim like Dr. Stanton. That's all he said, Eric."

"When did Katra get the call?"

"Just now, I assume. Just get over there."

"Try to locate Jackie. She's either home or at O'Banyan's. Tell her to meet me there."

"Will do. See you at the scene."

He dressed and rushed out, got into his car, and drove to

the address. In twenty minutes he pulled up to the blighted apartment house and found a police squad car sitting out front, and the crime-scene-unit van pulled in behind him. Dr. Hunter emerged with a couple of evidence technicians.

"Did Dr. Katra call you?" asked Brannon.

"Yes, he did."

"From here?"

"From the apartment on the fourteenth floor, yes."

"Did he give you any details?"

"No, just wanted me to be here."

No fire trucks had come, but some tenants had vacated the building, and they stood about complaining of fire odors, but no flames were visible anywhere.

As soon as they stepped into the hallway, Brannon and Angelica smelled the odors, horribly similar to those that they'd encountered within Dr. Renea Stanton's vehicle.

"Whoever this guy is, he leaves a stink trail," Brannon said to Angelica, trying to keep a sense of dread from overwhelming him.

Together, Brannon and Hunter rode up the elevator. The rattling elevator noise tightened Brannon's already tried nerves, and as they rose the stench only increased. "Smell familiar?" he asked her. "How did Katra find the victim?"

"Said he got an anonymous tip."

"Strange someone would call the ME instead of the cops."

"We get our share of weird calls, too, Detective."

When they stepped from the elevator, there were people taking the other elevator down, boarding with treasured items in their hands. Someone was asking, "Is there or isn't there a fire in the building?"

"We being evacuated or what?"

"What's going on?"

Some tenants had gathered in the hallway, gawking and gossiping about the occupant in 14-C. Fire sirens sounded from outside now. Someone had finally called it in as a fire. Then two uniformed policemen staggered from 14-C, choking on the odors. Brannon identified himself and said, "Keep everyone back fellas."

"Never seen anything like this kind of shit in my six years on the force, Detective. ME's inside already."

Dr. Adib Katra stepped out into the hallway, his eyes meeting theirs. "It appears the work of the same man."

Katra stood in his civilian white suit, discolored with soot and black smudges. He wore rubber gloves also smeared with black soot. He explained to Brannon, "Another missing woman under strange circumstances. This time teeth, an ankle and foot left behind."

"Another spontaneous human combustion, Doctor?" asked Brannon, watching his reaction.

"Or as Osterman says, someone who wants us to believe it so."

"Who's the victim?"

"A Mrs. Krueshicki. Door was unlocked, I entered when I got no response. I warn you, what is inside . . . it's difficult."

Brannon squinted at Katra, and the two exchanged a curious and questioning look until Adib broke off eye contact.

"I understand you got an anonymous call, sir. Was that at your office or on your cell phone?"

He hesitated. "Cell phone."

"Hmmm . . . wonder how they got your number. Not likely anyone here would have your private number."

"I suspect they fooled someone at the reception. I leave my number for call forwarding."

Eric nodded, accepting this for the moment. "Where were you when you got the call?"

"Am I a suspect of some sort? Why all these questions, Detective?"

"Sorry, Doctor. Just trying to get the picture."

"The picture is inside that door." Adib pointed to the apartment. "Look, I was having dinner at Caruso's—alone—when the call came over."

"Perhaps the guy who did this made the call," suggested Brannon.

"How do you suppose he got your number?" asked Angelica.

"Cleverly, I suspect," replied Adib. Katra then returned to the apartment, his cane tapping, looking a good deal stronger than the last time Brannon had seen him.

Brannon and Angelica followed Dr. Katra into the apartment, each fighting with the straps of a filtered mask. The two of them were immediately stopped by the black outline of a human form against the stark white of the refrigerator door, arms raised as if fending off an attacker. The picture Adib had alluded to, painted in that stuff the little ME had called human creosote. A soapy grease created of superheated human body fat. At the center of the figure, smeared in greasy black, were the letters *H-A-R-I*.

Dr. Katra then pointed out a handful of teeth, an ankle and foot, blackened by fire, all lying scattered at the foot of the fridge. He did not tell Brannon that the smoked ankle and foot, the largest remaining part of the victim, had been returned to the ashes from across the room, that he had unconsciously lifted it and handled the part which Hari had either thrown or kicked away after the combustion.

The ceiling above the fridge was also smoked and some of the gooey stuff dripped from there to the floor.

"What the hell is an h-a-r-i?" He spelled it out. "Some kind of terrorist group I haven't heard about?"

"Hari," Adib read it as one word. "I don't know," he lied. Lately, nothing is making any sense."

The scene of the crime, in many ways, proved worse than what they had found inside Stanton's car. The victim's shape silhouetted in dark, sooty outline against her bare, white refrigerator made Brannon feel as if some residue of the woman remained, staring over their shoulders, seeing if they were getting it right. Dr. Katra pointed to a smaller ball of blackness on the living room ceiling wholly unattached to the other strange stain, and on a much smaller scale.

Brannon asked, "What time was it that you got the call, Doctor?"

"Just after I left the lab, about seven-thirty, I believe."

"Suppose the caller is our guy, Doctor, why do you suppose he called you?"

"Why are you assuming it was the killer who called me?"

"A strange type like this likes to play games, leaving messages on the refrigerator. Hari . . . isn't that an Indian name? Maybe he saw you at the last scene, saw your reaction. Wanted to put it to you."

Adib shook his head at this. "I cannot say. Perhaps he was watching us at the last scene; perhaps he saw my weakness there and wished to play on it, yes." The thought terrified Adib. "Whoever called, it was a male with a gruff voice," Adib continued to lie, trying to extricate himself from the detective's questioning. He dared not attempt to explain that he had not been telephoned but had had a telepathic message. He had seen the street sign in his mind.

"He must have made inquiries, and somehow tricked someone into giving out Dr. Katra's number." Angelica came to his defense. She had been absorbed by the awful sight painted on the white surface of the refrigerator when she heard Brannon drilling Dr. Katra. It had taken her a moment to realize what was going on.

"Angelica, anyone asking you how to get in touch with me today?" Adib asked her.

She firmly replied, "Only the usual forty or fifty calls, Dr. Katra."

"It might help us locate the caller to check on your phone records. Perhaps we can pinpoint the origin."

"Do whatever you think best, Detective."

Brannon relaxed his questioning, thinking what Adib Katra said made a strange sort of logic, but the good doctor was also going to pains to prove it, and he was shaken by the questioning. It recalled how he had acted at the Stanton crime scene, how his assistant had had to take over for him. Adib Katra was acting strangely to say the least, and his coincidentally being near the scene—perhaps ten or eleven blocks over—when he got the call only made Brannon more suspicious. In fact, the doctor's body language added to Brannon's suspicions. Brannon knew the signs; he had interrogated hundreds of suspects over the years.

In the back of his mind in a file marked LATER, Eric Brannon put away the notion that in some peculiar way, Medical Examiner Katra was somehow involved or connected to the killings or the killer, even if tenuously so. He was hiding something. Brannon made a mental note to put Jackie on to checking with the incoming phone calls for Katra for the time in question, to see which had been forwarded and from where they had originated.

Katra's being too Johnny-on-the-spot here, ahead of even the patrol officers, made Brannon wary. He also recalled how Adib had prematurely called out the makeup of the chemicals smeared all over Dr. Stanton's interior windows, before any tests were run. Katra had called it without taking time to analyze the residue, a departure from his usual professional stance and thoroughness. Why? Brannon, like most detectives, couldn't leave a why hanging; he knew he must pursue Katra, who seemed to have some sort of weird track on these strange cases of so-called spontaneous combustion.

Brannon lifted a picture of a heavyset woman with gray hair and a massive pair of shoulders. She also had a pair of angry eyes lost in a masculine face, bloated most likely with liquor and a lifetime of cigarettes. In fact, empty bottles lay about everywhere, along with ashtrays filled with remnant cigarettes.

"Mrs. Krueshicki, the missing occupant," said Katra.

"Who ID'd her?"

"I had a visit from the superintendent. Poor fellow collapsed when he saw this place. He's lying in a bed in an apartment down the hall. He saw nothing, knows nothing."

"Yes, that's her picture," came a voice from the doorway. It was a man in a T-shirt drenched in sweat.

"This is Mr. Lambert, the super," said Katra to Brannon. "Perhaps you have questions for *him*?" Katra then took Angelica Hunter aside and began whispering to her.

"She was a mean old bitch," said the super, "but nobody deserves dying like this, nobody." He fought to get his breath, and he held both hands against his neck as if afraid of his head tumbling off. "Spontaneous human combustion, ain't it? Dr. Katra told me all about it. Has to do with the buildup of acids in the stomach, right, something called dia-phones, I think, yeah, diaphones."

"That is one theory, yes," said Dr. Katra, reassuring the man.

Brannon lifted a smashed frame, shards of glass falling like beads from it. "Looks like somebody took a photo."

"Her daughters," said the super between panting and pac-ing. "She kept the picture right there. Anytime they come to visit, the three of them would fight."

"Missing picture could mean the daughters may be in dan-ger. You know where they live?" asked Brannon.

"Fort Lauderdale, I think."

"Know their names?"

"Gilda . . . Hilda, I think. She never talked about 'em, and they seldom came to visit except to get her to sign this or that paper. They wanted her to go to a nursing home, but she refused."

"Man it's like a sauna in here," complained Brannon. He began searching for the woman's phone book.

"Her AC's been out. Weird, 'cause I spoke to the AC guy with Seminole. He was s'pose to get on it, but I guess he knocked off instead."

Brannon made a note to check on the dispatcher's records with Seminole Air. Maybe the man had seen something. Brannon then found the victim's phone book, and he located the address and number for the women. It appeared they lived together. He'd normally contact the next of kin to ID the body, but how now? he wondered.

He took the name and single address of the two sisters to one of the cops in the hallway. "Put a unit on the address until one of us can talk to the daughters."

"How do we tell them what happened? We don't know what's happened," replied the cop.

"Leave that to the detective squad. Tell them nothing. Just put a watch on the place. See anyone suspicious, call me immediately."

Firemen had begun to spill out of the stairwell. "Tell the fire guys it's a false alarm under control."

He then saw Ames and Jackie coming off the elevator. He met them halfway. "Whoever this guy is, he's working overtime. This could be a kill-spree night for the maniac."

Jackie asked, "Word is out it's a spontaneous human combustion. Any idea how the old girl might be related to Stanton?"

"No evidence to suggest they had anything in common."

"Who knows? Maybe she was a patient of Stanton's, and maybe this killer or abductor or collector or whatever he is was a patient as well," she suggested.

When Brannon returned to the room, he saw Hunter and Katra again engaged in disagreement, immediately silenced when they saw he had reentered with Ames and Hale. The two newcomers were too overwhelmed by the odors and sights here to have noticed, but Brannon did take notice. Something definitely odd was going on between the ME and his assistant. In an effort to cover, Hunter loudly asked, "How the hell do we process a crime scene like this, Dr. Katra?"

"Protocol . . . like any other," he firmly replied. "Grid it out, and follow protocol. Get lots of pictures. Now, as I said, Doctor, it's your case. I am turning it over entirely to you, and I trust you will do a fine job."

"All right, sir, if you're certain," she replied.

"You are managing well on the last case, and continuity is important."

Yes, yes . . . I will concede that."

Brannon didn't believe the charade for a moment. Both of them were covering the true gist of their argument with this conversation. Katra now stepped out into the hall, guided by an instinct to get away from the lingering odors here. The odors affected everyone, but secretly, they affected him tenfold. The snake within writhed and circled about where it had lain dormant for so long, excited by the closeness of the *Shakir* and its other half, and the odors seeping down to it.

Ames and Hale looked at Brannon, both of them stricken

by what they witnessed here. Brannon offered Jackie a quick way out, handing her an address on the daughters. "You want to break the news to her next of kin?"

It was usually a duty no one relished, but Jackie jumped at the chance to leave this place. Brannon walked her to the door. "Find out if the old woman had ever gone to Memorial or Saint Sebastian's or had anything to do with Dr. Stanton—or anyone else at either hospital for that matter. And run Dr. Katra's name by them for the hell of it."

"Katra?"

"Just do it."

Jackie shrugged and disappeared into the elevator and was gone. Brannon saw that Dr. Katra was now besieged by a neighbor lady with blue hair just outside the door, asking him, "What about Sam's cat? I tell you, she had a lovely Persian cat, answers to the name Lemondrop."

"Not anymore, my dear. I'm afraid the cat is lost to us."

Brannon wondered at Katra's choice of words, but he chalked it up to his meaning that the cat may have slipped out the door at any time. But then Brannon's eyes wandered back to the smaller ball of soot on the living-room ceiling.

Brannon watched Katra leaving, his cane tapping, looking rigid, as if holding himself together with bands of wire. He looked to have aged ten years since all of this had begun. Still, he had put up a good front here tonight, looking stronger than he had at the Stanton crime scene.

"Just a minute, Dr. Katra," called out Brannon. He caught Katra at the elevator. "I want to talk to you, perhaps tomorrow, Doctor, about the call you got to come here, see if we can pinpoint anything about the caller, and I've got a few questions about the old woman, Dr. Stanton, and your take on all this."

"Of course, my office at seven-fifteen a.m. and don't be a second late."

Katra's response surprised Brannon. He stepped back and watched as the elevator doors closed on the dark man, and for a millisecond, he thought he saw some strange movement in the man's black pupils, as if there were a pair of eyes behind Katra's eyes looking out at him.

Brannon returned to the crime scene to find Captain Ames with his head out a window, vomiting.

8

It was past nine when Brannon returned to the apartment to speak with Dr. Angelica Hunter, and still the odor in and around the apartment had yet to subside. *Alive and still pungent as ever*, he thought. He wondered if the apartment would be inhabitable ever again. No amount of ammonia and bleach could touch this, he told himself.

"Smells like odors I encountered in the war, but something about that one odor I can't fathom . . . nothing like it in my experience," he said to Hunter, making her look up from some vials she'd been labeling and placing into an evidence box. "You getting anything useful?"

"All I can tell you, Detective, is that what went on here—as out of the norm as it is . . . well, it's the same as what happened in Stanton's car."

"Leave it to science to point out the obvious."

Ames interrupted them, saying, "Thought you ought to know. Carl Osterman's in a coma at Miami General, a single-vehicle accident on his way home."

"We got word at the lab earlier," said Hunter.

"Sorry to hear it," said Brannon.

Ames breathed deeply and said, "So calling in Shelby Harne turns out to be a godsend. Harne says Carl wasn't being completely honest with us."

"How so? He says he can find not a trace of chemicals other than those found in the human body, no butane, no propane, no man-made chemical accelerants in the car—only animal-fat accelerants."

"That's all our lab has found either," said Hunter. She saw Brannon's confused reaction, and she was not disappointed. "Now you can join the rest of us who don't have a clue in hell as to what's really going on here."

The three of them fell silent for the moment. She finally said, "I know, it makes no sense, but this killer has found a catalyst that somehow ignites human fatty tissues."

"Spontaneous combustion," asked Ames. "That ought to play well with the brass upstairs."

Brannon's eyes widened. "You're serious? Spontaneous human combustion? Renea Stanton and the old woman died of spontaneous combustion? Is that Adib's judgment or yours, Dr. Hunter?"

"For lack of a better term, and any additional information at this time, that's my opinion. Take it or leave it."

"And Dr. Katra?"

"Yes. That's what Adib is sticking by. So far it's the only reasonable, if unscientific *unexplainable* explanation."

Brannon looked her in the eye. "But what do you really think, Dr. Hunter?"

"I told you what I think."

"No, you told me what Dr. Katra thinks, what he's locked down on."

She made no response, which spoke volumes to Brannon.

"So, I'm right. Not even you and Dr. Katra can agree on what we're looking at here, can you?"

"I didn't want to accept it, but Adib is adamant. He wants me to accept it. And since this morning, the bone fragment and blood and serum tests we ran assure us that what was left inside Stanton's vehicle was what was left . . . of Stanton."

"Good Christ, are you sure?" asked Ames.

"That . . . that smudge was her?" Eric gasped.

"I'm sorry about your friend, but what we had at the scene

was no abduction. She was there; she simply was in another *form*."

"Another form?"

"The brittle black Styrofoam and grease. That was her, and this," she pointed at the refrigerator, "is all that's left of the woman who lived here. This and the ankle and foot and a few teeth."

"Doesn't amount to much."

"No, and that's baffling, too. There's not enough left of either woman to weigh up as an entire body. That should be the case if they were simply transformed from solid to gas as Adib says they were. Matter, even when transformed, remains constant. So what happened to the rest of these women?"

"Adib has no answer to that?" asked Ames.

"He wouldn't hazard a guess, but he agreed there's a large discrepancy in body mass."

"And you two have no idea what set off these combustions?" asked Ames.

She shook her head.

Ames said, "And I had hoped to God Osterman was right."

"About what?" asked Brannon.

"Some new accelerant, possibly developed through space technology. He was in touch with NASA."

"Anything?"

"NASA says nothing that could accomplish this. Shelby agrees."

"In the confines of the car, in Stanton's case, you'd think we'd have found more mass, but no, damn it . . . no." Hunter sounded like a frustrated child unable to place a square into a round hole.

"So what're you saying, Dr. Hunter? That whoever is doing this is somehow taking the bulk of the bodies he combusts with him? Maybe in an urn?" asked Ames.

"In essence, yes."

"How? If they're being evaporated into gaseous form?" asked Eric.

"Your guess is as good as mine, but he is somehow capturing the—this mass I am speaking of—and he's taking it off with him when he goes. Somehow, he captures the gases, likely in some sort of vacuum."

Brannon looked away, shaking his head. "OK . . . OK, supposing you're on to something here Dr. Hunter, and you're right about this SHC stuff, but if so, the old woman's body would have gone up in one flashover at the ceiling. All the soot ought to be centered in one place, at the fridge. So explain to me about that spot at the center of the ceiling."

"I understand there's a missing cat."

"Cat? He combusted the old woman's cat, too?" asked Ames.

"Could be."

"Now that pisses me off," joked Brannon, trying to ease the situation with cop humor.

She managed a half smile and stood, drenched in perspiration, her blouse sticking to her below the soot-smudged white lab coat she wore. Brannon again thought her beauty at odds with her profession. Their eyes met for a moment.

"I'm out of here," said Ames. "I want your report on Stanton on my desk as soon as possible, Dr. Hunter. As for this mess . . . when you can, please . . ."

"Yes, sir, Captain. ASAP."

After Ames left, Brannon asked her, "You got any notion why Dr. Katra is, you know, sitting out on this case?"

"He's hardly sitting it out. He's been under a lot of stress lately, so I sat him down. He's staying put from now on until he feels better, working the case from the lab, that's all."

Brannon had heard differently from what patches of conversation he had caught. But he only nodded, her reply making him only more suspicious of Katra. "Let's get out of here," he suggested.

"I have to take all my findings directly back to headquarters, follow—"

"Rigorous and exacting protocol, I know. Chain of evidence. Let me drive you, then."

"Not necessary. I have the crime-unit van downstairs."

"Yeah, of course."

"But later, if you want to get a drink, talk," she suggested.

"I'd like that."

"After I've had a shower. Come by my place in"—she looked at her watch—"in say an hour and a half. There's a nice place just a block from my apartment."

"What's the address?"

"Some cop." She jotted it down on a pad and ripped it off and handed it to him. "Don't be late."

"Count on it . . . I mean, no . . . I mean sure."

Finally home alone, far from the death scene, Dr. Adib Shakar, aka Katra, sat with a double shot of bourbon in his apartment, nude, meditating and concentrating hard to block any mental energy he thought might be remotely connected with his nemesis, Hari Shakir.

He wondered how he was to keep up the facade of being Dr. Adib Katra, ME extraordinaire and forensic genius for Miami, and at the same time prepare himself for his own suicide, and at the same time prevent his arch enemy from breaking through to him before he could have his body turned into an unclean and decaying vessel, so as to end any possibility of its being used by the monster.

All of the sadness, all of the loneliness of his existence, all of the aloneness and silence of knowledge of this threat to the known universe, and how he must prepare to end any possibility of Hari's growing any stronger than the superbeing he had already become . . . it all proved a delicate balancing act, both mentally and physically draining. He was a man on a unicycle balancing sixteen plates in the air at once, all spinning, any one of which could destroy the balance of all power in nature.

He stood and went to a bookshelf, and, removing several volumes, he found the vault at the back. He had not used the combination in years, but he remembered it as if it were yesterday when he had placed the key and his will into the vault.

He thought of years ago, when he had first left India and

home for Europe. Tracked down there, he had come to America to escape Hari Shakir, to escape any attempt he might make to *mate* with him. Now he sensed Hari was not only near—extremely near—but that Hari had the instincts and the edge on him; Hari had sniffed him out from an ocean away. It could be a matter of days or even hours before the awful possibility that Hari located him. He could not let this happen.

From the vault, Adib, his hands shaking, pulled forth a small metal box that held his will and a key to a safe-deposit box at the bank wherein lie proof of his extraordinary claims, perhaps the only proof anyone might believe—the ancient scrolls that told the entire story of the Shakar and the Shakir families and how their fate was forever and inextricably entwined and entangled with the hungry ancient one—the Kundalini serpent god. The two-headed, circular creature whose body could never be filled, not with the entire world, and who was without beginning or end as both ends were the same—one the *Shakir,* the other the *Shakar.* The all-consuming beast to whom the ancient scryers paid homage. Both Adib's uncle and his uncle's friend, Kalie, had warned that if the beast of two heads ever became the beast of four heads—uniting *Shakir* and *Shakar* serpents, the union would represent the power of the four elements, earth, wind, fire, and water. The creature would create a black and endless void of all life if given full sway.

The scrolls were his only proof to the outside world—and Angelica in particular—that he was not mad; they would be the only proof Dr. Hunter might understand, but she must get them interpreted, and if so, she might follow his admittedly insane-sounding instructions for the absolute annihilation of his human form to keep it, even in death, out of the reach of the snake god.

Since the ancient recipe for this ritual suicide involved horrible, unspeakable acts against the body, no modern person like Angelica would understand or carry out the ritual without grave reservations. No one could in a place like America possibly understand the desecration of a body; no one aside from a scryer of old could begin to, and where might he find one in Miami, Florida?

He opened the box and held the key up to his eyes with the reverence of a priest looking at a holy relic.

He had a great deal to set in motion. He had a great deal to prepare. He prayed that Angelica and her new friend Detective Brannon would be strong enough to carry out his dying wishes.

Eric Brannon and Anegelica Hunter had walked from her high-rise apartment and down the street to Heidigger's Experiment, a bar and grill on the corner. Neither one wanted to sit down, both still keyed up over the day's events. So they played the electronic pinball machines and the space ball police action game. As they did so, they talked, now on a first-name basis.

"Really, Angelica, what's going on with Dr. Katra?" he asked.

"Whataya deaf? I told you, he's just coming off an illness, flu bug and now he's battling gastroenteritis, and he's edgy as hell."

"He seems unable to handle these fire deaths."

"Hey, no ME likes fried corpses, but this? Besides, he's just not feeling well, and it doesn't take a rocket scientist to figure that if you're battling a stomach and digestive-tract problem, and you have to breathe in the odors we've been encountering, it's going to get to you."

"It seems more than that, to me."

"What're you driving at, Eric?"

"How'd he get to the old woman's apartment ahead of us?"

"The phone call, and he was in the vicinity. What are you supposing up there in that cop's brain of yours? Give it a rest."

"Sorry . . . didn't mean to offend you. I got the impression he checked out the scene a long time before he made the call to Ames."

"And how do you know that?"

"First cops on call found him out on the fire escape, having a smoke. I got there in twenty minutes. He had already canvassed the place and talked to the superintendent."

"Adib works fast when he's at his best."

"But you just said he's not at his best."

"Are you baiting me?"

"Sorry."

"I think it may have something to do with family . . . back in India. He said something about getting some bad news. Likely someone died."

"Yeah, most likely."

Brannon missed a key shot on the electronic board, and the bright ball, which was actually a light-emitting diode on the pinball surface, slipped past his guns. "Damn it," he cursed. He turned to her and stared into her eyes. "Look, is there any remote chance at all that what we found in Stanton's car and at the Krueshicki apartment, that it was all planted? The grease spray painted on, the bones scattered by hand like Carl Osterman said?"

"A number of tests show the bones in the shoe in the car were from a middle-aged, female Caucasian, approximately five nine, a hundred twenty-five to a hundred thirty pounds, give or take. To be more certain, I pulled blood from the bone marrow and matched it with her medical records and bingo, the blood type was a match."

Brannon's eyes diminished and his face paled; he was still trying to come to terms with Renea Stanton's death. They found a table and seats and ordered another round of drinks.

"I'll run the same tests on Mrs. Krueshicki's bone fragments tomorrow but . . ."

"Yeah, I get the picture. What about fingerprint evidence? Anything?"

"Oddest thing."

"What's that?" His eyes lit with some small hope. "You've got something for us to run through VICAP?"

"No, no prints, but we picked up some weird *scales* embedded in some of the creosote."

"Scales, like fish scales?"

"Snake scales."

"No shit. Spontaneous combustion and snake scales. Now we'll have to go canvassing every damn pet store in the city. Tell me, Angelica, what's *your* best guess?"

"At the moment, no explanation. But forensic investigation does not necessarily exclude *paranormal* possibilities."

"Do you believe in paranormal activities? That they surround human experience, envelop us in a web of extrasensory input and output?"

"I believe there is more between heaven and earth than I see in my telescopes, if that's what you mean. Then again, someday we might want to find a *logical* explanation for what ignites a human body spontaneously."

"Maybe this g'damn heat has played some role . . . but that doesn't explain the snake scales, does it?"

"Nor does a heat wave explain how spontaneous human combustions have been reported in the UK and other cooler climates," she countered.

"Tell me you've been reading up on it."

"I've been reading up on it."

They looked across at one another. "Hell, I keep seeing birds dropping off from this heat we're in," he began. "Why don't they spontaneously combust?"

"Couldn't tell ya," she replied, "maybe not enough carbon in their little bodies?"

"Carbon?"

"We're carbon-based units of energy, Eric. The major accelerant found at the scene was carbon. Osterman knew that, and it had to play havoc with his logical mind. It's as if the very substance we are made up of was the cause of the combustion."

Brannon was not exaggerating about the birds. Miami's parks were littered with their carcasses from the heat wave and lack of drinking water. The Miami river carried countless dead birds out to sea along its course. On close inspection, environmentalists said the birds were bleeding at the beak, their lungs having exploded, unable to take in the super-heated oxygen. The heat wave had only worsened in the past few days. The only good outcome was that the flies had begun to die off, but the night had been silenced of crickets as well, creating an eerie feel to life in general, since the usual insect buzz had all but disappeared.

Only die-hard environmentalist groups voiced concerns over the insect population having disappeared, but no one missed the mosquitoes, centipedes, scorpions, spiders, and palmetto bugs. Even the mice, rats, armadillos, possums, and raccoons were going near extinct as a result of the unprecedented heat.

The horror stories involving the heat filled the airways, and stories and rumors about people going up in smoke *had* begun to circulate as a result of fire investigations going on during the heat wave, some rumored to be cases of spontaneous human combustion. But so far none of the newspapers or TV shows were speculating on how Stanton and Mrs. Krueshicki had died. The only reason for this: that police had kept the manner in which these two had died out of the hands of the press, so far. It was likely only a matter of time that the old woman's daughters would sell their story to some reality TV program or Jonathan Frakes's *Beyond Belief*.

Brannon was surprised the secret had been kept as long as it had, given the number of technicians and cops who'd witnessed different aspects of the two cases. "Before all this started, Angelica," began Brannon, "what was your take on spontaneous human combustion?"

"Most medical people refuse to accept SC as any sort of answer, and most of the so-called evidence has been anecdotal, you know, like UFO stories. Hardly conclusive. Studies into it have been stymied. No one wants to foot the bill to burn cadavers."

"What does your gut tell you?"

"That I'm hungry. Give me that menu."

They ordered light meals from the appetizer menu, and, while they waited on the food, Angelica explained how she had personally gone over every scrap of material collected from Stanton's vehicle. "It's the most bizarre case I've ever encountered, and having the Krueshicki case atop it," she said, "I could retire right now with enough to fill my memoir as an ME for a major American city."

"Let's consider the known facts in the cases. What kind of power turns a solid into super-heated gases?"

"Wood, cloth, flame-resistant materials, and metals are all high on the flash-point scale, when heat ignites a given material. For the human body, that initial flame has to be five hundred degrees Fahrenheit. Bodies incinerate completely to ash at between fourteen and fifteen thousand degrees."

He stared hard across at her. "So what mechanism or organism on earth can multiply five hundred degrees by ten, then focus that energy directly at someone and suck up all the evidence before anyone knows anything or sees anything?"

"People are almost ninety percent H-two-O. Water boils at two hundred twelve Fahrenheit? Yeah, so to heat a person to flash point, into a kind of combustion, you'd have to go well beyond boil point. Only thing that could vaporize that human soup into gas would be the temperatures found in a crematorium. No wand torch can touch that figure, not even a bloody bazooka or flamethrower can do that."

Brannon considered this, sipping at his drink.

She continued. "Within the kiln walls of a crematorium, the oven instantly dries out the flesh, evaporates the liquid within the cells, so that H-two-O in the blood and elsewhere will go to vapor instantly, followed by the proteins and carbons and bam! You're left with a pile of quicklime, potash, nitrogen, phosphorous, carbon, and calcium—all in ashen form—not gaseous, although a great deal of smoke escapes via the filtered vents before it's belched out into the cosmos."

"How did those kinds of temperatures get into a car and an apartment? And there were no ashes at either site except in . . . in that black Styrofoam form. Are you saying that the temperatures were higher than fifteen thousand?"

"Maybe . . ."

"But how? And how'd it become so focused, concentrated on the body and not the surroundings?"

"The crematoriums all across Florida have one aim, Eric, to leave not a trace of the body, not so much as a knuckle or finger joint. Besides, good sense and the law prevail, forcing the crematoriums to burn at fifteen thousand degrees for two reasons."

"And what are those?"

"To control environmental pollutants and to have a 'clean burn'—one in which the deceased could be at once scooped into an urn without anything rattling. When bones and teeth are left, they call it a poor ignite."

"A poor ignite?" he repeated.

"Too much time elapsing. Failing to ignite a truly self-supporting fire. People in the business call this the *fire wall*. If you don't immediately hit the fire wall, you'll have the enamel of teeth and portions of bone all mixed in with the ashes."

"So the human corpses you and I have seen were somehow instantaneously combusted?" asked Brannon.

"Then there's the fusion of metal cut from Dr. Stanton's car," she continued. "Ames called in a consultant, Shelby Harne, and he did a pyrolysis report on the metal sample."

Harne had not shown up at the Krueshicki apartment. He had a wife passing away with cancer, and he'd told Ames that he would look in on the crime scene the following day. "So, what did Shelby conclude?"

"He found an ionization of the electrons in the metal, making them all positive. No negatives. That makes them wild and random at once. Turned the metal into a kind of soupy sponge before it was suddenly cooled to become the misshapen lump we now have. Harne calls for temperatures nearing thirteen and possibly fourteen thousand degrees for that to occur. It fits within the range of a crematorium. Question is how?"

"Old Shelby hasn't a clue how?"

"Says such temperatures can be likened to dipping someone into the core of a nuclear reactor. The superheated condition charging through the electrons of the victim's body set off a chain reaction. It explains the methane—the ozone burn at each scene intermingled with the odor of burnt flesh."

"Isn't ozone formed when oxygen is subjected to intense high-voltage electrical discharges, as with lightning strikes?" asked Brannon.

"Good, you remember your basic science experiment. It's the cause of the unmistakable odor of impending rain clouds. But again, what can call up the electrolyte power to bombard a carbon-based creature such as myself into giving up all my g'damn atoms? It amounts to total chemical and electrical annihilation."

"I thought only God had such power," he said.

"You think he's behind these strange deaths?"

"And with that unsettling thought, how about another drink?"

"Shelby doesn't even believe his own findings," she confided.

"Either that or he doesn't want to."

9

Brannon walked Angelica home, and along the way they conversed more about the unsettling case. "Hopefully, it all amounts to some strange unknowable natural phenomenon, and hopefully, Eric, it's found its last victim."

"I *hope* we've seen the last of it, but I wouldn't bet my badge on it."

"Your logical side, like mine, wants to know there's some weird-assed chemical genius psycho behind the killings, right?"

He stopped and took her hands in his below the streetlamp. "What's the alternative? That nature is behind these killings?"

"What's more horrible to contemplate? A new form of natural disaster like sentient ball lightning out of the blue? Might make it easier to sleep at night to believe that it *is* some human monster rather than random strikes from God."

"Then again," he replied, his eyebrows rising, "maybe not."

"Are you about to kiss me?" she asked.

He took her in his arms and they shared a passionate moment. "Whoa, I need to come up for air," she finally said, pulling back.

They continued to her condo, where he rode up with her and she asked him in. There they shared a final drink, and she played her phone messages. Two telemarketers, an old boyfriend, and one message from Dr. Adib Katra, telling her that she would have to open up in the morning. Eric only caught snatches of it, but Katra's unmistakable voice sounded a bit strange . . . shaky, a stutter here and there.

She returned to the living room, saying, "That was Adib. He called to tell me he wouldn't be in, and that he wants me to take on his usual routine tomorrow. Wants me to open his mail, even. Call him if there's anything important. I tell you, he's really not himself."

"That's odd. He told me to meet him tomorrow at seven-fifteen. Must've taken a turn for the worst to take off at a time like this. I know your morgue is stacked with heat-wave victims."

"Yeah, timing is lousy, but I've been after him for a long time to look after his own health first. Hopefully, he's going to see his doctor." Angelica then looked at her watch. "My, it's past one, and I have to be in by seven now. Damn it, you'll have to go. I've gotta get some sleep."

"Hey, I can take a hint." But he took her in his arms again, and they kissed. Breaking it off, he made his way to the door, saying good night. "Can I call you in the morning?" he asked.

She smiled. "I should hope so."

It had begun with a twisting, coiling pain in his abdomen, and Adib Shakar knew instantly that *he* had not called up his personal serpent god, but that some power outside him had awakened the Kundalini within him. An impossibility? No, not if Hari Shakir was near enough, and apparently, he was extremely near.

He must be the most alone man on the face of the planet, Adib Shakar told himself, referring both to himself and to Shakir, his spiritual dark half. At forty-eight, Adib Shakar and Hari Shakir—born on the same day—had lived far longer than he had thought possible on this plane, given the creature residing within him, and given the other creature stalking him. In any mirror a dark little man stared back at Shakar; a small man in stature without a single distinguishing feature save the enormous, coiled snake tattoo residing at his vitals. It was an enormous and fascinating depiction of a two-headed king cobra, coiled, its heads meeting above the naval. It was a tattoo placed there at birth and retouched at age thirteen, and from there it had grown with his body to become fatter, but it had faded from its original brilliance, since he had not done anything to it since his thirteenth year in India. No one in America had ever seen it, but in India, following ancient custom, the family members gathered every few years to view it and retell the old stories of the power of the Kundalini to do both good and evil in the universe. If a man learned the ways of the Kundalini, he could control his mind and spirit, his body and heart as no other on earth, to be truly fulfilled in life, and he could spread godliness to all he touched.

Despite the family devotion to the secret powers of the Kundalini, Shakar still maintained his Hindu faith, even despite having spent half his adult life in a country that routinely considered his faith little more than a complex superstition, populated as it was with a pantheon of gods and rituals no Westerner could ever fully appreciate or understand. He was fond of pointing out that there was no Satan in Hindu belief, some mischief-making gods, yes, but nothing of the evil found in Christianity—the Antichrist. Even Shakir was no Satan, as evil as he had become, and the Kundalini itself? No, not Satan, but rather a force of nature, not evil in and of itself. In fact, for it to be evil, it required the human component, and as Hari Shakir fed on his human victims, so the serpent inside became more . . . what was the word?—serpentine.

As a boy growing up in the streets of Calcutta, where his family had gone to hide him in plain sight of the creature that stalked them, blending in as it were, Adib had learned how to be cunning, how to survive. But the moment he had looked into Dr. Stanton's vehicle, he was a boy again, a boy being chased by his worst nightmare. He had not seen such a death as this since his having left Calcutta for the second time. He had first left the city of his childhood at age eighteen, but he had returned as an adult and a doctor. He had been filled with visions of having the wherewithal to help his people. It was, after all, the city of Mother Teresa. As ugly as the city was, it evoked the best in human nature right alongside the worst. Charles Dickens could have done a lot with Calcutta, he often joked to anyone interested in understanding the City of Joy.

But he had had to flee Calcutta, learning from his last living relative that the *Shakir* had closed in on them once again, and that he must escape. While he did not wish to believe his great uncle, as he did not want to leave the city, he immediately thought of America again. Still, he argued to stay and face the evil and any consequences head-on; he did not, at the time, fully believe in all the family stories and legends.

"Showing is necessary," said his uncle, exasperated, frustrated, and afraid. "Come with me."

His uncle guided him to a back alley in the heart of the city. Against a dirty brick wall, a horrid sight—the blackened outline of a man with his arms and hands held over his eyes.

His kinsman explained, "What few bones left of the man, Adib, have been gathered up by the human rats inhabiting this place—to throw into their pitiful soups! But be assured, this is the work of the Kundalini residing in Hari Shakir, he who feeds on humans."

"How can this be?"

"Touch it, touch the image." His uncle forced him to the wall, where he smelled the human flesh adhering to the stone, and his fingers registered it as a kind of human paint. "If you put it below your microscope, Adib, it would be telling you the same as I am telling you."

Adib stared from his blackened finger as it came away from the wall, and at his great uncle. He could say nothing.

"Now come along with me." His uncle next took him to see an old woman deep in the most vile part of the city. The old woman was cooking a stew, and Adib's uncle pushed past her to fish into her stew for the contents. He pulled forth a ladle spilling over with bone and sinew.

"What do you see here, Adib?"

"They . . . they look like human finger bones."

"It is what is left of another street person, a beggar that the *Shakir* made a meal of. You know how the man was found?"

"Enlighten me, Father." Shakar often used the special endearment for this man who had earned it.

"He was not found at all; he was like you saw on the wall, but he was melted into the street. All that remained of him were the bones gathered up by this wretched woman to use to flavor her water. I tell you the Kundalini comes for you now."

The old woman blanched white at the pronouncement of the name in her hovel of a home.

"You must leave Calcutta, tonight."

"Have there been others killed in this manner?"

"Three that we know of, and so he gathers strength and knowledge with each feeding. He will soon know of you. Tell me, have you had movement in your groin, in your back and pelvic area?"

"Yes, as if something were stirred inside me. Yes."

"These are signals. Shakir is close. You must flee the city."

Adib had returned to Europe on a ship he'd boarded the next night. Under his new identity as Katra, he furthered his studies in medicine at Oxford, and he only left when again his insides stirred and his instincts told him it was time to flee again. He found passage on a ship bound for America. That had seemed a lifetime ago, and he had lived in peace in Miami for so many pleasant years now.

Today he was the keeper of the medical examiner's office in Miami, Florida. Certainly, the climate suited him better than had Paris or London. His ancestors were proud, looking on from the next plane; Adib had not only eluded Shakir for a lifetime, but he had made something of himself in the bargain and had given something valuable to society—his service—and he had not succumbed to the enticements of the serpent god.

But his time had run out; he knew it in his innermost heart. A wave of utter depression swept over him. He felt the hopelessness in the pit of his being, where the snake of his own evil side dwelled. His life had been one long waiting, one long nightmare. On the one hand, he had achieved something in staying ahead of the awful karma meted out to him, and on the other, maintaining control over his own personal demon from within had had its rewards.

The retouching of the tattoo of the snake had been a rite of passage into manhood, to mark him not as prey, but to mark him so as he would never let his guard down. Still, he remained a marked man, and it was difficult being the last of a dynasty believed to have gone extinct in the thirteenth century.

The overwhelming feeling of knowing that his uncle and close associates of his uncle had become victims of the Kundalini could not be denied. The fact simply sat on his heart like a gargoyle. It was the only explanation of how the thing had found him here in America. For his uncle remained the only one on the planet who knew of his whereabouts, and even then, he had not known of Miami or that Adib was the city's coroner. Adib had only written him once from England, telling him he was bound for America, and even then he hadn't told him where in America.

Adib's certainty over his uncle's death in Calcutta only added fuel to the fire of depression filling him. His uncle had no doubt vanished in the manner of combustion, caught by the Kundalini, knowing that if he were consumed by Shakir, then the Kundalini would know of Adib's whereabouts.

This must be how Adib had been found. Shakir must have gone back and forth between Calcutta and Oxford, London and Paris, finally back to England to find someone there who knew of his passage on the ship coming over to Miami. It could be a clerk, a sailor, a steward, or his uncle's friend, the scryer of Basra marketplace. Adib had met him once, and he had told Adib his fortune, that he would one day live in a place called City of Sun and be an important man. In any event, it appeared the monster had somehow found Adib. This knowledge had no doubt—as legend had it—passed into the evil serpent's consciousness when it fed, and the Oxford and London area of the UK had seen strange epidemics of spontaneous human combustions over the past few years.

Calcutta had been a city of despair, not joy, one that had begun its existence as a jute factory. By the time Adib's family had arrived—in essence to hide Adib amid the teeming population of other children there—the city had seventy thousand inhabitants, all scrunched into a ghetto area hardly larger than three American football fields. Among the crowded mass of humanity people formed alliances and neighborhoods along religious lines—according to sects and creeds. Sixty-three percent of Calcutta's population had been Muslims, thirty-seven percent Hindus, with islands and pockets of Sikhs, Jains, Christians, and Buddhists, all living in relative harmony.

When still a young man, believing he could make a difference there, Adib had performed an operation in a poorly equipped hospital, and the place reminded him of his university reading of Dante's *Inferno*. Before Shakar's eyes, a leper placed his stump of a leg onto the table, and from beneath the filthy rag bandage, maggots crawled into the light. As Adib removed the makeshift bandage, bits of rotted flesh, green and black, pulled away like sticky glue against the bandage. Finally, beneath this, the bone peeked, parched and brittle as if found in a desert.

Armed with forceps and a saw, Adib felt he could only do the work of a butcher; he had no morphine, curare cost too much on the black market and was unavailable otherwise, and what little alcohol they had was under constant threat from thieves. Some resold it to other facilities, while others drank it as if it were distilled liquor.

Amputations were an hourly occurrence in the Calcutta hospital where he had been employed. In fact, the need for amputations reminded him of field hospitals in the books he'd read on the American Civil War. Adib had had to work with primitive grinding tools and saws with broken handles. Even now, a world away and working on the dead in Miami, whenever Adib had to use the state-of-the-art, handheld electronic saw to cut into flesh and bone, he felt his teeth gnash at the recall of conditions in Calcutta.

Adib could see it as if it were only yesterday. He had shivered when his saw chewed into the humerous, and he still felt the empty pit of his stomach as the limb came away—*a lifeless object save for the still-living cells and the parasitic creatures living off it.*

"I bait the dogs with this, I have a meal," said the man of his leg. Adib heard the man's voice again as if it were yesterday, speaking of his own useless, severed limb in such horrid terms. The man had insisted the leg be wrapped for easy transport. Adib argued that it should be burned as gangrenous so as to not spread any further disease. But the man screamed how it was his and his alone to do with as he wished. He looped it with thread himself and hobbled off with it thrown over his shoulder, the twine a harness. He no doubt meant to sell the limb for what he could get from anyone on the street for dog meal or soap, diseased or not.

It was a nightmare that returned to Adib Shakar often in his work under the harsh light of his modern facility here in Miami, but now it had begun to haunt him in the dark as well. Still, the ills of Calcutta proved a bedtime story beside the god—presumed mythical by everyone else—the Kundalini, the creature that now stalked the last of the Shakars.

"How many innocent lives will it feed on to get to me?" he asked the empty room. "Worse yet, how many will it consume *after* it gets to me?"

He thought of Angelica, and how like a daughter she had become to him. He had dared not have children; he would not bring a child into this world to live the kind of life that had been bequeathed to him. So teaching young Angelica, molding her into an excellent forensic scientist, had become a passion. Lately, he had had to distance himself from her, however, and he feared for her, and at the same time, he knew that she sensed he'd not been himself. He settled her mind with a few generalities about failing health and a death in the family back in India. It certainly wasn't a lie.

But he had snapped at her the other day, and he felt sorry for having done so. She had spoken out in that purely American way of condescending without being in the least aware she was doing so. What had it been that she'd said?

They had been going over findings from the Stanton bones, when Angelica had said, "It's all so . . . so strange, this case, Dr. Katra."

"It is indeed, Angelica."

"So much so that I can fully understand your need to distance yourself from the findings. A little R and R may be called for."

"R and R?"

"Rest and relaxation, Doctor."

"Do I look that tired!"

The words *rest* and *relaxation* had irked him, but he honed in on *strange* instead, repeating it and saying, "You say the case is strange. Strange by whose standard? In India, no one would bat an eye at what you Americans call strange. In Calcutta this death of Dr. Stanton would be just another occurrence, but here it must be flowered up, blown out of all proportion so it can be labeled as beyond belief, abnormal, strange."

"Doctor, I only meant—"

"As if Americans valued human life more, but who is it spends billions each year to protect a population from itself? There are more people murdered in one day in this country than all of India in a year. So, Dr. Hunter, who is to say what is strange and what is not?"

"I didn't mean to imply any sense of superiority, Dr. Katra. I just don't comprehend the kind of force that can incinerate a woman and leave her car virtually untouched."

Angelica was hurt, but he could only storm away. He felt badly that their last significant conversation at the second such crime scene had ended with her thinking he was upset with her still. Clearly, he was not, but he knew that she might be left to think otherwise after his death by suicide, and he did not wish to leave this impression with Angelica. But he had little time for such niceties now, and he imagined no opportunity to talk to her before his death.

He did have to speak with her, however, to be certain that she and no one else found his body. He had to be certain of her whereabouts tomorrow morning. Before anyone else saw him in death, she must see for herself the evidence that a creature no one in Miami was equipped to deal with was afoot, and that only through his suicide and the ritual removal of his body from this plane might the serpent *Shakir* shrivel up and die out of a sense of hopelessness of its own short-circuited destiny.

However, it was not enough that Adib should kill himself, he must be assured that his body be dealt with properly—made unholy—and the only person in Miami he knew to be capable and put aside squeamishness was Angelica.

He feared going to her and telling her all this; feared she would simply take him for a crack-up, a lunatic. The taped confessional in which she would see Adib actually take his own life in his attempt to destroy the serpent within himself would gain her attention. The discovery of the serpent within him, below the tattoo, would convince her of the need for action. If not, then the key to the lockbox and its contents, the scrolls, would convince her. It must.

He had called her at home, but there had been no answer. He left the all-important order for Angelica to open up in the morning for him and to check his mail. Now he had a great deal to accomplish before she should discover his body. He must write up his wishes, based on the ritual list in as plain English as she could understand. He had committed it to memory.

Beside him, where he sat in the lotus position in his apartment, lay the scimitar normally kept hanging on his wall. The elongated knife had come down to him with the scrolls, as a kind of ancient solution should it come to this. Sanctified and purified, it was the only blade from which a wound to the Kundalini could not heal. It was also the blade of choice in the event his body were to undergo the ancient sacrificial ritual outlined in the scrolls.

He intended to use the blade on the serpent within him; if he were lucky, he might sever its two heads from its body before he died of his wounds. If not, perhaps on autopsy, Angelica—his spiritual daughter—would see what he *really* was, and she would destroy what remained of the serpent in her modern procedure for desecrating a corpse; either way, it would be done as he wished. But how was he to convince her of the absolute necessity of it all? It would be a good beginning to a new life in a nirvana he had long suspected he deserved, despite the normal consequences of suicide in his religious beliefs. In this instance, none of the *normal* rules or faith applied or mattered, least of all the commandment against suicide. If it should end the life of the Kundalini, he should be a hero in the next life if not this one.

Angelica Hunter felt her energy drain the moment she hit the bed, but her brain kept racing with images out of control, images of charred bone fragments, teeth, toes, fingers embedded in iron, and acrid smoke. Her most nagging suspicions she had shared with no one, only hinting at them with Brannon. A suspicion was only that, a suspicion: usually an illogical, nagging mistrust of the facts and circumstances. In this case, she held suspicions about Dr. Adib Katra, as obviously Brannon did. She could not, however, formulate those suspicions, and she had no idea what he was guilty of, save a sudden bad temper and a sudden run for cover. And now? Now he planned not to even show up tomorrow morning at the lab with the team in the midst of the most baffling case they or anyone else had ever seen. It simply didn't compute with what she knew of Adib's basic character.

Adib had been right from the beginning, *too* right. He knew everything at the scene in advance, all that she had told Brannon, he had heatedly told her, *before* any tests were run, and before Shelby Harne had seen the melted steering column, keys, fingers, and toe bones in the shoe tip. It had troubled her at both scenes. At the Stanton scene, she thought him too hasty to label it SC, and she still did. At the old woman's apartment it had been a sad case of I told you so. She imagined Dr. Katra out making a deal with *Ripley's Believe It or Not* right now, but she knew that wasn't his style.

Still, lately, he had been acting so peculiarly, but she could not lay any evil at his doorstep; he was, after all, the gentlest soul she had ever known.

Then she began again to consider the evening with Eric Brannon. She liked him. She had known him for a long time, but seeing him today, his softer side at the scene of Stanton's apparent death, she felt she had never really gotten to know him. When he had asked her for drinks, she had willingly accepted.

He'd left a little too easily even though it had been at her insistence, and while he held her and kissed her with great passion, she had to consider their first encounter a "poor ignite."

"Think a cop and an ME is a bad equation?" she asked her image in the mirror as she pounded her pillows.

She had enjoyed his company tonight. Still, she had doubts about their ever becoming a real couple. While they might have a chance at passion, igniting their own self-supporting fire, could they sustain a relationship? What was Eric Brannon's *fire wall*?

Thinking about Brannon and a possible relationship with him took her mind off the horrible sights and odors she had been subject to today, and it took her mind off the problems that seemed to be brewing between her and Adib. With these unsettling thoughts put at bay, she willed herself to stop thinking and somehow she fell into a deep sleep.

Adib Shakar had dressed and come back to the crime lab, bringing with him the scimitar, the metal box, and his suicide note. He had come in through the garage, taking the service elevator up to the thirteenth floor, bypassing any metal detectors. He now worked his final preparations inside Autopsy

Room Number One, the place he had chosen as his place to die. It was close to the freezers, and the quicker his body was turned to ice after death, the better.

He stared at himself in the monitor overhead. He tried not to think of the pain his death and the discovery of his body here would bring on Angelica, instead concentrating on the absolute necessity of his actions now. Overnight he had felt the *Shakir* even closer. He feared the other serpent would come crashing through the door at any moment.

He now snatched a magnifying mirror on wheels and a swivel arm to within reach of his left hand. Earlier he had placed the running water-hose on a hook over the slab to run down over the wounds he meant to inflict on himself. He had also turned on the overhead camera, and it recorded his every preparation and would record his suicide as well.

He disrobed and climbed onto the cold, stainless-steel slab. Using time well, in the silent, empty autopsy room, he had prepared everything so as to be able to perform the operation on himself. He had placed everything he needed on a metal table pulled close to him, within reach, where he now lay naked. The ritual scimitar lay close at hand, beside the metal box holding his last will and testament and the key.

As Adib raised the scimitar over the enormous snake tattoo coiled about his navel, he felt the snake within writhing at what he contemplated, both his and its death by his own hand. The thing fought him mentally, enticing him away from such thoughts, and Adib again saw his awful reflection in the overhead monitor that he had switched on to film the suicide. The large tattoo of the two-headed snake began to undulate with its real counterpart beneath the skin.

Adib fought to maintain control of the beast as he had all these years. He concentrated on Angelica's face, and he prayed that someday Angelica would understand why he had left his remains for her alone to discover. He spoke these sentiments into the camera now for her, adding, "Dispose of my body as I request. Do not deviate from it."

Dr. Adib Shakar wished that he could tell Angelica in some strange telepathic sense, right this moment, the truth, how he was of an ancient Indian family that had done war with the Kundalini Shakirs since the earliest known times. He knew that the heat-seeking monster, which had taken so many lives here and elsewhere only to get at him, would stop at nothing to find him alive or dead. Angelica must be made to accept the truth.

Adib's uncle had prepared him well; he now held a healthy respect and fear of the Kundalini since those lessons so long ago in Calcutta. He knew even as a boy that when and if he ever came into contact with Hari Shakir, not only would he be consumed, so would Hari Shakir—a man whom he had never met, but who remained a figure populating Adib's every nightmare. He didn't fear sacrifice any longer; his entire life had been sacrificed to this ancient curse, as had Hari's, but he did fear for the human race. The end result being a god of chaos coming into power.

Shakar had little choice left him.

He had thought himself safe after all these years, but there was no safe place, no haven, however far from India. There was no safe haven for mankind either unless it came at a precious price, the cost of his own life.

His mind repeated it over and over to himself until he said it aloud for the camera. "I must destroy myself in order to destroy the snake god within me, to end any hope of the beast within coming to power."

After writing a letter filled with directions to Angelica on how best to dispose of his remains, Adib had come back to the crime lab and had told everyone in the place to leave, claiming there was an escaped virus and so a quarantine. None of his underlings questioned him on the matter, most rushing to vacate the premises. By the time they were out of the building, they'd find their shift over, and they would go home. Others coming on would heed the quarantine long enough for Angelica to arrive—in less than an hour.

At his side where he lay on the same slab he had so often worked over, Adib left the note for Angelica. In it, he detailed a precise list of wishes which he labeled *MUSTS*. He left them for his young assistant, believing she of all people would carry them out.

When she entered, she would be the first human outside his family that had ever seen the snake tattoo coiled about his abdomen. She would find him splayed open, and hopefully she would find the dead snake residing in him, if he timed the strikes to himself perfectly.

He looked at his image in the swivel-arm magnifying mirror that he had pulled across the slab, studying the movement of the snake below his skin, trying to determine where the two heads might be. He would catch a glimpse of the flared cobra head and then it was gone. Time was running out.

He mentally worked to calm himself, so that the snake would come back to its normal resting place, outlined by the enormous, intricate, and exotic two-headed snake tattoo coiled in a realistic pose about his naval. A beautifully wrought and executed tattoo, something not done by one of the tattoo parlors at a kiosk in Calcutta but in the village of his forefathers.

He tried to imagine Angelica's reaction to his desperate plan. He imagined her awe at the size of the wound, the size of the dead snake in the wound, the tattoo itself. She had no knowledge of any of this or what it represented. "I should have schooled you in the lore of the Kundalini serpent god," he said into the camera.

But he hadn't wanted to deal with it; had become too complacent over the years here in Miami. For a time, he had thought it ended.

The tattoo appeared dim with age and the dusky skin. The dragon-headed cobralike image was done in crude and startling colors, bright reds, oranges, greens, and the scales of the creature seemed alive as the real snake inside circled, uneasy.

Angelica, like any Christian, would struggle with what the man she knew as Dr. Katra wanted from her. He asked among other *MUSTS* in large letters in his final communiqué to her, that she refrigerate his body and keep it in a frozen state until such time as she was to use the DIAL program on it to slice it into countless sheer sections and film them onto computer, creating a three-dimensional map of his body for scientific study. He wondered if she would read any further, believing him to be out of his mind at the time of writing these requests. He had written the medical procedure, *laser-sectioning,* and had written that he meant to leave his body for forensic study in capital letters, so that she would see that he was donating his body for scientific use in teaching interns. *Purpose behind the madness? But why suicide . . . to end his life against all he believed?* Angelica would scream.

She had never refused him a request, had never questioned him on essentials and procedures ever, and they shared a common friendship that had stood the test of apprentice and teacher, and due in greater part to her kind nature more than his own, they had avoided a hundred-odd fights.

"I have grown to trust you, Angelica," he said to the camera, the scimitar lightly playing over his abdomen. "In the end, I trust that you alone will carry out my final wishes to the letter, without fail or hesitance. I want you to carry it out immediately, and I pray you will. My last will is in the box along with a key, and it is dated almost ten years before now, predating my suicide." He wondered if she and others would see it as apparent *psychosis* and suicide. "The will," he continued, "is binding. The bank drawer key is for you to use. My real name is Adib Shakar, and I have given years of thought to my desire to turn over this body to science. Do not, under any circumstances, use any of my organs for donation or implant, Dr. Hunter. You must not disobey this bedside death wish. I repeat, after my corpse is frozen, the entire body is to be sliced into dissected disks, that you will film and place into the computer for analysis and study alone, from the brain to the toes. Once filmed, all the sections you've cut me into are to be discarded in our acid bath. Every inch of me. Understood? It is the only way. I can't stress enough, no organ donation."

So Hunter would discover the body and find the shakily scribbled notes and the tape, and she would immediately balk at what he asked of her. It was a good thing, a good way for his body to be used and destroyed at the same time, a modern method of ritual sacrifice that would avoid her having to humiliate the body as called for in the ancient sacrificial rites. Once the body was frozen, it was easily cut pepperoni fashion by the laser saw. Filmed into the computer as three-dimensional images, it would create a blueprint for study.

"In a sense, dear Angelica, this will give me life even in death, albeit an electronic life. Is that not like me, the Adib Katra you know, to leave the institution such a gift?"

Once each of the cross sections of his frozen body were cut and scanned into the computer, young interns and Angelica, indeed, anyone needing to do an autopsy could turn to computer-aided assistance in the form of digital graphics. Every cell and every artery and bone, cross-sectioned and filmed. It would mean a great deal to the crime lab, everyone. They'd be able to create a graphic image of every organ in the adult male. Such a program, if done correctly, could save hours upon hours of time in laboratory dissection. Through the magic of computer graphics, the city of Miami would have a state of the art program to rival that of the FBI's, all thanks to Dr. Katra's generous donation of his body to science. It would represent a magnificent gesture, but there was a catch, a final stipulation. The final insult to his remains, the acid bath.

"The alternative desecration of the body is in my will, and you will find it far less agreeable," he said to Angelica as he addressed the tape.

He knew that Angelica—grief-stricken at the sudden loss of her friend and mentor, and wishing to do his bidding— would feel she could only go so far. Unlike everyone else, she might not applaud his leaving his body to science. Given all that he had told her of his religion, she would not think it a grand or noble gesture. Even if she did as he requested, she would condemn him for his action this day.

He again felt a wave of horror and empathy wash over him at the thought of her finding him here in the manner he must leave this world.

He poised the long pointed scimitar over the head of the snake tattoo, awaiting the moment. He had meditated and chanted and prepared himself for this moment, the tape recording it all—the instant when he must tear himself to shreds along the lines of the snake tattoo, to attempt to kill the Kundalini within him and to end the psychic thread being created between it and Hari Shakir's serpent.

In a hundred different reflecting points around the room filled with stainless steel, a hundred images of Adib Shakar sent the scimitar down into his bowels. His prone body caught the blood-spray response as Shakar, screaming, sliced into the serpent deep within a second time, then a weak third as his blood mixed with the water spray he'd placed over himself.

The scimitar's huge handle formed a cross over the body where it had been plunged, and an unusual low keening welled up from the abdomen along with a strange gaseous cloud.

10

Angelica Hunter drove into the underground parking lot and took the elevator up. She'd seen some people milling about the front of the building, but, paying no heed, had used her passkey to enter the lot. From there, she took the stairs one flight up to the morgue and lab.

She'd had Adib Katra on her mind even before her clock radio came on to rouse her this morning. Something had happened to Katra the last several days, something that had him moving about like a nervous ferret, muttering, shaking his head, talking to himself, and now this.

In the several years that she and Adib Katra had worked side by side, Angelica had never let her mentor and friend down, and she was not about to start now. She had gotten up early and rushed to the lab to be on time to open up. When she got there, she was surprised to learn that the skeleton crew of the night shift had long since vacated, a breech of protocol. Someone was always on duty at the crime lab and adjacent morgue. It was standard procedure, good form. She recalled the people milling about outside. Had there been a bomb scare? She'd seen no evidence of police.

Leaving the crime lab unattended simply was not done. As a result, she had never entered the premises when there wasn't *someone* on board. She opened up Adib's office and made a quick succession of phone calls, and she learned that she was absolutely alone. She then saw the large note scribbled to her lying atop his mail: *ANGELICA—GO TO AUTOPSY ROOM #1.*

Foul-up in scheduling, she imagined. Someone must've gotten miffed, just left the lab empty. She'd know soon enough.

Even under the best of circumstances—a large enough staff, manageable caseloads, and just maybe a *corpus delecti*—crime-lab workups took time—a lot of time. Still Angelica Hunter knew quite well that even in a normal autopsy, there was always reason to take more time, to, as Dr. Katra always said, "be twice-times thorough."

She still had some tests to be run on materials and items taken at the Krueshicki crime scene and apparently they were sitting idle someplace. She'd like to go check on them, but there wasn't a soul to speak to. Now this strange note in Adib's shaky hand.

She felt a genuine affection for Adib; he had taught her more in the past several years than any single individual on the planet. His knowledge of forensic medicine and medicine in general proved staggering, astounding. She wanted to live up to his expectations, and he had treated her with the utmost respect and professional courtesy at all times, until recently, until the Stanton thing. Prior to this peculiar case, he had made her feel like more than his top assistant in the lab; he had made her feel like family. They had shared so much about religion, philosophy, history, and science. They exchanged cultural information as well. He was always hungry to know such strange things as how a silly game like golf evolved from wooden clubs and a canvas ball in ancient Scotland to become a multibillion dollar industry in America, and if such things had cosmic purpose. They had attended ballets and football games together, and she had been in his home, and he in hers.

She had a number of tests to set up, and she had a great deal of delegating to do when the others would arrive around eight, so for now, she would see what was so important in Autopsy One. She started for the room when the phone rang. Since it was Dr. Katra's line, she thought better of picking it up. Doing so would likely entangle her and she needed some time to get settled here and to figure out what was going on. Where the hell was everyone? Then she heard *her* phone ringing.

"Almost a normal day," she muttered in response.

God, was it really only a few days ago that all seemed right and orderly in the world, everything obeying the laws of nature? But things fall apart, she reminded herself of a favorite phrase used by her father, whose entire life had been a series of failures, not from which he had learned, but from which *she* had learned. In a backhanded, ass-backward sort of way, she owed all her success to her father. Failed marriages, failed businesses, failed dreams—they led him into drink, depression, and an early grave. He'd been right in sync with his simple philosophy—married to it—things fall apart. Things did at times unravel, dislodge, vibrate to pieces— often over a long and seemingly safe period, as with relationships. And most people chalked such things up to stock psychobabble pop-labeling as in "identity crisis" or "midlife crisis," when in fact it was as simple as her father had said: change comes and things fall apart; but she had added a new and positive outlook to the grim one—that change was not crisis but an opportunity for growth.

By the time she got to the phone, it had stopped ringing. No message.

Change, growth, permutations and mutations . . . the world was filled with the evidence of it, but Homo sapiens being so into the self and so fixated on the *me, my, myself, and mine* actually believed there could be stability in an unstable world, despite the evidence in air, sea, land and all other living organisms. The world only appeared stable. The sky only appeared gentle overhead, the sun warm, friendly, pleasant from the distance of billions of miles. All true and unshakable to the mind of man due his limited senses.

Einstein's theory of relativity was right on. All things were related, so the volcano was as much a part of the stability of earth as the placid lake. Even that lump of metal keys and ignition taken from Dr. Renea Stanton's car, she thought, staring at it where it lay on a shelf, tagged, only looked stable. The lump of metal appeared as inanimate as any metal, but it had gone through a bizarre metamorphosis, the atoms pulsating, warring, coming unglued, decaying, changing unseen to the naked eye.

How much had occurred over the past few days without her understanding, without her perceiving? Could the mystery of spontaneous human combustion be solved if she could just open her mind to it?

Meanwhile, with heat-related deaths in the city at an all-time high, space in the morgue was limited, the cadavers backing up. It was unlike Adib to disappear at a time like this, when every pair of hands was needed, and it again struck her as strange that everyone on the night shift had left without waiting for someone to take charge.

An eerie sense enveloped her, some nagging fear at the back of her brain saying that things just weren't right, when she heard the elevator in the hallway ping. Someone stopping on her floor. She flashed on the image of the old woman outlined in her own fatty tissue against her refrigerator. Then she felt it, a sudden overwhelming feeling of being transported back to the moment as two figures in protective ware and gas masks stepped off the elevator.

Through a mechanical device, one of them said, "Dr. Hunter. You *are* here. You've got to vacate the building. Some sort of virus loose."

It was Irene Williams, a black intern, alongside Roy Marks, another intern. "Dr. Katra ordered everyone out, and then he didn't follow us, so we came back for him in these getups, and somebody said they saw you come in through the underground lot, so . . ."

"If there were a loose virus, alarms would be going off. Katra's not even here."

"He was here; he gave the order to get out."

"He would have hit the alarm if there was a—" she looked

down at the paper in her hand. Again she read: *GO TO AU-TOPSY ROOM #1.*

"You can get out of those outfits and get to work," she told them. "I'm not going anywhere." She went through the lab for the autopsy room.

Eric Brannon had gotten successive messages both at home and on his office number from Dr. Adib Katra that were made *after* the doctor's call to Angelica, and in his messages, Adib insisted Eric be at his lab at seven-fifteen a.m. if he still wanted answers to all of his questions. He had stressed the time. Disregarding the message Katra had left Angelica, that he would not be in, Eric had come to the crime lab in search of the doctor. Outside, he had found a milling crowd and security guards, a story about a loose virus, but that Dr. Hunter was seen going into the building. He had called up to her office while security tried Katra's, but no answer.

He had a mental gunnysack full of questions he'd been hoarding up for Katra, and now this.

Ames had been up early this morning, too, and he and Shelby Harne had shared coffee in the captain's office, so Brannon had taken a moment to stop in and pick the old fire investigator's brain. Harne was fascinated with the case, and he had had time now to look over Stanton's impounded car and the apartment at 126 Magnolia. He was fascinated to learn that the fire in the apartment had been so concentrated in a given area that it had set off no alarms.

"I checked the alarm, and it should have sounded, especially with the flash point evident over the refrigerator."

"Explain the concept of flash point to me, Shelby," Ames had asked.

"Flash point is when the needle indicators tell me at what point on the thermometer a material ignites spontaneously, or in other words vaporizes."

"Vaporizes?"

"In essence to become part of the super fire, part of the heat."

"I see, I think."

"Really, Lou, the idea of spontaneous ignition of a human being, is . . . well . . . as ridiculous as say spontaneous ignition of an automobile."

"Then you don't think it possible without a catalyst?" Eric had asked.

"I've seen all manner of fires, some that have never been solved, but a pure SHC without a match of some sort. I can't see it."

"You mean, there first has to be a spark to begin the combustion."

"Exactly, a causative factor, a catalyst like you said."

"Gotcha."

"Look, Eric, under enough force of heat any material, other than a handful of inorganics, can be turned into flame, just like that." He demonstrated with a thumbnail against a match, lighting his pipe. "See what I mean? It's just a matter of *degree*. But of course, how did that much heat suddenly focus like a lightning strike inside the old woman's place and inside Stanton's car? I haven't one goddamned clue."

So here Eric stood, back at the ME's office, stepping off the elevator and looking for answers he believed he could only get from Dr. Adib Katra.

Instead he was greeted by two heavily suited up interns disrobing in the hallway. "Dr. Katra here?"

"Doesn't appear to be. Dr. Hunter's back that way," said the young woman.

"I'll find her. Thanks."

He saw her from the back and called out, "Angelica. Wait up."

She held the door to Autopsy Room One in her hand. "Eric? You're here."

"Katra asked me to see him about now. Is he here yet?"

"Maybe, I'm not sure. He asked me to open up at seven, but someone said he'd been here, so . . . come along."

"He's not in his office?"

"No, I just came from there."

"He left word on my answering machine that he wanted to see me, at seven-fifteen, here at his lab. Said he intended to make everything clear to you and to me."

"He said that?" She smelled the coppery scent of blood wafting through the door from the darkened interior. "What's that odor?"

Eric stepped ahead of her and entered the room, she following. The door closed behind them. Eric saw the body on the slab under a lamp and the light from an overhead video screen that reflected the still body. He saw the huge cross of the knife's hilt at the gut, and he saw the dark skin and the colorful tattoo kept awash beneath a running hose. "What kind of an autopsy are you in the middle of here, Doctor?"

She switched on the overhead lights, her brain disbelieving what her eyes displayed before her—Dr. Katra's ravaged nude body. She collapsed and Brannon caught her in his arms.

"It's Katra," she said, coming to. She recalled how odd it had been that the night shift had disappeared before her arrival. She mentioned it now to Brannon. "Only Dr. Katra could make that happen." She again buried her face in his chest, and Eric Brannon helped her to her feet. As he held her face against his chest, he stared at the mutilated body of the dark little Indian man they had known for so long.

"It appears he set this all up for my . . . for me to find," she said, trembling, "but why? Why, Eric?"

Brannon studied the weapon, recognizing its type: a long, double-edge razor-sharp, serrated knife—a scimitar in fact—remained upright over a number of wounds kept clean of blood by a constant flow of water from an overhead hose. The water sprayed clean the dead man's wounds and an exotic, huge tattoo of a coiled two-headed cobra around what would have been his abdomen, before being shredded open. The blood ran to the moat around the table and down through the funnels that took it to a drainage exit in the floor.

"That's his knife. He kept it on his wall at home. I've seen it on several occasions."

"Look at the size of that tattoo; it's almost larger than he is."

"I never knew he had it, the tattoo." She managed another look at the awful sight.

It looked as if Katra had not only wielded the knife himself, Eric thought, but that he had taped the event as well. It looked as if he were trying to cut off the scaled serpent that made a rainbow of color out of his gut.

Angelica didn't know where to look, as Adib Katra's stomach was splayed open, the lips of three separate ghastly wounds puckering up at them, one secured by the knife.

"Nooo! Nooo!" The pain of Angelica's wail, the anguish of it stabbed at Eric's heart. She cried out repeatedly, pulling away from Brannon now, going to Adib, looking into his pained features, her hands poised over him, begging him to answer her repeated *whys*.

"Careful of the knife. Don't disturb a thing; even if it is suicide, it's gotta be treated as a crime scene."

"Suicide? No, No! He wouldn't do that!" she now shouted. "Not Adib. He loved life. Someone . . . one of the night-shift crew. The real reason they're all gone before I got here. One of them went berserk. Adib would not kill himself; it flies in the face of everything he believed, not to mention his religion."

Eric cautiously stepped closer to the body. He reached out to her, but she was inconsolable. She wanted to throw herself against Katra, bind his wounds, plead with him, talk him back to life, but the color of his skin, save for the tattoo, was ashen and pale with death, yet when she caressed his face, he was still warm to the touch.

"He's only been dead for a short time, less than an hour," she said.

"Look, the camera is on. He filmed it all, including our discovery."

She looked up at the camera, shaking her head. "He wanted me to find him like this? Why?" She looked at the tray table beside him across from her and saw the box and the letter. She then glanced at the magnifying mirror, its arm swung out across the slab above the abdomen, carefully placed there as if he had used the looking glass to direct the knife.

Eric read her mind. "He had it directed at his abdomen, at the tattoo, and he taped his own death."

She again stared at the evidence, making the circle of confusion in her head go around again. "The camera and the swivel magnifying mirror are used in autopsies." She shoved the mirror on wheels away, went to the hose and cut it off, all to Eric's pleas to touch nothing. She reached a panel on the wall and turned off the video recorder.

"You shouldn't've touched anything, Doctor."

"Why not? It's all on tape." She had put on a pair of surgical gloves, and, before he could stop her, she removed the blade from Katra. Brannon thought he saw Katra's abdomen swell imperceptibly with the relief of having the huge scimitar removed, but such a notion was crazy, and he lost the thought when a loud crash filled the room.

Angelica had tossed the blade onto the metal tray table, spattering blood on the folded letter. The noise sent up a clatter in the room.

"Damn him! Damn him!" she cried out.

A silence filled the room now. Brannon pointed to the wounds. "His cuts are all localized over the snake's throat. It's as if . . ."

"Yeah, as if he were attempting to cut off the two heads of the tattoo," she finished his sentence.

"Let's reserve judgment until we look at the tape. Decide from it." Brannon lifted the letter with care, unfolded it and said, "It's addressed to you. Says his will and a key are in the box and meant for you as well."

She came around to look at the items on the table. She opened the box and found his will with an attached list of do's and don'ts regarding the disposal of his body. She took the letter from Brannon, which simply read, *Read the will and attachment. I leave my remains to science for laser sectioning and computer mapping, using the DIAL program. You must follow my directions for handling my remains pre-*

cisely and without deviation. Time is of the essence. Do not delay. And Angelica, I had no other choice. I am sorry. Read the will and strictly adhere to it. Use the key for further information.

"Get it all, the box, the will, the key, and the tape," she said, unnerved, shaken, and going for the supply room. She quickly reentered with a sheet. "I'm going to lock this room. We'll view the tape in my office."

"We're already guilty of disturbing the crime scene, Doctor."

"I can't stay in here another moment. Please, Eric." Her eyes were fixed, adamant. She opened the sheet with a flurry, and it cascaded over the corpse, completely covering him.

Eric gave in, popped the tape, and carried it with the other items out the door, and she locked it behind them. "I don't want anyone else seeing him like that," she told him.

They made it to her office and put the tape in the VCR and watched the horrid suicide. Adib Katra claimed his real name was Adib Shakar, and he spoke of a lunatic plot against him by some other family called the Shakirs. He spoke of a snake god that resided inside a man named Hari Shakir, who Adib claimed killed Stanton and the others, but that this man was driven by a beast within his body called the Kundalini, a serpent god in ancient Hindu culture.

He indicated his stomach, pointing at the tattoo, and in the tape it seemed to undulate with his heavy breathing. From Adib's features, it was apparent the man was in great duress. He spoke of how he wanted his body sliced into millimeter-thin sections, digitally filmed onto computer and turned into a learning tool for interns. Then he spoke of an acid bath for the disposal of the remains once the sectioning of the body had been completed.

"I put it all in writing, attached to my will and dated today," the dead man spoke from the video. "The only other alternative, to keep the monster of Hari Shakir from reanimating my own beast within is the ritual desecration of this body. Pleasant for no one," he insisted on the tape. "My modern medical answer of laser sectioning and disposing of the layers in acid, will be faster and far cleaner."

"What the fuck is he talking about?" asked Brannon, stopping the tape.

"The procedure he's talking about makes sense, but the reasons for it are . . . are . . ."

"Insane?"

"Play the rest."

They again listened to Adib's image on the tape. "I know this is a shocking revelation for you, while I have had a lifetime to prepare. I can only imagine how difficult this is for you to understand. But you must obey my last wishes to the letter. The alternative method of ritual desecration of my body I only describe to you in order to persuade you to use the modern means at your disposal. The ancient methods are brutal on the senses of the family who survive, and you are my only family, Angelica. I fear, actually, I know you will cringe and recoil at using the filthy methods necessary to keep the beast from overtaking my remains. Trust me, use the laser."

Then Adib lifted the scimitar and quickly, in three successive pounding movements, brought it down into his abdomen at the two-headed snake.

Eric forced himself to watch every second of tape, and he heard a strange, eerie noise escape the man's abdomen, like the squeal of a dying animal, and a gaseous cloud rose from the three self-inflicted wounds.

"Did you see that?" Eric asked Angelica.

"He must have gone insane."

He ran the tape back. "Watch . . . some gas escaping the wounds."

"It's not unheard of that gas will escape an abdominal wound, accompanied by sound, Eric. I . . . I can't watch anymore. Turn it off."

He froze the frame on Adib's anguished end. "What does he say in the pages attached to his will?"

"Most of it is repeating what he said on the tape. He means to be understood in one regard, how he wants his remains handled."

"And the key?"

"Safe-deposit box. Says my name is on it along with his. I knew nothing about it."

Brannon ran the tape again on silent while she continued reading through the pages Adib had attached to the will. She read aloud, "You will find all the answers you seek with the Chase Manhattan key. I am so extremely sorry, dear Angelica, to have to put you through this. I know it is a great burden, and I should have prepared you for it. But you must trust me as you have never trusted anyone before, and you must follow my instructions for the speedy corruption and disposal of my body. If you do not, then the horrible deaths that have begun in the city will be only a prelude to spontaneous combustion of human beings becoming a daily, perhaps an hourly event."

"I knew he was hiding something, but this sounds . . ." Brannon whispered, where he sat staring at the tape.

"Insane, I know. This *is* insane," she replied, seeing that the will attachments were dated just as he said, while the will was dated almost ten years before. She stared at the shaky handwriting on the first page of the new material. "Jesus," she groaned.

"What is it?"

"A list of steps. Things he says I must do to corrupt his body if I do not go through with the laser sectioning to dispose of his remains."

"What exactly does it say?"

She read from the list: "Using the scimitar, a sanctified, purified blade, which alone might weaken the Kundalini, you must decapitate the head and stuff both mouth and esophagus with maggots to hasten decay of the flesh and organs. . . . You must bury the decapitated head in a swamp or at sea. . . . You must sever hands, feet, and genitals again with the scimitar—and bury each at a separate crossroads. You must remove heart and lungs to be fed to dogs in separate locations. . . . Torso and any other remains you must throw into a body of unclean water and in no circumstance pray over the body."

"Bizarre. Real strange, Angelica. I knew he wasn't acting right in the head."

"Listen to this." She read on from Adib's list: "I'm sure the authorities would put you away for carrying through with this ancient ritual, so please dissect me millimeter by millimeter via the electronic laser as directed in my video will. It will be far easier for you to take this route. You can then say that you did it for research and scientific reasons with my blessings—all true and all aboveboard. Again, I repeat, no organ harvesting, and use no fire, no cremation. This is vital. And time is of the essence. Do not delay my wishes. Begin the freezing and the sectioning immediately, I beg you."

"Let me see that." Brannon studied the words, shaking his head. "Craziest damn thing I've ever heard," he muttered as he froze the tape again.

Angelica took a deep breath and said, "It's all insane, and it all began with those SHC deaths. Think of it, a devout Hindu leaves instructions for how his body—the receptacle for his soul—is to be desecrated. Doesn't fit with tradition—cremation, pyres, fire, and heat lifting the soul skyward? None of it makes any sense whatsoever. And how am I supposed to follow his wishes?"

"You don't have to. After all, he could hardly have been in his right mind when he did this. It's not binding on you."

Eric stared at the man's handwriting. He felt the strident note obvious in the words, the urgency, obsession, and something that rang of a place beyond desperation.

She felt unsure what she should do. Flipping through the will, he had stipulated that if he died before age fifty, that his remains were to be disposed of in the ancient manner of desecration. "The will itself predates laser sectioning. It was not a reality at the time."

Brannon now read, "The final stipulation. No burial, no cremation. In fact, I stress *no fire* of any sort can be used. Instead, the acid bath MUST be used or the unclean waters of the Florida Everglades."

Angelica shook her head. "All this goes against the man's

religion. Unclean water . . . an acid bath? Desecration of the body, a desecration of the life cradle, as he called it."

Brannon, not knowing what to say to this, looked up again at where he had stopped the tape. A frame of Adib stabbing himself.

She paced the room. "This means he'd be unable to return to the cycle of life to resume a search of the perfect karma and the perfect nirvana. A Hindu desecrating his own body finds himself in a limbo from which there is no return or escape—an eternal waiting room."

"What I don't know about Hinduism could fill a football stadium," said Brannon.

"He wanted me to be the one to discover his body, and he wanted you here to support me. He carefully timed our arrival and arranged for this."

"Where did he get that enormous tattoo?"

She shrugged. "I never knew he had it."

"Never seen a single tattoo so large before."

"From the look of it, it's been on for some time. Explains why he would never shower here on the premises. He must've been ashamed of it."

"What's to be ashamed of. It is . . . was beautiful before he hacked into it."

"It may speak to his state of mind that he chose to hack into the tattoo and not simply cut his wrists. All this time, hiding so many secrets . . . down to his real name, Shakar."

"Angelica, if you feel you have to honor his last wishes—"

"They predate his madness! They're fucking listed in his will."

"—then do as he says, this sectioning thing. The other way, you'd be violating more laws than I can count."

"So what do I do now?"

"When in doubt, do nothing. Do you have any better solution for the moment?"

"Nothing . . . do nothing . . . not right away at least. I'm not going to desecrate his body in any weird ritual severing of parts, I can tell you that much is for damned sure."

"What about the key?"

"Says it's to a safe-deposit box at Chase Manhattan, just down the street. Says I am a cosigner for the key, so I will have no trouble getting in. Says he forged my name on it years ago."

"This just gets stranger by the moment."

"I've got to call Crysta Conover and Don Porter to cover here, and I don't want anyone else touching Dr. Katra's body or seeing how he died, at least not for now. I want to salvage what I can of his memory here."

"I understand your wanting to keep this quiet, Angelica, but it's going to get out no matter what."

"Not by my doing."

"I've got to call this in, Angelica," he said to her.

"Wait . . . at least wait until we find out the contents of the safe-deposit box." She stared deeply into his eyes, tearstains dotting her cheeks.

Eric bit his lip, shaking his head.

"Please. It might give us some insights into why he's done this terrible thing."

"Waiting won't change things, and it is a crime scene. I've got to follow normal procedures just like you."

"Do what you have to. I'm going to the bank."

"Not without me, and not before we call it in. Any further delay and you and I will be under suspicion. Understood?" He had grabbed her hands to make his plea. "Look, we're both law enforcement, and we discovered the body, so that makes us first on scene, so it's my case automatically. We can dictate who comes and goes if you're strong enough to handle the scene, but that's all."

"All right, all right, I'll be strong enough, and I'll take the crime-scene photos myself. I don't want to find them on the goddamn Internet."

She snatched out her cell phone and called in the people she needed to cover the offices. Brannon turned off the video screen, took out the tape, and placed it with the other items taken from the death room. He toyed with the notion of returning everything to where they had found it, but he decided such an action would only make things worse in the long run. The end of the tape showed them discovering the body and the placement of everything in the room.

Angelica fought for the strength she needed to see everything through. She focused in on a series of questions filtering through her mind. "Who is this Hari Shakir that he talks about on the tape?" she asked.

"Probably the same Hari who left his name on the dead woman's fridge last night. Maybe Hari and Adib are one and the same, a schizo. I mean the way Adib had been running around. I'd give you odds we won't find any record of a call being patched through from here to his cell phone anytime around seven-thirty last night."

"No, Adib never demonstrated any schizophrenic tendencies. You have to be wrong."

"You mean before the Stanton crime scene? Or before coming to America? I've been asking myself, did Adib know Renea's killer, and perhaps then the method, the weapon, the wherewithal? All of it? Somehow, Angelica, he's connected, and his actions and words have proven that."

She glared at him. "Perhaps we'll learn more from information he kept in the lockbox in that vault? All of this cloak and dagger seems so remote from the man I had always known and loved."

"Perhaps you didn't really know Adib, not really; maybe you only knew that part of him that he wanted you to know and no more."

Her teeth set, her jaw quivering at this, she knew that if she did not steel herself, she feared this betrayal could be a finishing blow to her insides.

Brannon went to her, held her, and she clutched him, sobbing, releasing her hold on the confusion and hurt and sorrow all at once.

Eric Brannon had called it in to Captain Ames and his partner, Jackie Hale, breaking the startling and tragic news of Katra's death, characterizing it as a suicide. On arrival, assessing the scene, Ames suggested that Angelica sit the investigation out since she was so close to the victim and had admittedly, in a moment of emotional turmoil, removed the knife from the victim. Angelica, with Eric's backing, insisted she be lead forensic investigator on the case. After some debate, Ames backed off his stance, and Angelica took control, surprising everyone with her backbone and stamina.

She strongly dictated who came into the crime scene, protecting it of any further contamination.

Out of respect for Adib's memory and standing, the scene was kept as discreet as possible. Still rumors ran rampant throughout the building.

As Jackie and Ames looked over the carnage Dr. Katra had meted out on himself, Eric confessed to having removed items from the room.

"What items were removed from the room?" Ames wanted to know, angry at this development.

"Lou, we had to leave the room, and I didn't want the tape to disappear or the suicide note, so we took them to Dr. Hunter's office."

"This was after she placed the knife on the table there?"

"Yes, sir. At least she was wearing gloves."

Jackie stood shaking her head. "We'll want to see this tape and note."

"Can we . . . can we please keep the details of the tape and the note out of the press?" Angelica asked. "I don't want his memory smeared."

"None of us wants that, Dr. Hunter, I can assure you," Lou Ames said.

While Angelica locked the room behind them, Ames asked, "Don't you want to place his body in a freezer compartment?"

"I'll have to make arrangements. Everything's full, including the walk-in freezer.

"Heat-wave victims," Ames said knowingly.

"Along with the usual deaths, it's caused a situation. No room in the inn. But we'll find space."

They went to Angelica's office, and while Eric showed them what had been removed from the room, and shared the tape with them, Angelica took her findings to Irene Williams in the lab, asking her to process the findings. Eric saw the young black woman almost crumple under the confirmed news of Adib's death.

"Jackie, if you get a chance anytime today," Eric said to his partner, "would you check on incoming phone records to the lab for last night, looking for a call around seven-thirty p.m., which was supposedly patched through from here to Dr. Katra's cellular phone?"

"Sure . . . just as soon as I see this tape."

"And follow up on that lead we had on the Seminole AC man; see if we can talk to him. If he was in the building at the time, he may have seen something."

"Will do."

When Angelica returned, she found Brannon staring again at the tape left by Katra, and alternately studying the reactions of his fellow detectives, Ames and Jackie. Ames grit his teeth while Jackie Hale grimaced through the tape, their horror clearly relayed.

"This is unbelievable," said Jackie. She got up and began looking over the additional materials left by Adib, studying the suicide note and going for the will now. "It's all so off-the-wall bizarre, you know."

Ames ran the tape again. After finishing, he said, "The stress, the heat wave . . . the overcrowded workload . . . *something* got to this man."

"We may have additional information with this key he left," said Eric. "Dr. Hunter is the only one who can get it from a lockbox. While you two look over all this material, I'm going to escort Dr. Hunter to the bank and back. She's still pretty shaken up."

"She hardly looks shaken up to me," said Jackie. "In fact, Doctor, you look surprisingly in control. Oh, I mean that as a compliment. I know if it were me finding Eric in that autopsy room with a weird tattoo, his stomach ripped open, leaving behind all this unusual information, and me coming up on the body . . . hell, I'd freak out."

"Afraid I already did my freaking out before you arrived, Detective."

"Well, you put up a hell of a front. I can't imagine what's going on inside you."

"Just stark devastation. Frankly, I don't think it's fully hit me yet."

"Are you sure, Dr. Hunter," said Ames, "that you're able to handle the case, your responsibilities?"

She hesitated only a moment. "Yes . . . unequivocally, yes."

"All right, Eric, escort Dr. Hunter to the bank and get back here as quickly as you can."

Eric saw that Jackie was busily sizing up the meaningful looks he was giving Angelica Hunter. Jackie was trying to read him. He ignored this, took Angelica's arm, and led her from the room. They were soon standing at the elevators, waiting. From where they stood, they could look through glass partitions to see the crime-scene tape over the sealed door to Autopsy Room One.

11

When Angelica had gotten the needed help into the office to cover the day-to-day, she had stipulated that Autopsy Room One remain unused, a closed crime scene for the time being, and that no one was to go into the room where Katra's body lay beneath a sheet. She told her assistants that Dr. Katra had suddenly passed away, but she had not given out any details. For the time being, she would allow them to come to their own conclusions—heart attack brought on by the stress of the job, one guessed, while the other said something about a virus.

Word had gotten around that Dr. Katra had cleared out the place by telling everyone there was a virulent virus breach. Talk had already begun that Dr. Katra had been acting irrationally. Angelica had asked the two top internists left in charge, Crysta Conover and Don Porter, to not add any fuel to the floating gossip, as she called it. She left strict instructions that no one, including them, was to disturb the body, that she and police investigators alone would handle the matter until further notice. She also asked Don Porter to free up space in a freezer somewhere for Dr. Katra's body.

Porter had asked, "Is it possible that Dr. Katra had some sort of brain tumor?"

"It's possible. We won't know without a complete autopsy."

Crysta said, "I heard it was some sort of virus infecting his brain."

"Like I said, we won't know until we do an autopsy."

"I'd like to assist," said Crysta.

"Me, too," volunteered Porter.

She had nodded, thanking them. "We'll see when the time comes."

It was then that she had returned to her office, and from there she and Eric had gone in search of what lay in the bank vault.

On the elevator going down, Eric asked her about this rumor of a virus having killed Adib, and she replied, "It's easier to let the rumor stand than trying to explain the truth. Besides, it might insure that they steer clear of the room. Hell and for all we know, he may be carrying some sort of virus that drove him to this senseless act."

Passing a bright-faced young receptionist and an aged security guard, they exited the building, going for the Chase Manhattan Bank. Outside they hit a wall of heat that threatened to stop them. The entire state, along with all the Southeast, had become one gigantic bake oven, the asphalt land of Miami simmering like a stew under a sun that boiled flesh.

"Gotta wonder if this damned heat wave caused Adib's brain to haywire," he said over the noise of traffic as they entered the flow of pedestrians on the sidewalk. "Each damn degree up the thermometer anywhere else is no big deal, but here now in Miami it's a killer."

"Sure . . . sure . . . his brain was deep-fried. That answers all our questions, so we can shrug it off and safely sleep at night." Her tone was bitter. "I'm sorry . . . just upset."

It was undeniably hot at 114 degrees Fahrenheit already this morning, and Eric wondered how hot the brain fluid was allowed to get before bubbling. He thought of the absolute combustion of last night's victim in her apartment with no AC.

Angelica spoke over the noise of the city. "I saw it on tape with my own eyes, but it's unimaginable that Adib Katra would commit suicide."

"You didn't know him, Angelica. You only thought you did."

She seethed in silence, trying at accept the unacceptable. "I hate him for what he did."

"Obviously, he believed he was somehow responsible for the way Stanton and the others died."

She thrust the key to his eyes. "Whatever secrets he may have been harboring, he's obviously revealing them now. Eric, I know all the literature on suicide, and he doesn't fit your police profile of a typical checkout, so please, spare me the statistics and the bullshit."

"So OK, I'll shut up."

She pushed through the doors at Chase Manhattan, going directly for the safe-deposit boxes, where an officious woman had her sign in on an electronic card, and, just as Adib had said, there was her name, well forged, right alongside his.

She began to grow even angrier with herself than with Adib for what he had done. If he were thinking dark thoughts, why hadn't he confided in her? If he were feeling suicidal depression, why had she not seen it coming?

They entered the safe-deposit area, and she said, "I have to do this alone, Eric."

"But Adib wanted me with you, for support."

"Give me a few minutes."

"All right, a few minutes, but then I'm coming in," he insisted.

She located the box. As she stood before number 1426, Angelica imagined that she had *failed* Adib. The notion made her so angry at herself for being so stupid, so self-absorbed, so blind that she hadn't seen any of this coming. She was building an anger for herself so large now that she hadn't much left over for Adib's senseless act.

She opened the large box to find the usual stash of envelopes filled with stocks, bonds, private papers such as birth certificate, a passport, some foreign money and coins, old costume jewelry, an emerald, and a diamond ring. She placed it all into one bag she had brought with her for the purpose, knowing she'd have to turn it over to police. Then she saw it, an ancient parchment, thick and grainy, looking like a goatskin, rolled tightly and bound with a cloth tie. She carefully loosed the tie around the parchment and unrolled it. The edges crumbled at her touch. She could not imagine the age of the document, but she could instantly see that it was in a strange language, possibly Sanskrit, she imagined, but also, rolled neatly within the scroll, Adib had left some simple, lined paper with handwriting to explain. On the parchment itself, at the top, three names stared at her: *Shakar, Shakir,* and *Kundalini.* A lurid picture of two entwined two-headed serpents, combining as one, also jumped off the page at her, as each serpent was a likeness of the tattoo on Shakar's abdomen.

She sat now before the strange scroll, a magical sort of document that belonged under glass in some museum somewhere—another secret kept from her like the tattoo. It felt so wrong, so odd, so unlike the man she had known to be involved to this degree in some sort of mystical religious sect, even if his culture supported such mysticism throughout its past, for he was far and away the most scientific man she had ever known.

But here she sat in this privacy room alongside a vault in modern Miami staring at an ancient Indian Sanskrit scroll, wondering what it had meant to Adib, and wondering why he had directed her here.

She considered tucking it back away, putting the box back in its numbered little tomb, and walking out of there. Instead, she read the handwritten note Adib had rolled inside the parchment. Again it was his handwriting, dated the same year as his will.

If I should die, Hari Shakir will come to claim my body; he will claim to be a relative, but he is not. He must not, under any circumstances have any opportunity to be within the same room as my body. In fact, before that can happen, you must destroy my shell and everything that you find within it. You must corrupt and destroy my remains. Shakir must not know my body in any sense of the word. He must never be allowed to come into contact with the beast within me, my personal Kundalini. Adhere to my requests, each and every one of them. Otherwise, should Shakir's beast become one with mine, the world as you know it will cease to exist. I am in death as I have always been in life final sustenance for the serpent Hari carries within his body. Hari Shakir and his serpent god are responsible for untold numbers of spontaneous human combustions.

Although they seemed the words of a madman, Angelica found herself wrapped in a strange curiosity, and she found herself absorbing the insane fairy tale left her, a brief translation of the scrolls, a story about two family dynasties in the ancient world of India. She was again caught up in the insanity of it all, how so learned a man as Dr. Adib Katra could believe in such *nonsense,* that he was being stalked by a creature that breathed a fire that cremated human victims. But then the forensic evidence at two crime scenes had, in effect, supported the case for SHC.

The man now calling himself Shakar claimed that he had some sort of spiritual kinship to this serpent god called the Kundalini, and that it was here to claim him, and if it should get hold of him, *alive or dead,* before his body was corrupted, that this creature would take over rule of the world and feed at will on its most preferred prey—humans.

She heard Adib's voice inside her head say, "Don't under any circumstances disobey me."

She was startled when Brannon found her and tapped on the glass, inviting himself into the private booth. "What've you found?"

"More craziness," she said.

"Pour on more, you mean?"

She handed him the letter of explanation of the scrolls.

"You think these scrolls are authentic?" he asked after glancing over the brief translation.

"They look real enough. I think it may be Sanskrit from

the look of it," she offered. "But this story is just too fantastic to have any merit."

"And our spontaneous combustion murders? A day ago, they would have been science fiction, a car and an apartment heated to fifteen thousand degrees."

"Are you saying you believe this shit?"

"Not entirely, no, but suppose it's half a truth, say he really does have a brother or cousin or something who has it in for him? The guy comes here under a heat wave, sets up some kind of newly invented jet stream of superheated fire or some gizmo that turns people into a chemical fire and whoosh."

"An electrochemical fire that uses only the body's own chemicals as fuel, you mean. Do you hear how mad all this is? You're throwing out all the evidence I told you about last night. And me . . . I'm still unable to believe Adib's killed himself. He was so spiritual, and he spoke about the transmigration of souls, how the process relies on cremation, the fire to carry the soul into the next world, so what does he do with his body? He asks me to corrupt it with maggots, severe the private parts, grind and hack him to pieces, scatter it all in a muddy swamp or do the laser sectioning. What kind of drug was he on? I'm having a blood test done, and I want a brain scan for a lesion, a tumor, something to explain this hallucinogenic nonsense."

"Why did he . . . you know, leave you in charge as . . . as . . ."

"Executor of his remains?"

She got up, gathering all that Adib had wanted her to have into a cloth bag she'd brought for the purpose. "He once told me that he could not ever, under any circumstances be an organ donor. It had slipped out once while we were working, and I was going on about how much human tissue we literally buried in any given day, materials that could save sight, hearing, life itself. Adib argued that every man had a right to make his own decisions about the dispensation of his body."

"I guess he had given it some thought."

"He told me how life in India for most of the population was. He told me about the economic bondage that began at birth for many, parents selling off promised body parts to the highest bidder."

"Sounds bleak."

"We could talk and we could disagree, and we remained close. And he once confided that I was the only one he trusted to understand his position. Now this, the event of his death, and he wants me to follow his wishes and to the letter."

"Jesus . . . he really set you up for a big fall then, didn't he? How could he imagine you could carry out such wishes?"

"Maybe he thought you'd be my accomplice. I don't know. I had no idea he was carrying around this mythological nonsense, and that he wanted some ancient scatological rights performed to keep his body from being used as some sort of host for this Kundalini creature he speaks of. I think all promises are off at this point. My thinking is I can laser dissect the man, but that's as far as I can go."

"And the acid bath?"

"I don't see myself going that far, no."

"What do you usually do with such medical waste . . . I mean, what would be left after the dissecting?"

"We usually burn it."

"He specifically asked not to be burned."

Ignoring this, she said, "I still wonder if I could have done something—anything—to help Adib?"

The recriminations hit her in successive waves. Brannon recognized this and assured her. "No one could have seen this coming; no one who knew Dr. Katra would have ever taken him for a suicide."

Brannon guided her out and past the shining bars of the vault, through the bank, and out into the street. They stood now below a searing sun. She felt better out in the light, and even the heat felt good, for it felt real. None of what she'd discovered in the vault felt real.

Brannon took her by the arm and guided her across the street, where a small municipal park fronted the port area and ships as large as buildings sat in slips where passengers boarded. "Those people have the right idea—get out of Miami for a while."

She sniffed back tears and found herself leaning into him. Brannon made her comfortable on his shoulder as they sat on a park bench listening to the sounds of ships rigging and birds at play, and he slipped an arm around her. Angelica nestled there for a long moment and cried for the loss of her friend and teacher.

Eric said, "I think we need to sit down with an expert of some sort who can decipher the scrolls for us, maybe someone at Miami U . . ."

"To understand the Sanskrit text we'd need a translator, but I don't want it getting out that Dr. Katra had gone insane. I don't want his reputation destroyed." She immediately felt a need to protect the man's legacy in Miami, asking Brannon, "What good would it serve to embarrass his memory?"

Brannon realized that it was obvious to her that Katra or Shakar, for whatever reason, had left this life in an insane state of mind. "Still, I'd like to get some expert to look the scrolls over; see what he says about it," countered Brannon.

"As long as we can keep it discreet. I'd like to use an old friend of mine, a Dr. Helen McAllister. She'll keep it quiet. But first, I've got to get back to the lab, autopsy Adib's body."

"Then you're not going to treat it as he requested?"

"If there's a brain tumor or some other cause of this insanity, I want to know about it."

"Wouldn't that show up in the laser sectioning?"

"Yes, it would."

"Then why not put him on ice for now? We know what killed him; we have it on tape. That'll buy you time. You're in no shape to autopsy your friend now anyway."

"Yes, of course, you're right, Eric, and thank you."

"For what?"

"Being a rock for me . . . being here for me."

He hugged her to him. "We're going to get you through this."

*   *   *

They returned to a stunned Lou Ames and Jackie Hale, who had had time to read everything and were shocked at the list of items Katra had made for the ritual desecration of his body. By now everyone agreed that Dr. Katra—Shakar, as he called himself—had gone mad and had committed an act of the insane. Ames told Dr. Hunter that he would leave the disposal of Katra's remains up to her after the proper time had elapsed to locate any possible family members. Angelica assured him that she would follow proper procedure with respect to both the man's wishes and his remains, despite Katra's warning that no one claiming to be family should be allowed near his remains: *Hari will come to claim the body. He will know psychically that I am dead, and if he learns I am here, he will come to fuse with the serpent within. Hopefully, the serpent is by the time of your reading these words already dead and unable to fuse. But to ensure this, destroy my body as prescribed.*

Ames took Angelica's hand and warmly shook it, telling her how sorry he was about all this. Then he asked about the lockbox contents.

Angelica gently lifted the scrolls from her bag, and poured out the rest of the items found in the lockbox across her desk. She extended the scrolls to Ames, explaining them.

"We'd like to take the scrolls and Adib's notes on them to an expert, Captain," Eric said. "Get better informed."

"You have someone in mind?"

"Yes, sir, at the university."

"An old friend of mine," said Angelica.

"In that case," said Captain Ames, "I've got to get back to HQ, and Jackie will log the tape and all these other items in as evidence of the suicide. So, we'll see you back at the precinct later."

"I need the knife," Angelica said, "to take measurements." She recalled how important the scimitar was to Adib's plans, and the notion it was somehow sanctified and purified as the only weapon useful against his inner demons. Something in her wanted to hold on to it for now. "We know it's the knife he used, but I want to be thorough."

"Understood. You can log it in after your lab analysis, but see to it that it doesn't disappear."

Eric saw that Jackie had paled, and he sensed that she had seen enough for one morning. They placed the tape and the will into evidence bags, confiscating these, and Ames assured Angelica, "These items will be treated with dignity and discretion, Dr. Hunter, you can be assured."

"Thank you, Captain Ames. I just don't want that tape showing up on the Internet or some TV newscast."

"The official police report will read death by suicide," added Jackie, "and after a reasonable time has passed, the tape will be destroyed."

"We won't let it out of our control," Ames reassured her. "Like you, we all respected Adib."

Adib's death had already sent shock waves through the law-enforcement community. A general wave of sadness nestled over the crime lab. Rumors continued to abound.

Eric stepped out into the hallway with Jackie, asking if she had had time to look into the phone records at the crime-lab dispatch.

"I called over there the moment you left, and according to their records no such call was forwarded at that time. The lady I talked to said it's rare they would pass along a call to Dr. Katra's cell phone, that it would have to be a very important call, and there were none of an urgent nature at that time last night."

"Then why did he lie about it? Was there a call at all? And if not, how did he know of the crime scene before anyone else?"

"This just may end up as one of those mysteries that never finds a solution, Eric. Tell me, what's going on between you and Dr. Hunter?"

"This case."

"Hmmmpf! You're talking to a detective, Detective."

"All right, so there's some attraction. Happy?"

"Yeah . . . yeah, and I hope it works out for you this time."

"Thanks."

"I'm going to recanvass Stanton's hospital. Got a few new questions on my mind," she said.

"Don't forget to check on Seminole dispatch. See who was in Krueshicki's neighborhood last night. Speaking of which, how'd it go with the woman's daughters?"

"They're anxious to get into her place, get her things out. They have no idea what they're about to walk into. I told them to get a police escort when the scene is released. Right now it still has tape on it."

"They didn't seem surprised?"

"Oh, yeah, they were, but they took it in stride. One of them told me she always expected her mother to catch herself on fire with a cigarette one day. As for enemies, they gave me a long list."

They parted, Eric returning to Angelica's office. "Helen can only see us if we get over there right now. She's got to catch a flight to Houston."

"Let's do it then."

Angelica left word she would be at the University of Miami, and that she would return in an hour, at which time they would perform the autopsy on Adib Katra slash Shakar.

On the elevator going down, Eric asked, "Won't an autopsy violate the trust he—Adib—placed in you?"

"Like I said . . . with his having committed suicide, all bets are off."

The University of Miami was not far, and, taking his vehicle, they journeyed to the tree-lined campus with its winding small streets filled with fraternity and sorority houses. Angelica had called ahead and set up an appointment with a Dr. Helen McAllister, a Ph.D. in ancient languages, religions, and customs, someone Angelica knew from her days in college. She sounded dubious as to what they had, undoubtedly thinking the scrolls a fraud of some sort, but she was intrigued when told they'd been part of an estate. All this Angelica explained as they drove to the university.

Brannon then dropped a remark about how no one could ever really know anyone these days, referring to Adib Katra now Adib Shakar.

She replied, "I knew a man who reveled in life, valued life and family and tradition by all outward appearances. He quoted his parents often, and although they passed away years ago, he spoke of them as if they were always nearby. What else can I tell you? He proved a man steeped in the culture and faith of his people—Hinduism. And he loved Indian cuisine."

"Who doesn't?"

She then said, "Dr. Shakar treated me like a daughter. He took a personal interest in me . . . helped me out on many an occasion. He would take me to an Indian restaurant here in Miami where I had the best lamb curry I've ever eaten."

They fell silent a moment.

Brannon said, "Bad things happen to good people."

"Blindingly fast," she agreed.

"Unfortunately, we both see it all the time in our line of work."

She nodded and sniffed back a tear. "Yeah, lightning strikes without warning." Angelica knew this fact, knew it when news of her fiancé's disappearance had reached her. Tom, a Navy pilot, had disappeared during a routine air mission that ended with a search for his body. A lightning storm had changed her and her life forever. That had been four years ago. It'd kept her from getting too close to anyone, save Adib. Now this.

Adib Katra was dead. The lightning this time had been swift, and the emotional explosion came in waves now. She feared she would break down and never regain control.

"I know it's gotta be extremely difficult for you, Angelica."

"It's not just that he died, but the manner of his death, hacking away at his own insides to destroy what?"

"Some kind of supernatural beast within him, or so he obsessed about."

Thoughts over Adib continued to fill her mind, as they did Brannon's.

"Creepy . . . that stuff he wrote about . . . real creepy stuff," said Brannon.

"Why, because it's unbelievable? Or because it might have some truth to it?"

When they arrived at the university, they located McAllister's office, a small semi-darkened room filled with what appeared to be a lifetime's collection of books, maps, manuscripts, and papers—wall-to-wall and to the ceiling. The doctor had to clear off chairs for them to sit in, but she had prepared coffee, and she made a show of how little she and Angelica had seen of one another lately. "You've been such a stranger."

"Rather busy . . . due mostly to the heat wave."

Angelica introduced Eric. For the next fifteen minutes, the expert in ancient documents poured over the parchment scrolls left behind by Adib Katra. She had to go back and forth between several reference books to decode the words, although she was an expert on Sanskrit. She looked up at them, staring, saying, "This is a rare find . . . rare indeed. It's a dialect I'm not terribly familiar with, but here goes: It all tells a story of two families, a kind of cosmic fairy tale about a feud between them. Tells of the Kundalini."

"And what is a kun-dal-lini?" asked Eric.

"A two-headed serpent god that lives within mankind— dormant until awakened through ritual. It feeds through a kind of supernatural, superheated fire that literally combusts its victims. The creature devoured all mankind at one point, and left alone with itself and starving, it finally ate itself, but its seed remained behind. Like the flood stories, there was a new awakening of mankind. Mankind again flourished, thanks to the beneficence of Vishnu, the Hindu god of all things. But then two ruling families, the Shakirs and the Shakars, related by blood, began to worship the snake god, and a cult or sect was formed around it, rekindling its power."

"That's the point at which the scrolls were written?"

"It appears so. Nine hundred B.C. if my translation is correct."

"I've never heard of this serpent god until now," said Eric. "This Kundalini."

"It's a well-known god in the Hindu pantheon, one that controls by entangling itself inside a host male in each family. It says that if the two serpent gods living within these two men should ever come into contact, that this god—which feeds on the fire of flesh—will take control of all mankind, that it will feed on mankind as we feed on cattle."

"It says all that," replied Brannon, recalling what Katra had written, imagining how Katra had taken the story and applied it to himself and his tattoo. It all seemed so fantastic and strange.

"Yes, it says all that," replied Dr. McAllister, "and more. Goes on to say that dead or alive, this thing can make use of the body of either Shakir or Shakar, if the two should ever join . . . even in death . . . it's all about contact."

"Dr. Katra believed this was happening," Angelica said. "He killed himself and left a note to me, saying he had no choice, that this *thing*—he called it some sort of *spirit kin*— was within proximity."

Helen McAllister replied, "Strange that someone in this day and age would act on such a religious superstition, especially if it means suicide, but then Katra was Hindu, right? And it is an ancient belief system—a somewhat beautiful one at that. If he was a Shakar, as he claimed, the scrolls say that if this thing had reached him alive, it would have taken him over. Says here his only resistance begins with his death, but that his resistance cannot end there, that you must perform a ritual in which you cut his body into countless pieces."

"What does that say about the man's state of mind?" asked Brannon.

"Any shrink worth his or her salt will tell you, Detective, that the man died in the midst of a psychosis, likely . . . likely brought on . . . that is triggered by a traumatic event, most likely an event that, you know, opens a can of worms he's buried since early childhood."

"Perhaps something about the odor of burnt flesh," suggested Angelica, "something about the way the victim's fat was reduced to grease, that disgusting human creosote we placed on swabs and under slides."

Brannon then described the doctor's last two crime scenes. He added, "Prior to this, I had never seen Katra shaken by anything, not even when we brought him that severed head. Took him only a half a day to ID the head, and we located the body, the killer, and the weapon the next day. But this. . . . And I keep coming back to how did he know the black, fired grease in Stanton's car was, you know, human fatty tissue?"

Angelica replied, "He was extremely good; I learned so much from him."

"You realize, you two risk being arrested for mutilating a corpse should you follow Dr. Katra's directions for disposing of the body," the professor said.

"Katra thought of everything, including that." Angelica explained how he'd made the request to have his body laser sectioned into filmable partitions and scanned to create a computer map of the entire cadaver. "It would not break any laws, as his written final wish is to leave his body to science."

"And in dicing it up, he escapes this so-called serpent god that he's fixated on, thinking there's some supernatural force that has it in for him, right?" asked McAllister, frowning.

"That about covers it. After the dicing and the scanning, he asks that the chips we make of him be thrown into an acid vat until all that remains is scum."

"Which means his suicide is for all eternity," said McAllister.

"Whataya mean, all eternity?" asked Brannon.

"The man condemns his soul to never return, to never achieve the next level, never to find nirvana if his remains are not allowed to go skyward in fire," she replied. "When his people cremate their loved ones, the fumes and cinders that go skyward carry the soul upward so that it can return and begin anew on the path to enlightenment and attainment, you see, but by scattering and destroying all tangible evidence he ever existed, not a trace of himself to be left behind, outside a computer program . . . well. . . ."

"He loses all that," Brannon said thoughtfully. "Are you sure, Angelica, that he was orthodox? Orthodox Hindu?"

"He practiced his faith, yes."

"I see why you're reluctant to do as he requested."

Angelica turned to McAllister, her hands in the universal gesture of prayer, pleading that McAllister keep this entirely to herself.

"I assure you, it will go no further, Angelica. Trust me. No one would believe it even if I were inclined to tell the story."

"Thank you, Helen, for everything. We've taken enough of your time. Again, thank you for your help." Angelica stood to leave.

Eric did likewise. Angelica began to gather the scrolls.

"Those beautiful scrolls should be placed under glass in our museum here," said Helen. "It's a rare parchment."

"Sorry," countered Eric. "I'm sure it's as rare as you say, but it's evidence for the moment. Maybe when all this is over, you and Dr. Hunter can discuss other arrangements for the document."

"Yes, do let me hear, Angelica, Detective." Dr. McAllister, smiling up at them, now stood and extended her hand. "I hope I was of help."

Angelica, depression creating a sad aura around her, allowed Helen to hug her. They said their good-byes and Eric led her out. "I've got to get back to the lab, Eric."

"Right, not a problem."

12

In the silent morgue, in the half-light, with no one to see, Dr. Adib Shakar's body began a strange, odd quaking at its core, and beneath the sheet came an undulating and rippling, indicating life, movement.

The lights in the room came on, instantly freezing the movement.

Young Crysta Conover had located Dr. Katra's keys in his desk, and she had come both reluctantly and curiously into the room, with an itch to see Dr. Katra in his present state. Knowing nothing of what had happened, she had been unable to get past the police when they were here, but now that everything had settled down, she and Donald were to assist in the autopsy. She had never autopsied anyone she actually knew before, and to steel herself, she thought it best to prep the body for the autopsy, get as used to being around the dead man as possible. She didn't want to freak out and let Dr. Hunter down. Meanwhile Donald Porter was off trying to free up a freezer compartment for the body. With him off seeing to that, she had come here.

She was, after all, a medical student specializing in forensics, and while Porter had been left in charge, that had only occurred because she had gone down to the cafeteria at a crucial moment when Dr. Hunter had had to leave.

Young Crysta still couldn't believe the news that Dr. Katra was actually dead; she had had a genuine affection for the medical examiner. He had been an excellent teacher, patient and kind at all times.

Crysta now inched closer to the shape beneath the shroud. She started when she thought she saw a ripple beneath the sheet. She became chilled and spooked below the bright lights of the "meatball room" as the interns referred to it.

Inching closer, she saw a trick of light play over the sheet, another ripple, another slight undulation. It was enough. She backed from the room, turning out the light.

"What the hell am I afraid of?" she asked herself. "It's just a muscle spasm, a contraction. Happens all the time in the dead." She decided to walk back in and do what she had come to do, have a look at the body, determine, if she could, the truth of how the doctor had died.

She stepped back inside and flicked the light back on, but this time it flickered and died. *Damn blackouts again. The generator ought to kick in anytime.* She flicked the lights up and down but no use.

She stepped closer to the body beneath the sheet, drawn to it now. Whatever sort of contraction or muscle spasm she'd witnessed seemed now gone, but suddenly it appeared again. Something more than a simple muscle spasm, something moving, slithering, something just beneath the surface of the sheet, gliding beneath that white-and-gray wrinkled surface. Whatever it was, it preferred the semi-darkness to the bright lights. It began moving more freely now, as if. . . . As if it believed no one was watching.

Some small voice at the back of her head told Crysta to leave it alone, just as Dr. Hunter had said to leave the body alone until she arrived back. But Crysta couldn't leave it alone. Still, her hand, poised to rip the sheet away, seemed unable to act now.

She rushed away and found young Dr. Donald Porter, and, tugging at him, she said, "I need you, Don, now."

"Right here, now, like this?" he joked while wheeling a body from the freezer. He had a flashlight lit and lying atop the corpse he was moving. The lights all over the building had dimmed. Porter was pushing bodies around, trying to make room in the overcrowded walk-in freezer.

"Don, I need your help," she repeated, tugging at him until he relented.

"All right, what is it?"

"Come with me and bring that flashlight."

"You finally see my charms?" he continued to joke.

"It's Katra's body. I saw something strange and I want confirmation."

"Confirmation of what? He's dead."

"I know that, you know that . . . but . . . but there's something alive in Autopsy One, beneath the sheet."

He blew out a long breath of exasperated air and stared at her. "Oldest lesson in the book, Crysta, muscle spasms. And what're you up to? You know you're not to go near the body, according to our new fearless leader."

"This was more than a muscle spasm, and don't you think it strange that Dr. Hunter didn't ask us to prep the room for autopsy?"

"She said stay out of the room until she got back."

By the time they got to the room, Don had his arm draped over her shoulder and was saying that he could think of better ways to spend their time.

"You're sick, you know that? I need you for support. That's all. Now come and have a look." She tore loose from him and opened the door, urging him inside. The lights here were still of no use. She grabbed the flashlight and, feeling bolder, Crysta again stepped toward Katra's body.

"I wanted to see him, and I came in and I saw something odd."

"What's odd," said Porter, "is that Dr. Hunter was the only medical professional in the whole building that got a glimpse of his body. Then she tells us to stay clear of it. Spread some nonsense about possible CDC interest," he replied, "but then police filed in and out. Something's not right."

"Donald, she didn't start the rumor about the Center for Disease Control coming in. Forget about that. Look, I saw movement beneath the sheet, like . . . I don't know, like *breathing*. Suppose he really isn't dead?"

"That'd be a corker." Porter, equally curious about Dr. Katra's condition and the circumstances surrounding his surprising demise, asked, "Was it a heart attack or what? Somebody said heart attack but some of the cops were talking suicide. Do you believe that?"

"One way to find out. Dr. Porter—"

The young interns went toward the body now, when suddenly the room was flooded with light, the generator having kicked in. The glaringly bright light seemed to trigger a sudden spasm in the body, and it was as if an invisible wire snatched off the sheet, which cascaded off Katra's mutilated corpse. The young interns gasped in tandem at the horrid sight of the wounds over the tattooed surface of his abdomen.

"Look at that fucking tattoo!" cried Porter. "Beautiful, at least it was!"

"To hell with the tattoo. Look at those wounds . . . look at the knife wounds."

They had found far more than they had bargained for—a large mass of swelling coiled around the man's naval, filling in the enormous tattoo of the coiled snake, fleshing it out—bloating it with life that wiggled and stretched and pushed at the envelope of skin, and from the open wounds, there appeared some sort of odd movement as well.

"Something's just not right about this," Crysta nervously said.

"Tell me about it."

"Maybe we shoulda done as Dr. Hunter asked. This is too weird. Could be a disease. Let's get out of here."

"No . . . wait. I'm putting on a tape; get this on film. Could be important. Hell, could make *Real TV*."

Crysta knew what a film and photo nut he was, and she wondered at his reasoning. "Forget about it. Let's just go."

He popped in a tape and switched on the overhead cameras, saying "Just in case; who knows. With all the talk of spontaneous human combustions, maybe the old man's about to go up! If we catch it on tape, hell, you got any idea how much that tape would be worth?"

As he flicked on the camera, Porter heard Crysta's sudden gasp, stopping him in his tracks.

"Something's alive inside him; he's obviously dead, but something is moving inside Dr. Katra's corpse!" she screamed. "How the fuck do you explain that?"

"I wouldn't know how to put it on a protocol sheet, would you?" he only half joked, his eyes bulging at the movement inside the mutilated abdomen.

"There's got to be some logical explanation . . . some scientific answer."

"You really think so?"

"No . . . not really," she whimpered.

"Some hell of a tattoo the old man was hiding, huh?"

"He wasn't so old."

"I heard he was looking at fifty, but he looked like seventy."

"That's not so old, not nowadays."

"He's dead, Crysta; that's old. You don't get any older than your death date."

"There . . . there it went again. That movement like . . . like . . ."

"Like his intestines are filling out the tattoo," finished Porter. I saw it, too. This is damned strange shit; it's like something out of Edgar Allan Poe. It's got to be that his intestines are bloating."

"Like a bad drug trip," she countered, yet she inched closer to the cadaver.

"Let's take the high road here and just wait for Dr. Hunter. Obviously, she knows more about how he died, and if there is some sort of disease element here . . ."

She shook her head. "No, he's been stabbed, multiple times by the look of it."

"That doesn't explain the creepy internal hoedown going on inside him."

"You think Hunter can explain it?"

"Don't know, but your tape's not running," she said, pointing.

"Shit." He returned to hit the record button again. "Must be a worn contact point."

"Something's definitely alive inside him and moving around. It's like a slick eel. I've heard of eels getting into bodies and popping out at the most inconvenient times during an autopsy, but . . ."

"That'd have to be a drowning death, dear. He doesn't look to be a drowning victim."

"Damn it, I'm trying to make suggestions, comparisons."

"Look, look!"

"Whatever the hell it is, it's trying to get out."

It bulged at Katra's abdomen. Swelling up, dropping back, swelling up, dropping back, like something trying to hatch.

She placed a stethoscope against Katra's abdomen, listening, hearing a strong but strange response, a kind of pulsing.

"Get away from the body, Crysta," Porter suddenly said in a grave tone. "You were right the first time. Let's wait for Dr. Hunter to get back."

Porter felt a strange sense of danger come over him with the scent of something ancient, an unusual odor that had infiltrated the place, making him stare up at the ventilation duct to see if the fan was operating or not. Looking back at Crysta, suddenly he saw his young friend vaporized and sucked into the wounds of the cadaver. It happened so fast and the flame was so intense and powerful and brilliant that it sent Porter staggering back against the counter, where he knocked over bandages, sutures, beakers as he fell to the floor.

Katra's body rumbled and quaked, and, somewhere from far away, Porter imagined Crysta's scream, but there had been no time for a scream. He scratched and clawed his way from the room, knocking over things in his way as he went crashing through the door. On the other side, he came face-to-face with Dr. Hunter, the horror of his twisted features reflected in her clear green eyes.

"What the hell's happened? What's going on, Don! Where's Crysta? And what's that odor?"

Brannon immediately called it: "Ozone . . . same as in the two cases of SHC we've investigated."

"The odor of spontaneous combustion," she conceded.

Porter tried to dash away, but Brannon grabbed him and put him into an armlock and returned him to Angelica. "Answer Dr. Hunter."

"It . . . the   corpse . . . Katra . . . swallowed   her   up through . . . through his wounds!"

"What? What are you talking about?"

"I saw her one second, and she was gone the next. Whatever that thing was . . . is. . . . She . . . she was poking at it in his stomach with a damn stethoscope when—God, I pleaded with her to leave it alone—whatever it was, it . . . it turned her into a ball of gases and sucked her in through the man's open wounds. God!"

Now the ozone odor seeped through the autopsy-room door. Angelica pushed the door open, about to enter.

"Don't! Don't go near it," shouted the lanky Porter. "It's supernatural what happened in there." He pulled free of Brannon, but Eric stood in his way. Together, the three of them entered the autopsy room, Brannon having to force Porter. They stared across at the body, seeing that the tattoo was splattered with a black greasy residue now and a dark smoke had painted the ceiling directly over Adib's abdomen. Atop the abdomen lay Conover's mangled stethoscope, gnarled, melted, and entangled into a locket and chain she had always worn about her neck. The ugly metal obelisk with stems bounced about the abdomen as the thing inside undulated, as if feeding.

"Son of a bitch," moaned Angelica. "I should have listened to Adib. Put the body on ice immediately. This is my fault."

Brannon held his weapon extended toward the sunken snake. "Everything he said, there's truth in it after all . . . and Katra is guilty of at least one death we now know of."

"Adib obviously held this thing in check all these years through sheer willpower and ritual. Apparently now all bets *are* off." Angelica felt a great remorse over what had happened to Crysta Conover, but she needed to think clearly how to contain the situation. "We've got to get him to the freezer."

As she said this, the stethoscope jiggled and fell to the floor with a clatter, unnerving them all.

Brannon, too, had watched the dancing stethoscope, and he added, "That fucking thing wants out. It wants us! I filmed it . . . got it on tape." He pointed to the overhead camera.

"It can't live long in a dead body, hoping prey will come to it. It's struggling to find a way to survive," said Angelica. "We've got to find a way to deal with the body."

"Don't go near it, Dr. Hunter!" Porter screamed. "Look, if you don't believe me, how suddenly it can strike, look at the tape. We got it on tape!"

Porter inched his way around the room, steering clear of the cadaver. He reached the wall and hit rewind on the camera he had used. His hands shaking badly, he finally stopped the tape and replayed it.

In a moment they found Crysta, with her back to the camera on an overhead shot. They caught glimpses of the rippling movement beneath the skin, and they heard Porter telling her to wait for Angelica's return, and to get away from the body, when she leaned in over the wounds and suddenly the tape showed a brilliant blue-white light that came and went in an instant, and with its diminishing, Crysta was no longer in the room.

"This thing is instantaneous death," muttered Brannon.

"His body is . . . is . . ." began Porter.

"Carrying something, we know. Something as lethal as this creature that's *supposedly* chasing him," said Brannon. "Maybe it's been Adib all along, Adib and this creature that killed your intern."

"What're you suggesting, Eric? That Shakar is Shakir? That he left the name Hari on that refrigerator door? That he combusted those two women and all those victims the fire department's been investigating? That Adib's been behind all of this all along, a murderer?"

"Help me understand any other possibility; hell, I can

hardly wrap my mind around this video we've just viewed, can you?"

"That tape is proof he's telling the truth, proof that we've got to follow his instructions to the letter, Eric."

"It only proves that Adib Katra or Adib Shakar or whatever his name is, is as dangerous in death as he was in life. Suppose he was behind the other deaths, Angelica? We've got to consider it possible. I knew when I saw him at Stanton's car. He acted the part of a guilty man."

"I won't believe it. I can sooner believe his version of events, that there is someone stalking him with this same ability to combust people at will."

"Why didn't it combust you, Dr. Hunter, when you did the prelim and determination of death?" asked Porter.

She considered this carefully, and recalled that her examination had concentrated on the wounds, and she had taken the knife and replaced it carefully into each wound, taking measurements against it. She had to answer Porter with, "I don't know . . . maybe it was in a weakened condition, a stasis period? We don't know what we're dealing with here."

Brannon asked, "What do you propose doing with the body now since whatever is inside him will devour anyone who gets too near it?"

"It may well be just trying to understand its new status, what has happened to its host organism."

"And you had no inkling of this before now?" he asked.

"It must've been dormant during my preliminary exam. I didn't see it, and I certainly didn't smell it. I didn't have a close encounter with it, whereas Crysta did."

"But it doesn't figure. You took the knife out of him. You were close during the exam. A number of us were."

She shook her head. "I don't know. Maybe it was still stunned and weak from the attack? Who knows? Now are you two men going to help me get Katra into cold storage or not?"

"How? We can't lay hands on the body," countered Porter. "If we do, we go the way of Crysta."

Brannon agreed. "Absorbed into the man's decaying body, for all eternity for all we know."

"Christ, poor Crysta," moaned Porter.

"We've got to find a way to get him into a freezer compartment," she insisted. "The sooner we freeze him, the sooner we can carry out the sectioning."

"I wouldn't touch him for all the wealth in the world, and neither should you," argued Porter.

She suddenly brightened and turned to them. "I've got it. Porter, get that canister of liquid nitrogen in the lab and attach a wand to it. We'll first freeze the damned thing inside Adib, and then we'll refrigerate the corpse. Once frozen, this thing may go dormant."

"And then what?" asked Porter.

"And then we laser dissect him from top to bottom, just as he asked in the first place. Now, Porter, prepare the liquid nitro."

"Frozen . . . we freeze the devilish creature," muttered Porter, going for the three-foot-high liquid nitrogen canister.

"How can you be sure it will work?" asked Brannon. "This thing has blown temperatures to Fahrenheit fifteen thousand, remember?"

"We freeze him until he's a solid block of ice; it's necessary anyway for the laser cutting to work. We'll eventually have him in hundreds of quarter-inch-thick sections. This thing inside him is going to perish as a result. Trust me."

"And the acid bath?" he asked.

"We do it."

"How soon do you do the operation?" asked Brannon.

"As soon as he's safe to handle. We'll gauge him . . . wait until he's one solid mass. Frozen through, I doubt the creature could blow out a candle much less a human life."

"You realize that if the SHCs end after this, that we'll have to conclude that Adib will have been responsible all along?"

"Only if the combustions end can we assume that," she replied defensively, but Brannon's new theory of the crime once again shook her faith in Adib.

After seeing Crysta spontaneously combust on the tape,

she could not believe even Adib capable of controlling such a force locked away inside him. "Perhaps, after so many years of controlling this force, he simply snapped. That beast began to dictate and win out over his will, his heart and his mind."

"That's believable after seeing what happened on that tape."

"Still, in the end, the true heart of the man, in an effort to save others, won out when he had attempted to slay his dragon." This redeemed him in her eyes; after all, he had attempted to finally put an end to it all, even if he had failed.

Porter returned with the canister and wand, his hands shaking. Brannon took it from Porter and covered the abdomen in liquid nitrogen spray, and it worked perfectly to render the tattoo of the cobra invisible beneath the layer of ice crystals. It also rendered the living undulating cobra inside Katra-Shakar silent and still.

Porter reached up and popped the tape, and Angelica wheeled in a table on wheels to accept the body and transport it to the waiting freezer. On the table lay a large scanner of a sort Brannon had never see before.

"What the hell's that? A cattle prod?" asked Brannon.

"A wireless handheld sonogram device. I want a better look at this thing inside him, don't you? Get him on the table."

With gloved hands Brannon and Porter heaved Katra's body onto the table.

They guided Adib's body out of the autopsy room toward the walk-in freezer as Angelica waved the sonogram wand across Adib's body, concentrating it over the tattoo.

She stared at the small screen at the images she was getting as she worked to keep up while the table was wheeled toward the freezer. "I hope you cleared a space for him, Don."

"I did . . . I did, the walk-in unit has room now."

"You mean you did something I asked? If you and Crysta had done as I asked, she'd be alive now."

"And you'd be dead," Eric said from across Adib's body. She continued to scan over Adib's abdomen, and she stared again at the readings she was getting. A snakelike creature with two flared heads—one at each end—coiled about Adib's insides, masquerading as a second set of intestines it appeared, stretching, just as his tattoo did in two directions, down to the private parts and up toward the spine. Its breathing and movement had been severely limited by the liquid nitrogen bath and the cold all around it now.

"We can put these readings into the computer and have a slowed-down version of this thing that killed Crysta," said Angelica.

They wheeled Adib's body into the freezer, and Angelica threw the lock on it. "Secure for the time being," she said.

Porter took the handheld, wireless sonogram device from her. "I'll scan that onto disk, and we can run an image enhancer on it."

"We'll get a look at this anomaly," she told Brannon.

They followed Porter to a computer screen where he plugged in the sonogram device. It worked like a digital camera.

She made some phone calls, getting other locations to take some of the overload with respect to the bodies piling up from the heat wave. Brannon found coffee for the two of them. After this they were looking over Porter's shoulder at his computer screen.

The scarecrow-thin Porter could hardly contain himself, hopping in his seat at what was coming into view. The two heads of the snake were at opposite ends of the creature, and spurs of fleshy tentacles shot off the trunk in all directions, many of these having actual suckers for adhering to the spinal cord, the ribs, muscle, and tissue. It had small and large tentacles, but one fat primary trunk that coiled about the stomach like Adib's tattoo. Strangely enough, it undulated with life within the dead carcass.

"What the hell is that thing?" Porter begged.

"It's nothing I'm trained on," Angelica replied. "Nothing you'll see in Gray's *Anatomy* or in a pathology book. It's something absolutely foreign to us."

"An alien?" asked Porter. "You mean it's finally happened? Alien beings are infiltrating our bodies and—"

"No, no, Don, it's not that kind of alien. At least, I don't think so."

"This is all so unbelievable," said Brannon.

"One hell of a tapeworm the old man was feeding," muttered Porter.

"Our first look at the real enemy," added Brannon.

"At least we know freezing has some effect. A first step in defeating this thing," she said. "If we can find a way to kill this snake inside Adib, maybe we stand a chance with what's out there."

"Yeah, if there is another one of these things inside another human being, like Adib claimed."

Porter asked them what they were talking about. They looked at one another. "Dr. Katra claimed that he was being stalked by another man capable of combusting people, a man who carried a snakelike creature inside him as well," she explained.

"He left a confessional tape," said Brannon.

"Can I see it?"

"Confiscated, at my precinct lockup."

"But you two have seen it?" he asked.

"Yes, we have," she said.

"God, what we don't know about what we're dealing with could fill a cruise ship," Brannon said, exasperated.

They all stared again at the unusual life-form pulsating in grainy black and white on the monitor. "Damn thing has zero pigmentation, gray-brown like the intestines."

"Camouflaged as intestines," she suggested.

They sat, mesmerized, watching the living serpent inside the corpse as it swam around the man's insides, coiling here, stretching there, strangely like a fetus, but this fat, hungry life appeared to be seeking a way out, an escape route. . . .

"Porter," Brannon said, "you're sworn to secrecy until Dr. Hunter can do the sectioning. Got that?"

"Sectioning? You're going to do a sectioning on Dr. Katra with that thing inside him?"

"I want you to assist, Dr. Porter. May I depend on you?" she asked.

"Absolutely, yes. A complete sectioning. I've never had the pleasure."

"Keep it to yourself. We'll do it around ten tonight. The body will have had time by then to freeze entirely through. I set the freezer to rise to a whopping one hundred fifty below zero. By ten tonight, he should be a solid block of ice for the procedure."

"Again, Dr. Porter, keep all details of this to yourself for now," repeated Brannon.

"Detective Brannon is right, Porter. No one, and I mean absolutely no one is to know about this until we're done with the laser sectioning on the body. We can't lose any time."

"What about notifying next of kin?" asked Porter.

"He had none according to his last statement. Still, someone comes asking for Adib's body, and we could have trouble going ahead with the procedure. Fact is, he believed someone would come looking for his body, the other serpent man, so we want to do this thing before anyone can slow or stop us."

"So . . . we do this on the Q.T.," said Brannon.

"We've got it on tape. People will understand in the long run," Porter tried to reassure them, and then he added, "That tape's going to be worth a fortune."

"I don't want to hear that kind of talk, Don," she said, glaring at the young intern. "We have to think about Crysta's family."

"I was . . . only thinking of Crysta's family. What's going to happen with her family. I mean her sister calls her like every day, and her mother's always in contact. How are we going to deal with that?"

"She's disappeared."

"Disappeared," he replied.

"Keep it that simple and that factual, Don, and you won't have to lie to them," Brannon firmly said.

"Disappeared."

"Yeah, disappeared. For the time being," she said, adding,

"We can try to level with the family after the procedure, after we rid the world of this thing."

"All right," he said, swallowing hard.

"I think it's a wise choice of action," Brannon said to the two of them. "We keep the details among us alone, until which time, as a group, we are all comfortable in disclosing the entire story. After which, we may all be out of work and labeled as nutcases."

She looked at her watch. "Porter, be here by nine-thirty, and don't be late. Eric, if you want to be on hand, we could use you as a witness."

"Count on it."

13

Mrs. Tyrone Smith, aged thirty-one, wondered who could be knocking at her apartment door this time of night; it was nearing 8:40 P.M. She dared not open the door, not in her neighborhood. She looked through the peephole and saw a dark-skinned man in a brown Seminole AC company uniform, his shirt proclaiming him simply as Randy, and while he was dark-skinned, he hadn't the features of an African-American. She guessed him to be one of those Arabs that were getting all the good jobs these days. A flash of thought about how different her life might be today if her no-account, absentee husband, Tyrone Smith, had a halfway decent job just once in his life, maybe a tough supervisor to keep him on track, then maybe she and little Ty would be a far sight better off today.

But life had not been kind to them, and neither had Tyrone. The last time she saw Tyrone, they had had a horrible fight, one that had sent neighbors rushing in, and one that had ended up in a 911 call, but Tyrone bugged out faster than the cops were able to get there, so no one had seen him in the area for over a week.

She imagined Tyrone passed out on some friend's sofa somewhere on a cocaine high. He was no use.

"Here to speak with Mr. Shakar," said the man on her stoop.

"Mr. who?"

"Shakar."

"Shack? He's calling himself Shack these days. That'd be Tyrone. Fool got himself a Muslim name, least he said it was Muslim. Muhammad Abdulla Shakar."

"That is right. He is the one I must see."

"Look, if he owes money, he ain't here to pay it, and I ain't got it, so you may's well forget it."

"No, you misunderstand, I have money for Mr. Shakar."

"You on business for the Seminole company?" she shouted through the door.

"No, no . . . I owe Shakar money . . . gambling debt."

"Really? How much?"

"Three hundred dollars, all here, we square."

She undid all but the chain lock and cracked the door open only slightly, the chain dangling at his black, mesmerizing eyes. "You can just hand it through to me, and I'll see Tyrone gets it."

"Why do you call him Tyrone? How do I know it is Shakar who gets money?"

"There ain't no Shakar here, only Tyrone, Tyrone Smith. Like I told you, he upped and changed his name on the street. He just likes to playact he's some important somebody, and he can't do that unless he pretends to be somebody else. I'm his wife . . . so whatever you come to give Tyrone, you can just turn over to me."

Hari Shakir smiled, trying to put the frail-looking young woman at ease, and he said, "Are you sure?"

"Yes, yes, I'm sure of it."

"Here then," he said, holding out a small pouch.

She reached for it and Hari grabbed hold of her wrist. Hari's lips parted and she saw some flicker of movement— his tongue?—that looked as if it had eyes. An hallucination? The man's grin both repulsed and fascinated the woman. Inside the blue light that engulfed her, milliseconds before she was vaporized into gases, she saw the snake's head clearly, its fangs dripping a white substance as creamy white as Tyrone's semen.

Then she saw that she was still whole and of substance, and the vision of herself being turned to smoke and inhaled by a demonic serpent had vanished. She pulled from the man's grip and grabbed up her Bible, thrusting it before her and shouting, "Get thee away from my door, Satan! You get away from this house! Devil . . . the Devil himself!"

"Then tell me where Shakar is."

"I tell you, I don't know where that bastard is. I knowed one day he'd bring hell raining down on me. Mama warned me 'bout him, but I wouldn't listen." She held the Bible higher, like a talisman before her.

"Your book can't save you." Hari said, touching the book and igniting it. It plumed into a ball of flame that was instantly sucked through the crack of the door and instantly swallowed up by Shakir, and Mrs. Smith realized the awful hallucination was somehow a premonition, one placed there in her brain merely to torment her, for he meant to do to her what he'd done to her Bible. All in an instant of recall, she saw it and heard his suggestion in her ear. "Come be mine."

Hari's tongue darted through the open door and stung her in the face, burning her like acid. She tried to slam the door on the damnable tongue, but he rammed the chain lock from the door with his weight against it, and she fell back instead.

She backed away, her cheek searing as if hit by acid. She crawled deeper into the interior, her eyes never leaving him, as she pleaded, "Don't hurt my baby . . . don't hurt my baby."

When she finally backed into a wall and knocked over an end table, he gently helped her to her feet and wrapped his arms around the trembling little woman and smoked her into black air that he instantly sucked down into his being, and he felt the snake serpent enlarge with the consuming of the woman.

Mrs. Tyrone Smith went to flash point so instantaneously that Hari could not inhale fast enough to capture all the creosote created from her bodily fluids and fatty tissues, so some of her wound up washing the wall where she'd stood, creating a kind of black chalk outline. The meltdown of this one was, however, so intense she'd left no large fragments behind when she had gone from solid to gaseous form. Still, a flaming finger on the hand that had clasped the sofa went spiraling sideways and landed on the cushions, igniting it at the moment of her combustion, an unusual happenstance, Hari thought.

Hari curiously studied the burning sofa. Flames would bring attention. He grabbed up a flowered afghan and buried the flames with it, pounding them down. This done, he dipped his fingers into the black soot of what remained of Mrs. Smith-Shakar. Using his blackened finger, he wrote in black, gummy creosote the series of letters: *A-D-I-B*.

"Ahhh, closure," Hari said to the empty room, the wall blackened with the smoke of the sudden combustion, the air laden with ozone. "Now, didn't she say something about a child?" He walked toward the back of the apartment but was stopped by the Kundalini's voice inside his head.

The woman knew nothing of Adib Shakar; she was telling the truth. Hari was wasting their time in this place.

Hari knew that in consuming Mrs. Smith the creature also consumed her mind and memory, so the serpent knew what it was talking about. He decided it best to get out of there before someone saw him, but what about the kid in the back room, likely sleeping? It wouldn't take but a moment.

Hari felt the growing insatiable appetite of his master. Both of them wanted to find Shakar, but the need to consume other beings was also a passion now. *One more morsel for tonight,* the god within told Hari.

Hari was halfway down the hall, going for the back bedrooms in search of little Tyrone Smith II, his name given up to Hari during the combustion of his mother, unaware that the afghan he had left on the couch and the couch itself had reignited. His attention was focused on the noise emanating from the child's bedroom.

He snatched the doorknob and twisted it. Locked. He concentrated and, holding firm, he turned the lock into flame.

The metal and wood instantly compromised, it crumbled away in incinerated ash, leaving a large hole. He stepped into a darkened room with the window raised, the drapes without life. No air stirring, no more sound. He rushed to the window to find the boy scrambling down the fire escape, already two floors below, too far ahead of him to catch.

From behind him, he heard the sound of a breathing fire, the whoosh of it as it crawled up along the peeling paint on the walls. Returning the way he had come, he saw that the fire was out of control, and the letters he had left on the wall were being eaten by the flames.

He stepped through the smoke and fire, allowing it to claim the place, going back out the front door and down the stairs for the exit.

Young Tyrone Smith was six years old, and he knew the boogeyman when he saw him. He had peeked out his bedroom door to see what all the shouting was about when he saw the dark man with the strange look on his face grab his mother's Bible and turn it into flame. He knew instantly it was a bad thing, because he knew his mother loved that book, and next he saw the man—who must be the Devil, since his mother had said so—turn her into flame. With his door closed and locked now, little Ty heard the man's footsteps in the corridor coming for him. That's when the boy quietly and tearfully opened his window and climbed out onto the fire escape. He realized for the first time in his life why people called the metal staircase a fire escape.

He moved as fast as his trembling little body could take him. He found his way down the stairs, and, at the bottom, he hadn't the weight to pull the final set to the ground. He hung in midair from the bottom rung, knowing he must swing to his right, leap for a Dumpster not quite below him. Staring up through the stairwell from where he had come, he searched for any sign of the Devil. No one was there. Maybe he had fooled Satan.

He swayed his body to and fro several times when his grip

was lost and he fell onto the closed Dumpster. The noise rattled the alleyway and frightened a cat that raced squealing away. Some neighbors' lights came on.

Tyrone ignored his bruised side and slid down the side of the Dumpster and crouched there, scanning both ways along the alley for the Devil.

Then he saw him, at the end of the alley, searching for Tyrone. The boy huddled where he was and stopped breathing. Tyrone knew he was cut off from getting to his aunt's apartment next door, that the Devil man stood between him and the doorbell. Nor did he dare shout out to his aunt Latisha, or throw rocks at her bedroom window, which he could see was dark, telling him she was asleep.

He wanted to run, but he was afraid of the man who breathed fire.

He remained huddled in back of the Dumpster, the sound of a rat coming near. This sound was replaced by footsteps coming toward him, and then the Devil called out, "Tyrone? Come out, Tyrone. Don't you want to be with your mother?"

Tyrone's hand found a broken Jack Daniel's bottle. He lifted it and climbed to his feet. He would only have one chance to escape in the opposite direction. He felt the vibration and heard the thunderclap in his ear—the Devil's hand had come crashing down on the Dumpster, sending up a deafening noise. Tyrone bolted out and threw the bottle, striking the Devil in the face and drawing blood, and the boy ran down the alley, found the backyard chain-lock fence to the building next door and scrambled through the unlocked gate, leaving it swinging on its metal hinges with its "Beware of Dog" sign rattling. Tyrone knew the Doberman was called Dobbie by its owner, and kids in the neighborhood said the dog guarded a treasure buried at the foot of the tree. Dobbie now fought his chain, tugging to get loose, its gaze *not* on Tyrone but on the man at the gate.

Tyrone danced around the dog and hit the back door running, but it was locked. Banging on it roused no one, and when he turned, he saw his only avenue of escape were the wooden steps nailed to the tall poplar tree a generation ago.

They didn't look like they would hold, but Tyrone had seen boys twice his size use them to shinny up this tree.

He leapt up onto the wooden slats of the stairwell to the upper branches. One of these branches overhung his aunt's tiny patio, where she kept her bike on the fourth floor.

Tyrone worked hand over hand, pulling himself along. He had always wanted to climb this tree, seeing the neighborhood boys do it, but fear had always held him back.

As he shinnied up, the barking dog had aroused neighbors and lights were going on all over the building. Looking down, Tyrone saw that Dobbie had somehow broken his restraint. Tyrone watched the dog leap at the Devil, and the Devil grabbed him by the neck and roasted Dobbie into a blue flame of fumes, and the barking was instantly stilled.

The Devil then stood at the bottom of the tree, his white teeth showing in a grin as Tyrone worked tirelessly to get to the next landing, his aunt's level. Tyrone knew the wire screen was blowing in the wind, almost completely torn away. He'd have no trouble getting onto the patio once he got there. But he feared the Devil would turn the huge tree into flame with him on it, should he touch it before Tyrone leapt off.

Then Tyrone was there at his aunt's back door, and the lights were on, and his aunt was unlocking the sliding-glass door. Having heard the commotion of the dog, having seen Tyrone in the tree, she rushed out shouting, "Tyrone! Child, what're you doing?" She rushed to the edge and leaned over it, reaching out to him.

"It's the Devil, down there! He's kilt Mama, and now he's trying to kill me!"

She saw the dark shape at the bottom of the tree, and she saw him calmly turn and walk away without a word, and the silence of that damned dog belonging to the Jeffersons was eerie.

She grabbed Tyrone up into her arms, asking him, "Who is that chasing you?" She wondered if the boy's father had gotten them all into trouble with some serious drug lord as she watched the strange dark man stop at the gate, turn and stare up at them. In the distance, she heard fire trucks approaching.

Tyrone trembled in her arms, and she asked all her questions at once. "What's happened to your mama, Tyrone? And what's this nonsense about the Devil? And how did you get up that tree this time of night all by yourself?"

Tyrone finally felt somewhat safe in his aunt's arms, sobbing, telling her the most amazing tale she had ever heard, and she wondered how much was fact, how much the exaggeration of a six-year-old.

She got on the phone to tell her sister where the little one was while Tyrone kept shouting some nonsense about the Devil having come to his house, that he had burned up and eaten his mother.

No one answered the phone. The boy was hysterical and in tears. Maybe something awful had happened. Maybe Tyrone senior was the Devil that the boy was talking about.

Latisha Warner feared going over to the side window, hearing the fire sirens stopping below. She saw the strobing lights, and she saw the flames shooting from her sister's apartment and the floor above hers. People all over the neighborhood were now filling the windows and shouting as if it the fire were a Monday night football game.

"Oh, my God! Shauna!" she cried out for her sister. Still holding Tyrone close, she again cried out. "Ho m'God, m'God, m'God, your mama's in a burning apartment! You gotta be a good boy and stay for a while with Winnie next door. I gotta go help your mama outta that building!"

"But Mama ain't there. The Devil man burned her up and ate her right down his throat, just like he did the dog. I saw it. . . . I saw it!"

She tugged the boy by the hand. "You gotta go by Mrs. Johnson, Tyrone. I gotta be free to see about this!"

She rushed to her neighbor's door with Tyrone in her arms. The sheer terror coming off the boy told her she couldn't handle everything alone. She pleaded for her neighbor and best friend to take Tyrone while she rushed to her sister's apartment, but Tyrone didn't want to let her go, clinging to her, pleading that she would get burned up, too.

Latisha pulled herself free and rushed out of her building and toward her sister's place. She ran out into the blaring noise and flashing lights and into a dark-skinned man dressed in a brown uniform, bouncing off him and onto the apartment steps. He was of the same general appearance as the man she had seen walk from her backyard, and the notion frightened her. He offered his hand and apologized. "I am so sorry. Please, let me help you up."

She refused any help, using the railing instead. He laid his hand on the railing and it grew hot to her touch. She yanked her hand away.

Then she met his gaze, dark and mysterious, the pupils seeming to move like spinning orbs, reflecting the strobing fire-engine lights, when she saw her reflection standing still, frozen in his eyes. In the next instant, she saw her reflection turn into Shauna's. Unable to catch her breath, she tried to scream, but it only came out as a gasp. She backed off as more people spilled from her building, coming out to watch the show; the others moved past them, their focus elsewhere.

"Good night, Latisha," he coldly said, and she watched him casually walk away from the fire as if nothing were happening, going toward a van with the Seminole Indian logo on its side.

Her lips quivering, fear like a ball inside her, she asked aloud, "How did he know my name?"

"Who? Who're you talking about?" asked Winnie Johnson, who had come out after her, Tyrone in her arms, Winnie's two older girls holding on to her nightgown.

"Him," she said, pointing, but the van and the stranger had vanished behind another fire truck that had pulled up.

Regaining herself, she pushed through displaced people from Shauna's building being herded away by firemen setting up a safe zone. All this to the sound of more fire trucks approaching.

She shouted her sister's name over the den of noise.

Oblivious of the firemen telling her to get back, Latisha

raced toward the burning building, still screaming her sister's name.

Tyrone fought his way out of Winnie's arms and raced after his aunt, crying, "Don't go in there! The Devil's still in there. He eats fire!"

Unlike other firemen, Shelby Harne never raced to a fire. He didn't have to. He was in cleanup position, batting third. First came the firefighters—sirens and red trucks deploying at the scene—setting up in rapid time to do mortal combat with the enemy flames, while their squad leaders and captains organized the assault, battle per battle. Then came the second wave, backup units to be used if the first units could not contain the blaze. It was only after the flames were beaten down and conquered that fire investigators entered the war zone.

And so he casually drove to the Woodhaven section of the city, following the chatter on the radio. Sounded as if things were already under control.

Woodhaven, like a lot of neighborhoods in Miami-Dade, had been cut out of the lush Florida countryside back in the fifties. Where once whole forests of palm trees and juniper stood above saw grass, now acres and acres of blacktop roads, parking lots, apartment houses, strip malls, and wood-frame homes stood on the flat plain. Not so much as a gradual slope or a single fine old tree could be found in the area. The only relief to the eye were a handful of planned parks where children's swings and slides resided over scrub grass and sand. Most of the houses here had aluminum awnings that winked in sun and moonlight.

Fences, stone steps, garden gnomes, little windmills, the obligatory pink metal flamingos, weeds, and dead brown patches of grass all whirred by in kaleidoscope fashion outside Shelby's car window. He paid little heed, but he did see an oncoming Seminole AC van with its signature logo: an Indian image with his bow about to fire an arrow in the form of an icicle. Shelby tried to get the number on the weaving van, but he had to pay attention instead to avoiding the bastard. He snatched his wheel to the right so as to not make contact with the SOB at the wheel of the van—a dark-skinned guy with wild eyes who looked to be on some sort of high.

Shelby continued, silently cursing the idiot behind the wheel.

In another few minutes, he saw the billowing black smoke over the tops of the houses ahead. He'd been enjoying a corned beef on rye and shooting the breeze with a friend at Dan's Fan City. Dan, the owner, was the friend. They were in heated argument about city politics when Shelby's beeper went off. While he was in semi-retirement, the heat wave had him working overtime, and he'd been called in as a consultant by the MPD on the weird fires Dr. Katra had characterized as SHC—spontaneous human combustion. Then on top of that the department had lost Carl Osterman to a DUI and a coma.

He instantly called in on his cellular and learned it was a four-alarm blaze, which in this heat could turn into enormous trouble, enough trouble in fact to take out a whole city block unless attacked quickly and vigorously. He learned it was at Winslow and Cernan in Woodhaven. Fires broke out there more often than he cared to think about, and the area was a danger to police and firefighters alike on any given night. Tonight, in this heat, anything could happen, including a race riot.

When Dan asked him if he was going to the fire, he replied, "Gonna finish my sandwich first. It'll be some time before this one's cool enough to walk through."

And so he had finished his sandwich and his Pepsi Cola.

By the time Shelby arrived on scene, one apartment house was completely in cinders, and a second one abutting it was going that way; the streets were littered with police, holding back people who had been evacuated from both buildings. Many of the people out of home were women and children, and they sent up a wail of human anguish to the night sky.

Shelby Harne had in his long career learned that on scene,

he, like any investigator, had to remain aloof and professional, and to try not to get sucked into the overwhelming grief and pain left in the wake of fire. He could hardly do his job, determine if the cause of the blaze was a poor receptacle, a frayed wire, a cigarette gone astray, or intentional arson, if he allowed emotions to get in his way. He would have none of it. The seeming lack of sentiment and empathy might displease people, but there it was; how to live as long as he had as a fireman and not lose his sanity.

Shelby now climbed from his unmarked car, and on closer inspection, he saw that at least the second fire was contained, thanks more to the lack of wind than anything the firefighters had done. Exactly how and where the fire had begun could take days, weeks even, to decipher, given that the eleven-story structure had pancaked in on itself. Unless they had an eyewitness somewhere in this crowd, but Shelby doubted it. He would need a team, and they would have to work it out in a three-dimensional grid like archeologists, trying to rebuild a past event. He'd need some of those computer whiz kids to know precisely where the fire had started, unless he got damned lucky, unless the hot spot cried out to them. Most certainly, he'd want to get a sniffer in here.

He got on his cellular phone and called to have a dog at the ready for whenever the man in charge gave him the go-ahead to enter the smoldering ruins. Then he looked about for the man who *was* in charge, and he saw Captain Luther Vanick, who somehow made shouting look calm. The captain waved and bullhorned and directed the show. At a moment when he let the bullhorn drop to his side, he acknowledged Shelby's presence with a firm nod. "It's a bit early for you just yet, Shelby."

"Looks like this coulda been a lot worse."

"Got a kid to thank for that, I hear."

"A kid?"

"Six-year-old who escaped apartment six-D, but the kid's mother never came out. Poor kid says the Devil got her."

"I guess that's one way to look at it."

"We set up a fire wall between the two buildings to offset

any further damage. The first place is going to be nothing but a pile of rubble. Going to make your job damned hard, but at least we know the epicenter was six-D."

"Maybe the kid can direct us to it," Shelby joked. "Do you have building specs?"

"They're on the way. You'll have 'em in an hour."

As Vanick said it, the devastated building they'd given up on to save the other, continued to collapse—now its outer brick facing tumbling. The onlookers gave a collective groan.

The structure could not have been much to begin with, Shelby thought. Both he and Vanick knew from experiences right here in this area that some early developers had paid no heed whatsoever to fire safety codes. Instead a lot of money had passed through a lot of hands.

"It'd be a blessing in disguise if all these old buildings could be brought down," said Vanick.

"My sentiments exactly."

"But in the meantime, where would the inhabitants go?"

"Don't know. City can only do so much. Already have every school gymnasium in the city being used as temporary shelters. Any place is better than living in a tinderbox about to go, and given this heat."

"You'd think we could catch a sea breeze one of these nights, not that we want one tonight."

"Yeah, agreed." The two veterans knew that the fire under these warm conditions would have spread faster if given some wind to work with.

Shelby thought Vanick a good captain. While some said he was overly rule conscious, too conservative, too easily unnerved by fire, Shelby knew better. Vanick, like him, had seen his share of injuries and fatalities, enough to know that any fire called for a healthy respect of the red stuff. A little positive fear saved a great deal more lives than recklessness and bravado.

Vanick's face was smoke blackened and grim. "You know, Shelby, I wouldn't rule out that the kid—the one who's looking like the little hero—he coulda been playing with a lighter, matches, a candle, or something else, and it got out of control. A neighbor who saw the flames saw the kid climbing down the fire escape at the same time. You know, beating it."

"I'll have to have a talk with the kid."

"They've got him and his aunt in back of a squad car behind the safe zone. The two of them became hysterical. The aunt tried to run into the burning building, and the kid was trying to stop her when my boys scooped them both up."

"Is the kid talking?"

"No, not to anyone but his aunt, or so I hear."

Shelby glanced to where several squad cars were parked, their strobe lights sending crazy shadows everywhere, and in the backseat of one cruiser, he saw the sad little black boy, his head against the windowpane. His eyes looked as unresponsive as two large marshmallows.

"I'll see what I can do." Shelby sauntered toward where the boy stared vacant into the night. He felt grateful in the sense that he would have first dibs at the kid, but, as he neared the squad car, he saw that Detective Eric Brannon was in the front seat, already interrogating the kid.

Brannon looked up, seeing Shelby Harne, and he climbed from the cruiser, intercepting the old fire investigator with a slight wave of the hand.

Shelby asked, "Doing fire detail work now, son? Let me see that badge of yours again!"

"Just made curious when I heard the kid claimed his mother was killed by a fire-breathing Devil man."

"Is that right? Kids say the darndest things."

"Yeah, but the aunt saw a man chase the boy to her apartment door from the fire scene. Says the kid was terrorized by him. Says the boy climbed a tree four stories high to get to her back door."

"Is that right?"

Brannon continued. "He claims his mother was turned into a flame, and that this Devil did the same to his mother's Bible."

"And here I heard the boy wasn't talking."

"He's *not,* not now. In a kind of posttraumatic shock, Shelby. All I could get was what the aunt told me he told her."

Shelby pursed his lips and nodded. "And so says the distraught aunt? Sister of the deceased. . . ."

"The boy's six, Shelby, and he needs medical attention."

"Does he have a history with fire? Does he play with fire? That's all I want to know at the moment."

"Does he like to play with fire?" Eric repeated the question. "What did you like to play with as a boy, Shelby?"

"Touché. But explain to me, Eric, who declared this a murder investigation?"

"I was on my way home when I heard the call. I swung by."

He nodded. "You should've let me have a go at the kid first, Brannon. As to this posttraumatic shock stuff . . . how do you know he's not faking it?"

"You ever see a grown man in shock, say a fireman who's just seen his buddy turned to toast?"

"Yeah, matter of fact, I have."

"And another thing, Shelby. When you question the kid, take a good strong whiff of the air inside that cruiser where he's been for a half hour."

"Don't worry. I may be old but my nose still works, and I have heard the 'Devil did it' defense a thousand times, Brannon. Poor old worn out Lucifer, the alibi of the centuries—Satan, Leviathan, Asmodeus, whatever the hell you want to call him, he always gets made out the bad guy when people decide they can't take responsibility for their own actions."

"Did I tell you that the kid is six, Shelby?"

"Six or sixteen, like I said, the 'Devil made me do it' defense is as old as the Bible."

"Look, his story is similar to the Krueshicki crime scene. There we suspect a cat was combusted and then the woman. Substitute the Bible and it's the same MO. The creep alights her Bible then smokes her."

"With a torch that burns fifteen thousand degrees? No such

thing, so I guess we have to believe the kid . . . who believes the Devil did it."

Brannon had been contemplating since leaving the crime lab that perhaps Adib Katra's death would put an end to the strange human combustion deaths. He wanted to believe the SHCs had been the result of one man's madness, and that with Adib now gone, the spontaneous combustions would end, regardless of how they were achieved.

Brannon had seen how Crysta Conover had been literally smoked into Adib's wounds by the snakelike creature revealed on the sonogram, and the more he had watched the tape, the more he thought the old ME's crazy story about another man, capable of far worse, stalking him, could be the rantings of a schizophrenic. That perhaps Adib was both men, Shakar and Shakir. But Brannon was sure that explaining any of this to Shelby would not get any results.

Brannon had gone home to get some rest and await the ten o'clock appointment to witness the strange sectioning of Dr. Adib Katra. But he had gotten a call from Jackie, and she had informed him that there had been a Seminole AC man dispatched to the address and apartment where Mrs. Krueshicki had died, and that he was missing along with his van now for almost twenty-four hours. Digesting this news and unable to rest, Brannon got up, made a light dinner, and monitored the police radio band he kept in his kitchen to catch any reports of suspicious fires. He hadn't been interested in the apartment fire until he overheard one cop on the scene reporting in that a little kid claimed his mother and her Bible had been turned into blue flame and sucked down the throat of Satan.

"All right, Shelby, I'm going to level with you, but nothing gets repeated, understood?"

Shelby smiled wide. "Fire away."

"We've got evidence on tape of an actual spontaneous human combustion that proves what happened to Stanton and the others is SHC."

Shelby looked unimpressed. "Who're we?"

"Dr. Hunter and I."

"What about Katra? What's he think of all this mumbo jumbo?"

"Fact is, he was so convinced of it, Shelby, that he . . ."

"That he what?"

"Sometime in the early morning hours, he committed suicide as a direct result of these murders by SHC. And the tape we have in our possession, well it is a tape of an actual spontaneous human combustion."

"Something for the Fox channel to televise, huh, Detective?"

"Listen to me, what this boy described about the last moments of his mother's life fits in with the tape evidence."

"You must be working too hard, Brannon."

"Kid told his aunt the Devil was wearing a brown uniform with an American Indian on it. Sound familiar? Seminole AC, Shelby, the Devil was wearing an SAC uniform, and he smoked a Bible, and then he smoked the woman."

Shelby's face went from a smile to a confused frown. "That's a little bit strange."

"What? The fact I believe there might be some truth in the kid's statement to his aunt?"

"No . . . no . . . just that, well, I was near run off the road by a guy in a SAC truck not five, ten minutes from here. You suppose he wanted to combust me?" joked Shelby, laughing now.

"Which direction? I'm serious, Shelby. Which direction was he coming from?"

"From straight out of here as fast as he could go, but the fire's been burning for over half an hour."

"So he likes to watch."

Shelby nodded. "Most fire bugs do it so they can watch us all run around like fools."

"The kid described a SAC guy, I'm telling you, down to the uniform and stitched name patch."

"You mean his aunt did."

"All right, his aunt then."

"Did she get a name?"

"He heard his mother call him Randy, and I got on the horn. Dispatch put me through to SAC."

"And?"

"Turns out SAC has a missing man, a Randy Meyers . . . hasn't shown up for work, and a van's gone missing. I put out an all-points bulletin on the van only five minutes ago."

"Hell of a coincidence all round, I'd say." Shelby chewed on an unlit pipe, considering it all. "OK, say I believe the kid for a moment, did he say if he was a white man or a black man?"

"Said he was a dark man."

"The guy rushing off was dark-skinned. He could be the crazoid who's planting all these bones around town and setting fires to simulate spontaneous combustions."

Brannon realized that even though Shelby had found unexplainable levels of heat to Stanton's ignition, he, like most men in his profession, simply could not admit to a fire without a causative factor.

Brannon thought of the APB he had put out on the van, urging radio cars within a ten-mile radius of his location to be especially vigilant. "If located, keep in sight, acknowledge location and await backup, and nobody is to approach until I am on scene. Got that?" he had ordered.

"Think I'll go have a heart-to-heart with the little boy now," said Harne, "but I do want to see that tape of yours, maybe tomorrow?"

Brannon watched Harne amble off toward the kid in the car.

While Brannon awaited word from anyone about the missing Seminole van, he paced, an uneasy feeling growing inside him the size and temperament of an angry rhinoceros. In his mind, he revisited each nightmare moment in this bizarre chain of events since that first call he and Jackie had gotten regarding Dr. Renea Stanton's car, in which she had been assaulted with some unknown fire source, something unknown even to the veteran firemen like Shelby. The trail then led to the old woman who'd died horribly in her apartment, and now this—a mother dead in a fire, her son telling a bizarre story.

Brannon tried to make sense of it all, until fifteen minutes later when the Seminole AC truck was located. Dispatch gave the disheartening news. "It appears abandoned, Detective. They want to know if you wish them to secure it and search it."

"No . . . no . . . tell them to hold until I get there."

Just then a man rushed the police line, shouting and causing a scuffle. Someone else shouted that it was the kid's father, to let Mr. Smith through, to reunite the boy with his father.

Then the man identified himself as the boy's father, calling himself Muhammad Shakar.

The name instantly caught Brannon's attention—Shakar. Coincidence? Far too much of it for the detective's palate. Brannon shouted for the uniformed cops to release the man calling himself Shakar into his custody.

Sporting a bruise over his right eye from the scuffle at the control line, Tyrone senior shouted, "Why you all got my boy in back of a cruiser! Where's my woman?" Then he snatched the car door open and began cursing at Latisha.

Brannon grabbed him and pulled him away from Latisha and the boy, and, holding him by the lapels, he shoved Smith-Shakar hard into the cruiser, telling him to shut up and listen. He then informed the gangly black man, "Your wife has died in a fire, and your son is a material witness against the man who set the fire. And right now your sister-in-law is the only one the boy can talk to. He's had enough fright for one night."

"OK, OK . . . easy, man!"

"Now, I want you to act like a man here. Can you do that? Do you understand how important it is that you take responsibility for that boy now?"

Tyrone crumpled to the street, his head in his hands. Brannon kneeled beside him. "You need to be strong for the boy's sake."

Tyrone looked into Brannon's eyes.

"He needs you now more than he's ever needed anyone."

"I know that. I see that."

"Can you act on it? Can you be a man here tonight?"

"Yes, I can."

"You're all the hope he's got aside from a loving aunt, and you really ought to value her as well. She tried to save her sister. She had to be subdued by two firemen. Now your son has seen enough to last him. He needs to see you now like a rock for him, Mr. Smith."

Tyrone looked for a moment as if he would correct the name, but instead he replied, "I'm here ain't I? I love Ty. I'll do right by him." He wiped his own tears and calmly went to his son and held him in his arms.

Brannon followed the man and asked him why he had referred to himself as Shakar. "Got in with some brothers in the Muslim way, you know. Been taking the program. Changed my slave name."

"I see."

"Why you ask?"

"I have an outside suspicion that whoever harmed your wife, sir, was in fact here to harm you."

"Don't you think I know that?" Tyrone's eyes grew wide, as if he mulled over his worst enemy, as if to say, I know exactly who you mean.

Brannon quickly tried to dispel this notion. "But I believe the man who did this to your wife was in fact after someone else named Shakar. We have good reason to suspect as much."

His eyes grew wider. "Whoa up! You saying that 'cause I changed my name all this happened to my woman?"

"Case of mistaken identity, yes sir."

Brannon could not have explained it to him if he tried. He simply said, "You got a good-looking, healthy son there, Tyrone. You want to give him all your attention from here on out."

Brannon stepped away from the family and told uniformed policemen that he wanted the man and his son placed into twenty-four-hour protective custody.

"I gotta go check out that Seminole van," he told the uniformed cops. "If my partner should show up, send her on."

Brannon drove off for the location of the van. As he drove to the location, he thought of Randy Meyers, the Seminole worker who had gone missing now for twenty-four hours. Randy had a history of drinking, and a coworker had been trying to keep his disappearance hush-hush until this became untenable.

At the scene where the van had been abandoned, Brannon found additional, strange evidence of the fire-eating creature he so wanted to disbelieve possible, the monster of the scrolls. The back interior doors were scorched and blackened with that same human soot they had found in Dr. Stanton's car, at the Krueshicki apartment, and it would likely also be found in trace amounts in the rubble of the Smith apartment. Whatever thing was behind all this, it left a trail of terror and fire. It meant Brannon had to eat his words and tell Angelica that there was indeed a second serpent stalking Adib, just as Katra had said. These deaths were the work of evil incarnate.

Brannon's partner, Jackie, found him looking over the empty and abandoned van. "Look familiar?" he asked.

"Eerily so," she replied. "What the hell's going on in our city, Eric? Shit like this," she pointed at the interior of the van, "makes you half believe in that crazy story Katra fed us."

Brannon stepped away from the stench of Randy Meyers's abandoned van. Leaning against his car, he tried to put the timing together. While Adib Katra could conceivably have been the catalyst in Stanton's and Krueshicki's deaths, and possibly the AC repairman, he could not have been setting anyone ablaze tonight. Yet Harne had seen a dark-skinned man driving a Seminole AC van away from the fire scene at the Smith place. Perhaps it was the man Adib had warned them about, Hari Shakir, that Harne had seen tonight. And if the kid's story was true, the Devil was wearing a light brown uniform like those worn by Seminole repairmen.

Was it Adib's Hari Shakir?

"You know something you're not telling me, Eric. Something you're holding out. What is it?"

"Jackie, if I told you what I suspected, you wouldn't believe me."

"Try me."

"All right, damn it. It's just like Adib says in the deathbed confession he made."

"That these deaths are caused by a guy named Hari Shakir, and that he's carrying around some kind of serpent beast within him that torches people and turns them into this?" She continued to stare into the blackened interior of the van, where a scattering of small bones and teeth lay amid the black soot.

"I've seen it happen, spontaneous human combustion, at the crime lab. We have it on tape."

Shaking her head over this, she said, "Sure . . . meanwhile, I've found our killer, Eric. Adib must have known the guy."

"What're you talking about?"

"Well I did some old-fashioned police work, *Detective* Brannon," she said in a mocking tone.

"Is that right?"

"While you've been chasing fire alarms, I went back to Memorial and asked about anyone on the payroll named Hari Shakir, and guess what?"

Brannon straightened at this. "He was working there?"

"A Hari Shakir signed on as an assistant to maintenance two weeks before Dr. Stanton was killed."

"Son of a bitch."

"Hari disappeared after his shift the night Dr. Stanton was killed. They haven't seen or heard from him since."

"Good work, Jackie."

"I simply took what we learned from Adib on the tape and retraced our steps. Now we just have to cuff him before he can use his g'damn flamethrower or whatever it is on us."

"We have to find the fucker first."

"I have an address on him. Shall we pay Hari a visit?"

"Let's do it. Let's go see the bastard."

They had the uniformed officers impound the AC van, and,

getting into Eric's car, they rushed off for the address she had on Hari Shakir.

Inside the cab of the car as the streetlights danced over the windshield, Brannon said, "This guy is dangerous, Jackie. We still don't understand what it is we're dealing with."

"Wanna call for backup?"

"Wouldn't hurt to have a SWAT team on hand, and tell them to bring a canister of liquid nitrogen with a wand attachment."

"What the hell're you talking about, liquid nitrogen?"

"Bullets may bring this Hari down, but if he's got this serpent thing inside him that I saw inside Adib Shakir, it will need freezing."

"Freezing?"

"Just make the request. Tell them it's a special-needs case."

"I'll see what I can do." She had difficulty making dispatch understand her request. Finally she got off the radio and said, "All set. They'll meet us at the scene. Now, do you want to explain this liquid-nitrogen thing?"

"At the crime lab earlier today Dr. Hunter, an intern named Porter, and I . . . we all witnessed a young woman combusted before our eyes, Jackie. This thing is real, this thing Adib spoke of on the tape. The thing inside him, even from his dead body, attacked this woman and turned her into smoke and sucked her into Katra's open wounds."

"You saw this happen before your eyes?"

"On tape."

"Ahhh . . . well . . . they are doing wonders with special effects these days."

"No, this really happened. A fire-raining, fire-breathing ancient Indian serpent. I've seen it inside Adib Katra's body. We contained it with liquid nitrogen, and I watched Angelica film it using a sonogram device. It's a strange supernatural serpent, and, according to Adib, this Hari character has one of these snakes inside him, too."

"This is all very fucking confusing, Eric."

"I know."

"I don't believe in fairy tales, Eric, and neither did you until you began spending time with Hunter."

"What's that supposed to mean?"

"You can't really believe all this fire-breathing dragon insane shit Katra fed her, can you? Tape or no tape."

"You haven't seen what kind of power this thing can unleash. I have. And just suppose this Shakir guy we're talking about . . . suppose he's carrying around the same kind of power I saw released from Adib's corpse? It's the only answer left as to how these people died."

"Eric, all I know is that once we get our hands on this creep, he's going to fold just like they all do. He's going to turn out to be some low-life loner who can't get it up, only this son of a whore's maybe a failed chemistry major. I tell you, once we take him down, all this weird-assed serpent cult stuff will vanish. Now, let's pick the creep up."

"Trust me, Jackie. Whatever you do, you don't want to touch this guy."

"We have to cuff him . . . may even have to subdue him."

"Just let me handle him, all right?"

"Sure . . . sure, you can take the collar."

Brannon considered the appearance of what he contemplated. If he shot Shakir on sight, he would likely go to prison for his actions, and still it would not guarantee the death of the beast within Shakir. It was a sacrifice he was willing to take if he could end Shakir's kill spree, but then what of the serpent?

"Just follow my lead," he told Jackie, "and trust me."

14

They were met at 224 Sewell Street by backup units, and a SWAT team had already been deployed around the building, but no one had any liquid nitrogen tanks. The SWAT team captain explained that on getting the message, he had thought it a mistake and had ignored it.

"Do you want to explain to me why you need liquid nitrogen on hand, Detective Brannon?"

"Let's just go in, shall we?" said Jackie, marching off and into the building, going for the apartment. Eric trailed after her, his weapon drawn, saying, "I told you to follow my lead."

Four of the SWAT members pursued them into the building, the chief saying his men would go in first, but Jackie had gotten a lead on everyone, and she was already pounding on the door, shouting, "Police, open up!"

A battering ram was brought up.

Jackie called out again demanding, "Hari Shakir, open up!"

The superintendent called out to them, "He's not in! Please, don't destroy the door! He hasn't been back for a while."

Everyone relaxed. "How long?" asked Jackie.

"All day and all night, I think. Hope he hasn't skipped out like the guy before him," replied the thin little man.

"We've got enough probable cause to break it in, so you want to open it, do so now," said Eric.

"This place is within walking distance of the hospital where Shakir worked and Stanton died," Jackie pointed out. "He's our man."

Outside, backup units and SWAT members watched the exits, including the roof and fire escape.

The door swung open to the faint odor of ozone. "No one home," muttered Brannon as they entered.

Behind them the superintendent said, "Tenant before him skipped out without a sign. Made a mess of the place. This guy Hari's been a good tenant, picked up the rent like it was a sublet, and he even said he'd clean up the mess Jackson left behind. I got no complaints. What's he done? Whataya want him for?"

Jackie glared at the little man and said, "Multiple murder, so if and when you see him, give us a call." She pushed a card into his trembling hand.

They began an extensive search of the dingy little place. Every room turned up bare, every closet the same. Nothing. No flamethrowers, no torches, no mechanical devices, not even a television or radio. The refrigerator and cupboards were absolutely empty save for spoiled milk and rotting vegetables.

"Eric . . . over here," Jackie called out, flashing her light onto the heavy drapes at a window overlooking the street.

Against the drapes, looking like the shroud of Turin, they saw an anguished face and the outline of a man.

"When's the last time you saw Mr. Shakir?" asked Eric.

"Late yesterday. Looked like he was going off to the hospital. Looked like he had a lot on his mind."

"Is Dr. Katra's story about a guy named Hari Shakir stalking him taking on any more meaning for you, Jackie?" asked Eric.

"This guy and Katra are somehow linked, Eric, like he said on the tape, but I'm still having a hell of a time wrapping my mind around this case, and what you said happened at the hospital." She lifted the drape with the barrel of her gun.

Sooty, Styrofoam-like ash rained from the old cloth. At the foot of the drapes, concealed behind them, a half a foot and a few fingers lay.

"Why didn't the drapes go up in flames?" she asked. "A refrigerator I can see, but this?"

Brannon saw a newspaper peeking from beneath the bed, and he fished it out with his heel. It was folded on a story covering Carl Osterman's accident. The report said that he had been investigating a suspicious car fire hours before the accident. "Hari's showing a little too much interest in Osterman. Let's put a surveillance on the apartment and get over to County General."

Hari Shakir had slipped back into his apartment at Sewell Street without alerting the nosey neighbors or the superintendent, and he had changed back into one of his blue Memorial maintenance uniforms before coming to County General Hospital in search of Chief Carl Osterman. The uniform's smiley-face patch with his name on it put people at ease. At reception he asked for Carl Osterman's room number. The receptionist said it was past visiting hours, but he convinced her that it was the only time he could look in on his old friend, and that the comatose fireman had saved his little girl a year earlier. He told her he worked long hours at Memorial. She gave him a tag and clearance.

"Do you know if there is a medical professional named Shakar working here?" he asked as an afterthought.

"Hmmm . . . no, I don't believe so." She scanned a registry. "No, sorry."

Hari had felt the growing fear that Adib had done something drastic, that he had wounded the beast within himself and possibly had killed himself out of some misguided desperation. The sense of it was deep felt, and the snake within Hari had become extremely agitated and absolutely impatient. He wanted information, and he wanted it now.

Hari felt a terror growing within him. While he wanted completion and wholeness just as the snake god wanted it, still a lingering fear of that moment could not be denied. He wondered how much of himself would survive in the consciousness of the beast, despite its promises to him.

He rode the elevator up and stepped off at the third floor, finding it quiet. No one at the nurses' station except an elderly woman working over a report at her computer. Another nurse was darting into a lounge area. Hari located room 312.

Inside room 312 Leonard Pasternak lay in a full-body cast, his body elevated, and he had a view of the comatose patient across from him there at County General. He could not speak, as his jaw was wired. The motorcycle accident had left him in horrible shape, and his doctors were talking about years of rehabilitation. Tired of watching TV, he had little to keep his mind occupied, so when anyone came into the room, he was instantly curious.

He watched a man in a pair of blue jeans and a dark shirt—looking like a service uniform—come in to see the comatose fireman in the other bed. Perhaps it was another in the endless trail of firemen come to pay their respects. Leonard watched the upright man bend over the other bed and stare down at Osterman. In the semi-darkness of the room, the visitor appeared black.

Leonard looked out from bandages encircling his face. For a moment the visitor regarded him, staring at the full-body cast, when he asked, "Is this the fireman, Osterman?"

Leonard could not reply, unable to even shake his head as it was in a medical vise grip. He picked up the marker and paper the nurse had provided, and with his one good hand, he began to write but stopped short. If this guy was visiting Osterman and knew him, why didn't he recognize the man? Leonard was unsure what to write, what to ask the stranger.

"He saved my child's life," lied Hari.

Leonard wanted to nod but couldn't. He wrote instead, holding the pad up to Hari's black eyes, noticing how they seemed to pierce the darkness.

Are you a friend? Was struck over, replaced by: *Yes, that's him.*

"Good . . . I have found him. The newspapers said he has

worked thirty years with the Miami fire department. He must know a lot of medical people. Perhaps he knows Adib Shakar."

Leonard didn't know how to answer this, so he let it go. He didn't like the way the dark-skinned foreign-looking man talked. Something creepy in his accent and those penetrating eyes. They seemed to glow in the darkness.

Then the seemingly grateful man turned back to Osterman and said, "I am Hari, and I have come for you."

The last thing Leonard saw before the eruption of flame and gas over Osterman's body was this Hari fellow taking the fireman's hands in his. Suddenly the dark stranger's form became larger, his skin rigid and scaly, and then *whoosh,* a flashover of light and Osterman was turned into a gaseous cloud. Leonard's eyes widened even further as he watched these gases being consumed by the dark stranger. A small rain of black gunk had slapped onto Leonard's body cast as a result of the quiet explosion centered over Osterman's co-matose body. Amazingly, no alarms or water sprinklers went off, only the monitor for Osterman's vital signs. The IV drip that had been in his arm dangled loose and was dripping on the floor now.

Leonard shook and tore at the contraptions holding him in place, but he had no escape. His hands scrambled for the buzzer to call for help, and he struggled to locate it, fumbling until he found it. But he hit the TV button instead, an episode of *Law & Order* filling the screen. Finally his fingers found the call button on the console. He repeatedly buzzed, as ter-rified gibberish spewed from his mouth. His knuckles became white from holding so tightly to the tenuous lifeline of the buzzer. Unable to scream, unable to run, his heart alone raced, his eyes wide with fear as the man calling himself Hari turned to him with a flared head and snake eyes, grin-ning.

"I think this time I will get useful information," Hari Shakir said to Leonard. He then took the buzzer from Leon-ard's one useful hand and dangled it away from him. He pointed at a smiley-face patch on his uniform. "Have a nice day."

Shakir turned to leave, but he ducked behind the door instead when a nurse rushed into the room, choking on the acrid odors left behind by the combustion, and she stared at the blackened canoe-sized hole in the bed all the way through to the floor beneath the bed where Osterman had been. She reached out and placed a light finger on a gnarled bone dangling at the foot of the hole. The bone was hot to her touch, and she cringed back as it fell into the seared folds of the mattress.

Leonard tried to scream and rattle the metal trapeze, the bars and chains surrounding him, attempting to alert her, but she was in shock, and he was helpless in his cast.

Hari stepped from the darkness, and she wheeled to face him. Hari wrapped his arms around the nurse, and she imploded into a gaseous ball that he seemed to absorb through his serpentlike scaly pores.

Leonard had not seen Hari's transformation so well the first time, as his back was to him, but now he saw the man's head and face had taken on the shape and features of a king cobra, his tongue darting out, his mouth wide and sucking down the gases that the nurse had become.

"Michelle," said Hari, knowing her name and her mind.

Hari returned to the door, peeking out. Unable to turn his head, Leonard's eyes alone tracked the monster.

Choking on the odors filling the room, Leonard struggled to find the coiled wire of the buzzer, and when he retrieved the thing, he continued to squeeze it madly, his heart pounding, his eyes fixed on the blackened hole where Osterman had been. Hari had stepped out of his line of vision, and for a moment, Leonard thought perhaps he would be spared, and he wondered who would believe the insane story he was left holding.

Then he sensed someone behind him, another nurse perhaps come to help him, standing silently, likely paralyzed by the sight of what was left of Osterman—a few bones dangling amid the black hole.

Whoever had come into the room, stepped into Leonard's view, and Leonard's heart stopped. It was the same man who had turned Osterman and Michelle into cinders and the black gel that had exploded onto Leonard's cast.

Hari's smile curled in sinister derision at Leonard's plight. "I should let you live to tell your story . . . but I am curious now how to suck you out of there."

Leonard pleaded in unintelligible gibberish as the thing took hold of his one free hand, and it plunged its serpent's tongue into his screaming mouth. Leonard felt the rush of heat rise from within him, putting pressure on the cast all round him. Neither the nurse nor Osterman knew what had hit them, she being taken totally by surprise, and he being in a coma, but Leonard knew how he was dying and the knowledge of it tortured his last moments on earth.

The only thing left hanging over Leonard's bed was the cast itself, the interior filled with soot that peeked out through the eye sockets and mouth, and a few fissures that had opened up during the combustion that had occurred inside the cast. It was an interesting and satisfying burn, Hari thought. With the loss of Leonard's weight on the cast, the chain holding his left leg had come crashing down, breaking part of the cast at the leg, spilling out some of the human creosote onto the sheets and floor. A few loose bandages and the metal parts that had held the man in place dangled like a strange mobile under the airflow of a ventilation duct.

Hari took a moment to congratulate himself. It was the perfect burn that Hari and the serpent had always longed for.

The bed itself had been untouched, unlike Osterman's.

Hari stepped from the room, the odors spilling out behind him. He closed the door and made his way to the stairwell. An elderly nurse wearing a face mask was reassuring patients spilling from their rooms, asking for calm, telling them maintenance was on the way. When she spied Hari about to duck into the stairwell, she shouted, "Are you here to have a look-see about the odors coming through the vents? Should we call the fire department?"

She had telephoned maintenance and she'd assumed Hari

was their answer. *These night-shift guys were useless,* she thought. "What're we going to do about it?"

"I already took care of it, ma'am," said Hari, going through the door. "The odor is maybe displeasing but it won't kill you."

"What the hell is it?"

"Is coming from room three one two, burnt-out machine."

"Oh, yeah, it does have a machine odor to it, and I did send Michelle to check on a failed monitor. We'll have to get another one."

"That is not my department, madam," Hari said, sliding through the door as other nurses and a doctor rushed past, going for the source of the problem.

The elderly nurse wracked her brain for why she hadn't answered the buzzer light on bed two in the room. She'd become so sick and tired of Pasternak's unintelligible whining. All hours of the day and night, the body-cast patient wanted special attention, a straw tipped here, a scratch there, someone to raise him, lower him, position his pillow when there was no way he could even feel his damned pillow. Classic case of the boy who cried wolf, and she had simply stopped responding. But how would that look now? How would it play out if the drunken fireman died because she hadn't responded quickly enough, waiting for Michelle and sending her down to the room, while she had gone for coffee.

Her thoughts were answered by screams coming from 312. The doctors and nurses who'd rushed to the room had all staggered back out into the hallway, gasping for air. The doctor shouted, "They're all gone! The patients are gone!"

"And where's Michelle?" asked one of the nurses.

Hari heard the commotion as he went down to the stairwell toward the main floor and exits below. Hari dashed for a rear exit, and, when he got outside in the heat, he felt much better. But his mind, for the moment, was filled with conflicting images, all speeding through his consciousness, the lives and memories of Leonard and Michelle in his way. He had to awaken the memories of the fireman now inside him, to search his mind for information. See what he knew of a man named Adib Shakar.

Eric and Jackie had rushed to the hospital where Osterman had been admitted. Flashing his badge, Brannon asked for Osterman's room.

The receptionist keyed in the name into her computer. She sat below an air duct, remarking on an unpleasant odor, when she said, "Three one two. What is that awful smell?" she added.

Brannon and Jackie knew the odor wafting across to their side of the counter. "It's him! He's here!" shouted Brannon, racing for the elevator.

The odor of death permeated the elevator car they rode up, and, finding the third floor, they pushed past confused patients. The detectives had their weapons drawn as they ran for 312. There they found two nurses dazed, struggling to come to terms with what they'd discovered, while a doctor was on a cell phone, calling for police. "Christ, we're too late. He's come and gone!"

Jackie agreed. "He's damn sure been here."

They ushered the nurses back and rushed the room, choking on the acrid odors and the horrible sights awaiting them. The air in the room was supercharged with ozone, far more than any previous scene, and this told them two things: the body count was higher than at any other crime scene, and that if they had only gotten there a few minutes earlier, they may have been able to save Osterman.

They stood frozen in the doorway, staring at the bizarre scene of the full-body cast suspended in air over the one bed. The twisted apparatus around Pasternak's bed was still twirling in the wind below an air duct, and the black Jell-O residue covered what they only now realized was an *empty* full-body cast. Through a broken-away leg, soot and debris had poured, revealing that Leonard Pasternak had combusted within the confines of the cast. Stepping closer, the detectives leaned in over the empty eye sockets and empty mouth.

"Jesus, Eric, this poor bastard had no chance whatsoever."

"You think Osterman did? Shit, the man was in a coma."

"From coma to combustion."

They looked across at Osterman's bed, a hollowed-out center of blackened materials outlining where his form had been.

Jackie stepped around Pasternak's bed, going closer to Carl's, when she slipped and fell into a circle of charred human fatty tissues on the floor there. "Fuck!" she shouted, frustrated and dirtied.

Eric helped her to her feet, her clothing and hands discolored. He grabbed a towel lying over the back of a chair, and, while she cleaned up, he examined what she had slipped on. He lifted a small ankle and foot. An ankle bracelet had been seared into the flesh, and the toenails still shone bright with pink nail polish beneath the soot. "Call Ripley's. You were tripped by a dead nurse," he said.

She ignored this, her eyes fixed on what remained of Osterman.

"Like to see what Shelby Harne makes of this," Eric said, followed by a coughing jag. His mouth and nose were filled to choking in the highly charged atmosphere of the room. Osterman's bed looked like a burnt-out canoe, the outline of his body evident, far more visible than the poor fellow who had died inside the walls of his own cast.

Above Osterman's bed and above the area where the nurse had died, Eric made out the telltale sign of the stain of superheated gases, but not so over Pasternak's bed. Any afterburn would be on the roof of the cast itself. Solidified ash like that found in Stanton's car was everywhere.

Nurse Matilda Ernhardt timidly peeked in to the room, struggling to say something to the detectives. "There was a man here," she struggled to say between broken gasps, "a dark-skinned, tall man . . . looked like perhaps he was . . . Pakistani. Name on his uniform was Hari. I thought he was working maintenance, but I checked. They never heard of him."

"Of course, he's wearing his maintenance uniform from

Memorial," Jackie said. She then asked the nurse, "Was he carrying anything? A device of some sort like a flame-thrower?"

"No . . . nothing . . . not a thing."

Brannon had seen and heard enough. He marched Jackie and the nurse outside. "Lock this room until a forensic investigation team can go over it," he told the nurse. He then took Jackie aside. "You saw what happened in there. You saw how this guy turns people into that black Jell-O shit you slipped in. We're on the trail of something *not* human. The same something Adib warned us about."

"Whatever Hari Shakir is, we were just behind the bastard. He came here for a reason, to find Osterman! Why?"

Other people in the building had come to have a look at the carnage in 312. Brannon cursed that they had been held up for as long as they had in the hospital room, but it had been such an assault on the senses, he understood their having slowed in their chase of Hari.

"Maybe Carl stumbled onto something that pointed to this Hari Shakir. Who knows?"

"But Carl was in a coma."

"And Hari wanted to make sure he never came out of it."

"Well . . . the bastard's long gone by now. So, what do we do next, Eric?"

"You heard the nurse. He wasn't carrying any kind of acetylene torch. This is all balled up with Adib Katra—Shakar, he called himself on the tape."

"All right, I admit it's certainly looking like this guy is trying to get at Adib, but Adib's dead now."

"You don't have all the facts. That fire tonight at the Smith residence, turns out Smith had changed his name to *Shakar*. And there's that compelling tape in Angelica's possession I want you to see. This damn thing wants Adib dead or alive."

Jackie thought about this, and she thought of all that she had seen and heard on Katra's tape, and all that she had read from his will and the suicide note left to Dr. Hunter. "So we're supposed to be chasing an ancient serpent beast out of Adib's scrolls?"

"I only know it's real and if half what Adib said is true, we've got to get back to Angelica and see that Katra's body is destroyed according to his wishes tonight."

"You think this Hari character is on his way there?"

"I don't know, but his goal is to find Adib, like I said, dead or alive, so let's get over there."

They went for Brannon's unmarked car and raced from the lot to the police crime lab. He called ahead, dispatch putting him through to Angelica. "We have to do that laser sectioning thing on Adib's body now! No more delays. Prep the body."

"What's happened, Eric?"

"This thing Adib warned us about is on a rampage. It just blew away Carl Osterman and any poor schmuck who happened to be in the room with him. This thing is getting closer, into our circle of acquaintances. In fact, he could be on his way to your location now."

"All right, the body should be ready for sectioning."

"Angelica, be careful.

"I'll take every precaution."

Eric hung up the radio and said to his partner, "I just want one clean shot at this Hari guy."

"What about the mess left back there at County?" asked Jackie as they raced through a red light, their strobe and siren stopping traffic.

"Call it in to Ames. Tell him to get Shelby Harne and a team of evidence techs to process it. Right now, we need to get back to the crime lab. Angelica has frozen Adib's body and is planning the sectioning tonight, and she needs us as witnesses and armed guards."

Jackie asked, "Supposing Katra and this Hari guy are sharing the same psychosis?"

"Good theory. But even if it is some aberrant shared madness, psychosis, I'm still right, Jackie. He'll *target* Adib or rather his remains as part of that psychosis. But it goes beyond a warped mental state. It's physical too, the tattoo, the

DNA, the damned snake crawling around inside Adib that I told you about."

"I want to see this sonogram you're talking about."

"The sonogram Angelica made clearly shows something's alive inside Katra's body, a snake of some sort, and the damn thing has two heads."

"God, I can't believe all of this, Eric."

He shook his head vehemently. "No, neither can I, but it's all true, and if you're hunting this thing with me, then you need to know the nature of the beast."

Brannon put the gas pedal to the floorboard, speeding across another intersection.

Hari Shakir felt an overwhelming sense that something had changed. Throughout the week he had felt closer to Adib Shakar than ever before. His serpent had been telepathically aware of this truth. It had sent out powerful signals to its brother, and there was a sense of certainty that Shakar had gotten the messages. But now there was none of that, and Hari feared the worst, that Shakar had destroyed himself and possibly the serpent within him.

Getting information out of Osterman was painstakingly slow and difficult. Hari had found a small neighborhood park, empty of anyone, and he sat in the playground on the jungle gym, his head in his hands, feeling battered and bruised from the frightening idea that he had spent his entire life in pursuit of a goal that his other half could so easily put to an end.

But Hari was not giving up, and neither was the serpent within him. Osterman's coma had clouded his knowledge, but it was still in there for Hari to find. He need only search diligently, but he feared time was running out.

"It's a cruel fate I have been brought to," he said to the night, "spending a lifetime in search of my brother."

Hari heard someone rummaging around the alleyway behind him. It sounded human, but he had no appetite, and he must focus on the task at hand.

*   *   *

Eric and Jackie tore into the lot and found their way up to the crime lab and morgue on the thirteenth floor, the clock reading 9:46 P.M. When Angelica saw them coming, she rushed up to Brannon, who said, "We can't delay. This thing's killed five more people tonight, and it's in heat to find Adib's body."

"We've got a problem, Eric."

"What's that?"

"Adib's body isn't ready yet."

"What? Why not?"

"I thought my thermometer on the freezer door was lying, but I ran a check on it with the DIAL laser."

"Dial?" asked Jackie, curious.

"DIAL—Diagrammatic Imaging Autopsy by Laser. It's the program we use for laser sectioning, and it's telling me the body's not yet ready."

"He hasn't frozen in all this time?" Brannon was stunned. "What happened? It's been what, four, five hours in the freezer."

"A problem with the cooling system. It shut down but no alarm went off, and no one realized it for several hours. Heat wave has caught up to us. No brownout this time, just a system failure to the freezer units, which are all connected."

"Jesus . . ." Brannon looked in through the freezer door at Adib's body. "So he only looks frozen?"

"Right, Adib's body is frozen but not frozen solid. The body must be absolutely rock hard throughout if we're to section it."

"What about putting him into a cryogenics tank? Doesn't that work on liquid nitro?"

"Yes, and that would work, if we had one. The closest cryogenics storage facility is in Orlando, and then Atlanta, but they are going to want a lot of paperwork, and prepara-tion could take longer than we have. Besides, moving him, as you know, could get someone killed."

Hearing this, Jackie asked, "What're you saying?"

"If the body thaws, it becomes a danger to anyone touching it."

"Like a contagion?" she asked.

"Worse yet. You'll have to see the tape to believe it," replied Angelica.

"He's like a ticking bomb," said Eric to his partner. Then he turned to Angelica. "I want Jackie to see the sonogram, too. In your office, while we figure out what to do about the body."

"Can't you exchange Adib's body with another corpse in one of the drawers?" asked Jackie.

"They're all on the same system, run by computer. It's stopped producing cold. I've been on the phone to get a computer-savvy repairman in and he's on his way. But I don't think Adib will be ready before morning."

"Morning? We don't have that kind of time. I think this Hari Shakir is right on our heels."

"Everything we need for the laser sectioning is here; fact is, no other facility in the city has DIAL. We either do it here or we don't do it at all."

"Let's see that tape and sonogram," said Jackie.

Angelica dropped her gaze and nodded. "This way." She led them to her office, and she spent some time searching for the tape. "Something's wrong. . . ."

"What is it?" asked Eric.

"The tape is gone, along with the sonogram of the snake. Damn . . . damn it's got to be Porter. The jerk's a video buff. Likely made copies by now, and he probably thought he could get them back before they were missed."

Brannon clenched his fist. "Porter's likely looking for the highest bidder, no doubt. Shit."

"Weasel," muttered Angelica.

"Give me his home address. I'll pay him a visit," Brannon suggested.

Angelica shook her head. "Let's see if he's got the balls to show up for the sectioning first."

"All right . . . OK."

Angelica told Jackie about the taped death of the intern

and more about the sonogram done of the thing inside Adib's body. "After all that, I laid down here for a nap and woke up to the freezer problem. Where the hell is that repairman?"

Angelica made some fresh coffee at the countertop in her office. Brannon and Jackie joined her for a cup, and Brannon described the suspicious fire in Woodhaven, Jackie's discovery of a man using the name Hari Shakir who had been working at Memorial Hospital, and their discovery at his apartment. "Which led us to County General, where Carl Osterman was combusted the same way as the others."

"It's getting closer to Adib with each feeding, almost as if . . . as if it interrogates its victims before killing," Angelica mused.

"It's not exactly being selective," said Jackie. "It killed two others in the room with Osterman, and Osterman wasn't talking to anybody. He was in a coma."

"Strange," she replied. "It bears out Adib's words. I had an unsettling nightmare while I dozed, that Adib's soul, his core being would be stolen if I could not save it."

"His soul?" asked Jackie.

"I know it sounds foolish. Nightmares generally are, but they are also highly symbolic."

"I would have thought his soul had long departed the body by now," said Eric.

"Perhaps not . . . not so long as the serpent inside lives. At least, that's what my dream was saying."

Jackie choked on her coffee. "Your dream told you his soul was somehow trapped with the serpent, inside his own corpse?"

"Dreams are symbolic—representational, abstract—right?" Angelica replied.

"Go on."

"It's not so much Adib's body it wants, this thing inside him and this thing chasing him, but his soul, his being."

Brannon whistled. "If you're right . . . what happens to the souls of Hari Shakir's victims?" asked Eric, when suddenly alarms went off in the building. "What the hell is that?"

"Fire alarms . . . Any other night, I'd say it was a false

alarm. But at the moment, with that thing after Adib's body?" asked Angelica. "I wouldn't gamble on it."

"But you have been experiencing electrical problems, outages, the freezer shutdown," he replied.

"Yeah, most likely the heat wave," Jackie said, unconvinced of it herself.

Angelica got on the phone and called down to the lobby at the main desk. "That's odd."

"No answer?" asked Jackie.

"Nothing. There's always someone on duty."

"Try security," suggested Jackie with Eric looking on.

Lights dimmed, flickered like so many candles vying for air to live on. Then the lights went out altogether. "What the hell?" Brannon said, the alarms still blaring. "I got a bad feeling about this."

Angelica dialed for security and found the lines busy. "Something's wrong. Earlier I took the precaution of asking reception to let me know if anyone comes in claiming to be related to Dr. Katra. I hope it has nothing to do with these alarms."

"Try security again. If we get no answer, we've got to find a way out of here with Adib's body." Brannon stared out her office window to the street below, seeing people spilling from the building. "One way or another, it looks like we need to get out of the building."

Jackie and Angelica stared out the window. A police car now pulled up to the entrance below. "Let me get this straight," said Jackie. "You two intend on taking Adib out of here? Suppose it is a false alarm? Or a small contained fire? What happens if you two race out with a body in tow? We're already hip deep in shit with Captain Ames for leaving the scene of a crime at General, and now we're plotting this?"

Still no answer came from security.

The elevator doors opened and Hari boarded for the thirteenth-floor morgue, knowing from Deana Hughes that she'd been warned about Hari, and he learned that an Adib Katra, the city medical examiner, lay dead somewhere in the morgue and that he was of Indian descent. Was Katra and Shakar one and the same person? Had Shakar killed himself in a rash and foolish attempt to escape his destiny? Hari felt the Shakar serpent nearby, and the body was near . . . inside a dysfunctional cooler.

Hari felt a great elation come over him. At last, the time of union had arrived.

But the elevator was dead. The fire alarms had shut them down. Hari cursed, stepped out of the open door and stared at the stunned security guard who held his gun up to him. An errant shot was fired, missing Hari, who ducked into the stairwell.

He came face-to-face with Donald Porter.

Dr. Donald Porter could only think to save himself. He had overheard enough of the killer's conversation with his victim to know what this man named Hari wanted—Adib Katra's remains. "Thirteenth floor . . . thirteenth floor refrigeration room," he blurted out.

People were crowding down the stairwell toward them in a flood of confusion and out into the lobby. "Take me to my brother, Adib," Hari ordered Porter. "I feel his coldness . . . his aloneness. We belong together."

Porter fingered the wand of the fire extinguisher that he held behind him now, thinking it a pitiful weapon, but hoping surprise might save him. Quaking and fearful, suspecting that he'd be killed no matter what, Porter thrust the wand into Hari's face and fired its contents into his black eyes. He then swung the canister into the man's skull and dashed out into the lobby, joining the crowd pushing out.

Alarms continued to go off everywhere. Uniformed security guards had come rushing to the aide of the receptionist, but not a scrap of her could be found, and Porter went to grab a phone to call upstairs to warn Dr. Hunter of what was on its way. He ran behind the reception desk, grabbed a phone, and dropped to the floor to hide, then his hands registered the fact that the phone was a mass of melted plastic and misshapen metal parts, and his eyes fell on a right lower leg, ankle, and charred foot still in its shoe—what was left of Deana. The leg dangled from her chair by a pool of black glue.

Porter backed out and raced for the security-checkpoint phones. Old Bennett, the security guard, was shaken but ushering people out. Porter got on the phone, calling for Angelica.

As he dialed, Porter replayed everything in his mind, wondering if he could have prevented it, but there seemed nothing he could have done differently.

He had earlier made his way to the elevators with the tapes he meant to replace before anyone noticed their having been *borrowed*. Standing, waiting at the elevators, he'd begun to worry, when he overheard the man asking about Adib Katra. He had looked across the lobby to see that it was a man in a maintenance uniform who had gone through the checkpoint just ahead of him, and he noticed just how dirty, sooty even, the uniform was, as if the man had just climbed out of a chimney.

Deana Hughes, the short brunette at the reception desk, was insisting that the man sign in before going any further. The man reluctantly turned from the direction where he pointed and muttered, "Katra . . ."

The tall, dark man then went to her. He took the pen and roster she extended, and he stared at the offering.

"Perhaps I can direct you," she had said.

"I am here to fix everything." He signed in and she read upside down.

"Oh, you mean the refrigeration units upstairs?" replied Deana.

"These are in the morgue on the thirteenth floor, I am told."

Porter saw no tools, no work order, nothing. He immediately became suspicious.

"Dr. Katra sent for you?" Porter had asked, stepping in.

"He called our company, yes. I am hearing all good things about Dr. Katra."

The stranger seemed to be going through some rehearsed lines, but struggling both with the language and fragmented memories.

"I was told to see him. I understand he and I come from the same province in India. We have much in common."

"And who told you this?"

Porter noticed the receptionist looked nervous, and her hand went beneath the counter. She looked as if she might panic. "I'll just call upstairs to see if Dr. Katra is in," she lied.

Porter realized that Deana had pressed a silent alarm, and he knew that security would be on its way. He decided that Dr. Hunter must have left word to stall anyone asking after Adib or his remains.

"A mutual friend, a fireman told me about Adib."

And you just happen to work in cooling systems, Porter thought. Don reached for his cell phone, deciding he should call Dr. Hunter to let her know what was going on here, when he realized that he'd left the phone in his car. He silently cursed his forgetfulness and wracked his brain for what to do now. The only security guard in sight was the old man checking people through the metal detector. Old Mr. Bennett was the closest man with a weapon, but the security guard's attention remained on getting people through the checkpoint. It was late, and Niles Bennett was shorthanded and partially deaf.

Porter saw the dark man's agitation growing with each punch Deana made on the telephone keypad, and then he saw the strange man grab the receptionist by the hand, saying, "No call, no need to call!"

"I can't let you into that area without clearance, sir," said Deana.

"Enough!" he shouted, losing his temper.

Porter had then seen two security officers on their way to the desk, but they were at a distance.

Hari held firm to the girl's wrist, stopping her call, while Porter insisted he let go of her.

"I'll take care of this *my* way," he said.

Porter was about to grab the man when a searing ball of fire and gases replaced Deana's hands and arms, and then rocketed through her body, consuming all of her.

Porter's eyes had met Deana's at the instant before her entire body was consumed. Her last words were swallowed in the combustion, going unheard.

That was when Porter felt the enormity of the terror and that the incineration had occurred so instantaneously that no one else had witnessed it. Porter had then stumbled back, slipping into the stairwell, where he stashed the tapes and discovered the fire extinguisher. No fire extinguisher had ever looked so small to him before. Seconds before the monster plowed through the door, he had taken the canister from the wall and placed it behind him.

He knew he would relive Deana's death and his narrow escape over and over for the rest of his life. But for now he was on the phone, desperately trying to warn Dr. Hunter of the true nature of the disturbance that everyone else assumed was a fire in the building.

15

Upstairs at the crime lab and morgue, Brannon and Angelica recognized the odors wafting up through the ventilation and elevator shafts, the unmistakable odors they had experienced at the spontaneous combustion crime scenes. With alarms still going off, Jackie, too, sniffed the air, asking, "Is that what I think it is?"

"Damn it, it's him!" said Brannon. "He's here, now!"

The intercom had then come alive with a security guard's warning that someone had entered the building with a bomb of some sort. "It's got to be him, this Hari Shakir guy," said Brannon, pulling out his nine-millimeter Glock. "Come on, Jackie, let's get this mother."

Jackie pulled her gun as well. "I'm with you this time. Shoot first, ask questions later."

Angelica's office phone rang insistently, adding to the alarm. She picked it up, and Donald Porter was on the other end. "Dr. Hunter! A man looking for Dr. Katra . . . claimed to be related . . . just . . . just smoked Deana in a spontaneous combustion at the reception desk! It's a madhouse down here."

Lights flickered on and off again, the alarms still blaring.

"Does he know what floor we're on?" asked Angelica.

"Yes and you've got to get out of there. This thing isn't

human! It swallowed Deana like it did Crysta. Get out the back stairs. The elevators are down due to the alarms!"

"Get to security! Make sure we have power to the service elevator!" she told Porter.

"Just take the stairs!"

"Don't argue, Porter, just do it!"

"OK, OK, just get clear of there. This guy touches you, you're cinders!"

She dropped the phone on its cradle and said to the others, "He's come for Adib's body and the serpent! He's on the stairwell."

"We'll meet him on the stairwell," said Eric.

"No! Our first priority is to safeguard Adib's body, so put away your John Wayne act and help me. We can't risk Shakir's getting near Adib. Given his apparent power, Shakir could heat him and eat him in one fell swoop."

She raced for the cooler, and Eric holstered his weapon and rushed after Angelica. Jackie remained behind, shouting, "I'll just cover you from here."

"We take him down the service elevator, through the underground garage. My Explorer's there," Angelica said as she tore open the freezer door.

Angelica grabbed the table that Katra's body lay on. She kicked off the safety and began wheeling it through the doors. Brannon grabbed the other end, helping her guide the metal table.

"Go, go, go!" shouted Angelica.

Brannon shouted to Jackie as they wheeled the body toward the back corridor and elevator. "Come on, Hale! Don't be a hero. Stick with us."

"God, I hope that elevator's operating," Jackie replied, ignoring him, standing her ground.

"The service car is on a separate line, so we may get lucky," Angelica shouted back over the den of the alarms.

"Where the hell're you going to take the body?" Jackie asked over her shoulder, still standing near the stairwell door, keeping watch through the small window.

Angelica didn't slow. "Anywhere . . . I don't know. We'll figure it out."

"We'll need a cold-storage unit with no questions asked," said Brannon, who locked eyes with Jackie, a knowing look on his face.

"My dad's grocery," she said. "He has a meat locker," she explained to Angelica. "I'll call him, tell him to expect us. Get that elevator up here!" Jackie speed dialed her father on her cellular phone and told him to expect them, and that they had need of his meat locker.

"For what?" he asked.

"No time to explain, Dad, just expect us."

Eric again shouted at Jackie, "Come on! Come with us, now!"

"The scrolls and the scimitar," said Angelica.

"Where are they?" he asked.

"Damn it, I forgot about them. They're locked in the safe in my office, where I should have had those tapes."

"Forget 'em! He's after the body," Eric assured her.

Jackie was on her cell phone again, this time to Ames, trying to explain their situation, sounding insane, when the stairwell door pounded open and into her, knocking her to the floor, her telephone and gun skidding away from her. They all saw the dark-skinned man with the blue-black hair and fixed black pupils coming at Jackie. She crawled to her gun, got up on her knees and pointed the weapon, shouting, "Police, stop!"

Eric aimed his weapon as well, saying, "Back this way, Jackie."

"Deana at reception sent me up. I am Hari *Katra*," he said, "and I am here to claim my brother's remains." Hari saw Angelica and Eric at the end of the corridor with the shrouded body. Seeing the body, knowing it was Adib Shakar's body, filled him with a longing, and it seemed as if he saw no one else nor the guns pointed at him.

"We know you're Hari Shakir," Jackie said, rising from the floor, standing in Brannon's line of fire.

"Back out of there, Jackie!" Eric called to her. "Do it! Do

it, now! You're too close to him, and you're blocking any shot I might have!"

Jackie began backing away, saying, "We know you killed Dr. Stanton and the others. Now get down on all fours and kiss the fucking floor, now!"

"Adib . . . Adib Katra has died," he pointed to the body now at the end of the corridor. "He is the *Shakar*." Hari felt a coldness come over him with the realization that it was true, that Adib had indeed committed suicide rather than join with him.

"Fell right into our trap, didn't you?" shouted Jackie. "Adib Katra's alive and well. We simply baited you here," she lied, trying to buy them time as Angelica pounded for the elevator to rise to them and open.

"Get the hell away from him, Jackie!" ordered Brannon.

Hari Shakir had taken in everything, his eyes roving from the body to Brannon, Angelica, and back to Jackie, the only barriers left. Hari's form suddenly enlarged and his long, undulating stride closed any distance between Jackie and himself. Brannon watched the scales come up from the lower layers of Hari's skin to replace his epidermal layer. His head flared wide, his nostrils enlarged with his burning eyes. It all happened in the blink of an eye.

Jackie opened fire, and from behind her Brannon fired, emptying his clip, but the bullets were absorbed and the wounds healed over even as they were made.

Hari bellowed, "My serpent god protects me! Unlike Adib, I feed my god, and it makes me strong."

"Son of a bitch is unstoppable! Get Back!" Brannon screamed while Angelica frantically cursed the elevator doors. Seeing Hari's resistance to gunfire, Jackie now back-pedaled over her cell phone, slipping on it. This sent her right leg skidding, and she went to one knee, still firing, when Shakir took hold of her.

It had all happened in such lightning speed that Jackie had not seen or felt his touch before she'd erupted into a fireball of superheated gases, the ignite blowing out window partitions beside the beast and discoloring the floor and ceiling where Jackie had been.

Angelica continued to hammer on the elevator button, screaming at watching Jackie Hale ignite into that strange gaseous form she had only theorized about and seen on tape. Seeing it occur in real time, here like this, terrified and weakened the onlookers. Brannon cursed the creature and fired through the blinding, choking smoke, his nostrils filling with the odor of acrid ozone. He watched horrified as the creature now sucked in what was left of Jackie. For that brief moment, he and Angelica saw the two-headed creature rise from the throat, taking in all the gases.

Finally the elevator doors opened and Angelica yanked the table with Adib's body inside, where the sheet fell, partially in, partially out of the cab. Angelica stared at the cold corpse, icicles dripping from it.

Brannon continued to rain bullets into Shakir's body with little result. The serpent man staggered forward, his skin hardened and thick with the scales of the supernormal beast.

Angelica repeatedly and hysterically screamed, "Move! Now! Get the fuck on the elevator! Now!"

Brannon finally stopped firing and stepped into the elevator car just as Angelica pressed CLOSE on the light panel. Eric snatched the sheet inside just as the two doors met, and Hari's weight slammed into the doors, causing the entire car to shake as Angelica pressed for a descent to the parking garage. Brannon felt the heat of the monster's touch through the door and drew his hands away, shouting, "Son of a bitch!"

Even as they dropped to the floor below, they could hear the roaring curses and anger of the monster overhead. They heard the splashes of molten metal from the steel service doors overhead raining down like lava on the top of the elevator cab, sizzling as they cooled.

Brannon looked across Adib's body at Angelica, and his pain and grief was written on his face. Exhausted, he doubled over and said, "Why didn't she listen to me? Bastard thing killed Jackie!"

"I'm so sorry, Eric. You did everything you could."

"Such a horrible way to die, and I was helpless . . . couldn't touch it."

"We've got to stay focused, Eric. The important thing now is . . . we have to keep Adib's body away from Shakir, and we have to keep it on ice."

He nodded, saying nothing, perspiration dripping from him. He was shaken.

"Outer door to the garage will be locked this time of night," she said. "No one without a passkey gets through. The only way to access the garage from this direction is through the service elevator. He'll be sealed for a short while before he figures out how to find us again, if we can keep the elevator out of his hands."

The fire alarms had shut down, and the elevator carrying Angelica, Brannon, and Adib's corpse was filled with an eerie silence. In that strange tranquility, trapped there with the body, the tattoo, and the serpent within him, they could hear one another's heartbeat. The telltale odor of ozone followed them down the shaft.

Angelica lifted the shroud that had fallen off Adib's body and again covered him. They got off at the parking level and wheeled Katra's body against the open door, jamming it open, holding it there until Eric found a discarded Pepsi bottle to prop it open with. This effectively put the elevator out of use for the monster.

"It all happened so damnably fast," Brannon muttered.

"You did all you could, Eric," she repeated.

"I pumped an entire clip into him. Jackie hit him six times at close range before he . . . before he grabbed her."

"You couldn't know that bullets would be useless against this thing."

"It all happened so fast," he repeated, dazed.

"We've got to keep moving, Eric. Imagine what would happen if that thing could increase its power by joining with the other serpent like Adib warned . . . like the scrolls foretell."

They rushed the body to her Explorer, and, struggling with

the slippery surface of Adib's still-frozen shell, they placed it in the rear. While his corpse was not frozen through, it was as stiff as wood.

The man chasing them hadn't slowed, having reacted to the bullets as if they were bee stings. And now they heard his footfalls pounding down the stairwell.

As they finished loading Adib's body into the Explorer, Brannon saw the heavy metal door that kept Hari Shakir at bay. It had reddened up and was dissolving into molten metal, a large hole being cut.

She climbed behind the wheel, and Brannon, coming around back of the vehicle, saw Hari Shakir emerge through the molten metal and into the lot.

Taking hold of the stainless-steel table that had carried Adib's body, Brannon sent it hurtling at Shakir, who became tangled in it as a myriad of tentacles had sprung from the man's body, reaching out toward Eric. Brannon leapt into the car even as Angelica pulled from the parking space. While Eric was still only halfway in the car, the door hanging open, she rammed into Shakir, the sudden impact stunning the monster and sending him below the car.

"Get us the hell outta here!" Brannon shouted.

She didn't slow but rather steamrolled the rear wheels up and over Shakir where he had fallen, thumping over his body in reverse. Shoving it into forward, her back tires pounded over him again, sending him into a roll along the pavement while a parking lot attendant looked on in horror.

In the rearview, Angelica said, "My God, he's getting up."

Brannon looked through the rear window to see Shakir rising from the pavement behind them.

Angelica drove for the exit and the Explorer sped past the electronic eye that opened the underground door. She had to slow down to await the rising gate or smash into its metal mesh. Brannon turned in his seat to stare helplessly as the tall, black parking lot attendant rushed to the injured man, helping him stand when the attendant burst into a ball of gases.

Brannon hung his head, unable to do a thing about what

he had witnessed here any more than he had been able to help Jackie upstairs.

They tore from the building and out into the teeming street traffic, for the moment safe. Around the corner at the front of the building, they could see the multicolored lights of police cars and fire trucks. While Brannon normally welcomed police backup, the reality sank deep. No one among the authorities would understand or believe their plight, and this only made their task more lonely.

Angelica and Eric came around the back of Hale's IGA grocery store, where Eric rang the delivery bell. He spoke into an intercom, identifying himself and getting a buzz. Eric entered to find Graham Hale, Jackie's retired cop father who owned the store, smiling back at him and asking, "What kind of need do you have for my meat locker, Brannon? And where's my little girl?"

He was expecting them, but he was expecting Jackie as well. "Jackie got the call through to you, did she?" he asked, wondering how to break the bad news to him.

"Yeah, she sounded rushed. Tried to call her back but got no answer. She all right?"

Brannon dropped his eyes.

"What? Give it to me straight, Brannon."

"Jackie fought her last monster tonight, Mr. Hale."

His face went ashen, his features stricken. "Whataya mean?"

"She died in the line of duty."

He collapsed to one knee, pulling over a display with him. "My God . . . my God. Where is she? I want to go to her. Where is she?"

Eric rushed to him and dropped to his level, letting out a long sigh. "There's no way that can be arranged, sir."

"The hell you say. What happened? You were supposed to cover her back, Brannon! What the fuck happened?" He pushed Brannon away and pulled himself to the countertop.

"Did she tell you what we needed the freezer for?" Brannon asked.

"Answer my fucking question, Brannon!"

"We've got a body that needs to be refrigerated now, Mr. Hale. As soon as I secure it, we'll talk. I need a table on wheels. You have one?"

"Back storage room," he muttered, following him back. "Where is she, Eric? What's happened to her?"

"Did she tell you about the Stanton case, the Krueshicki fire, sir?"

"The car, the apartment with the fridge, yeah. She was stumped. She asked me my advice."

"The guy we were chasing, sir, *he* found us."

"I told her to go back to the first victim, talk to everyone close to the first victim again if need be," he muttered. Then he shouted, "Who is it, Brannon? I want the motherfucker's name! I'll kill the son of a bitch with my own hands."

"We're going to get the bastard, sir. I promise you."

"You're telling me she died in a fire, a combustion like she described happened to Stanton and the others?" he asked. "She died like that?" Hale was stunned, his mouth hanging open. Tears began filling his eyes, and he turned away.

Brannon wheeled the table out to the Explorer where Angelica sat with the air at full blast. When he and Angelica returned to the store with Adib Katra's body, Angelica saw that Hale had crumpled under the news of Jackie's death. She and Brannon watched the bereaved father looking like a confused fish on a line. He thrashed about, looking for something to smash.

"We have an unusual request of you, Mr. Hale. We need to leave a body in your ice locker for a few hours, until we can figure out our next move."

Hale paid no attention to the fact they had just wheeled in Adib Katra's body and were placing it into his meat locker. "There's got to be *something* left of her?" he said, still dazed, Brannon's words not registering with him.

"This is Dr. Hunter with the ME's office," Brannon said.

"As soon as we can safely remove Dr. Katra's body, sir, we will do so."

"Safely," he repeated, "a body?"

"A very special body."

"But not my Jackie? She doesn't have . . . there isn't anything left of her body, is there?"

Angelica took the man's hands in hers. "I'm afraid not, and I'm so sorry, sir, for your loss."

His eyes were vacant, removed. He staggered to a corner of the store and slumped down, crossing himself with his arms as if cold. Someone came through the door, and Brannon rushed forward, telling the teenaged customer that the place was closed.

The young man who entered protested, but Brannon flashed his badge and said, "Beat it."

The teen left, cursing under his breath, and Brannon closed the door, locked it, and placed a sign on it.

Brannon again went to Hale, and the two men stared into one another's eyes for a long moment. "Tell me you didn't get her killed, Eric," Hale said, his eyes like gray steel.

"I was there, sir," said Angelica, "and Eric did all that was humanly possible to save her."

"And she died fighting?"

"That she did."

Brannon said, "You're all closed up now, so go home, Mr. Hale. We're just going to use your freezer for the night. Have to baby-sit that corpse."

"Whatever you say, Brannon. Jackie thought the world of you."

The old man ambled off toward the back, still shaken, looking as if he might collapse.

"Make sure there's no problem with the controls on the meat locker," Brannon said to Angelica. Together, they returned to stare through the window at Adib, now lying amid the carcasses hanging from hooks there.

Angelica looked back over her shoulder at the broken father. Hale had resurfaced and was going toward the front again. "It's so sad," she said to Eric.

Another irate customer began knocking on the storefront doors.

The alleyway behind the store had been baking. The trip from the morgue had raised Adib's body temperature.

"Safe for the time being," said Brannon, ignoring the banging up front.

"Yeah, but for how long? How did that thing find Adib in the first place?" She looked into his eyes as if the answer might be there.

He breathed heavily, went to a freezer unit and snatched out a Pepsi for each of them. "I don't know."

"Adib was using another name, and, according to Porter, Shakir asked for Adib Katra at the reception desk. So he must've somehow put two and two together, that Katra and Shakar are one and the same."

"But how? It's been stumbling around, killing off people left and right, and suddenly it finds its way direct to Adib?"

"Maybe it has something to do with Adib's death," he said.

The customer outside had given up and the pounding ended.

"How do you mean?" he asked between sips.

"That this Hari does have a kind of kinship to Adib, and he feels Adib's death on a deeper subconscious level than we normally see, like the way twins often can feel one another at great distances . . . that he's somehow psychically connected to Adib."

"Or that serpent within him," said Eric, considering this.

They stepped away from the cooler. Brannon told her of the attempt on a man named Tyrone Shakar earlier, about the boy who saw his mother torched. "Then it somehow found its way to Carl Osterman."

"And from Osterman, it came almost directly to us, to the lab. . . ."

"He didn't come immediately from Osterman's death, but soon after, yes."

"But Osterman couldn't't've told him a thing."

"I know. . . . He was in a coma. Damnedest thing."

"What?"

"Jackie and I almost caught the bastard thing there. We were that close, and had we run into him there, I'd likely be dead now, too. I gotta wonder why was it her and not me? And Mr. Hale's wondering the same thing."

She stared into his eyes, a realization coming over her. "Eric, when this thing consumes people," she thoughtfully said, "have we considered what happens to their memories, their thoughts? All we see is the horrendous way they died, the loss of their *bodies* in a matter of an instant. What of their minds, their personalities, their souls—the very thing Adib was worried about losing to it?"

"What are you driving at?"

"Suppose this thing can somehow gather information from its victims? That it takes on their knowledge?"

"Our memories and thoughts? Good God . . . if that's true . . ."

Hale was up front, arguing with someone to go away, shouting, "Closed! Death in the family! Closed, damn you! Can't you read English!" Hale muttered back to Brannon, "Damned foreigners."

Brannon turned to find Hale at his front window, arguing with a dark-skinned man standing outside the locked door. "It's him!" shouted Angelica, recognizing the man outside as Hari Shakir.

"Get back! Get away from there, Graham!" shouted Brannon.

The windows burst in at Hale in a fiery explosion.

Hale wheeled around, staggering, revealing a hundred-plus shards of hot glass had embedded into him from the force exerted on the storefront's see-through doors.

"The body!" Brannon shouted. "We've got to get it out of here, now!"

Angelica tore open the freezer door and began wheeling Adib's body out the rear exit.

Hale had somehow staggered upright back to his counter and pulled out a huge shotgun. Rivulets of blood from the countless punctures painted Hale's face and white apron, and his unsteady, glass-punctured hands shook as he tried to pull the double-barreled shotgun's two triggers. Amazingly, he did so. The blasts slammed into Shakir's eyes and already-battered body. Blinded, screeching, still Shakir managed to transform into the creature that welled up from within, and with tentacles bursting from it, the thing reached out and grabbed hold of the end of the shotgun as Hale was reloading. He pulled the barrel as Hale fired, and the shot was again absorbed as the thing yanked the grocer over the counter, leaving the Formica top slick with the man's blood. With Hale's head held against the counter, Hari again became the snake god, scaly and huge, and he combusted the man, sucking in all his gases.

While Angelica rushed out the back with Adib's body, Brannon, who had seen the murder, had grabbed a can of lighter fluid and spread it around, igniting it along their path of escape out the rear. The flames created a wall of fire, giving them cover.

Brannon's last sight of the creature was it tearing the freezer door from its hinges.

Outside, Brannon closed the door behind them, and as Angelica wheeled Adib's body to the car, he tugged a Dumpster across the door. The roaring sound of a full-blown fire had erupted inside the store, bottles popping like gunshots, the water sprinklers and alarms going off, all hopefully adding to Shakir's confusion.

Brannon dropped what was left of the lighter fluid into the full Dumpster and set it ablaze. It shot up and covered their escape further.

Together, they placed Adib's body back into the Explorer and closed the rear door on him. Looking up, they saw Shakir yank open the door. With flames in back of him and flames in front of him, he roared and jumped into the blazing Dumpster, the force sending it and him directly at them.

Brannon and Angelica had leapt into the car as the flaming Dumpster threatened to tear into them, the creature crying out, "Give me Adib!"

Angelica started the engine on the first attempt and threw it into forward, the Explorer escaping a direct hit by the

Dumpster, which slammed into her bumper. Then they felt a loud thump on the rooftop.

As they raced from the rear alley, they could hear the paint atop the Explorer searing, and they could smell the metal as it was melting. Shakir had grabbed hold, but Angelica tore into a forty-five-degree turn from the alleyway, sending his body sprawling across the pavement.

Hari Shakir stood in the street, his clothing tattered and blackened by the store fire. Steam rose off him where he stood half naked while traffic weaved around him under the glare of the blazing flames shooting out the front of Hale's grocery store.

An explosion rocked the store and the street, the force sending glass and objects hurtling into Shakir, but he remained standing and defiant in front of the store. A Miami police cruiser pulled to within a few feet of him, two officers leaping out with their weapons trained on Hari.

He raised his hands in the universal gesture of defeat.

In the shadows created by the flames, he looked like Satan himself, Angelica thought as they careened around another corner and out of the monster's sight.

"Damn it, if I had my car, we could warn those two officers back there. They have no idea what they're up against."

"There's nothing we can do for them, Eric. No more than we could save Mr. Hale or Jackie or any of the others. We have one job to do now, to stay alive long enough to destroy this thing inside Adib before that damned beast gets anywhere near Adib's body ever again! That's twice now it's come close."

"What are we saying, Angelica? That no one's life is more important than our goal?"

"Unforgivable as it sounds, that's right; we're all expendable. Get used to it. Adib did. He gave his life to end it. He tried to destroy the serpent within him." She was crying now as she drove through the cityscape.

"Yeah but he failed." Brannon thought again of the expanding retinue of people consumed by the monster.

"Which only means we cannot fail, Eric."

"And how're we going to kill it now? What the hell're the two of us going to do against this thing?" asked Brannon.

"We've got to be faster and smarter than it. Eric, it followed us straight to Hale's. How did it *know* we'd take the body there?"

"How *did* it know? You tell me."

They sat in silence for a moment. "Then it's true, what I dreamed about," she said. "Adib tried to tell us that it takes on its victims' thought patterns or memories."

"Jackie led it to us?"

"I'm afraid so."

"Like Osterman led it to the crime lab?"

"Exactly."

"Then we're not safe anywhere, and neither are Adib's remains."

"Adib was telling the truth all along, and we were too blinded by rationality to pay heed." She almost ran into a city bus pulling from its stop.

"Calm down . . . calm down!" he repeated.

"OK . . . OK . . . calming down. But now what are we to do?"

"The scrolls," he said.

"What about them?"

"They represent our only way. The directions he gave to destroy his body are wrapped in the scrolls."

"The scimitar must be used on the serpent, just as Adib had been attempting when he killed himself." Angelica pulled to a red light.

Eric insisted she keep moving, "Don't slow down. We don't know where that thing is. Take a right." When they got through the light, he said, "We can't delay any longer. We have to desecrate his body in the ritual manner that Adib described."

"God . . . I hate the thought of it . . . such butchery, Eric."

"What choice do we have? It's the only way left."

"We'll need the scrolls and the scimitar."

"In your office safe."

"Damn it, we can't go back there. The authorities see us, they'll hold us for questioning."

He agreed. "They've got to be wondering what happened to us and Adib's body."

"Besides, Shakir may be watching the place."

"Yeah, but we've got to get the knife and the instructions. We do that, we could take the body out to the Everglades—Miami gangster's solution. It's the only way."

"But how do we get back into my office without being seen?"

"There's no going back to any place either of us normally habit," replied Eric as they now drove aimlessly through the city. "He will be there at every turn. It'd be nice to get help, but who's going to believe our reason for having run off with Adib's body?"

"I know who." She got on her cell phone, seeing that a message was left her. She checked it, hoping that it was Don Porter, the only other person that had seen the creature in its full fury.

The message was from Captain Ames, and, after listening to it, she said, "Your captain is screaming for you to check in with him."

"When this is over," said Eric.

She dialed Don Porter's phone at the crime lab, hoping to get lucky, that Porter might still be there. Don came on, asking where she was, and talking of the devastation done to the lab.

"Porter, shut up and listen! First, tell no one you've heard from me! No one, you understand?"

"Yes, understood, Dr. ah . . . Crane."

"Someone's there?" she asked.

"Outside in the hallway, Ames and some cops," he whispered.

She knew that Ames would never understand what she and Eric proposed. "Listen, Porter, I'm offering you a chance to redeem yourself over those stolen tapes."

"I have your originals tucked safely in my locker."

"Good, so are you still interested in helping me out here, Porter?"

"Anything, *ahhh* . . . Dr. Crane. You name it."

"I'll need your silence on this, Don."

"Anything . . . anything." He was still rattled by what he had witnessed.

"I'll need a bone saw and a full quart can of maggots from the freezer, the ones we use for training interns on time of death. Not the leeches, the maggots."

"Handheld bone saw and maggots. Got it."

"And Don, in my office, you know where the safe is. Take down this combination." She read it off to him. "Inside, you'll find a bag and inside that bag are some important papers and the knife Adib used to kill himself with. I need it all."

"Got it, Doctor."

"And come alone as fast as possible to the corner of"— she looked at the street sign they sat below—"Granada and Buena Vista. And tell no one. You have that?"

"Sure, no problem." Then he whispered, "But where's Adib's—"

"The less you know, Don, the better to keep you out of trouble. Now, do you know how to get here?"

"Yeah, be there in fifteen."

"Alone, Don! With what I need."

"Alone . . . got it."

She hung up. "I hope he doesn't come with the cavalry."

"Bone saw? To speed up the process? I thought we needed the scimitar for the cuts?"

"We may not be able to rely on the scimitar to go through bone. It's pretty damned old and likely dull. It may not sever a head as easily as slicing open an abdomen."

"Maggots, huh?"

"Adib said it wouldn't be pleasant."

"Sounds like the understatement of the century."

"It will be difficult to carry through with this, Eric, believe me."

"What's the alternative? We've got the AC as high as it

will go, and he's thawing out back there, and we don't know at what temperature that thing inside him will become active again. Wish we could get him to that cryogenics lab in Orlando."

"We'd never make it. No one is waiting for us to show up with this cadaver in tow, Eric. We don't have any options."

"Then we've got to do it the old-fashioned way." Eric rubbed at his weary neck.

"It's going to be ugly and difficult."

"And if we're caught during any stage of it?"

"We'd be put away as lunatics."

"We can't let Shakir win. He wins, the future of all mankind is ended."

"We have to do this thing and do it tonight," she agreed. "We'll need a place of impure waters."

"I know just the place in the swamp where we can get in close to a landfill."

16

Hari liked the fit of the Miami police uniform he now wore. He was enjoying the cruiser as well. Between the two seats, resting on its butt, and strapped in was a huge pump-action shotgun he kept banging his elbow on. He drove for the crime lab, hoping to pick up Hunter's and Brannon's trail there.

Earlier Hari had pretended surrender to the officers, and, when one had attempted to handcuff him, Hari, with his back to the man, extended his hands to accept the cuffs, but instead, he had grasped hold of the cop's hand and had turned him into smoke there in front of the blazing grocery store. The second officer was close enough to feel the heat and be splattered with some of the black goop Hari had made of his partner. He shakily fired into Hari several times before Hari took his gun from him and ordered him to strip down.

Hari had then turned to toss the clothes into the vehicle only to find the naked man racing off. He climbed into the cruiser and gave chase.

Since Hari had need of the cruiser and the uniform, he must catch the runaway cop. He didn't want the other man calling in to headquarters and putting out an APB on the cruiser.

Hari located him moments later a few blocks away in a

phone booth. Hari gunned the cruiser and smashed into the booth, turning the second officer into a sandwich of glass, brass, aluminum, and flesh. He was dead when Hari backed off him and drove away.

Now it was 1:42:02 A.M. according to the cruiser clock, and Hari was driving back to set up a surveillance of the police crime lab. As he drove, Hari recalled how he had felt when he had gotten that first instinctual feeling that Adib Shakar had killed himself. He thought about the pain of it, each thrust of the ritual scimitar, and he imagined the wounding and weakening of his twin serpent as well. The image of Adib's attack on himself and the serpent within had come full-blown to Hari's mind when he had been in proximity to the body. Adib had weakened the serpent, and the weakening had made it more difficult to locate Adib.

Hari had been so close at the crime lab, and in the basement garage, and then in the store. He replayed the seconds he had lain atop the speeding vehicle with Adib's body just below him. Hari's every cell, every organ, had felt the nearness of the precious few feet between himself and Shakar, lying dead beneath him, beneath the shroud in back of the car he'd watched disappear from his sight.

As he had stood in the street, staring after Shakar's self-appointed guardians, Hari and the beast within him recalled feeling their other half inside the car, calling out to him, urging him on. It loved him as much as he loved it. It wanted him as much as he wanted it.

The nearness to completion had created a feeling of sentimental pathos in Hari's serpent and human gut, a great well of expectation, a depth of connection with the being within as it opened its soul for a moment of grief and pain at the untold years of searching. And now here to be so close to the end. It created a mix of melancholy and ecstatic awe and wonder, the confusion of a god, and Hari realized for the first time that even the Kundalini had fears and doubts. To come so close and to be robbed of victory by humans. It was unthinkable. Hari feared the serpent's wrath if he should again meet with failure.

Hari felt the coldness of his brother serpent again; he felt it deep within. When he had been atop the vehicle for that short moment, he had felt how stiff, how cold and immovable his brother snake was, trapped within Shakar's body. He hated Adib Shakar for his cowardly act, his attempt to escape his destiny. But of course, it could not work. Hari would not allow it to work.

He wracked his insides, all of his recent kills, for ideas on how to pursue the ones Adib had cajoled into protecting his remains—Brannon and Hunter. He knew that they meant to destroy any chance he might have at reuniting Shakar with Shakir, that it was no longer a secretive matter between Adib and himself.

These thoughts filtered through Hari's mind as he drove on toward the crime lab.

"You are a damned fool, Adib, turning your back on the serpent all these years, and now the ultimate betrayal. Little black man with little vision," he cursed Shakar.

Adib's serpent would rise with the body's temperature in this heat. They could not protect themselves from it, much less him. They could not long keep his other half dormant. Furthermore, the one called Jackie knew her partner well, and she had an idea where he would next go, that he would want the scrolls and the scimitar, that he would want to follow Adib's directions for desecrating his body, and Dr. Hunter would have hidden them somewhere in her laboratory.

They had kept the AC in the car at its highest setting, and they were freezing while waiting for Porter. Where they sat, a nearby street gang, hanging about a children's park, was becoming curious, and one member started approaching the car on an apparent dare.

Brannon flashed his badge through the passenger-side glass.

"Yo man, why're you carrying a stiff around in the back of your car? Let me get that badge number."

Brannon dared not roll the window down as the heat outside would rush in. He shouted through the glass instead. "Beat it, kid." He reached back and straightened the sheet over Adib's body.

"Keep the windows up," she agreed. "We've got to keep it cold in here. Wish to hell I'd gotten tinted windows with this thing."

"We have to make a decision. Can't sit here like this for long before some John Q drops a coin on us. Porter's not coming. Maybe we should find another cold-storage place and put him on ice, or commandeer a refrigerated truck and make a dash for the Everglades with a stop at True Value for the tools we need."

"The fucking world depends for the moment on Don Porter," she said with a sigh.

"There's an enlarging puddle of water growing back of us," he said, staring back at Adib's covered body. "I'm serious. You just imagine that thing inside Adib getting loose inside the car with us."

"Stop worrying. The body will take hours to thaw out."

"Are you sure?"

"Look," she pointed out, directing his eye to Shakar's left hand and fingernails.

For the first time Brannon saw the ice crystals that had formed around the nails. "Yeah . . . I see."

"Of course, it'd been better to have kept him in cold storage overnight, but we don't have that option anymore, so . . . Where the hell's Porter?"

Angelica's phone rang. "It's me, Porter. I'm just around the corner. Had to shake a cop car tailing me from the lab."

"A cop tailing you from the lab?"

"Yeah . . ."

Overhearing this, Eric got on the phone. "Only one guy in the cruiser?"

"I really didn't look that closely."

"Be careful. That cop could be Hari Shakir."

"I shook him ten minutes ago."

She got back on the line. "Don, did you get what I asked for?"

"Absolutely, and more." Porter's car came around the corner, and he flashed his lights at them, playing James Bond. He parked nose to nose with them, getting out and coming toward them, carrying two bags. Brannon got out, rushing to get what they needed and get out of the area.

From all he could see the kid was alone, unshadowed, and except for the prying eyes of the gang watching from the swings at the park, no one paid them any attention.

Angelica slipped out, letting the AC continue to run. She opened the rear door to receive what they had requested. Porter handed over the bag with the scrolls and scimitar, then pleaded that Brannon take more care with the bone saw and the jar of maggots. "You don't want those suckers all over your car," he said, adding, "Oh, and there's one more thing we'll be needing."

Porter rushed back to his car and worked to pull a large, heavy canister with a wand attachment from the backseat. "I'll give Katra another liquid-nitro bath to cool his jets. Whataya say?"

"Good idea. Do it," she said.

With the rear hatchway open, Porter lifted the sheet covering Katra and gave him a liberal spraying of the cold-inducing chemical. The gray-white cloud from the spray spilled out the rear of the Explorer and filled the cab, keeping Brannon and Hunter outside, exposed and watchful. The cloud hanging over the vehicle looked like a strange, white fog, and their clothes were doused with it.

Porter worked the shroud back atop the cadaver, placed the canister and wand alongside the body, and backed out. "There's lots more left in the canister. We may need it later."

Porter noticed the blistered peeled paint and disfigured top of her car. "Jesus, what happened to your car, Doctor?"

"Never mind that. Don, you haven't seen us tonight."

"Wait, I want to go with you! Help out."

"No . . . we're going to take it from here," she firmly replied.

Porter gritted his teeth and said, "At least tell me where you're taking the body."

"The less you know, the better. Trust me," Brannon said, coming around to the driver's side and taking the wheel of the car. Angelica had stepped to the passenger side and slid in beside him.

"But I want to help!" Porter shouted.

They tore from the curb, and Porter stared across at the kids in the park who were staring back at him. He felt their eyes following as he returned to his car, anxious to get out of this neighborhood, when suddenly he saw a car speeding after Dr. Hunter and Detective Brannon. He immediately hopped into his own car and gave chase, following the phantom behind them. He got on his cell phone and dialed for Dr. Hunter. She picked up.

"You're being followed!"

"The cop that tailed you from the lab?" she asked.

"No . . . a gray Nissan two door. Maybe a ninety-eight. Can't make out the driver." The signal began to break up. "Some one else must've . . . fol . . . from . . . lab."

"You're breaking up, Porter," she told him. "Listen to me! I want you to break off this pursuit, Don. Do you hear me? We'll take care of it from here."

She got only static, unsure how much he had heard. Angelica imagined that Porter was making it up to lend credence to his reason for following them. She explained all this to Eric, and, exhausted, she lay her cheek against his shoulder as he drove.

Adib's body lie still and motionless behind them as the Explorer made its way out of the city.

Less than a quarter mile behind them, Don Porter pursued the car tailing them. The last few words between Don and Dr. Hunter had been visited with great static, telling him he was running out of seconds on his cellular again. What good would it do to call back? He'd best save it for when he needed it, he told himself.

As he had been speaking to Dr. Hunter, Porter had kept the mystery car in his sights. When he got off the phone, he turned on his radio to an ear-shattering, teeth-gnashing pounding of acid rock.

The boys hanging out at the park had been watching all the strange goings-on across the street, and they continued to debate the meaning of the white cloud of smoke that had engulfed the Ford Explorer, and what might have been inside the mysterious bags. Some thought a huge cache of cocaine had somehow exploded inside the car.

The one boy who had gone near the car claimed once again to have seen a dead body in the rear, and that they had sprayed the body with some sort of chemical. "Some kinda weird *Outer Limits* shit going on," he said to the others. The others didn't believe him about the body.

The debate raged on when a police cruiser eased by as if from nowhere. The park boys watched the police cruiser fall in behind Porter's car. They had seen a lot of strange things here tonight, and they expected the cop to pull over and question them, but he kept going, looking oblivious to everything, his black eyes and dark skin glistening in the heat. He was driving with his windows down, as if soaking up the heat.

Angelica and Brannon now barreled down U.S. 1 South, following the Atlantic coast for the Everglades. Brannon had vacationed in the area, and he had on more than one occasion been called out to the Everglades on homicide investigations. He knew the backwater bays far better than she.

"If anyone's following us like Porter said, they're either very good or we've lost them," he said, looking into the rearview mirror.

"I think Porter finally got the hint and went home for the night."

Eric drove on until he suddenly made a sharp turn onto a grassy nonroad in the middle of nowhere. "No lights behind us," he said.

They had been driving for two hours west-southwest of the city, going deep into the Florida Everglades to a remote area where Eric had gone boating and fishing as a child. Avoiding the tourists roads and motel strips, he found a sandy, overgrown weed patch of a road no longer in use except perhaps by fish and game officers in the area. The road was so narrow in spots she thought they would drive right into the marshy swamp, but finally it opened on a wide, flat clearing, what appeared to have once been a campground, long abandoned. In the distance, she saw some lights.

"Landfill I told you about. After we throw the torso in the swamp, we can bury select parts of him in the landfill."

They were several miles off-road here where Brannon came to a stop. With the Explorer facing forward, and a dead end of marshland ahead, they came to a standstill.

"God, I don't know if I can carry through with this," she said.

"There's no other choice. We'll do it together," he assured her.

They went to the rear of her Explorer to haul out Adib's body.

"I feel like we ought to say a prayer, but even that's forbidden," she said to Eric.

"No, we stick to the directions literally. No changes in the script."

"Wait! Don't touch him," she said, staring at the body where it lay under the weak interior light. "I thought I saw movement under the skin—chest area, as if the serpent is rising from the abdominal area toward the throat."

He flinched back, "Damn, you're right," he replied. "I see it."

They stared for a moment at the ominously strange-looking movement below the skin. "It's moving away from the cold spot, where Porter sprayed the abdomen," she suggested.

"It's looking for another way out, feeling cornered, as if it knows what we're planning for it." As he replied, Eric reached for the liquid-nitrogen wand, and then he sprayed the corpse again with it, giving it a liberal dousing. He then shoved the wand into the corpse's throat and opened the throttle again, filling Adib's throat with the cold. "In case it has any plans of coming out here," he said.

All movement ceased.

They both hesitated lifting the body, but finally they convinced one another it was safe to do so. They laid Adib out on the marshy saw grass.

"I'll get the things we need from the car," she said, going for the bone cutter, the maggots, the scimitar, and Adib's handwritten instructions. "We need to get those maggots into him, give them time to work."

"I say we start cutting immediately," he replied.

Brannon kept his light playing over the corpse, searching for any sign of movement. He imagined the serpent slipping out of Adib here and racing off into the swamp.

He decided they ought to have the liquid nitrogen canister at hand, and, turning to go after it, he heard Angelica scream from the car. He turned to find a flashlight and gun pointed at him.

"All I want are the scrolls!" shouted a female voice from behind the light. "I can offer you a deal."

Brannon made out the features. It was Dr. Helen McAllister from the university, and she had Angelica held as a hostage, a gun at her throat. McAllister had obviously followed Porter from the crime lab, and had followed them there.

"Don't do this, Helen!" Angelica choked out her words from the stranglehold the taller woman had on her.

"Turn over the scrolls, and I'll provide a way for you to dispose of Shakar's body that will be far more efficient than what you're planning here."

"And if we say no?" he asked.

"Then I simply kill you both and take the scrolls, Detective Eric! I don't want it to come to that. I'd much rather help you and *earn* my reward."

"Are you crazy, Dr. McAllister?" asked Brannon. "Do you know what's going on here? So many victims killed tonight alone. Imagine if this thing comes to full power. Your scrolls will be useless."

Angelica said, "We're all potentially going to die like the others if—"

"I've seen the results of this thing. I was at your crime lab, Angelica, when Hale was consumed. I saw the whole thing. I want it stopped as much as you, but I also want the scrolls."

"Then let us do what's needed here!" Angelica shouted.

"If I tell you that I have a solution to your problem, will you turn over the scrolls to me? That way, no one gets hurt."

"A better way to dispose of the body?" asked Eric, stalling for time, his hand itching for his gun.

"Desecrating Shakar's body. . . . I know that has to be loathsome for you both. I have an offer. Do you wish to hear it or not?"

"All right . . . all right. Enlighten us," replied Eric.

Angelica struggled to get free, but the woman held her firmly about the neck, the barrel of the gun at her temple.

"The National Accelerator Lab in Key Largo, the Genesis Lab . . . it's only a half hour from here. They have a nuclear accelerator chamber there. I can get you inside. All you need do is get the body to that accelerator chamber and pulverize it into particles."

"Does that make any sense, Angelica?" asked Brannon.

Choking against the hold McAllister had on her, Angelica calmed. "It could work, yes. But how do we get past security, much less gain access to this chamber?" she asked.

"I've made arrangements with the man in charge, Dr. Anwar Tapai, also of India. He understands the value of the scrolls and has a buyer."

"I'm sure he does," said Eric.

"Anwar is anxious to help. All we want in return are the scrolls."

Brannon tried to calculate the value of the scrolls. It must be astronomical, he thought, for McAllister to have conspired as she had. "All right . . . just let Angelica go."

"Throw your gun down, and put the body back into her car. We'll all go together. Do it," ordered McAllister.

Brannon reached into his shoulder holster, gingerly removed his Glock, but held on to it for a moment, considering his options. They stood below a star-filled sky, and Brannon could see deep shadows everywhere, and he heard the sound of small vermin and animals as they lurked about the swamp. "Drop the gun and put the body back into the car, Detective. We don't want to keep Shakar's body long in this heat."

In a moment Eric made out Don Porter inching forward from the gloom of a building fog nestling over the scene. Somewhere out of sight his and McAllister's cars waited. The two of them must have coasted in with their headlights off.

Against the moon, Don's thin form showed that he was carrying a crooked tree branch he'd picked up from somewhere along the way.

Brannon tossed his weapon down. "All right . . . we do it your way, but this guy Tapai better be real."

Eric hefted Adib's body back into the open rear of the Explorer beside the liquid-nitrogen tank. "How do we find this lab?" he was asking when a police car suddenly blinded them all with its beacon light. Porter was the closest one caught in the light, silhouetted with the club about to come down on McAllister. McAllister wheeled around with Angelica under her hold to stare back at the other intruders.

Brannon recalled the cops who had confronted Shakir, and he knew it was Hari behind the spotlight. Brannon stared at the marsh and swamp. There was only one way in and one way out.

Brannon slammed the rear door down on Adib's exposed body.

"Yo . . . y'all. . . . Is there a problem here?" asked the policeman.

Porter recognized Shakir's poorly disguised voice, shouting, "It's him! The Indian guy, the fire-breathing bastard that killed Deana! It's him!"

Porter threw the stick at Hari Shakir, whose silhouetted form was enlarging to twice his normal size in the police spotlight. They saw tentacles shoot from Hari's body, and two snake heads emerged from Hari's mouth. The creature had grown large with its night of gorging, and it rushed forward in a supernatural leap that overtook Porter in an instant, igniting him into a flare that burned as quickly as a blink.

Porter's scream disappeared with him into a gaseous flaming ball that lit up the surrounding woods like a lightning strike, but it caught nothing on fire.

Helen McAllister had released Angelica, standing frozen before the beast, her gun in hand, trembling. Eric shouted, "In the car, now!" as he leapt for the driver's seat. But while McAllister loosed her hold on Angelica, she remained caught in Hari's eyes, terrified at what she had witnessed.

Angelica ran for the Explorer and screamed for McAllister to get in the car while she herself climbed in, crowding in beside Eric, who was preparing to floor the Explorer in reverse, his arm slung over the seat as he stared back through the rear window. "This road dead-ends up ahead. We've only got one way to go. Fire that nitro over Adib's remains now! We're about to go through hell!"

With that he floored the Explorer, sending it out of neutral and into reverse, straight at Shakir, while Angelica climbed into the rear and shoved the wand into Adib's gaping mouth as she had seen Eric do, firing.

Even as Helen McAllister's body suddenly erupted into a fireball of gases, Eric sent the car over the monster.

Outside, Hari took the full brunt of the Explorer this time as Brannon ran him down, slicing through the superheated air of Helen McAllister's combustion. The interior of the car became hot, and they feared the body would thaw.

Angelica held tight to the wand, and, even as she bounced about, she continued pumping the liquid nitrogen into Adib's body. When they rumbled over Hari Shakir, the Explorer threatened to topple, but it righted itself, and Brannon tore away, still in reverse but off course. His bumper rammed into the police cruiser, tearing away one of its headlights. Shakir had pulled the cruiser into a position ahead of Porter's and McAllister's cars, blocking the only exit.

"Get out! We have to take the cruiser!"

They were both sweating and fearful of the thing within Adib coming out to consume them both there in the car. Eric leapt from the Explorer, some fifty yards from where he had run over Hari Shakir, and, checking for keys, he saw they were in the police cruiser's ignition. He tore open the rear door of the Explorer, shouting, "Get the cruiser door for me! Now!"

She had grabbed up the bags containing bone saw, maggots, scimitar, and scrolls, but she dropped the maggots and bone saw, breaking the jar on the floorboard, leaving both it and the bone saw.

He grabbed Adib's body, and she opened the rear door, where Brannon struggled to place him inside. Ahead of them, in the cruiser's spotlight, they watched the monster, half man, half snake slowly rise from the ground fog.

Angelica had tossed the scimitar and the scrolls into the cruiser as Eric climbed behind the wheel and unceremoniously shoved the liquid nitrogen onto the floorboard between her legs. "We damn well may need this." Eric then threw the Explorer's keys out into the swamp and shouted, "Seat belt!" as he rammed the gas pedal in reverse.

Hari Shakir matched the speed of the car as he now came at the retreating cruiser. Eric kept the spotlight in his eyes as he drove backward, until he swerved in a tight triangular clearing, going into a three-point turn, his wheels sending up swamp mud everywhere.

"The gun! Free it!"

"But it's useless against him!" she protested.

"Just do it!"

She had only just buckled in, and now Angelica grabbed and clawed at the straps holding the twelve-gauge pump-action Remington shotgun that stood upright on its stock between them there in the front seat, trying to determine how to release it, when she found the buckle and tore at it, ripping her nails.

In the tight space alongside the swamp, Eric executed the turn, as Angelica watched Hari Shakir from a few yards away leap lizardlike straight at them. She frenetically loosed the gun.

Halfway through their turn, Hari landed atop the hood like

some prehistoric jaguar, his black eyes roiling with a red fire, tentacles and suckers trying to take hold.

Spinning out and into a wider, more open area, the cruiser nearly missed going into the swamp. Eric kept up the centrifugal force, counting on the spin to keep Shakir off balance, hoping to throw him off the hood entirely.

Angelica stared out at the unnatural red-eyed creature staring at them through the windshield. It had three heads, two of them serpentine, the center one human but scaly. It's tentacles and suckers reached up over the top of the car in all directions. It sent its deadly tongues pounding on the windshield, searing it to a white heat, warming their faces and cracking the glass shield into a million arterial lines.

Eric gyrated the cruiser and, unable to see through the roadmap of cracks, grabbed the shotgun and pointed it at the windshield. "Hold the wheel!" he shouted, and she did so.

The first blast exploded into Shakir with the glass. Eric then pumped another thunderous blast through the destroyed windshield into the monster's three heads while the car spun in the controlled circle Angelica had maintained.

But the creature held on with suckers attached to the vehicle.

"Now fire the liquid nitro!" he shouted at Angelica.

Using the gaping hole in the windshield, Angelica sprayed the liquid nitrogen into Shakir's six eyes, blinding the snakes and him when Brannon simultaneously hit the brakes with all his might. The sudden blinding, combined with the sudden stop, sent Hari Shakir flying from the hood and into the swamp, muddy water spraying everywhere.

In the headlights they saw that Hari was impaled on a protruding branch from a fallen tree where he lay in the muck, staring up at the stars and moon. Yet he remained alive, kicking and fighting to right himself.

They watched for a moment in the headlights.

Eric said, "Give me the damned scimitar."

"What?"

"The scimitar! Give it to me!"

She shakily handed it to him.

"We should finish him here and now," said Eric, climbing from the car.

"No! We don't have the power, and Adib's body can't fall into its hands, Eric. Drive! Go! Go!"

He rushed at the staked creature, and, like a discus thrower, he let the scythe-shaped knife go with all his strength. The force sent the scimitar hurtling end over end, and it struck Hari Shakir in the forehead, embedded there in his skull. *"Strike!"* shouted Eric, rushing back to the car and hopping inside.

"Now can we go!" she pleaded.

Under the headlights, Hari looked dead. "I think this nightmare is finally over," he assured her.

She pointed out the destroyed windshield. "No . . . not quite."

Hari had reached up and yanked the scimitar from his head, dropping it into the swamp. Still impaled on the branch, he began ripping his body from the prison of the mammoth stake as a pair of alligators moved in on him. Shakir grabbed hold of one of the gators and combusted it over the water.

"Drive!" she shouted.

Eric stepped on the gas, and they peeled down the swamp access road. He had caught a glass fragment in his cheek, and the dash was littered with what remained of the fried and blown-away windshield. Using the butt end of the liquid-nitrogen canister, Angelica broke away any loose and dangling glass that would fall out in a good wind. When she saw the piece of glass embedded in Eric's face, she found a tissue in her bag and gently removed it.

She saw that blood had spattered the back of the rolled scrolls that had been pushed aside in her grab for the scimitar earlier. She took the scrolls and carefully placed them inside her purse. "Thank God we still have the scrolls," she managed to say, out of breath.

He held her hand as she continued to dab at the blood on his face. Both their hearts continued to race.

"That was close . . . too damned close," he muttered.

"Now we've got the added problem of the outside temperature flooding in," she said, indicating the windshield.

"You'll have to keep hitting Adib with the cold nitrogen."

"Pray for a miracle."

Eric reacted by gunning the cruiser again, and they raced out of the area. In his rearview, Eric watched the deadly creature crawling up out of the muck and climbing into the Explorer. "It likely knows how to hot-wire a car, given all the knowledge it's acquired. Damn thing."

"It's relentless. It killed Porter and Helen, and would have killed us if it hadn't been for you."

He put his hand over hers. "What do you think of this Genesis Lab McAllister mentioned?"

"It does have the only atom smasher in the state. As for dealing with this guy, Anwar Tapai, what choice have we? The knife and the bone cutter are back there in the swamp, not to mention the maggots."

"What about the principle of the thing? Can it work?" he asked.

"It has to, besides, as I said, I don't see we have any other choice."

They found the paved highway, U.S. 1, which would take them to Key Largo. "But is it possible to de-atomize this thing like McAllister suggested?"

"The nuclear accelerator she referred to simulates the atmosphere of space."

"Then it is theoretically sound . . . a logical plan?"

"Hell, logically, if we can get that thing into the chamber, decompress it, it should implode, given the pressures. If that doesn't kill it, if we can get the electron bombardment done . . . yes, nothing could withstand such an assault."

"Then let's do it."

"But getting Hari Shakir into the thing won't be easy."

"We bait him with Adib's body." Brannon wiped sweat from his brow.

"That's damned risky. If they were to mate before the atom smasher did its work, then the creature becomes all-powerful."

"And what alternative do we have? It's going to be dawn

soon, and we're out of options. How long can we go hauling a body around the state before we're arrested?"

"It found us at Hale's grocery," she thoughtfully said. "It'll find us at the Genesis Lab, too, thanks to McAllister."

He nodded, pushing the gas pedal to the floor and putting on the siren and lights. "We just have to get there first. Lay the trap."

They were both painfully aware that while they had the AC at full blast, the busted windshield sucked in warm air from outside. "Keep hitting the body with the nitro," he said.

She crawled to a kneeling position in her seat and shoved the wand through the metal partition between front and back seats. "If this stuff doesn't hold out, these bars are all that's left between us and Adib's serpent."

17

Angelica called ahead to the lab in Key Largo, getting Anwar Tapai on the line. He immediately recognized her name. "Helen told me to expect your call. Then you are prepared to accept our demands?"

"Yes, the scrolls for the use of the accelerator."

"Put Helen on."

"I'm afraid that's impossible, Dr. Tapai."

"What do you mean?"

"Helen McAllister is dead, sir."

"That's impossible! I just talked with her less than an hour ago. She said she had everything under control."

"She was killed by the monster of the scrolls tonight, only fifteen minutes ago."

"The monster of the scrolls? The Kundalini?" Tapai fell silent on the line. Angelica brought him up to date, telling him how Helen had been killed.

"Killed by a mythological beast?"

"There's nothing mythological about it, Dr. Tapai. It's as real as it is destructive, this thing we want to destroy in your chamber, sir, and it killed her."

"She tried to . . . to tell me that the Kundalini was alive and is here in actuality, but I failed to believe it. I'm still not sure I do."

"Unfortunately, Doctor, it is true, and it's growing in strength as it randomly kills. Can we count on your cooperation?"

"Helen told me of the scrolls, and I have known of the legends all my life, but I never believed them. She began following your investigation of these recent suspicious human combustions. She began to believe it had something to do with the scrolls she so wanted. She told me what she witnessed at your crime lab. She saw a man turn a woman into smoke and gases. She'd gone looking for you at your office, to try to persuade you to turn over the scrolls to her when alarms sounded. She said the accelerator would be needed."

"That thing she saw at the lab, Dr. Tapai, and again tonight, it is the living Kundalini. We need to implode it along with the body of Adib"—she hesitated—"Shakar. It is the only way now to send this monster back to hell. She told you all this, didn't she?"

"Yes, but I presumed there was another explanation. I am a scientist, not a believer in the supernatural gods of ancient India."

"Doctor, this thing kills anyone that gets in its way. You've got to help us. We have the body of the *Shakar,* and we are being pursued by the *Shakar,* sir, and it's tragically true. We want to lay a trap, using the body of Adib Shakar as bait. Do you understand our need, sir, and the need for this to be done immediately and in privacy?"

"I understand, and I will help."

"For the good of mankind, sir, that machine of yours represents our last and only hope."

"I will do it for Helen and for the scrolls, which belong on display in my country. Now tell me, what precisely do you need?"

"Access to the accelerator chamber immediately."

"In anticipation, I have already arranged for a private experiment, we will call it, being conducted. I am in charge here. Bring the scrolls with you," said Tapai.

"You'll get them when we know we have what we want,

Dr. Tapai. Now we're in a Miami police cruiser. Make sure we have clearance at the gate."

"Consider it done."

"Which entrance will get us to the chamber more quickly? We've got to get Shakar into that chamber, Dr. Tapai, and getting him there won't be easy. The thing has the ability to ignite a person at fifteen thousand degrees. Can your chamber withstand such temperatures?"

"It can, yes. Then all that Helen had said about this creature . . . it's true."

"Which entryway will lead us quickly to the chamber?" she asked.

"Come in through the south loading dock. How close are you?"

"Minutes away. We'll need a table on wheels, or better yet a refrigeration unit on wheels. Can you accommodate us?" she asked.

"A large refrigeration unit on wheels? For the body? Yes, we have portable units large enough for the job."

"Give me the phone," said Brannon, reaching for it. He introduced himself and said, "Dr. Tapai, we'll also need clearance through security, and you will want to tell your security to stand down and allow this . . . this assassin into our trap."

"I'm not sure I understand your plans for the accelerator, and I do not have the authority to tell security to stand down. That would take a committee."

"At least tell them at the gate not to slow us down. That it's an emergency, and for their own safety, they're not to stop the man pursuing us."

"I'll try."

"No, don't try, Doctor, do it! Tell them the man is highly contagious . . . tell them anything."

"I'll do what I can. Perhaps to explain our *special use* of the chamber, we'll call it a containment of a contagious disease."

"That sounds like a wise idea. Tell people we're with the Center for Disease Control, tell them whatever will work."

In the distance Angelica saw the lights of the U.S. National Accelerator Lab, the Genesis Lab created to study findings from NASA launches and to study the most elemental materials on earth in a man-made space-type environment. It was a facility created for nuclear bombardment of subatomic materials.

Angelica pointed out the huge pyramidal building and its lights to Eric. It was a modern skyscraper in the middle of a huge field, looking like a cross between a pyramid and a nuclear reactor.

"Impressive architecture."

"It's not the building we're interested in. It's the chamber."

"Tell me more about this chamber."

"It was built as part of the government's push to develop superconductive materials for NASA while it furthers the frontiers of the fairly new science of quantum physics," she explained. "They're heavily invested in creating antimatter in this mile-long chamber. I've flown over it. From the sky, it looks like a giant circle. It's one hell of a vacuum."

"How does it work?"

"By bombarding materials with protons, they've created antiprotons, and have in effect created the conditions that led to the creation of the universe. If they can create antimatter out of Adib's remains, and do the same for Hari Shakir, then we may have a chance at beating this thing."

"What exactly is antimatter? I thought it was science fiction, you know, *Star Trek* stuff."

"Antimatter is found in cosmic showers. It's theorized to exist in other galaxies beyond ours as black holes—places in the universe where only antimatter exists."

"Until now."

"The accelerator lab . . . only other place where it exists, but there it is controlled in the experimental chamber."

Pulling into the narrow security check, they had to weave through concrete barriers, but once they reached the actual checkpoint, they were waved down at gunpoint by a single officer who stared at the condition of the cruiser's windshield and at the body in the backseat.

"This isn't what we asked for," he said, tugging out his badge and flashing it at the security officer. He shouted to the officer, "We're here as guests of Dr. Tapai. The man in the rear is highly contagious. We have to quarantine him here! It's a medical emergency that could infect the entire state and possibly the nation, do you understand?"

The guard was hardly out of his teens, and his mouth hung open.

"I'm with the medical examiner's office," Angelica added. "Did Dr. Tapai tell you we were coming?"

The man nodded, stepped into his hut, radioed ahead, and opened the gate. Brannon said, "Lock the gate and get to a safer location. We're being followed by a dangerous terrorist also infected with the disease."

"Anthrax?" he asked.

"Far worse, son. Now do as I said."

"I'll get some help out here, sir," replied the young officer.

"He's extremely dangerous!" shouted Angelica as Brannon tore through the open gate.

"How do you warn people about this kind of danger?" she asked Brannon.

"At the moment, our larger concern has to be destroying Adib's body."

"I hope we can trust this Dr. Anwar Tapai to live up to our bargain," she said.

"Well, he didn't balk at the idea of our using his facility to nuke a body and to set a trap for the serpent."

"One thing to agree to it over the phone, another to carry through. We're asking him to stand by while we pulverize a dead man, a live one, and two serpents, to send them into a black hole of nothingness."

"You think he'll freak?" asked Brannon, searching for the south loading dock.

"Depends on how badly he wants those scrolls," she said, patting her purse.

They pulled up to the south loading dock, which Tapai had told them to come to. The labs here ran day and night. It was 3:26 A.M., and they studied the dark-skinned doctor in the white lab coat, an Indian like Adib and Shakir.

It didn't surprise Angelica to know that Helen was involved with a prominent man like Tapai. Helen liked successful men, and she was into everything Indian. Dr. Tapai must have been her lover, and being Hindu, knowing something of the value of the scrolls, he would've been her first choice to come to with her wild scheme. Tapai waved them on. He stood beside a lone security officer, who had a gun on his hip.

The sight of the shattered windshield drew interest from the security guard. "Man, what the hell happened to your cruiser?"

"We have to move fast!" shouted Angelica, getting from the car. "We've got a contagious situation that needs containing! Get that freezer down here!"

Brannon had climbed from the car, the shotgun in hand. "We're being pursued by a terrorist using a biological agent," he said, hefting the shotgun and then lowering it to the hood of the car, saying, "Conventional weapons are no use against this thing."

Both Tapai and the guard regarded Eric and Angelica with reserved suspicion. The young security guard had obviously been debriefed by Dr. Tapai. He looked in Tapai's direction for a nod, and, getting it, he helped the doctor wheel the freezer unit—an upright the size of a refrigerator—down the ramp to the car, its wheels spinning. It appeared that Tapai, a large man with gray beard and thick glasses, had made some special arrangements with the guard.

"Just how contagious is the dead guy in the cruiser?" asked the guard.

Tapai swallowed hard on seeing Katra's body and the snake tattoo. He looked into Angelica's eyes and said, "So . . . this is the *Shakar,* the one who committed suicide to avoid a union with the other. Just as foretold in the scrolls, which I will take from you now."

"No . . . not until we see a good-faith effort that you are committed to helping us, Dr. Tapai."

"Then we have a standoff."

Brannon grabbed for Wheeler's gun as he raised it, and he knocked Wheeler down, wrenching the gun free and throwing it away. "We're wasting precious time here. Get us to the accelerator."

Tapai looked again at Adib's body.

"Dr. Adib Katra," said Angelica, "medical examiner for the city of Miami. A fine man."

"My God, Katra . . . I knew of him by reputation."

"Help me get Dr. Katra's body into the cooler," said Brannon to Wheeler.

The young security officer held back, not wanting to touch the body, fearful of the disease. "It's contained," said Brannon, "so long as it remains cold. Now help me get him into the damn freezer."

Dr. Tapai handed Wheeler a pair of surgical gloves, which he quickly placed on. Angelica looked on from the other side of the car, opening the back door and readying the liquid nitrogen should they need it.

Brannon saw that the crystals along the outer skin and beneath the nails had evaporated. "Damn, he's not so stiff anymore," he muttered to Angelica.

She replied, "All of you, stand back." She placed the wand over Adib's chest and opened the spray, but in a moment it only sputtered. "Damn, we've run out. Get him into that cooling unit, fast."

Brannon and Wheeler began to inch Adib's body from the cruiser.

Tapai said to Angelica, "My dear Helen. She was obsessed with the scrolls for their monetary value. When she contacted me, I told her how much they would bring from the National Museum of India. Tell me, did she suffer?"

"It was . . . Her death was instantaneous."

Brannon had Adib's legs, and Wheeler, no longer hesitating, grabbed the upper torso as Brannon slid the body from the backseat. Together, they carried the more supple, less stiff body to the freezer unit. "If he moves, drop him!" said Brannon to Wheeler.

"How's he gonna move? He's dead."

"I mean at the slightest hint of movement, Wheeler! If he moves, drop him and back off. You got that?"

Wheeler shrugged as he worked.

In a moment they had the body standing in the cooler, Brannon and Angelica breathing more calmly. Brannon was about to close the door when Adib's body quivered and a hand fell out. Wheeler, acting on reflex, lurched to catch and right the problem even as Eric shouted, "Don't!"

Wheeler watched the dead man's mouth gape open, and he saw an enormous snake's tongue strike him in the eyes, combusting him, sucking the fumes into the cooling unit and into Adib's body.

Tapai gasped and fell back on his knees, staring, frozen.

"Jesus Christ!" screamed Brannon, who'd immediately shoved the door closed, ramming home the lock, cutting off the trail of gases, causing Wheeler's smoke-blackened fatty acids to paint the area around the door handle and seal. Both Wheeler's naked and untouched lower legs and feet remained intact, unaffected by the fire, lying crisscrossed at the foot of the door.

Tapai was on his behind now, his features ashen, terrified. He had been standing close to Wheeler, and his lab coat, like Eric's right hand and arm, was sooty from the combustion. Tapai blubbered, unable to fashion words until he managed to say, "Oh my God, oh my God!"

The metal door and lock held, but Brannon felt the heat surrounding the area around the black paint that had been Wheeler. Brannon pointed to Wheeler's leftover extremities, and shouted, "Is that enough proof for you, Dr. Tapai? I've seen with my own eyes now six such deaths in the past few hours. This thing is real, and is a threat to us all, Doctor."

"Damn it!" said Angelica, realizing the controls for the freezer unit were set on low. She switched the gauge to its coldest setting.

"If Adib's body has warmed enough to allow that snake to grab Wheeler," asked Eric, "what's to keep the thing inside there?"

"It's likely marshaled all its strength for the attack on

Wheeler, but is still in a weakened condition. It most certainly doesn't have Shakir's power."

"In the event you're wrong, Angelica, let's get the damned thing to the accelerator."

"It knows it can be killed; it's been wounded by the scimitar, and it's trying to stay alive for as long as it can."

"And it knows how close Shakir is," said Eric. "It's buying time."

"I see now that it's all horribly true," said Tapai. "The Kundalini does exist, and it is here." Tapai's voice had taken on a sense of desperation.

"Now you know why we want you to pull your people back, allow us to bait this thing's other half into the chamber," explained Angelica.

"Using Shakar's body and his serpent to bait Shakir and his, yes . . . I completely understand now. Such power . . . it is amazing, dazzling. I saw the serpent rise and disappear in the blink of an eye. Poor young Wheeler didn't know what hit him."

Angelica, wanting to impress Tapai with what lay ahead of them, said, "There's another far stronger serpent after us, and if it unites with this one, we're all going out the same way as Wheeler, Doctor. Is that understood?"

From the distant security gate, they heard gunfire. "He's here, damn him! Shakir is right behind us!" shouted Brannon.

"Get up and show us the way to the chamber, Dr. Tapai, now," Angelica said, tugging at the man.

Tapai climbed to his feet and said, "This way, quickly."

Brannon grabbed the shotgun, and he and Angelica lent their combined weight to the refrigeration unit as they pushed it up the ramp and through the door. Dr. Tapai bolted the delivery door behind them.

On the inside, they came upon another security guard, who held a gun on them. "Hand over the shotgun, butt first! Now!"

Brannon did as ordered. "We're not the enemy."

"Someone's breached the gate, and Wheeler's away from

his post, and now I find you here. What's going on here, Dr. Tapai? What's in the freezer?"

"We don't have time for this!" shouted Angelica. "This is Detective Brannon, Miami police, and I'm the ranking medical examiner for Miami, and we're working with the CDC—" she lied even as she showed him her credentials.

Tapai added, "There is a terrorist pursuing these people, attempting to get hold of bioharzardous material now safely inside the freezer."

"Biohazard? Terrorist?"

"They got your man at the gate moments ago, and they got Wheeler," shouted Brannon, displaying his badge.

Dr. Tapai said, "Stand down, Larry. It's an emergency."

Larry went to the bank of monitors Wheeler was supposed to be watching. Still holding a gun on them, Larry rewound the tape monitoring the gate.

While he was working with the tape, the guard asked, "Where're you taking this hazardous material, Dr. Tapai?"

"Larry, we have to render what's in the cooler harmless. Let us pass, now!"

"I don't think so, Dr. Tapai, not without word from Security Chief Bell, and I don't have that. And no one's running around the building with a shotgun, Detective," he said to Brannon.

Tapai protested, "But there are terrorists behind us, attempting to get their hands on this material."

They all heard a soft whoosh like a sudden eruption of fire coming from the monitor. They saw the outer gate standing open, the security hutch alongside it appearing empty, and a plume of fire had blackened the booth's window all around.

"He's gotten through the gate," said Brannon. "Run the tape back. You'll see what we're up against."

Larry did so.

At the security gate Hari Shakir had zigzagged around the maze of barriers at a high speed and pulled calmly up to the security checkpoint. He could almost read the pimply faced guard's thoughts: *No one's given clearance for this guy.* Standing behind his hutch window, the guard had put out a hand for the car to stop, and Hari, dirty from the swamp, pulled up in the Explorer he had hot-wired, smiling wide. He had a large healed scar on his forehead where the scimitar had embedded itself, and his hair was falling out. The stress and strain of this night on his body had been grim and difficult.

"State your business, sir," the young officer said.

"I'm here to see Tapai. Tell him McAllister is here to see him."

"McAllister. I'll have to see if you're on Dr. Tapai's list. Procedure."

The young officer stalled for time. Backup was supposed to be on the way. Then he saw the name McAllister on the list, but it was a Helen McAllister.

"Are you Helen?"

"Allen . . . must be a mistake."

"Frankly, sir, with your ethnic appearance, you don't look like a McAllister, whether it's Allen or Helen, if you don't mind my saying."

"But I do mind." Shakir reached out and grabbed the man's wrist, and the guard reacted instantly, lifting the gun he had held poised just below the lip of the window. Recalling what Brannon and Hunter had said about contagious disease, he fired a round into Hari's face, and for a millisecond the kid thought himself safe, but Shakir only grinned as the guard watched the wound heal over. The guard found himself unable to pull away from Shakir's grip. Shakir then turned him into flame and gases, sucking him through the hutch window, and through the car window, and into his throat. Hari then casually climbed from the car and worked the controls to open the gate.

No alarms had gone off, but he saw two surveillance cameras had recorded the event. He might expect more resistance ahead. As he drove, he mined the dead guard for details to guide him.

18

When Larry Earnhardt, the security guard inside, saw what had happened to the other man at the gate, he asked repeatedly, "What'd I see? What'd I just see? What do you know about this guy? What kind of explosives does he have? Does he have a name?" shouted Larry as he watched Tapai usher them out.

Brannon shouted back over his shoulder to Larry, "There's no way you or your men can stop this guy with conventional weapons. Let him through to the accelerator."

"The hell I will," muttered Larry, hefting the Remington shotgun.

Angelica shouted, "Allow him to follow us to the accelerator. We'll make our stand against him there."

Tapai led Brannon and Angelica down the corridor, past a series of doors to a waiting elevator. "This will take us down to the nuclear accelerator facility," he explained.

Brannon pushed Adib's body onto the elevator, and, as the doors were closing, they heard the inhuman pounding on the delivery room door where Larry stood with the shotgun poised.

The elevator descended to the lower level.

"Shakir knows what McAllister knows," Angelica explained to Tapai, "so he knows we're baiting him in, using the accelerator. He'll come at us with some caution."

"I hope we know what we're doing," said Eric. "What if Hari doesn't go for it?"

"He will . . . he has to," replied Angelica. "Besides, he's grown arrogant."

"No longer satisfied with remaining in the shadows," agreed Eric.

She added, "He wants completion, and he knows if he isn't successful tonight, that we'll have destroyed Adib's body nonetheless."

"He doesn't think we stand a chance," said Brannon.

The elevator doors opened on a wide corridor and they stepped off, Eric shoving the refrigeration unit ahead of him. "He thinks he can get to us before we can destroy the body."

"And he may be right," she warned, "if he gets to the body before we can throw the switch."

Brannon turned to Tapai. "How well did McAllister know the layout?"

Tapai halted and grabbed Angelica by the arm. "Are you two saying that Helen . . . that some part of Helen actually does live on in this creature?"

Angelica saw the horror of the idea envelop Tapai's every sensibility.

"I remember as a child in India being told that the Kundalini has the power to imprison the souls of its victims," he replied. "By combusting its victims and swallowing the fumes before the soul has any chance of escape."

"Perhaps when we destroy it, we free Helen and the others from its hold."

"And if it joins with Shakar? According to the legends, Helen will have a share in the creature's immortality," added Tapai.

"I can't say," she replied, "but if it is so, it could be an ugly immortality."

Brannon repeated the question Angelica had put to Tapai. "How well did Helen McAllister know the layout here?"

"It's how he finds us," Angelica said. "Please, answer the question."

"I gave her a tour once, similar to the usual visitor's tour but of course behind the scenes. She was confused by all the talk of quarks and protons, but she understood the principle of turning matter into antimatter."

"Then we have to assume Shakir will quickly find us," said Angelica.

"She was lost down here, and we came from another direction, my office. I explained to her that the chamber is like a bicycle wheel with a series of spokes—corridors leading to and from it. Each corridor is lettered A through Z. A and Z are at the beginning and end of the accelerator loop, alongside one another. We'll bait it at A with the open airlock, and place the bait at the airlock terminal at Z."

They entered a restricted area, and Dr. Tapai placed his eye against a retinal scanner. The door opened, and they plowed through. They stood in a darkened control room with the refrigeration unit.

"Here we are," said Tapai. "A beautiful mechanism engineered to simulate conditions in the universe that led to the creation of matter and antimatter."

They watched Tapai quickly readjust switches, and he turned on all the lights. "I had everyone evacuate this area earlier in anticipation of your arrival," he explained. "We'll want your pursuer to believe that the accelerator is not only shut down but inoperable for the time being. Look at the screen."

Angelica and Eric had exchanged a look, both of them deciding that all earlier preparations Tapai had made had been for their benefit, not to combat the monster. Overhead, the large screen read CONDITION ZERO—24 HOUR SHUTDOWN.

"It's a bogus message, only true of this control room. I have a secondary control room at my disposal."

"Would McAllister know of the other control room?" asked Angelica.

"No, she would not."

"Then Shakir won't know of it either."

Tapai pointed down at the enormous accelerator tube.

"I've managed to make it appear as harmless as I can." Angelica and Brannon were staring out the control-room window, down at the huge, glass tube in the shape of a racetrack going in both directions.

"You're looking down on Airlock Corridor Z to your right, A is just below us. We bait Shakir with the open airlock here at Corridor A, and place Adib's body in at the next airlock at Z."

"Shakir will be able to see the body from here," she said, staring down at the next airlock corridor that Tapai referred to as Z.

"Exactly. When he finds the control room is shut down, the chamber open and appearing harmless and inoperable, he'll rush in after his goal."

"If he goes for the trap," said Eric.

"He'll see the body inside. It will lure him in," Tapai added.

They studied the perimeter corridor of the underground mile-long accelerator.

"I shut down all activity in the chamber when I got your call," began Dr. Tapai. "Made some people most unhappy, but I managed to clear the control room for our *experiment*."

The enormity of the accelerator settled over Angelica and Eric as they continued to stare down the length of it, while Dr. Tapai continued to monitor the equipment. "It's a perfect trap," he said.

"Now all we need do is to lay out the bait," added Eric.

"Come along, this way." Tapai pushed open another door, which led into an interior hallway between offices.

Angelica and Brannon had followed with the refrigeration unit, and together they found an elevator door. An overhead sign blinked in red light: OUT OF ORDER. "Part of my ruse," said Tapai. "We don't want him coming this way but going down to the airlock and into the chamber from here, bypassing this area altogether. Once he enters Airlock A, we'll close it behind him. He'll have no escape from the vacuum and the bombardment."

When they boarded the elevator, they saw the panel read

alphabetically from A to Z. "This isn't an up-down elevator but a horizontal transport. It runs around the accelerator to each of the airlocks. Mostly used for maintenance and for checking on the cameras stationed at each corridor."

"Just so long as it will get us to Airlock Z," she said.

"It will take us there and to the auxiliary control room. I only hope this creature can read."

"It reads all right," said Brannon, recalling the newspaper story about Osterman.

They were soon at the second control room, Brannon pushing the refrigeration unit ahead of him. They had also arrived at the airlock at Corridor Z, and from this vantage point they again stared into the huge glass chamber. This control area overlooked the accelerator at Airlock Z. Angelica saw that specialized electron-microscope cameras were mounted every twenty yards to snap pictures of the invisible world of atomic molecules inside the chamber.

"How thick is the glass?" asked Eric.

"Twelve inches. It's the same as on NASA spacecraft, and it can resist temperatures well over fifteen thousand degrees, as when reentering Earth's atmosphere."

"Are you sure this can work, Dr. Tapai?" asked Eric.

"I believe it can work, that it is theoretically possible to disassemble this creature by bombardment with subatomic particles. That any mass can be reduced by a shower of antimatter if the settings are high enough."

"Theoretically?" asked Brannon.

"We don't know what we're dealing with here, Detective. Helen merely wanted to know if it were theoretically possible to *implode* a person or animal inside the chamber—that the vacuum alone would kill this thing, and perhaps it will, but I'm taking no chances now. The vacuum will be achieved at the same instant that the bombardment will hit."

"It sounds as if Helen prepared you somewhat for what was headed your way, Doctor," said Angelica.

"I had two calls from Helen. She had read about the spontaneous combustions, and when you two came to visit with the scrolls, she had become obsessed with getting those scrolls. She followed you, and apparently she saw an actual spontaneous human combustion brought on by this thing that chased you from your crime lab, Dr. Hunter."

"And the second call?"

"She realized what difficulty you were in, running off with the *Shakar* body in tow, not knowing how you could keep ahead of that monster. So she proposed the accelerator for the scrolls."

"And you had no trouble embracing the idea?"

"On the contrary, I had a great deal of trouble embracing it. We . . . we argued. She was a strong-willed woman. I gave in, but I believed we were dealing with something human, not a mythological beast."

"Are you saying she went to my office to negotiate the idea of the accelerator?" asked Angelica.

"Yes, she did. On her second call to me, she told me to turn on the TV to Channel Two. And there was a report of three people in one room who had died in apparent spontaneous human combustions all at once at County General in Miami. Further proof of the impossible, she claimed."

"You still didn't believe her?" she asked.

"At that time, Helen said she meant to strike a deal with you."

"The accelerator time for the scrolls?"

"She asked me to convince you that we could implode and atomize a human body." Tapai paced the secondary control room. "I remained skeptical, but I made preparations. Then I got your call that Helen was dead, and that you were on your way here. But until I saw what happened to Wheeler, I could not fathom the reality of it all."

"So she didn't know how you planned to trap this thing?"

"I didn't know myself until I got the call from you. I immediately set the secondary, auxiliary control room to override everything. It operates on another set of commands, my commands at the moment. Come now. We've got to get down to the Z corridor airlock. That's where you'll place the bait."

As they made their way down to Airlock Z, Brannon

asked, "Suppose he discovers the first control room? Can he do any harm from there?"

"Control of the airlocks and the chamber itself has been diverted to the secondary here. I assure you, it can't be restored back to the primary until twenty-four hours have elapsed. It's a fail-safe measure in case of emergency, as we have now—biohazardous material. Once atomized, the debris will be sucked into a container that will be buried along with other hazardous material."

"At a nuclear dump site?" she asked.

Eric asked, "You've got everything figured out, don't you, Dr. Tapai?"

"No, not really. None of us knows what will happen when and if that creature is showered with antimatter particles. And after seeing what the one half of this thing is capable of, I want to recalibrate the amount of the bombardment. But first, we need to put Katra's body inside."

Tapai pushed through a door and out onto a gently sloping ramp that would take them to the chamber itself and Airlock Z at the bottom of the ramp. As Brannon carefully maneuvered the freezer unit, Angelica whispered to him, "Keep your eye on Tapai. Everything in this place requires his retina and code."

"Yeah, we lose him, we lose the war."

"I hate having to trust him."

"I'm afraid we're at his mercy."

"Just be careful."

Angelica had watched Tapai punch in the code that had opened Airlock A, and she had memorize it, just in case. She didn't know what she might do about the retinal access to the controls.

"We must get in and out quickly," Tapai was saying, his hand poised over the airlock keypad, but a sudden squeal of alarms going off in the building stayed his hand.

"Do not worry," said Tapai. "The secondary control room is designed to run under any circumstances."

Angelica searched Tapai's eyes for any sign of deception, but his black eyes proved inscrutable. She unconsciously clutched the bag holding the scrolls strapped around her neck.

More and louder alarms went off all around them.

"It's him!" shouted Brannon. "He's in the building, setting off fire alarms."

"Agreed, we've got to work fast," said Tapai.

Holding up a hand to the others, Angelica said, "But first we have to make a *difficult* decision."

"What's left to decide?" Eric asked.

"We can quickly and surely destroy Adib's body and thereby render it useless to this monster right now," she replied. "Baiting the pursuer, anything could go wrong. Suppose Shakir gets to Adib's remains and bonds with the other serpent *before* we can shower them with the antimatter?"

"Then we've lost," Eric said. "He'll blow that chamber all to hell."

"There are no guarantees," agreed Tapai, keying in the code to open the exterior airlock door, "but I say we must try to rid the world of both these serpents, now. Before we make a decision, give me the scrolls," said Tapai, his hand out. "Let me read them, now!"

"You can read Sanskrit?"

"Yes, and I recall something important. I must see the scrolls. It may be crucial to our decision."

She stared into his eyes, trying to read the black pupils. She slowly removed the scrolls and handed them over.

Tapai's lips moved as he read the scrolls. "Here it is, yes, just as a story told to me in childhood, it is written here."

"What? What is it?"

"It says here that if the serpent is destroyed in its entirety, then all the souls trapped within are released. Is that incentive enough to carry through with your plan?"

Angelica nodded, "That's incentive enough, yes."

"Then we go for broke," said Eric. "Besides, I really want to see Hari Shakir fry."

"Then we are agreed." Tapai rerolled the Sanskrit parchment in his hands.

"All right," Angelica replied, "but we've got to time this

to the moment. We don't know how much time it takes for those two serpents to merge into one being."

Eric asked, "How quickly can the subatomic rain be turned on, Dr. Tapai?"

"It is just a matter of a switch, but it will take a few minutes to restore the absolute vacuum, and to bring the chamber up to the desired level of bombardment, a level we have never attempted before. Two human bodies carrying that thing . . . it's a large mass."

"So far, Dr. Tapai, this thing has defied all the laws of nature, and it is only at half power," she said. Angelica bit her lower lip, adding, "The fate of the world rests in our hands."

Just then a white-haired man in a lab coat came through a corridor door and shouted at Tapai, asking, "Dr. Tapai, what in God's kingdom is going on here? Who are these people, and what's in that storage unit that's hazardous? Security called me. I had to tell them I had no idea what you were up to."

Angelica took the opportunity to whisk the scrolls back from Tapai.

"Dr. Strohner, we are in the midst of a bomb detonating. Security has been breached, so please, we must do as the police tell us. Show him your badges, officers."

They flashed their credentials for the old man. He glared back. "If you can be here, Dr. Tapai, then so can I."

"Dr. Karl Strohner, my chief rival," Tapai said, shrugging. "Now please, out, Dr. Strohner. Go through Corridor Z. For your own safety, get out of the building as quickly as you can."

"I'm not buying it, Dr. Tapai. You knew about this before anyone, almost an hour ago, when you asked everyone to shut down their projects and vacate the control room. Yet the head of security knows nothing, and now alarms are sounding."

Eric went to Strohner, ushering him through a doorway and into the adjoining hall, telling him to evacuate. "Get to the nearest exit. Those alarms are for a biohazardous bomb threat, Doctor. Move it!"

As the old man left, he mumbled about this being highly irregular, and that he would bring Tapai before the review committee.

Eric returned to Tapai and Angelica, still at the chamber airlock, the exterior door open and waiting for them to enter. Tapai went again to the keypad and retinal scanner. He had already keyed in the code, and he now pressed his eye against the scanner. "State-of-the-art retinal scanner technology, Dr. Hunter," he said, seeing her take notice. "Won't accept anyone's eye who hasn't been cleared, and the eye must be *living*."

The airlock door plunged upward with a whoosh. Tapai held them in place. "When you go inside, the exterior door would normally close behind you, but I have quit that command, to allow you an open retreat, without waiting for any timers. Normally you'd be wearing a space suit and oxygen, and the doors would open and close in careful sequence for decompression, but since there is no vacuum at the moment inside the chamber, you're not going to go through decompression."

Tapai started away, but Angelica grabbed his arm. "Where will you be?" she asked.

He stared down the chamber back toward Airlock A, as if looking for Shakir to step into the chamber at any moment. "I'll be able to monitor things better from the control room," he suggested, rushing off.

"Now we really have to trust the man," said Eric. "Stay out of the airlock, understand? No matter what happens."

Eric stepped in, pushing the cold-storage unit ahead of him, entering the glass bridge to the inner chamber. Once inside, the interior door opened, and he saw that Dr. Tapai had indeed arranged for the exterior door to remain open as well. "All is a go, Dr. Tapai," he said over the intercom in the airlock.

"Place your bait inside," replied Tapai, "and get out fast.

Hopefully, he will follow the course we have laid out for him."

"You believe he'll stop to destroy the controls before he steps inside?" asked Brannon.

"As we might anticipate, yes, but I assure you, he cannot override the controls from there, not now. We have him."

Hari had driven straight for the loading dock where he saw the patrol cruiser. Hari pulled into the loading bay and went for the door, finding it locked.

He placed his hands on the door and concentrated, and the metal surface began to soften and turn to a molten Jell-O, starting to drip away. It took only minutes for the superheated molecules of the door to begin to dissipate altogether, and leave a large enough hole for Hari to reach in and lift the thick dead bolt laid across the door.

He stood at the end of a corridor, staring at an office of security monitors, but no one appeared to be home.

McAllister had not been in this area of the building before, but the security guard had. McAllister's friend Tapai had given her a personal tour that didn't include this place. He knew Tapai by facial features, and he knew him to be a scientist with the highest-ranking security clearance, the man in charge of the accelerator chamber. Hari didn't understand exactly how it worked, but he knew that McAllister and the others thought this oversized oven a possible answer to their prayers, an instrument that might destroy Adib Shakar's remains, and so destroy Hari by denying him his chance to touch with Shakar.

Already they had tried and failed. They had failed to destroy Adib at the crime lab, had failed at the swamp, and now he must insure that they fail here.

He knew they would be baiting him at the chamber. McAllister had knowledge of the plot. She understood little about the inner workings of the accelerator, but she understood its general purpose, and the purpose to which Adib's guardians meant to put it—to destroy Adib's remains along with Hari's own Kundalini half if they could. However, Mc-Allister lacked specific knowledge of exactly how to get to the accelerator from here. Where was the damn thing in the building? The lower-level security guard didn't know the way either.

Someone here must be able to direct him.

Hari caught a glimpse of himself in a glass reflection as he passed a partitioned area where the small security office held monitors linked to cameras trained on every corner of the building, inside and out. Hari knew he smelled of swamp water, and that he looked dirty and unkempt from his mad night of searching, that his body looked haggard and ashen.

Larry Earnhardt leapt up from behind a desk and began firing a shotgun. Hari walked into the shower of buckshot, stunning the man, holding him with his eyes. Crossing the distance between them, Hari grabbed the gun at its barrel, and, using his other hand, he looped his fingers around the guard's wrist, as if measuring it. He sent a searing but controlled combustion through the gun and up to the man's wrist, turning gun and wrist into a fireball of heated metal and scorched flesh.

The stub of hand and gun came away from the man's body, and Hari grinned, holding it up to the other man's eyes. The security guard screamed and pleaded, "Merciful God . . . God have mercy."

"Mercy? I'll give you mercy. Take me to the accelerator chamber, or I'll take your other hand and work my way up from there one limb at a time."

Hari then saw Brannon, Hunter, and Tapai on one of the monitor screens. "There! There they are. Where is that?"

"East wing to the accelerator. They're going for the accelerator."

"Take me to them, now!" He took Larry hostage, his finger to his head. "Or else I fry your brain next."

A team of other security officers suddenly rushed into the corridor, and they all pointed guns at Hari, but they also stared at Larry's stub of a wrist, blackened and cauterized by the fire that had sliced his hand off. "Unless you have a grenade launcher, get the hell outta here!" shouted Larry.

"You know we can't do that, Larry!" replied Richard Bell, head of security.

"A bullet to the face, and now buckshot to the torso, and it only puts holes in his clothes, chief! So back off!"

"Identify yourself!" ordered Bell, a tall black man.

"I am Hari Shakir, and I have come for what is mine!"

"Don't piss him off. Let us by," pleaded Larry. "They don't pay us enough for this, Jim, Pat, Mike, Joe."

"He's only got a finger pointed at you, Larry," Bell shouted, reaching out to strike Hari with the butt of his gun.

Tired of the games, Hari suddenly sent out a lizardlike tongue that slapped Bell in the face. The others watched Bell go up in smoke and gas, and they trembled on seeing Shakir swallow these gases down his throat. It happened so quickly the others could not believe what they had seen, and Larry had been painted with the blackened residue of Richard Bell. Hari's form, in that moment of explosion, had taken on the shape and scales of a dragonlike beast, but was it an explosion? It had concentrated entirely on the single security guard. He was completely combusted while Hari Shakir remained untouched by the heat that had seared mustaches and skin from the others who were closest to the combustion.

The closest had been Larry. His uniform blackened with grease, Larry dropped to his knees, and, using his good hand, he drew his thirty-eight and shoved it to his temple, killing himself for fear of going out the way Bell had.

Hari tossed him aside.

Hari then turned his attention on the other guards, all of whom backed off as Hari came toward them. They opened fire, but Larry had been right. Bullets hardly slowed this inhuman thing before them.

Hari grabbed one, combusted him, and this time it set off alarms all over the building. The remaining security guards fled back through the corridor and through a door that opened on a huge open-air foyer flush with tropical plants and a pond—the reception area, darkened and closed to the public at this hour, filling with people rushing from offices, reacting to the alarms and trying to get out of the building.

Overhead, at the very top floor, a giant skylight showed the stars and the heavens. Beneath these stars, on the ground floor of the building, Hari turned yet another human being into a brief flare.

People now raced for the exits, knocking one another aside, trampling others. Some fell into the pond, some slid on the stone tiles. Between the alarms and the screams, it had turned into bedlam.

"I haven't time for this!" Hari told himself.

Hari grabbed hold of yet another guard and held him firm, controlling the urge to combust and feed on him, and promising, "I will not harm you. I will not turn you into a human torch if only you will point the way to the accelerator."

"There, Corridor A through M," he said, pointing and pleading on his knees for his life.

Hari saw the letters of the alphabet on overhead signs, like airport terminal designations, pointing out the way to the visitors' viewing area.

"Don't be worried. I can be your friend," Hari said to the man. "What is your name?"

"D-D-Daniel."

"Well . . . Daniel, you wouldn't lie to me, would you?"

"No . . . no."

"Do I have to consume you to have the truth out of you?"

"No, no, no! A, it's Corridor A."

He smiled. "Not to worry. I was, after all, invited by Dr. Tapai."

Hari then consumed the man to the horror of everyone around them. He then rushed for the designation Corridor A. As he did so, he realized that Daniel had been withholding the crucial added knowledge Chief Bell provided, that it was LLCA—Lower Level Corridor A—that he wanted.

As he caught the elevator, he pictured the layout of the place in his mind. He had it; he knew where the control room was. If he could shut it down with fire, then the damned thing would be inoperable, and he will have won. Nothing could stop him now from getting at Shakar's remains and the living organism still within Adib.

19

Eric Brannon slapped the side of the refrigeration unit, saying, "Do we open it, or leave it for Hari Shakir to open?"

"He'll more readily come inside the chamber if he sees Adib's body," she replied.

Tapai spoke to them from the control room through an intercom in the airlock. "I agree with Dr. Hunter. Besides, we will want a direct shower of protons to strike the organic target directly. Are you ready?"

"All right, Angelica," shouted Eric over the alarms, "no sense in both of us being in harm's way. You hang back now where you are, and you, Dr. Tapai, be ready to close that airlock hatch as soon as I'm back inside."

Pushing Adib's body along ahead of him, Eric moved into the chamber itself now, the airlock portal behind him remaining open. Angelica watched from the relative safety of the corridor, staring through the glass.

Eric wheeled the refrigeration unit to the center of the chamber itself. Once he got out and Hari came in—and once the two airlocks were secured—the tubular chamber would be again a complete vacuum to simulate space, and if the decompression didn't kill the monster, then the bombardment would commence. But it must all be done before the two serpents could become one.

With these thoughts running through his mind, Eric realized the refrigeration unit exterior was again warming up. He quickly faced the door away from the airlock and himself, and he reached around to trip the lock, when Angelica said, "Careful, that thing inside gets stronger with each feeding, and it hasn't had time to freeze again."

Then he felt the heat coming off the metal container. It became so intense that he pulled away. "Damn thing is heating up the cooler."

"It's using stored energy and energy gained from Wheeler," she said, "to combat the cold."

The unit began to quake and then redden.

"Get out of there!" she shouted, rushing into the airlock.

Eric was struck by the charging, demolished refrigeration unit, which rocketed toward him when the door blew. Tapai watched from overhead as the refrigeration-unit door flew off in one direction, sending the unit into Brannon, bloodying him and knocking him down. The unit careened off on its rollers.

Adib's body had catapulted out, and it lay bloated where it had come to rest, some fifteen feet from Brannon, and writhing out of the abdominal wounds were the two raised heads of the creature. Its four eyes quickly assessed its new surroundings.

Angelica started to reach out a hand from the airlock to grasp hold of Eric when the airlock door came crashing down with a whoosh of air, almost taking her arm off.

A soft silence filled the vacuum chamber where Angelica had fallen back.

Angelica erupted, shouting, "Eric! Get away from it!"

Eric was laid out on his back a few feet from Adib's body, Eric's eyes wide, watching the two cobra heads lifting higher out of Adib's torn abdomen.

"Don't look at it! Run!"

But Brannon stared, mesmerized on seeing the snake's two separate heads with all its eyes focused on him. Angelica was right. The thing seemed strengthened by its having so recently fed on Wheeler, and obviously its time in the cooler hadn't been long enough.

The two cobra heads struck out at Eric just as he rolled away. The distance and the creature's continued attachment to Adib's body held the snake just out of reach. The snake released more of itself out into the world as Eric scrambled further from it.

Angelica screamed, "Open the airlock door, Tapai, now!"

Eric tore his gaze from the monster's double stare. He backed away from the liver-colored, thick-bodied serpent's licking tongues, consciously keeping his eyes from meeting the monster's again.

Adib's body was being dragged along behind the creature, which wanted it both ways: it wanted another meal, but it didn't want to give up the security of its dark lair, Adib's insides. It seemed wrapped about his backbone.

Eric had been backing away on his hands and rump, but he got up now and threw his body against the glass door of the airlock, coming face-to-face with Angelica on the other side.

From overhead, Tapai had stared in amazed horror at the creature. Cornered, it had come out. Horrified, Tapai had hit the airlock door, and it came crashing down, locking Eric inside with the beast, while Angelica screamed from inside the airlock.

"Tapai!" Eric's voice was muffled by the glass.

"You bastard, no! Open it! Tapai!" shouted Angelica, shaking her fists up at Tapai.

"We can't risk it, Brannon!" he shouted. "Get yourself down to the next airlock portal at Y intersection! Hurry! There is no time to lose. It will be open and waiting for you! Go!"

Brannon feared that the snake was freeing itself from Adib's decaying body, seeking any chance at life. It still had all its four eyes fixed on him.

Angelica continued to pummel the glass and to plead with Tapai to let Eric out here and now. Eric's hands pressed against the glass, against hers as the snake rose higher and higher behind him. "Behind you!" she shouted.

He pushed off the glass, spinning to his left bolting for the next airlock portal.

As he had pushed away from the glass, the snake plunged into it and Angelica saw Eric replaced by the two flared heads and the four mammoth snake eyes. The brown thing left a sticky, sizzling residue against the glass.

Fixed on Angelica's image now, the snake began burning the twelve-inch-thick glass, creating a stain of white heat in its attempt to get at her, but it was no match for the NASA glass. She taunted it, doing all she could to keep the serpent's attention from Eric while he ran for the next airlock. She pounded her fists into the glass directly at its eyes. Relenting, she then placed her cheek against the glass. "Come and get me! Focus on me, you motherfucking bastard of hell!"

"Good!" shouted Tapai. "Keep its attention off Brannon as long as possible."

As soon as Tapai said this, one of the monster's heads turned an eye toward the retreating detective, and it pulled away, going for Brannon, yanking its twin along with it, and the force dragged Adib's body behind it.

"Damn it, Tapai, the thing understands language. It learns from its prey. You may as well have signed Eric's death warrant."

It had left a large misshapen circle of superheated glass on the interior of the airlock door, but it had only penetrated the first layers of the glass.

Angelica tried to calculate the strength and mobility of the serpent. It appeared looped around Adib's spine, pulling the body along behind it, slowing its pursuit of Brannon. "It's afraid to be completely on its own, without a dark place to hide," she said aloud with the realization. "But it must feed."

Angelica turned to stare up at Tapai at the controls, shouting, "Get that third airlock opened, Dr. Tapai! You son of a bitch, now!" She raced from the airlock to join Tapai in the control room, where she could best watch Eric's progress and escape.

Tapai tripped the lock from where he sat, allowing her entry, and he said, "I had no choice! We have to keep that thing inside the chamber now."

"Get Eric out of there!" she shouted.

"I am working on a solution."

"We can't switch on the accelerator with Eric inside."

"Brace yourself. We may have to." Tapai was staring at a monitor, mesmerized by the snakelike creature with its host of tentacles and suckers exposed now, dazzled by its macabre connection to Adib's body.

Angelica watched Eric on the monitor, limping, bloody, without any defense, so far out of reach of the serpent's deadly tongue and tentacles. She shouted at Tapai, "Dying inside that chamber with that thing is not an option for Eric Brannon, Doctor!"

She switched on an intercom and said, "You can make it, Eric. It's moving slow, dragging Adib's body with it."

Tapai talked to him through the intercom. "You have only a small window of opportunity, Detective. Hurry! The portal will be open and waiting for you, but I will close it if the creature is too close."

Angelica watched the serpent again, its form elongating, undulating, slithering sidewinder style, each of its heads raised and hunting.

"Open it!" she screamed. "Open the fucking airlock!"

Tapai keyed in the necessary commands. "All it needs now is my retinal scan," he said.

"Do it!"

"The scrolls first," he said, indicating the bag around her neck. "Hand them over to me."

"You son of a bitch. You planned this all along!" She reached for the bag she'd kept around her neck, and she threw it at him. "Now open the goddamn airlock!"

He turned the bag inside out and dumped its contents on the floor. There were no scrolls in the bag.

On the monitor screen Eric continued his race for the exit. "We have a man's life at stake here!" she shouted.

"And you need my right eye. Now where are the scrolls?"

"Down there." She pointed to the chamber.

"Down there? *Inside* the chamber?"

"Take a close look at Eric's shirt."

He turned to the monitor and studied the bulge in Brannon's shirt. She said, "I insisted he take them. Passed them to him just before he left the airlock."

"But why? You fool! They're priceless."

"And they'll be just as priceless when Eric comes out with them."

He opened a drawer and pulled out a handgun. "I placed this here to use on myself, should anything go wrong. I'll use it, too, if I have to."

"Open the causeway, Tapai. We can destroy this thing, and you can have the scrolls if we time it right."

"The scrolls foretell this moment; the power of the Kundalini will overwhelm us all, but it will select one among us to survive, to do its bidding."

"No!"

"It is written in the scrolls." She saw the insanity in his eyes now, and she realized the allure of the supernatural power extended to Tapai, and the madness that told him he could control the beast. He had been lying to them all along.

"You can't be serious, Doctor. All of mankind is at stake."

"I intend to survive at any cost."

"This thing we're trying to kill is pure evil."

"It is an intelligent being. It will acknowledge my capturing it and my mercy on it. It will know that I am its chancellor, the keeper of the scrolls."

"Think of Helen and the others who gave their lives."

"It will reward me alone."

"Open the portal, please, Dr. Tapai!"

He pointed back toward Airlock A, where she saw Hari Shakir enter the chamber. "All parties are here."

"From the beginning . . . you had no intention of destroying the creature, did you?"

"Not once I learned it was truly him, the Kundalini. There

is no power on earth it cannot consume and make its own. The accelerator will only feed it more power. It can not be contained."

"If Shakir combusts Eric, the scrolls will burn with him. You need to get Eric out to have the scrolls, Doctor."

"Yes, yes!"

He placed the gun on the workstation panel and keyed in the sequence to close off Airlock A behind Shakir, sealing Hari Shakir inside the chamber along with Eric.

She grabbed the gun on the console, and he grabbed her hands. The gun exploded, killing Tapai, leaving him slumped in his chair.

"Oh my God, no! Damn it! Damn him!" she shouted.

She shakily grabbed his head by his gray hair and wheeled his body against the panel. She quickly maneuvered his head and his eye over the retinal scanner. But when she looked out on the chamber, she saw that Eric had already come and gone at the Y airlock, and that he was running for the X airlock. The sequence of numbers would be different, and she wasn't sure how sensitive the scanner would be to a dead retina.

She struggled to find the pattern in the airlock numbers. A, Z, now X. She guessed it to be identical except for the last two digits, which corresponded with the alphabet, twenty-six being Z, twenty-five being Y, and twenty-four being X. She keyed in the sequence she had memorized from earlier and replaced the last two digits with twenty-four. She then forced Tapai's right eye open and held it open with Band-Aids that had spilled from her bag. Angelica next brought the dead man's eye over the scanner. Her medical mind told her it could not work, that the sensitive mechanisms of the eye would already show up as dead.

She was right. The airlock doors remained closed. Eric was at Y, the serpent still in pursuit, and Hari Shakir in pursuit of it.

From behind her Angelica heard someone say, "Can I help you here?"

She wheeled and brought the gun up. It was Dr. Strohner.

"Detective Brannon is trapped in the chamber," she said.

"Yes, I know. I've been observing from the control room that is now useless. You need my retina."

Strohner joined her at the controls, looking over the settings. As he did so, he spoke. "I took refuge in the control room when I saw the strange man turn a young colleague into cinder and gases. And now I've got to be certain of what Tapai has done here. I have to check what he has the accelerator programmed for."

"The airlock first; get Eric free first." She held the gun now on Strohner.

"There is no time. I must check behind Tapai first."

"Do it then, and make it fast."

Strohner said, "I know what it wants, and I understand your dilemma. Our first priority must be to destroy that thing."

She stared down at the chamber, seeing that Shakir had arrived at the demolished refrigeration unit, and from there he called out, "My brother! I am here! We can unite!"

The snake tugging Adib's body would soon again be within striking distance of Eric. Brannon appeared out of breath, panting.

"We've got to get him out of there, Doctor, now."

From their vantage point, they could see that Adib's serpent was pulled by a psychic connection of sorts to its other half, but it was torn, one head studying Brannon, the other looking back down the tube toward Hari Shakir.

"You're lucky I returned," said Strohner, making rapid adjustments to the controls.

"All right . . . I have Tapai's program stopped."

"Stopped? What're you doing?" she asked. "Tapai said all the controls were set!"

"Set wrongly."

She lifted the gun and held it on Strohner. "Just get Eric out of there and put this accelerator in motion, now!"

"Trust me, Tapai never intended to destroy the creature.

He had the setting for clockwise-spinning *positively* charged proton bombardment. It will only feed the monster to positively attack it now! It can only increase its power inside the chamber, I assure you." Strohner shook his head. "The man was mad. He must have believed he could control that monster if he saved it from annihilation. Damn fool."

"He thought he could cooperate with it, using the scrolls." Angelica looked back at Tapai's body, another victim of the serpent.

"He was planning to shower it with positive matter, not antimatter. He meant to feed it!"

"The airlock!"

"Yes, of course!"

"Do it, now!"

Her eyes drifted to the airlock Brannon stood pounding on.

Hari Shakir had found the maze of this place confusing and he had feared running out of time. The alarms going off all around him had people scurrying about, but no one questioned him, since he had thrown a white lab coat with a security-clearance tag over himself. He had forced it from a woman he had encountered in the corridor, heading for the exits. He had first convinced her to give him the lab coat, and when she did, she began pleading for her life. He responded by consuming her. "Now you will live forever," he had said. "My gift to you and ultimately all mankind."

He hadn't seen the white-haired elderly Dr. Strohner witnessing this. He was too busy mining information from the woman. She knew precisely how to find the control room for the accelerator, and she knew how to shut it down. He rushed to the spot, and there he found the door locked against him. He pounded on it, claiming he needed immediate access.

An old man with snow-white beard, reminding Hari of a scryer he once consumed in India, came to a window and stared out at Hari where he stood in the corridor. The white-haired old man pointed skyward, drawing Hari's attention to a sign over the door that read: IN EVENT OF ALARM, ACCELERATOR CONTROLS ARE LOCKED DOWN.

Adib placed both hands on the metal door and began firing it, turning it flaming red, and suddenly it was molten, a large hole all around the lock opening up. "Adib! Adib!" he shouted as he rammed his hand through the supercharged heat, his skin covered now with scales.

From inside, Dr. Strohner shouted into the intercom for help from security, and, getting no response, he shouted for help from anyone.

Hari had pushed through the door now, and he stood facing Strohner. "You are not Dr. Tapai," Shakir said. "Where is Tapai?"

Strohner stared, his jaws in a vice grip of painful fear. He had been trying to determine what Tapai was up to when he had returned to the main control room to find it virtually useless.

With a glint in his eye Hari approached Strohner, reaching a hand toward him.

"Look down there at the chamber. It's what you're after. Go ahead, look!" said Strohner, pointing to the window overlooking the accelerator tube.

Hari stepped away from the old man and stared down at the scene. Just below him stood an open airlock, and at distance of perhaps a hundred yards there was another airlock, where Brannon and Hunter had placed a refrigeration unit. Hari had watched Brannon being hit by the refrigeration unit, and he had seen Adib's body tumble from it, and then he saw Adib's Kundalini rise from the body and strike out at Brannon.

Seeing it, Hari's insides raced with anticipation and desire. He had waited for this moment for so long, and now it was here. "The alarms have caused the chamber to be shut down?" he asked Strohner.

"Yes, for twenty-four hours, until everything can be thoroughly checked out," lied the old man, looking calmly back at the activity down at the next airlock. He had also witnessed the large, two-headed cobra rise from the body on the chamber floor. While Dr. Strohner gasped at the sight, Hari laughed in delight.

Hari had watched the drama below unfold as Brannon banged on the airlock, then he'd suddenly pushed away from the glass and was racing away while the woman struggled to maintain the creature's interest.

Brannon looked like a mouse in a maze with the beast in pursuit.

The other Kundalini's attack heartened Hari. His brother was not so different from himself after all. "A beautiful thing, is it not?" Hari asked the old man.

"It is that, yes . . . strangely beautiful."

"Obviously, the chamber is shut down at the moment, but is it inoperable?"

"Yes, it is," lied Strohner.

"Show me the control switch for closing that airlock."

Strohner did as asked.

Hari switched it on. No response. He then concentrated and set the control panel to melting under his hands. "That should insure the truth," he said, turning to reach out for Strohner.

But the old man had quietly cringed away through a door in a black corner. Hari pushed through the door and saw a row of offices, any one of which the old man may have ducked into, and then he saw the elevator that signaled itself out of service.

"To hell with the old fool," he said to himself, going back to the viewing window. He once again looked down on the rising Shakar Kundalini in the chamber below. The sight of it sent Hari rushing down to the disabled airlock portal A. At last, he thought, united with my brethren.

Dr. Karl Strohner had rushed into the lateral elevator, disregarding the safety alarms and the blinking out-of-order notice. He had determined that Anwar Tapai had sabotaged the control room, rendering it useless for at least twenty-four hours, and his fastest route to the auxiliary room from here was the lateral elevator.

Strohner didn't understand everything that was going on, but he had seen the supernatural at work, and he had pieced together what Tapai and the others were up to.

The elevator opened on another shocking scene, Tapai holding a gun on the young medical examiner from Miami. He heard their words and he saw the struggle for the gun, and he watched Tapai slump over, dead.

20

On first entering the chamber, Hari had slowed at the airlock, examining it, a bit fearful still of entering, suspicious of the setup. He torched the keypad controls he found there, and then he inched through the final portal. Holding his breath for a moment, he waited to see if anything would happen, if the airlock would close on him. Nothing happened.

Once he was sure he could exit and enter at will, Hari had then rushed down the chamber toward a final completion, the meshing of the two serpents to form the four-headed god Kundalini.

He felt the tug at his core, felt the nearness of the other half.

When he reached the refrigeration unit, he stared ahead at the next airlock chamber. He psychically called out to his other self, announcing his arrival. But the serpent kept up its tenacious pursuit of Brannon, dragging Adib's body with it. Brannon continued to run for the next airlock, having found yet another one locked. Hari listened to the conversation going between the airlock and the outside, and he searched for where the woman's voice was coming from.

"He's in the chamber, Eric. Hari Shakir is inside!" Angelica spoke to Brannon through the intercom. "Hurry!"

Panting, Brannon replied, "If you have to, throw the damn

switch, Angelica. There's too much at stake here."

"No, Eric! You're getting out of there."

The scrolls he'd placed in his disheveled shirt now fell as he ran for Airlock X. He stopped, trying to retrieve the scrolls. "Leave the damn things!" she screamed.

Brannon saw the creature that had crawled from Adib's body closing the distance between them. He turned and fled, leaving the scrolls behind. Up ahead, he saw the next airlock door swoosh open. He quickened his pace and the pursuing creature did likewise. "Be ready to drop that door as soon as I get inside!" he shouted.

Both of Strohner's shaking hands hovered above buttons on the control panel, one that would close the airlock door, and one which would create a vacuum and a shower of sub-atomic antimatter inside the vacuum at once.

Strohner and Angelica watched the deadly game play out below them. Brannon dove into the airlock chamber, and the door came crashing down, severing one of the serpent's heads. The thing lay there, silent, and appearing dead at Brannon's foot. He wanted to kick it away, but he didn't want to make contact with it. "Get me the hell outta here!" he shouted, and the outer airlock door opened. He literally rolled from the airlock, and the door closed behind him, trapping the head of the sickly brown, ashen, bug-eyed snake that had tracked him there.

He had heard how hundreds died each year from the venom of severed snake heads.

"He's safe now," said Strohner.

"Turn up this thing and let's see what we can do before Shakir completes his metamorphosis."

"Metamorphosis?" asked Strohner. "The only change this monster's going through will be annihilation."

While Brannon stared in at the torn and bleeding stub where the serpent's second head had been, he could see Angelica in the control room with Strohner. "Hit the juice!" he shouted up at them as Shakir came toward his final goal, the body and the serpent.

"It's missing a head, Shakir!" shouted Brannon, using the

intercom link on the airlock panel. "Can't really be whole and complete with only three heads and a stub now can you?"

Shakir stared down at the large, thick, flared head that flopped about like a dying fish in the airlock chamber. Brannon hoped it would buy them some time.

Hari smiled from his side of the glass, coming up to the airlock and staring down at the severed head between the two portals. Already, the thing was regenerating tissue and elongating itself.

"Watch and learn," said Hari, turning to take hold of the serpent that had now unraveled itself entirely from Adib Katra's body. Hari had torn his shirt away to reveal the enormous serpent tattooed on his abdomen, identical to Adib's. The detached two-headed serpent licked at Hari's tattoo, creating a layer of steam wherever the tongue touched. The stub of the second head was bleeding an acidic fluid. Tendrils climbed from out of the bloody stub and bore into Hari's tattooed abdomen. Hari swelled with the joy coming into his eyes, and he raised an arrogant finger to point at Eric where he stood just on the other side of the glass. The serpent that had left Adib's body had completely wrapped itself around Hari, and it undulated against his body in a sensual bonding, the snake beginning to disappear through the skin in a strange osmosis, melding with Hari.

Hari's skin began perspiring, glistening, and the heat being generated inside the chamber turned into a white-and-blue cloud surrounding Hari.

Disregarding all else, staring into Hari Shakir's contented eyes, Eric imagined a world entirely changed, entirely at the mercy of this mad being.

Brannon feared the worst . . . feared they had failed.

From overhead in the control room, Strohner and Angelica watched Adib Shakar's body implode, scattering parts of him all about the tube—blood, gristle, bone—until it all disappeared into finite atoms. The refrigeration unit had also imploded and was reduced to particle elements, all of which were spinning around the mile-long tube at incredible speeds. But Hari was in metamorphosis, *becoming* the Kundalini before their eyes, despite the bombardment. He had erected a blue fire wall around himself, a kind of shield.

Strohner replied, "We have achieved a complete vacuum! It should have destroyed this thing by implosion."

"It's not working on the monster!" she cried out.

"Turn this thing up!" shouted Brannon from where he stood.

In the control room, Strohner increased the antimatter electron bombardment, but it seemed to have little effect, other than holding the monster in place. If it was working, it seemed to be doing so one cell at a time.

"Antimatter particles differ from their counterpart occurring on earth," Strohner explained. "I've set the negatively charged antimatter in the chamber at the highest level possible. You can't get any more magnetically opposite with respect to spin."

"I have no idea what you're talking about, sir," she replied, watching him making more adjustments in the control levels.

"We live in a clockwise world, and due to the earth's atmosphere, antimatter spins counterclockwise. What we normally do in the chamber is to annihilate antimatter in collisions with clockwise-spinning positive matter. But in this case, my instincts tell me we need the opposite, counterclockwise spinning antimatter to attack this thing. Tapai would only have fed its strength using positive matter. He must have known that."

They looked down on the chamber where matter and antimatter were at war.

Small parts of Adib's body, a few remaining bone and teeth fragments, continued spinning around the mile-long tube, but they were now being disintegrated.

The serpent creature felt the pressure on its enlarged body almost immediately, as Hari's body had been completely transformed into the creature that defied death even here, in a vacuum that it prepared to burn its way from. It concentrated on one small area, firing the glass container, compromising each layer one at a time.

Brannon stood just outside the airlock, staring up through the portal at the swelling monster and the burning glass, and he felt the heat coming through to him. He shouted up at the control room, "Faster! Hit him with all you've got!"

They all watched the white heat of the monster as the bombardment of negatively charged antimatter showered the beast, beginning to penetrate its shield of superheat. The creature had for a brief moment shed all human form, showing itself. A three-headed hydra, with a fourth head being busily regenerated. Tentacles and suckers attached themselves to the glass, continuing to work on the integrity of the shell.

The creature had grown so large within the shroud of heat that it touched the one-story top of the chamber, and the three heads glared out through its giant eyes, and it began inhaling its own heat source, sucking in the antimatter bombardment as it did so.

The Kundalini felt the powerful pressure of the vacuum it found itself in, threatening to implode it. It had to escape now. It put all of its concentration on the hole it meant to burn through the glass to save itself from meltdown and implosion. It quaked and bloated, becoming elastic, getting large, contracting smaller, the process repeating itself as another layer of glass was breached, when suddenly the creature began to *come apart at the cellular seams.*

As the creature's cellular cohesion was compromised faster than the glass, the Kundalini flailed at its prison, ramming tentacled suckers against the sides and the top, threatening still to burn its way out. But the vacuum tube filled with the vapors of the decaying cellular structure of the monster itself now, its scales becoming invisible as each became subatomic particle matter, sucked into the invisible black hole of the antimatter created by Strohner.

The sound of the screaming, dying creature within the giant tube reverberated throughout the building. The heat against the glass increased in brilliance and temperature, threatening to melt a hole in the vacuum, when suddenly there was a great flash of light and Shakir and the Kundalini were gone, a trail of brown tissue, blood, cartilage, gristle, bone, blackened grease, and smoke scurrying off around the mile-long circle like a dragon seen in a cloud.

Angelica, Brannon, and Dr. Strohner watched as small bloody pieces of it floated on the nuclear wind created in the chamber, struggling to reach one another in a blind attempt to reconnect and join with other parts.

"Damn thing's tenacious; I'll give it that," said Strohner.

"Give it more power, all you've got!" Brannon cried out from the floor.

In the control room, Strohner replied, "It's at full power."

Soon all the torn pieces of floating matter that had been the Kundalini were disappearing into finite, invisible matter overwhelmed by antimatter.

"Thank God," Angelica called out, "It's gone! It's dead."

"Into the black hole we created for it. Dead only in the sense we transformed it into another form, into subatomic molecules," said Strohner. "But dead nonetheless."

"A fitting end, in view of what he did to his victims, and dead enough that it won't be doing any more smoking," agreed Angelica.

"Thank God!" Brannon slumped down against the glass, relieved and breathing deeply. Angelica kissed Dr. Strohner on the cheek, saying, "My God it's finally over."

"Not quite," replied Eric, looking over his shoulder at the remaining serpent head in the airlock chamber. "Nuke the son of a bitch!"

"The fourth head," Angelica said to Strohner. "We need to destroy it the same as the rest."

The control-room doors burst open and they found themselves surrounded by men with guns pointed. Angelica and Strohner were forced away from the controls, but Strohner protested. "You must let us finish what we have to do here! I must open the interior airlock door to destroy that thing in the airlock."

"It seems to me you've done enough damage here, Dr.

Strohner. Take them away," ordered the man in charge.

Through the glass, Angelica saw that Eric, too, was being held at gunpoint by a federal SWAT team. She made a dive for the airlock switch that Strohner proposed throwing, but she was grabbed and pulled away.

"You've got to let us finish what we started!" she shouted.

"Dr. Hunter is right! Let us finish our work here," added Dr. Strohner.

Below they watched a team of four in biohazard gear descend on the chamber and the airlock, while Eric was being held by armed guards. The men in protective suits stared down at the thing in the airlock.

Brannon, his hands in cuffs now, struggled to be heard. "That's all that is left of the damned thing, and it must be destroyed!"

One of the biohazard personnel turned to stare Eric in the eyes. Inside the suit stood a small, dark Indian woman. He saw the same intensity of spirit that he had always seen in Adib Shakar's eyes. "Detective Brannon, you and your friend, Dr. Hunter, are finished here. Go home to the life you have waiting for you. This is officially over."

"Who are you?"

"We will contain the outbreak from here."

"Outbreak? Is that what you're calling it? An outbreak? It's a monster."

"You've done a remarkable job, Detective, but now it is time to turn this over to us."

Eric looked up at one of the cameras stationed along the mile-long tube. Pointing, he said, "Check the building's monitor tapes. You'll see what it's capable of!"

"Believe me, Detective, I know what it is capable of. We were called in after the incident at County General Hospital—three fatalities there. We know how dangerous this hazard is, and we will take all necessary precautions."

"And just who the hell are we?"

"I am Dr. Irina Panjai, Center for Disease Control. We will contain the problem."

"What do you intend to do with it?"

"The ultimate fate of the creature is yet to be determined, but for now it will be safely stored away until which time as such determinations can be made in objective fashion, without passion ruling."

He stared hard at her, imagining the worst. "You're going to try to harness this thing? Aren't you? It can't be controlled, Dr. Panjai."

"I disagree. Dr. Adib Shakar controlled it all these years. There is a way." She turned to the SWAT team commander. "Get them all out of here," she said. "And get this airlock open."

"It must be destroyed, Doctor!"

"Please, let us do our job, now, Detective," countered Dr. Panjai.

"But I'm telling you, it can't be controlled. It's too risky."

"I have orders, Detective, and they come from the highest levels of government."

"It's madness to do anything but destroy it."

"No . . . not madness, Detective, faith." He saw a glint in her eye through the glass helmet dividing them. He then realized that all of her assistants were Indian as well.

Panjai returned her attention to the serpent in the chamber.

Eric was herded together with Angelica and Strohner toward the exit, the SWAT team leader shouting, "Get 'em all outta here, now!"

"It appears that they're taking it out of here to study it, learn what biochemical spark creates an SHC," he told the others.

Eric and the others were led out in cuffs. The building was now swarming with national guardsmen and federal marshals. As they walked out, they found it had become dawn, and the front of the building was barricaded with police and military vehicles, and a Miami helicopter was just landing.

Eric told Angelica and Strohner what little he had learned from Dr. Panjai.

"Damned fools," said Strohner.

Eric saw Captain Lou Ames and fire investigator Shelby Harne had climbed from the MPD helicopter, and they were arguing heatedly with FBI agents. Ames and Harne looked frustrated and fatigued, and their attempts to get any information from the feds appeared futile when Ames threw up his hands.

When he saw Eric and Angelica being led from the building in cuffs, Ames rushed to them. "Get these cuffs off, now!" he shouted at the men guarding Eric and Angelica.

As the cuffs came off, Ames told them, "Our deal is that we all vacate the grounds now or Eric faces charges."

"But they're playing with death in there, on a grand scale," said Angelica, pointing back at the building.

"There's nothing more you can do, Dr. Hunter. It's out of our hands now. Get aboard the chopper, all of you."

The three of them reluctantly but finally boarded the Miami PD helicopter with Lou and Shelby. Above the nuclear accelerator, looking down on the mile-long circle at the base of the building, they poured out their story to the Captain and the fire investigator. Harne explained to them that he had called the CDC when he saw what had happened at County General. "The guy smoked inside his body cast really captured their attention."

"Panjai you mean?" asked Eric. "The Indian woman."

"Yes, her most of all."

"She's inside now with the serpent head."

"They'll contain it, Eric. They have ways of containment, and they know from your experience that cold puts it into a dormant stage."

"Why didn't they take the opportunity to destroy it?" asked Angelica.

"They want it alive," replied Eric. "They want to know *how* it kills."

Shelby said, "They must want the biochemical formula for creating conditions right for a spontaneous human combustion. If they can learn that, they *will* harness its power."

Back at the accelerator chamber, Dr. Irina Panjai looked over the devastation and pieced together what had happened there. Dr. Panjai was in charge of the Biomark Laboratories in Miami and affiliated with the Center for Disease Control and the U.S. government. She had been called out from her Miami lab to have a look at the devastation caused in a room at County General Hospital where three lives were taken in an apparent burst of spontaneous human combustion. When she had examined the missing man in the full-body cast, she knew it was the work of the Kundalini.

Currently members of her team were taking samples of a black, oily substance, like that found at County General, adhering to areas all over the building. Other members stared down into the airlock where the only sign of life left in the chamber was the single serpent head.

"It looks positively prehistoric," said one.

"Strange tendrils . . . strange color," commented another.

"It is truly the serpent god," asked a third.

Dr. Panjai had ordered the accelerator be shut down, and the airlock doors opened. She had hoped to see more pieces of the creature in the chamber, but there were none visible. She stepped inside, breathing heavily into her mouthpiece and perspiring into her biohazard suit. She had spent her life in the faith of the Kundalini's existence, and in pursuit of any evidence she might bring to bear in order to rekindle the ancient cult of the Kundalini, to gather followers for its cause. And here was all her proof a few inches from her.

To gain complete control of the situation, Dr. Panjai had worked quickly over the last twenty-four hours, securing the necessary authority to move ahead with her plans to study the creature. She had lied to her superiors, telling them it was a new life-form, possibly of alien origin. She had faxed them photos taken at County General that displayed the awesome power of the force it was capable of, enticing them with the idea they might learn its secret for spontaneously combusting people. She had told them that she wanted to understand its power source, possibly duplicate it.

Thanks to the crime-scene photos, they had liked the idea, giving her full authority over the project—*for the time being*.

She only had one head from one of the serpents to work

with. The tapes, which were turned over to her, would, hopefully, tell her which one—Shakar or Shakir.

From a safe distance others watched Dr. Panjai's care with what remained of the monster they had been tracking. Panjai crouched in over the thick living serpent's head when she heard the voice inside her own head softly say, "Take me to the tomb of the *Shakar*."

She stared at it, ashen brown, fleshy. Tendrils shot off from the thing in various directions, some with suckers at the end. "My lovely extinct species." The snake's eye held her in a curious gaze. "I am here to help you."

Panjai opened the lid of a metal biohazard cooler, and, using tongs, she lifted the serpent's remains and placed what was left of the great Kundalini inside the container. She felt a rapport with it, hearing it speaking to her soul. "All secure now . . . nothing to worry about," she said, placing the lid over the container and securely locking it.

TWENTY-FOUR HOURS LATER

Eric was awakened by sunlight spilling in through Angelica's sheer drapes in her high-rise apartment. The sun played over her features, bathing her. He thought of her bravery and determination throughout their ordeal, and how like an angel she looked.

She released a sigh, still asleep in his arms. He tightened his hold on her and smelled her hair, breathing her in. The day before, once they had arrived at Angelica's apartment, they had finally allowed themselves to come down from the adrenaline high that had fueled their mad dash from the crime lab. Their race against Hari Shakir, the race that had taken them from Miami to the nuclear accelerator lab, had taken its toll on them.

After informing Ames of their suspicion that Porter had left a copy of the sonogram of the beast and a tape of Crysta Conover in his locker at the lab, and copies at his home, the captain informed them that the locker had been opened by the feds, the originals taken. He then promised to send two of his detectives to search Porter's apartment for the copies in the event they must prove themselves innocent of any wrongdoing in the matter.

Ames had put Dr. Strohner up for the night at a hotel, and he had seen to getting Angelica and Eric to her place. He had managed to keep their return to Miami quiet, calling no attention to them.

After showering, they had fallen into one another's arms. Eric, fondly recalling the lovemaking, gently touched her brow and ran his finger along her cheek, tracing the curve downward to her neck, when the phone startled her awake. He guardedly tightened his hold on her, saying, "It's OK, just the phone."

He lifted the receiver, saying hello.

"Eric, it's Lou Ames."

"Captain, good morning."

After a moment on the phone with Ames, Eric told Angelica, "Turn on your television, Channel Two News."

Angelica found the remote and clicked on the set. The screen was filled with chaos and fire trucks surrounding a building.

The newscaster in the foreground was saying, "No one yet knows the cause of the blaze, but this facility at Landis and Balmoral is being called a chemical fire. We are at the BioMark laboratories, and experts say there are sizeable stockpiles of chemicals as yet untouched by the blaze. Firemen are working desperately to end the fire before it can spread to other areas of the building, which could touch off another explosion. Two as yet unidentified bodies have been removed from the building."

"My God, that's Panjai's lab," said Angelica.

"Is it the work of the serpent?" Eric asked Ames.

"We only know that they killed two security officers—gunshots to the head, execution style. No evidence of any spontaneous combustion deaths, but Panjai, her three assistants, and the serpent head are missing."

"Gone? Gone where?"

"Anyone's guess."

"It's already begun again," said Angelica. "Damn them. Why didn't they let us destroy it while we had the chance?"

"Arrogance . . . I suspect, if not something more sinister."

"We suspect the fire was set to cover the theft."

"Where will she take it, and what will she do with it?"

"Only she knows that."

Epilogue

At the base of the altar lay the discarded biohazard waste container. Atop the altar lay Dr. Irina Panjai, naked except for the tattoo that encircled her abdomen about the naval—a four-headed serpent god, the completed, whole Kundalini in brilliant, freshly retouched colors. In one hand she held the writhing serpent's head saved from certain destruction, and in the other hand she waved a ritual scimitar. While she was surrounded by chanting followers, Irina felt completely alone with the serpent's head there on the sacrificial altar of the Shakars.

The flickering torches along the mildewed, spider-webbed stone walls in the tomb sent up shadows. The shadows of her followers on the ceiling and walls danced like so many joyous ancestors, urging her on. The tomb floor sent up dust beneath the feet of her stomping followers, littered as it was with the bones of those who had failed before her. A dry, choking air filled with ancient spores clawed at her lungs as she listened to the chant of "Kundalini, Kundalini, Kundalini," over and over.

As if to worship alongside her human followers, eyeless, sleeping serpents had risen out of the earthen floor to crawl over the bones and to wriggle up the sides of the altar.

Irina had created a worldwide network, a watch group for

the newly organized and modern Cult of the Kundalini when word was sent to her over the Internet of eyewitness accounts of men and women being spontaneously combusted in Calcutta. She had later gotten reports of spontaneous human combustion deaths in Great Britain, and then the newspapers were talking of such things in Miami. Now here she was, about to become one with the Kundalini in her homeland.

With all the life and hope she had brought into this place, the tomb itself began to breathe, coming alive. Irina felt as if she had come home.

Irina Panjai poised the ritual scimitar—one of several in the tomb—over her abdomen, prepared to make the incision with one hand, while in the other writhed the serpent, anxious to enter her. She and the serpent had had long telepathic discussions about this moment.

She intended the opposite of what Adib Shakar had done; she intended to insure the Kundalini's life span be her own, buying it time to heal, until they could find a way to bring it to full power, or at least allow it to live to its own potential. Something Adib Shakar had feared, but something she embraced.

She had spent her life in search of the Kundalini, and she had grown up in the region where the tombs of the *Shakir* and the *Shakar* stood. The old legends ran deep, and she had, as a young girl, heard family rumors that said there was Shakir blood in her family. If so, she might be the only hope of the Kundalini ever rising again. Perhaps it could never rise to its full potential, perhaps another Shakar could never be found, but she decided it was a risk worth taking. She wanted to share in the power of the serpent god.

She did not understand the reluctance of the Shakars to unite with the Shakirs. She held no fear of a new world ruled over by the Kundalini. There was so much worse found daily in the streets of Calcutta alone.

She had continued to be in near-constant telepathic communion on the long journey home from America. The creature's telepathic messages had cemented her mind to the plan she had already devised, giving a blessing to her decision.

Irina, like many in the region, had always worshipped the serpent god, offering prayers to him, burning sacrifices to him. Her faithful assistants and followers had come with her to the tomb, crowding inside, prepared to be taken by the serpent god if he chose to consume them through her body. All of them wanted to be used by him in the new quest for immortality and world dominion.

Irina's abdomen swelled with her breathing as she brought the knife down for the careful incision into the tattoo she had carried with her since childhood. She wanted to be the new conduit, her body and soul turned over to the serpent god. It was the logical culmination of her vigilance at finding the Kundalini and protecting it from complete annihilation.

With the serpent in one hand, and the knife in the other, she listened to the serpent's voice inside her head—*instructions.*

All instructions must be followed to the letter. . . .

The torches continued to entice the ancient Shakirs buried here into the dance of shadows all round her. The tomb continued to breathe. Irina felt a sense of déjà vu as the serpent moved under her touch.

Her followers stood row after row and chanted as she brought the knife across her abdomen, slicing from left to right, creating a direct path to her body for the serpent to take.

She placed the serpent in the blood oozing from the wound, and it calmly bored its way into her, seeking its new home.

In a matter of minutes Irina's wound healed over, and she felt the serpent coiling about her spine.

The #1 New York Times *bestselling author's*
all-time horror classic...

SHADOWLAND

PETER STRAUB

NOW WITH A NEW INTRODUCTION
BY THE AUTHOR

"Creepy from page one. I loved it."
—STEPHEN KING

COMING FROM BERKLEY MARCH 2003